THE WOMAN WHO DIDN'T

HC MICHAELS

SEQUEL HOUSE

For my sister, Ingrid.

I'm sorry for writing that letter to the newspaper when we were kids and signing it with your name.

ABOVE THE SURFACE

Detective Hooke was missing something. Thirty years in the job had taught him that his intuition was far more valuable than his case notes.

He flicked through the photos of the crime scene, despite having already burned every detail in his mind. He was *sure* he'd overlooked something.

The house was in one of Melbourne's wealthiest suburbs, making it an interesting place for a murder. The dead body lying on those highly polished tiles seemed out of place, like it was messing up the décor somehow.

The boys at the station had taken to calling it the White House, an appropriate name given it looked like someone had gone through the house with a bottle of bleach. It had white furniture, white rugs, white curtains, white walls and white roses in white vases. The splatter of bloodstained vomit looked almost artistic, pooling at the feet of a large marble statue of a goddess.

What a shame for such perfect lives to take such an imperfect turn. Two people who were the envy of all and now one of them was dead and the other facing a life locked behind bars.

The detective didn't know why he was so surprised. Nothing was ever as it seemed. That's why he often thought of life as a pond. No matter how much it shimmered on the surface, you can never know what secrets lurk beneath its murky depths.

His problem was that the surface of this case was proving difficult to break.

50 DAYS BEFORE THE BREAK

Skye spent the afternoon in front of the mirror rehearsing how to deliver the news to her husband.

"Theo, we need to talk. Theo, something terrible has happened. Theo, I don't know how to say this..."

Each approach started with his name and ended with her tears. There was no way to tell him without getting upset. She'd just have to come straight out with it.

As it turned out, she didn't have to tell him.

"I'm worried about you," he said, dumping his keys on the solid marble kitchen counter and draping his suit jacket over the back of a chair.

Skye bit back her annoyance. A jacket worth as much as some people's cars shouldn't be *draped*. It should be *hung,* preferably on a padded hanger.

"Why would you be worried about me?" She slid his dinner across to him, wincing as a jet of steam nipped at her thumb.

"Let it cool a bit." He pushed the plate aside and perched on a stool, the white leather of the seat squeaking as it took his weight.

She sighed. It'd taken her ages to plan this week's dinner menu, ensuring they got enough protein and vegetables without the sugar or fat. Not to mention all the time Linda spent cooking it.

"Tell me what's happening with you?" Theo reached across the counter for her hand.

Skye's pulse rate rose. *Not now!* She wasn't supposed to tell him like this. She wanted to wait until they were in bed with their laptops perched on their knees. He'd be wearing his Louis Vuitton reading glasses and he'd tip them down to the end of his nose when she said there was something they needed to talk about. She could imagine it so clearly.

"I'm fine. Really, I am." She took a picture of him with her mind. This was the face of a man who thought his wife was a healthy thirty-year-old woman. She'd never see this face again.

"You're not fine. Tell me, babe." He blinked as he waited for her to find her words.

She drew in a deep breath. "Really, I don't want you to worry about—"

"You have cancer, don't you?" Theo asked, the patience sliding from his voice.

"But how... how did you know?" Tears stung Skye's eyes. This was the downside of being married to a criminal lawyer. It was such an effort to get anything past him.

"So, it's true then?" he asked.

She nodded and Theo's handsome face filled with lines. For the first time since they'd been married, he looked his almost fifty years. He'd never looked his age. This was one of the reasons she'd been so madly attracted to such an older man. It gave him a certain virility, a power most other men could only dream of. If he could hold back time, then surely, he could do anything. He was like Kronos, the Greek god of time.

This was the name she called him in their most intimate moments as she raked her fingers through his dark locks, her body convulsing with pleasure, his black eyes smiling at her with adoration.

His eyes were always smiling at her.

Until now.

"Is it your ovaries?" he asked.

"Yes." She walked to his side of the counter and wrapped her arms around him.

"How bad is it?" He pulled her close and she caught the familiar scent of his aftershave. She inhaled, enjoying the manly smell of him, glad tonight wasn't one of the nights he went to the gym.

"How did you know?" she asked, stalling for time before she had to tell him how bad it really was.

"You fell asleep in bed last night with your laptop on. When I shut it down, I saw you were researching ovarian cancer." He dropped a kiss on her forehead. "At first I thought it was for your work..."

"You should've woken me if you were worried." She loosened the embrace so she could look at him.

"You seemed so peaceful," he said. "Besides, I didn't think anything of it until I got an email today about an anomaly on our credit card. When I checked, there was an invoice for an ultrasound. For a minute I thought maybe you were pregnant, but I know you'd never keep that from me. It had to be something you didn't want to tell me."

"Do you ever take time off from cracking cases?" She felt him tense. He normally liked it when she ribbed him about his dedication to his job.

"This wasn't a case I should've had to crack." Anger slipped into his voice to mingle with his concern. "You're my wife. You should've told me."

"Don't you normally use private investigators for that kind of thing?" She smiled to take the sting out of her words.

It didn't.

His body tensed even further, and he took a step away.

She'd never been happy about the way he tracked her down when they first met. He'd seen her being interviewed on a morning talk show and claimed to have nearly choked on his muesli. Unable to get her out of his head, he asked his private investigator to find out more about her.

She was surprised she'd made this kind of impact on him. She had the same long blonde hair, blue eyes, milky complexion and size six figure as any of the television presenters and Theo hadn't seemed to have had a problem with his muesli before.

"I did tell you." She reached for him and ran her manicured fingertips down his chest, trying to coax the tension from him. "I'm telling you now. We're talking, aren't we?"

"What did the doctor say?" he asked, relenting just a little underneath her touch. "Tell me exactly what he said."

"Oh Theo, I can't tell you." Skye took in a deep breath, feeling the beginnings of tears pricking the back of her eyes.

"Skye, tell me." He was frustrated, his normally calm voice cracking under the strain of his emotions. She knew there were prosecutors all over the city who'd tried unsuccessfully to break him like this in a courtroom, and she'd managed to do it with only a handful of words.

"They're going to take my ovaries." She dissolved into tears, burying her face in his firm chest. "We won't be able to have children."

"It doesn't matter," he said, running his hands down her back, his fingers catching in her hair. "It doesn't matter."

She knew that wasn't true. It did matter. It mattered a lot.

He'd been begging her to give him a child since they first met, a son to be more accurate. She sometimes wondered if that was what first attracted him to her—her young, pink ovaries filled with possibilities for the future. Would he still love her without them?

"We have Amber," he said, referring to his sixteen-year-old daughter from his first marriage. A daughter who made it very clear she didn't belong to Skye.

"Someone say my name?" Amber walked into the kitchen and opened a cupboard, reaching for an apple. "Why can't we have a fruit bowl on the counter like normal people? Oh, that's right. Apples aren't white."

"Amber, we just need a moment here, please," said Theo.

Amber looked across, her eyes widening like she was seeing them for the first time. "Why are you both crying? What's wrong?"

"Nothing." Skye pulled back from Theo and shook her head, trying to let him know to stay quiet. What could they possibly say to Amber? It wasn't like she'd care.

"Umm, it doesn't look like nothing." Amber stood frozen with the apple halfway to her mouth, waiting for an answer.

"She has to know, babe," said Theo.

"I have to know what?" Amber started to sound panicked. "Is Mum okay? Has something happened to her?"

"It's not your m-mother." Theo rubbed at his strong jawline. "It's—"

"It's me," interrupted Skye. She'd rather choose the words than have Theo do it for her. "I have cancer."

The panic on Amber's face worsened. She ran her hands through her dark curls, causing them to stand up even more than usual, as if they too were upset by the news. "Cancer? Oh my god."

"It's in her ovaries," said Theo. "But she's going to be okay."

"She can get her ovaries cut out, can't she?" Amber asked, directing her question at her father.

"Yes, Amber," said Skye, reminding her she was standing right there. "But I'll still need to have chemo to make sure they've got it all."

"Chemo! You mean you're going to lose your hair?" She ran to Skye and threw her arms around her waist, hugging her tightly.

"There are worse things than losing your hair." Skye patted her on the back with stiff, awkward movements as she tried to come to terms with this unexpected burst of affection.

"This is terrible," moaned Amber.

Skye turned her face as Amber's hair tickled her cheek. Amber looked so much like her Mauritian-born mother, especially with the weight she'd been putting on lately. She wished Theo would say something to her about it. Skye would be crucified if she dared mention anything.

"Amber, darling." Theo came over and placed his hands on his daughter's shoulders. "It's lovely you care so much, but I really need to talk to Skye about this if you don't mind?"

Amber untangled her arms from Skye's waist and stepped back, wiping mascara-stained tears across her cheeks until they blended in with the layers of her cheap foundation.

"I'm really sorry, Skye," she said.

Skye nodded. "It's okay, Amber. Thank you. I'll be fine. You'll see."

She watched her stepdaughter head out of the kitchen.

"Don't put it on Facebook!" Theo called after her.

"I'm not stupid!" she called back. "Besides, Facebook's for old people!"

Theo rolled his eyes and turned to Skye, pulling her into his arms once more.

"I'm scared," she said.

"Me too, babe." He pressed his cheek to the top of her head, and she wondered how that would feel when she had no hair.

They stood there in silence and Skye drank in the comfort he offered her, wishing she'd told him earlier.

"Skye." Theo cupped her face in his hands so he could look her in the eyes. "I love you. With your ovaries or without them. This doesn't change anything between us. I'll always love you. You don't need to have my babies. It doesn't matter."

Guilt wound its way through her core. Saying something didn't matter, didn't make it true.

This house would never know the sound of a toddler's footsteps echoing down the hallway. Her belly would never stretch to accommodate Theo's child. She would never know what it was like to push a tiny human from her body and hear its first cry.

There were so many things she'd never know and never do.

———

Amber flopped down on her bed with her phone held up in front of her face. She'd sent a message to her group chat when she heard raised voices.

Amber Manis
Drama in the kitchen! Going to investigate...

There were seven missed messages in the five minutes she'd been gone. Now that she knew what the drama was really about, she dreaded reading the replies. She considered deleting her original message, but there was no point. Everyone would have already seen it. Better not to write more, though. If her dad found out, he'd kill her. She never would've said anything if she'd known it was going to be a something actually serious! She'd thought maybe Skye wanted to paint the grass white.

Cait Spremic
Oh, I love a basic drama! Let us know what happens x
Tara Hearts
Hope ur ok Ambey Pambey
Chai Lyn
U can't just say that! What's happening???
Kelsey Bey
What's going on? Update please!
Alyssa Eve
Call me!!! x
Amelia More
Call me too x
Tilda East
Call me first!! ;)

Amber wiped away her tears as she decided what to say.

Amber Manis
Hard to explain on chat. I'll talk to you at school tomorrow x

She shoved her phone under her pillow before the temptation got too great, knowing her friends wouldn't be satisfied with that response.

Sure enough, her phone started buzzing with so many messages her pillow looked like it had a vibrate function. People did love a drama, especially when it involved a high-profile couple like her father and Skye. She wondered if they'd all be so interested if she had normal parents. She was certain if she messaged about her mother, the only response she'd get would be crickets chirping outside her window.

Anyway, she should be thinking about Skye's cancer right now, not her friends and whether or not their interest in her was genuine.

The situation was all a bit heavy. She'd never been close to Skye, but she couldn't wish cancer on someone. If it happened to her, then it could happen to anyone. Skye wasn't even that old. She was skinny, too, and fit. She did so much yoga she could practically bend herself inside out. And she didn't even drink, unless you count those tall glasses of green slime she downed each morning. She was a walking advertisement for healthy living.

It freaked Amber out. If Skye got cancer, then anyone could. What if her dad got it? Or her mum? Or even herself? Kids got cancer sometimes.

She started to cry again, grabbing for her phone and reading the growing stream of messages through her tears.

The girls really wanted to know what was going on. It wasn't fair to leave them out. Besides, this affected her, too, and she needed support just as much as Skye. Well, maybe not just as much, but still, she needed people to help her through this and how could they if she didn't tell them what was going on?

Her thumb got busy and she started to type.

49 DAYS BEFORE THE BREAK

Skye reached for her mother's hand and held it gently.

"It's me, Mum. It's Skye."

Her mother eyed her suspiciously, a look of mild panic flickering across her face as she tried to drudge up her memories.

Skye had grown used to that expression. It was the image she now associated with her mother's once beautifully composed face.

"I have a daughter named Skye." Her mother nodded proudly at having retrieved the memory.

Skye let out a slow breath. "That's me, Mum. I'm your daughter. I'm Skye."

She'd spent her entire life begging her mother for attention. *Look at me,* became the catchphrase of her childhood. It didn't matter what she was doing, she was always asking her mother to notice her. Nothing had changed in adulthood. She was still crying out to be seen.

"You're not my daughter." Her mother shook her head and pointed to a photo on her bedside table. "That's my daughter."

It was a photo taken on Skye's wedding day. Not her wedding to Theo, but when she'd married Dean. At her first wedding, she'd been the full bridezilla with a veil that trailed to the ground and a dress with a bodice sewn with so many imitation pearls she could barely stand up.

She'd looked quite different at her second wedding. She went without a veil, not wanting anything to distract from her gown, designed especially for her by Alex Perry. There were no imitation pearls on that masterpiece—or imitation anything. It was classic elegance with sweeping lengths of silk chiffon that clung to her body in all the right places.

Yet her mother's favourite photo was of her wearing her cheap beaded dress because that was the wedding she'd been at. By the time Skye had married Theo, her mother's dementia was so far gone it was impossible for her to attend.

"That's me, Mum." She held the photo next to her face. "See, I'm Skye."

"Don't touch my photo." Her mother snatched it from her and clutched it to her chest.

Skye noticed her nightgown wasn't buttoned up correctly but wouldn't dare try to fix it. The last time she'd tried to do that, her mother had slapped her hand away with surprising strength. In her prime, she'd been a principal dancer with the Australian Ballet, her grace and beauty enough to reduce an audience to tears. It was hard to reconcile that woman with the one in front of her now.

"Let me put this back." Skye tried to prise the frame from her mother's hands worried she might crack the glass and hurt herself.

This behaviour was just another thing to add to the list of things that didn't make sense. Her mother was holding that photo like she actually cared about her. How sad that the only love Skye had ever felt from her mother had come when she no longer knew who Skye was.

Managing to get hold of the frame, she set it back down on the bedside table behind the plate of brownies she'd baked the night before. That was one blessing of having dementia—calories were impossible to count. For the first time in her life, her mother was able to enjoy the wickedness that chocolate had to offer, without fear of ruining her figure. Unfortunately, Skye didn't have that same luxury.

She wondered if one day she'd let herself go and have the same rounded thighs and rolls of belly fat her mother now had.

"Skye." Her mother's eyes widened as she looked at her daughter.

"Yes, Mum. I'm here." She reached out and took her mother's

hand, tears stinging her eyes. She was being seen in her mother's dementia in a way she hadn't been seen before. It made her both incredibly joyful and painfully sad.

"You look gorgeous," her mother said.

Skye's emotions intensified. Her mother had never given her compliments growing up, instead preferring to remind her of her shortcomings, which had been a total waste of breath. Skye had already known her hips were too wide, her nose too long and she showed too much gum when she smiled. She hadn't needed her mother's constant reminders. Even as an adult when she'd shed every possible ounce of fat from her body, had her nose reconstructed and learnt to smile without parting her lips, her mother wasn't satisfied. There was always something else she could improve on.

Now, with thanks to dementia, suddenly, she was gorgeous.

It was these rare moments of warmth that made all the hours spent sitting by her mother's bedside worthwhile. It was like panning for gold and uncovering a diamond. She'd collect these precious gems and store them close to her heart.

Skye contemplated whether she should tell her mother about the cancer. It would feel so nice to have her take her in her arms and soothe her worries. She thought of the way other children's mothers fussed over them when they were unwell. If Amber had even the slightest sniffle, her mother would be on their doorstep with chicken soup and hugs and kisses to make her better.

Whenever she'd gotten sick as a child her mother had looked at her in disgust, ashamed at the way she'd succumbed to her weakness.

"*I couldn't get away with that at the ballet,*" she'd say. "*Once I danced on stage for three hours with a temperature of forty-three.*"

"*But I'm not in the ballet,*" Skye would complain.

"*Not with those thighs you're not!*"

Maybe now she was *gorgeous* her mother would care about things like her daughter being unwell.

"It's a shame about the glue, though," her mother said. "Messy stuff."

Skye's perfectly shaped brows pulled together. "What glue, Mum?"

"Someone came into my room last night and painted my feet with glue. Why would they do that?"

The moment was over. Her mother had disappeared beneath the blanket of her disease once more. There'd be no taking Skye in her arms and soothing her. If anyone was going to be doing any soothing, it'd be her.

"Nobody did that, Mum." Skye patted her hand, please to find she didn't pull away. "I promise. Nobody would do that to you."

Her mother looked at her with her familiar look of suspicion.

"I know it feels like they did," said Skye. "I know it feels real to you, but you need to trust me. Nobody painted you with glue."

Her mother pulled her hand away from Skye, holding it to her mouth. "Dean did it."

Of all the crazy things to say, it had to be that. Dean painting her feet with glue!

Skye knew for a fact her first husband hadn't done any such thing, mainly due to the fact he was dead. Perhaps he'd come back to do a spot of haunting? She knew of a few men who'd like to do that to their mother-in-law.

"Dean's dead," said Skye. "He didn't do it. Nobody did it."

"Dead?" Her mother's eyes filled with tears. "Dean's not dead."

"No, he's not dead." Skye sighed. Even though her mother's dementia had only just begun to take hold when Dean died, it was one detail she didn't seem to be able to keep a grasp of. Normally it was easier to just let her believe her beloved son-in-law was still alive. It was strange how she seemed to remember him, yet often had no idea who her daughter was.

Skye shook the thought away, unsure why she expected dementia to make sense. The whole point of it was that it was a muddled mess.

Her mother's diagnosis had been a cruel blow for someone still relatively young, leaving her confined to life in an aged care facility with people decades older than her as her peers. It was just as well she didn't realise what was happening to her most of the time.

"I almost forgot." Skye handed her mother a glossy program she'd had sent to her from the Australian Ballet.

Her mother liked looking at the photos and her doctors thought it would be good to encourage her to hold onto as many memories as possible from that time of her life.

Skye had sometimes wondered if she should bring in her mother's diaries. She'd found them when she'd cleaned out her home before selling it. She'd nearly missed them stacked up behind a pile of clothes in the bedroom. There were about a dozen volumes, dating right back to before Skye was born. Occasionally, Skye liked to flick through them, having read some of the entries over a hundred times.

She'd ultimately decided against bringing them to her mother. Some memories were better left buried.

"Is that me?" Her mother pointed to a photo of one of the ballerinas.

Skye leaned in for a better look. "No, Mum. You were even more beautiful than that."

"Was I?" Her mother smiled at the possibility.

Skye nodded.

She had been, too. Smoking hot, in fact. If only some of that warmth could've spread to her heart.

"But that was before Dean painted my feet with glue."

Skye kissed her mother and left her with her ballet program. It hurt too much to stay any longer.

———

Skye had a head full of thoughts of Dean when she returned home and carefully undid the buckles on her Christian Louboutin heels. She placed them neatly next to the sofa in her living room and sat down, glad she'd worn the shift dress she'd ordered online from Harrods. The fabric was soft and didn't crease easily.

Dean was her first love. The romantic side of her wished she could say he was her only love, but that wasn't true. She loved Theo, too. Although, there were differences in the love she felt for her two husbands.

If she weren't so exhausted, she'd reach for her phone and open the photo she kept of Dean in a secret folder. She didn't do it often, but sometimes the urge to look into his eyes was overwhelming. It helped to know there was a little piece of him close by.

Tucking her knees up, Skye hugged a cushion to her chest. Then, worried she'd get foundation on the white fabric, she put it back down. It didn't matter. A cushion was never going to take away the pain of Dean's death.

Some people saw it as disrespectful to his memory that she'd married Theo so quickly. But they didn't understand. She hadn't married Theo because she didn't love Dean, she'd married him because she *did*.

She looked over at the framed photo of Theo on the glass side table. It was taken at their engagement party and had caused quite a stir when it was published online, earning him the nickname, *George Clooney*. The resemblance wasn't all that far-fetched. He'd looked gorgeous in his Armani suit, his olive skin and dark features giving him the appearance of a man who'd just stepped off a luxury yacht after a summer in the Mediterranean.

Theo was handsome, rich, devoted, and could fuck like a prize bull. Sex with Dean had never been like that. He didn't fuck. He made love with tender caresses and soothing words whispered in her ear. With Theo it was hard, fast and dirty and turned her on in ways she never thought possible.

This was just another reason she found it hard to compare her two marriages. Not only were they with different men, but she was a different woman.

Her phone buzzed from within the depths of her Prada tote. She shuffled about for it, being careful not to chip a nail. She didn't have the energy to visit the salon to have it fixed.

She found the phone and saw Theo's name lit up on her screen.

"Hi, babe," she said, wondering how he was coping today. He'd taken her news badly. He was even more upset than she was.

"Hi, yourself." His sexy voice made her stomach twist into knots.

"You didn't wake me this morning." She was disappointed he'd let her sleep. It was one of the only times in their married life she'd woken without his hand sliding up the back of her silk camisole. Morning sex had become as routine as her green smoothie for breakfast.

"You need your rest," he said.

"I need you."

"Oh, babe." She could hear the sadness in his voice. He must have so many thoughts running through his mind.

"I'm okay." She tucked her feet up underneath herself and leant back on the sofa. "Really I am."

But he wasn't buying that. "You sound tired."

"I just visited Mum," she explained, trying to inject more energy into her voice. "You know how exhausting that can be."

"Did you tell her?" he asked, cautiously.

"What's the point?" She let out a long sigh. "It's not like she'll remember anyway."

"True. No sense in upsetting her," he agreed, always seeming to know the right thing to say. "How was she today?"

"Really good actually. Much better than usual." It was true. Despite her confusion over the glue on her feet, she hadn't sworn at Skye or tried to hurt her.

"Are you still..." He coughed.

Her stomach pulled into a different kind of knot and she sat up straight. "Am I still what?"

"Doesn't matter," he said quickly.

"It does. What were you going to ask me?" She drummed her fingernails on the arm of the sofa, suspecting she knew exactly what he'd wanted to say.

He hesitated. "I was just wondering if you're still going to get those tests done, with everything else that's going on now? It doesn't matter. I shouldn't have asked. We can talk about that later."

She'd made a deal with Theo when they were first married that she'd get tested to see if she had the gene responsible for her mother's dementia. If it was negative, they could go ahead and have a child. If it was positive, well...Theo refused to look at that as an option. His life was too charmed for that. It seemed he was wrong. Her cancer news hadn't just broken the charm, it'd smashed it to pieces.

"What's the point?" she asked. "I told you they're taking my ovaries."

"But we still need to know...for you. For your future."

She nodded despite the fact he couldn't see her. "Once all this is over, I'll do it, okay?"

"Whatever you want, babe. I'll support you either way."

She smiled, knowing this was true.

"Look, I've gotta run," he said. "I just wanted to check up on you. Make sure you're okay."

"I'm fine. I love you." She made a kiss sound, wishing he were there to receive it in person.

"Love you too, babe." He put a smile in his voice even though she knew he'd be frowning. "See you tonight."

She disconnected the call. Her poor Kronos. She hated hearing him like that. Not only did he have a sick wife to deal with, but he needed to let go of his dream of one day having a son. That would really be hurting him. Hopefully, he'd be able to come to terms with it and realise they could still have a full and happy life together.

She couldn't see the big deal in wanting to continue on the Manis name, anyway? It was only a surname. It wasn't like Theo was the King of England or anything. There were plenty of other blokes around called Manis who could continue on the name for him, his twin brother included.

Theo's first wife, Rin, hadn't had a problem providing him with an heir, even if she'd gotten the gender wrong. According to Theo, the whole reason Rin had become his first wife was because of Amber. He would never have married her if she hadn't fallen pregnant *accidentally*.

Clearly, Rin had wanted more of Theo than he'd been prepared to give, so she'd used everything in her arsenal to snare him. It'd backfired on her, though. Theo had packed his bags when Amber was only a few months old, telling Rin he couldn't possibly be a father when his legal career was only just starting to take off. Skye felt sorry for her for having been silly enough to believe it was possible to trap a man who didn't want to be locked in a cage. That kind of man always managed to find the key.

Poor Theo couldn't win. He'd rejected Rin when having children wasn't a priority and now it was, he was stuck married to a woman telling him she was soon to have two hollows where her ovaries had once been.

"Oh, you're home, Skye." Linda walked into the living room with a duster in her hand. That was the worst part of having someone clean your house. It was never your own. The garden was no different. There was always someone pottering around, sent by their landscaper to maintain the grounds. She hardly ever went out there, preferring to look at the garden from her windows.

She was going to have to tell Linda about the cancer, she supposed. Maybe she could get Theo to do it. She didn't have the energy for it right now. Besides, Linda was her housekeeper, not her friend. Did she really have to tell her at all?

"I'll be in the library if you need anything." Skye dragged herself off the sofa and picked up her shoes.

"I can do this later. Sorry to interrupt you." Linda took a step backwards and Skye frowned at a stain on her white apron.

Linda had been working for her since she first moved in with Theo. She didn't have any references when she'd applied for the job, but Skye had hired her anyway, mainly because she was older than Theo. She trusted Theo, of course, but it was always better to keep temptation as far away as possible.

"It's fine. I was about to get up anyway." Skye pinched her mouth into a smile. "I have some work to do."

It was true. She had an article to write for the media company she worked for. They ran a popular website full of witty stories about first world problems including health, parenting, sex and marriage.

In Skye's peak she had over three hundred thousand followers on Instagram, although lately her popularity had been waning. But those loyal followers who remained should know about her cancer. It wouldn't be right to keep it from them. Maybe she could give the story to Linda when she finished and tell her about it that way? It was so much easier to write words than to speak them.

"Would you like me to bring your lunch in there?" asked Linda.

"I'm not hungry today. I'll just have a mineral water, thanks."

It was at times like this she wondered if she should take up drinking something harder. Mineral water just wasn't going to cut it today.

Maybe a quick yoga session would clear her head before she started writing? Now wasn't the time to let her fitness slip. In the months to come she was going to need all her strength to stay standing on her two feet. She was lucky she had Theo to help hold her up.

———

Theo heard a loud gasp from outside his chambers. He went to investigate only to find his twin brother in front of his new assistant's desk. Jane was wide-eyed to see her boss standing before her wearing blue overalls and a three-day growth when she'd been certain he was at his desk, dressed in his expensive suit.

"Sorry, Jane," said Theo. "Forgot to tell you about my evil twin. This is George."

A deep blush crept up her cheeks and her eyeballs darted between them in the way people did whenever they stood side by side.

This reminder of how similar they looked made Theo feel uncomfortable. He saw several differences between them. For a start, they dressed in totally different styles. Shakespeare got it right when he said it's the clothes that maketh the man. What they wore made them look completely different. When not in his overalls, George dressed like a hobo. He also had a lot more grey starting to come through in his temples than Theo. And he could use a decent haircut. Not to mention his filthy fingernails or the leathery state of his skin after all those years working outdoors.

Really, they looked nothing alike. Jane needed new glasses if she'd mistaken George for Theo.

It was quarter past twelve, which meant George was on his lunch break—a concept as routine to George as it was foreign to Theo.

"Got a minute?" asked George, who headed to his chambers without waiting for an answer and plonked himself down in a chocolate brown leather armchair. It swallowed him, making his knees stick up at an extreme angle. He shifted his weight, not seeming to be able to find a comfortable position.

This was precisely why Theo liked those armchairs. They were stylish, adding to the overall upmarket look to the room, yet the moment anyone sat down, they began immediately planning when they could stand up. He was too busy to have people hanging around when he was trying to work. It was best to make them as uncomfortable as possible.

Theo returned to his desk and leant back in his chair. The reinforced spring system balanced his weight, delicately positioning him at exactly the right height at his computer. He'd paid a consultant a fortune to set it up like this for him.

"Nice of you to dress up," he said.

"I'm a plumber." George screwed up his face. "What do you expect? A tuxedo? Some of us have real jobs."

George hauled himself out of the armchair, opting instead for the sturdy metal seat on the other side of the desk. This was where Theo's clients normally sat. Many a worried man had squirmed in that chair as they wove the elaborate stories they wished to use as their defence.

Theo yawned. He didn't have the energy for brotherly banter about which one of them worked the hardest. They worked equally as hard. It was just that while Theo spent his days up to his armpits in the shit of society, George was up to his armpits in actual shit. Theo couldn't help it if figurative shit paid more than literal shit.

The news of Skye's cancer had sapped all his energy. For the first time, he understood what people meant when they said they were bone tired.

He looked out his window. The city of Melbourne loomed in front of him. Skye was out there somewhere. He hoped she was feeling better than he was.

"Earth to Theo." George clicked his fingers in front of Theo's face.

He blinked, bringing his brother into focus.

"Sorry, boofhead," said Theo.

"Don't call me that." George crossed his arms and huffed.

"Sorry, boofhead."

He knew this nickname annoyed him, which was precisely why he'd been calling him it for over three decades now. It'd started when George's first girlfriend dumped him, telling him he was a boofhead. Some names just stuck. That wasn't Theo's fault.

"What's going on?" asked George, seeming to decide to let the boofhead argument simmer for now.

"Nothing." Theo waved a hand dismissively. "It's fine."

"Bullshit. Are you forgetting we shared a womb? You can't hide anything from me." George leant back in the chair. "Now, spill it."

Just because they'd shared a womb, didn't mean they needed to share their every thought. Theo was too busy and confused to want to talk.

As fun as it had been growing up with an identical twin, it was far less enjoyable as an adult. Despite their competitive banter, he and George had a sixth sense about each other. While Skye had been telling him about her cancer, George was buzzing on his phone wondering what the hell was going on. He'd texted George back rather than call, knowing he'd never be able to hide it from his voice and not wanting to tell him about Skye until he had time to process it.

Which was precisely why George was making this appearance at his chambers. He should've just taken his call last night.

"I said, spill it," repeated George, waving his hand in front of Theo's glazed eyes.

Maybe it was better to just come out with it. George was going to keep probing until he came clean. He might even shut up for a moment if he told the truth.

"Skye's got cancer," he said as plainly as he could.

George stood up as his hand flew to his mouth. "You're fucking joking with me!"

Nope, looked like he wasn't going to shut up.

Theo fought the urge to cry. He hadn't cried in front of his brother since they were eight years old. He wasn't going to start now. It would only result in George calling him a pussy for as long as he'd been calling George boofhead.

"You're not joking, are you?" asked George.

What a stupid thing to say. Nobody would ever joke about their wife having cancer. Unless they hated their wife, which he most certainly did not.

"No, I'm not joking." Theo rolled his eyes.

"Fuck." George shook his head slowly. "Where is it? How bad? How long's she got?"

"Ovaries. Bad. Hopefully a long time yet. Cancer's not always terminal, you boofhead." He grimaced at the lack of filter between his brother's brain and his mouth. Sometimes he wasn't just a boofhead, he was a fucking dickhead.

George let out a long whistle. "I can't believe you didn't tell me."

"She only told me last night." Theo held up his palms. "I haven't told anyone."

"What about Amber?" George sat back down, seeming to have absorbed the worst of the shock.

"Well, Amber knows, of course," he said. "She was there when Skye told me."

"Did she chuck a party?" George asked.

Theo resisted another eye roll. "Come on, it's not that bad. Amber likes Skye deep down."

"Yeah, six foot deep down." George chuckled at his own joke.

"Enough, George." There was that lack of filter again, only this time he'd really hit a nerve. He could think of nothing worse than the two people he loved most not being able to stand each other. It was easier to just pretend they got along, like they did when he was around. Besides, it looked like Amber had been really affected by Skye's news. Maybe this cancer would bring them closer together. Something good had to come out of it.

"Mate, I'm sorry. I'm in shock, you know. I can't believe it. She's so young. I mean, if it was anyone it should be you or me or Sophie, god forbid." He made the sign of the cross three times, as was their mother's habit before she died.

Theo and George had gone to school with Sophie. She'd been married to George for over thirty years, longer than Skye had been alive. She was like a sister to Theo. Well, not quite. You didn't date your sister. Sophie had originally been his girlfriend, but when things didn't work out, she'd drifted over to George, who'd been more than happy to help mend her broken heart.

How different his life would be if he'd married Sophie. He could've, too. She was hot for him in those early days. She probably still was. Really, she couldn't be attracted to George and not him when people apparently thought they looked exactly the same. Strangely, he'd never really thought about it the other way around. Was Skye attracted to George? He pushed the thought from his mind.

Anyway, that thing with Sophie happened a very long time ago and they all told each other it was completely not weird. Although, if Theo was honest it was weird. *Very* weird. How many blokes could say they'd slept with their sister-in-law? Not that he could reconcile Sophie's solid fifty-year-old body with her sixteen-year-old small-breasted self.

"Will she still be able to have kids?" asked George.

Theo shook his head. "No."

"Not to worry. You've got Amber," George said warmly. "Besides, kids are overrated. Always taking your money, keeping you awake worrying until they get home, answering back."

"You know I wanted kids with Skye," Theo reminded him. "A son, perhaps."

"No idea why, mate." George wasn't letting it go. "If I had a woman like Skye, the last thing I'd want is to knock her up and ruin that tight little—"

"Enough!" He hated it when George spoke about Skye like she was a piece of meat. He'd always been jealous he earnt more money than him and now he was jealous of his wife. It was pathetic. They had the same DNA, for goodness sake. The same opportunities handed to them in life. It wasn't his fault if he'd made more out of what he'd been given than George had.

"You don't need to have a son." George sat forward in his chair. "Lukas will carry on the Manis name. Don't worry about it."

That was exactly what he was worried about. This was the one thing George had over him—he'd been the one to produce a child with a penis. He never bragged directly about it, but it was comments like these that showed just how proud he was.

Smug bastard.

"Yeah, whatever, little brother," he said reminding him who was the older twin.

"You know you were only born first because I pushed your dumb arse out of my way." George smirked at his comeback.

"Keep telling yourself that." He glanced at the clock, wondering how long George was going to stay. He had work to do. If George were a client, he'd have billed him hundreds of dollars for this visit so far.

"Look, you know conversation's not my strong point," said George, realising he was losing his twin's interest. "You're the fancy talker out of the two of us. Forget everything I said. I'm sorry to hear Skye's sick. I'm here for you."

"Thanks, boofhead."

"Given everything that's going on, I'm going to give you one free boofhead."

Theo grinned at him. "Gee, thanks mate."

"So, is she having chemo?"

Theo tried to remember exactly what Skye had told him. He really needed to write some dates down. "Surgery first, then chemo."

"Fuck. How are you going to cope with that, you big nancy boy?"

George was well aware of Theo's phobia of needles. He'd fainted a couple of years ago when Amber had to get a blood test.

"You know why I hate those things," said Theo.

George nodded. "Yeah, but we both saw Mum hooked up to those machines and you're the only one left having nightmares about it."

When their dad died of a stroke ten years ago, neither of them had known how lucky they were to lose him so quickly. Their mother had taken five long and torturous days to die from acute pancreatitis. She was hooked up to so many machines they could hardly get near her to kiss her or hold her hand. It would've been easier to cope with if she were at peace, but she was writhing in pain trying to rip the tubes from her body. A few times she succeeded, sending blood spurting all over her bed.

At the time, Theo had coped—he'd had to—but afterwards he'd gone into some kind of shock. Every time he saw a needle now, the memories came flooding back. It was too much to take.

He knew he had to get on top of his fear if he was going to support Skye through her treatment.

"I'll figure something out," he said, glancing at the lion tattoo poking out of the sleeve of George's tee-shirt. He'd gotten it the week after their mum died as a mark of respect, claiming she'd battled her disease with the courage of a lion. In that case, Theo thought he should've gotten a lioness tattoo. Or spent more than a hundred bucks and gotten an actual tattoo artist to do the work, instead of the no-hoper at the hepatitis factory down the road. It looked like some kind of kindergarten drawing.

"Maybe I'll get hypnotised," Theo said, only half-joking. He had to do something about his phobia eventually.

"Well, if you start quacking like a duck, I'll know what's happened." George tucked his hands into his armpits and flapped his arms.

"Very funny."

"I'll get Sophie to ring Skye and see if there's anything we can do for her." George let his arms fall. "Chicks are better at that kind of stuff than we are."

As the conversation dragged on, Theo casually pressed a button on his desk phone to signal Jane that he needed an interruption. This was usually reserved for clients. George was special today.

His phone beeped and Jane's voice came through a speaker. "Excuse me, but I have Mr Klein on line one. He says it's urgent."

"Tell him I'll be with him in a moment."

George took the hint and stood, punching Theo playfully on the arm. "I'll get out of your hair."

"Sorry boof. I appreciate your visit, but I have to take this call." He got up and hugged his brother. They slapped each other on the back to make sure it was a manly hug.

"Love you, mate," said George. "I mean it. I fucking love the shit out of you."

"Get out of here, you poof."

George walked to the door.

"Hey, boofhead," Theo called after him.

George turned to look at him, eyebrows raised.

"I fucking love you, too."

The truth was, he did.

Even if he was a first-rate boofhead.

47 DAYS BEFORE THE BREAK

"The Skye has no limit."
Skye Manis announces deadly cancer battle.

This isn't easy to write. You joined me on my journey when I was at my lowest point, stuck at the bottom of a mountain wondering how I would ever get to the top. With your help, I managed to not only climb to the summit, but I did the samba when I got there. I learnt that when it comes to me, the Skye really has no limit.

The last few years of my life have been wonderful. I have an adoring husband, a beautiful house and a career I love. I must also tell you that I have cancer.

That last part really sucks. I only just got the news recently, so forgive me for not announcing it sooner. I needed time to share it with Theo. As you can imagine, he's been very upset, but he's also been so supportive and understanding and I love him for it. He really is my knight in shining armour.

The cancer is in my ovaries. My treatment will mean I'll not only lose my hair, but the ability to have children. My heart is broken. I would have loved nothing more than to have had a baby with Theo.

Part of me wants to throw a tantrum, shake my fists in the air and declare to the world how brutally unfair this is. But ... I can't do that. Not to me and not to all of you who held my hand as I pieced my life back together when my first husband, Dean, was taken from me. I've thought a lot about Dean lately. His life ended so abruptly. One minute he was driving his car and the next he was gone. Just. Like. That. He was never given the chance to fight for his life. I have that chance. And fight is exactly what I intend to do.

I'm going to fight and I'm going to win. I'm going to do it for Dean. And Theo. And you. But most of all, I'm going to do it for me.

I know once again I'll be inundated with offers of help, but if I can ask one thing of all of you, it's this...look after yourself, get in touch with your body and learn what feels normal and what doesn't. Please visit your doctor if you suspect anything is wrong.

Ovarian cancer is a silent killer. Look out for feelings of bloating or pressure in your abdomen, pain during sex, changes in bowel habits, indigestion or bleeding outside your normal period. None of these symptoms are sexy, but neither is death. We need to talk about these things in loud voices instead of hushed, embarrassed tones.

So once again my life has taken an unexpected turn. Last time this happened, I was blind with grief. This time I'm going to stop and take in the view.

Hold your loved ones close. Live the life you dream of. And remember to smile. Life is beautiful.

Skye xx

———

Skye hit send on the email to her editor. She'd done it. It'd taken her three days to draft but she'd finally sent her cancer news out into the world. She felt like the bravest woman on the planet. She smiled so spontaneously she forgot to hide her gums.

It really was the most difficult story she ever had to write. Apart from the very first story she wrote about Dean's death—a brutally honest account of what it felt like to lose your partner.

Dean had been driving home from a work trip to Adelaide late one night and fell asleep on a particularly notorious stretch of Dukes Highway. It was unclear whether he died when his car struck the tree or if he'd managed to hang on while his ruptured fuel tank atomised the gasoline, leaking it into the crumpled cabin before it ignited on the cigarette he'd been smoking at the time. Smoking really was a health hazard.

Cars didn't normally explode into fireballs like they did in the movies, just as newlywed husbands didn't normally drive off roads and die. But the car had. And Dean did.

The body of the man she'd loved with all her heart was so burned and mangled in the car accident the coroner had to use dental records before he was prepared to issue a death certificate.

The story of Dean's death was the story that not only got Skye the job but made her famous. She quickly gained a huge following of women keen to hear updates on her journey. Just as quickly, she left her job in that putrid call centre. Each story she posted would receive thousands of sympathetic responses. The fact she'd only been married a month when Dean died was what seemed to fascinate people. She went from newlywed to widow before the moon had the chance to cross the sky.

She reflected on how the worst event of her life had directly resulted in the best thing to have ever happened to her. It launched her career. Maybe this time it would be the same.

Her success led to an independence she'd never had when she was married to Dean. It'd also led to a new husband.

Her destiny was sealed from the moment Theo choked on his muesli. He was a man who was used to getting what he wanted in life and he'd decided he wanted her. His private investigator tracked down her phone number and given that Theo had undergone extensive training in winning arguments (otherwise known as a law degree), it didn't take him long to convince her to go on a date with him. He didn't really give her much choice. Not that she'd wanted to say no. He was everything she'd been looking for, with the added advantage of being much older, which meant he worshipped her, complying with her every wish in order to keep her mouth smiling and legs open.

There weren't many men his age with a washboard stomach, a full head of dark hair and teeth so white they could light your path in a blackout. And he loved that she was so independent. The hot blood that thrummed through his veins had other ideas that didn't involve listening to her complain about being bored.

They were a match made in heaven.

Now, life was about to take yet another turn. Her waning popularity had been a direct result of her perfect life. Dramas were what interested people. Not mundane happiness.

Despite the horrible news contained in the story she'd just written, her editor was going to love it. It would be a hit. There was a whole new fan base out there who'd join her following. Women who'd also struggled with their health and could relate. Others who desperately wanted children, only to discover they weren't able to have any.

She'd cried as she wrote it, going through half a box of tissues as she wiped the tears from her eyes, but it expressed exactly what she wanted to say.

Now she'd submitted it, it was only a matter of time before her phone started ringing. The media would want to do interviews, her editor would want her to write follow-up pieces, and friends and fans would be offering their sympathy and support. It was all very overwhelming. At least it would keep her busy, leaving her no time to mope about being sorry for herself.

She felt like she'd launched a hurricane into the world and for the moment she was sitting quietly in its eye, waiting for it to sweep her away. She just hoped when it eventually blew over, she'd be able to land on her feet.

———

Amber was sitting at the kitchen counter, her headphones clamped to her ears, swaying to the beat of the music as she ate her toast. She'd planned to skip breakfast, given how much weight she'd gained lately, but she'd woken up famished, so decided to put off starving herself until after breakfast.

She noticed her father standing before her. His mouth was moving. He must be saying something to her.

She turned the volume down and raised her eyebrows at him. "What?"

"Amber, can you take those things off your head for one minute so I can talk to you?"

She groaned, wondering what she'd done wrong now.

"What, Dad?" Slipping her headphones to her neck, she grimaced as they caught in her hair. Her mum had the same uncontrollable curls and apologised regularly for passing them onto her. Everyone said it was uncanny how much they looked alike. She hated that. It wasn't that she thought her mum was ugly—she looked all right for a mum— it was just that she'd rather have taken after her father a little more. In a heartbeat she'd exchange her dark skin for her father's olive tones, her curls for his sleek locks and her rounded hips for his athletic frame.

"Just checking you're coping with the news about Skye?" he asked. "You seemed pretty upset when we told you."

She shrugged, needing more time to process her feelings. It was all a bit confusing.

Amber had many secrets, but how she felt about Skye wasn't one of them. All her friends knew. Even her father knew if he was forced to look at the situation without wearing his love goggles.

Skye had stolen her father right when she'd needed him most and part of Amber hated her for it. She'd ruined everything, including their house. She'd drained the life out of it, along with all the colour. Who in their right mind would decorate an entire house in white? It was ridiculous!

Amber was embarrassed to bring any of her friends home, not just because of their house and its battle with albinism, but because she couldn't stand for any of them to see the way her father fawned over Skye like he was some kind of lovesick teenager. Yuck! It was the grossest thing on the face of the earth.

Amber was sixteen. She should be the one thinking about sex, not him. He was halfway to one hundred for goodness sake.

She'd taken to wearing headphones around the house, particularly in the morning when the moaning coming from the master bedroom would echo around the quiet of the house, making her want to vomit. Thank goodness for modern technology.

"I was just shocked, I guess," she said.

It occurred to her that maybe she should ask him how he was coping but lost the thought as he spoke again.

"I know you two haven't always been the best of friends and it's been tough for you living here away from your mum, but it was really nice to see how much you cared." He smiled at her, waiting for her to melt at his compliment.

She shrugged again, wondering if this was a roundabout way for him to ask her to move back in with her mum. Which would be pretty inconvenient given her school was only a short distance from here— the whole reason she moved in with her dad and Skye in the first place.

"It was pretty random news," she said, trying to keep her responses short in case she said the wrong thing. *God! Why is it so freaking hard to hate someone with cancer?*

"You know Skye's story went live today, so you can tell your friends about it." He swiped half a piece of toast from her place and bit down. "Be careful what you say, of course."

"Like how? How careful?" Hopefully he didn't know about all the things she'd already said about it online.

"Oh, you know, just don't go into details. Leave that to Skye. You know she likes to control what information goes out about her in the press." He went to grab another piece of toast and she moved her plate away.

"Sure. I'll be careful what I say." She reached for her headphones, hoping he'd get the hint. She didn't really want to talk about Skye.

"Amber, I'm still talking to you." He tipped back her headphones.

"Careful!" she snapped, checking them for damage. She'd be lost without those things in this house.

He wiped his hands on a white tea-towel, which would be sure to upset Skye if she found out. Those things are for looking at, not for actual use. Her dad really should know that by now. "You know you can talk to me, don't you?"

Her eyes widened as she tried to hide her outrage. Talk to him! She'd love to if on the rare occasions he was home, he wasn't being monopolised by Skye. He'd become a stranger. She missed her old dad who used to take her to movie premieres, concerts and dinners at fancy restaurants. He was fun in those days. When she was little, he used to tickle her feet until she laughed so hard she could feel tears streaming down her cheeks.

"I'm fine, really, Dad." She forced a smile to her lips. "Don't worry about me. Just focus on Skye."

He nodded. "Okay, go back to whatever it is you're listening to that's so interesting."

She turned her head before he could see the tears sliding down her face. Her father still made her cry, only now her tears were never accompanied by laughter. How could you tell someone you missed them, when they'd so clearly chosen someone else?

———

Theo sat down on the ab crunch machine—his favourite piece of equipment at the gym. He'd already turned the resistance up high, planning to do at least a hundred crunches. Skye loved his abs. Hell, he loved his abs.

He didn't need to get a tattoo like George to tell the world anything about himself. His body was his tattoo. It symbolised his determination to succeed in life. He wasn't going to let something like turning fifty get in the way of that.

Fuck! Fifty. It seemed impossible.

He counted his crunches, trying to obliterate thoughts of his age from his mind.

One. Two. Three.

Stupid-arsed lion tattoo.

Four. Five. Six.

George probably only got it to piss him off, knowing how much needles freaked him out. Competitive prick.

Seven. Eight. Nine.

Anyway, there was no contest. If there were, he'd win hands down.

Ten. Eleven. Twelve.

He had a better job. A bigger house. A hotter wife.

Thirteen. Fourteen. Fifteen.

Skye.

Sixteen. Seventeen. Eighteen.

Shit. Skye. Fuckin' cancer.

Nineteen. Twenty. Twenty-one.

Fuck. Fuck. Fuck. Fuck. Fuck.

He finished his hundred crunches, one fuck for every crunch like he was praying some kind of demented rosary. He hadn't prayed to any actual god about this. He'd tried that when his mum died, and it hadn't helped. There was no reason to think it was going to help now.

Deciding to give his quads a good burn, he headed for the bikes. That should help with his anger. Normally he used his latest case as motivation, but not today. Skye drove him on as he pressed down on the pedals, spinning them faster and faster until his muscles screamed for mercy he wasn't prepared to offer.

The thought of Skye with cancer was like the devil nipping at his heels. If only he could outride it and leave behind his frustration, confusion and...grief. Yep, grief. It was like he was in mourning for someone who hadn't yet died.

Not that he thought Skye was going to die, but it was certainly possible.

Those two words—cancer and death—were linked together with handcuffs made from titanium. It was impossible to think of the C word without the D word directly following it, just like some kind of fucked up alphabet.

No, Skye wasn't going to die. It was just that everything else around him was shrivelling up, his cock included. He didn't want to touch her. He *couldn't* touch her. She had cancer. You can do lots of things to cancer. You can poison it with chemo, scorch it with radiation, cut it out of your body, but you sure as hell didn't fuck with it, let alone fuck it.

Sex would have to wait. Looking for it elsewhere wasn't an option in this marriage. He took his wedding vows seriously, having stuffed them up so majorly the first time around with Rin. He may as well have had his fingers crossed behind his back when he'd promised to stay faithful to her. If he could've paused the ceremony and dragged one of her hot bridesmaids out the back for a quickie, he would've relished the chance. That was pretty much exactly what he'd done, too, except it was a month after the ceremony, not actually during it.

He never should've married Rin. She was a nice woman. Just not the right sort of woman for him. He only married her because of Amber. Stupid really. Amber had coped just fine with them being divorced. She didn't need them to be together.

Rin seemed to be coping just fine these days, too. It'd been years since she'd called him in the middle of the night crying. He kept telling her she deserved better than him. Not that Skye didn't also deserve better. It was just that he gave Skye a better version of himself. Anyway, now Rin had Jeff to give her everything he hadn't been able.

Including a son. Two actually. She had two sons as well as another daughter. Maybe if he'd stayed with her a little longer, she'd have given him a son. Nah, she'd probably have pushed out six more daughters and he'd have been well and truly stuck with her then.

His quads were burning now, past the point of being ignored. Time to switch to the calf press. He didn't want to turn into one of those guys with puny calves. George had puny calves. He never went to the gym, claiming his job was his workout. It was sort of true. He had fairly impressive biceps from lifting all those pipes or digging all those holes or whatever it was that he did all day. Unfortunately, they were matched by his equally impressive beginnings of a pot belly. It seemed plumbers didn't have the need to do many sit-ups. George's kids were a worry, too. Not so much Beth, but Lukas. He was a very big boy. Sophie must be feeding him too much of her Greek cooking. She was a bloody good cook, but she was killing that boy. She was certainly killing his chances of ever getting a girlfriend. Nobody wants to date a fat bloke.

Theo lay down on the calf press and pushed up the weight platform, extending his legs, being careful not to lock his knees.

One. Two. Three.

Everyone had a son except him.

Four. Five. Six.

Everyone.

Seven. Eight. Nine.

My son this. My son that.

Ten. Eleven. Twelve.

Fuck you and all your sons.

Thirteen. Fourteen. Fifteen.

Maybe Amber would present him with a whole football team of grandsons one day.

Sixteen. Seventeen. Eighteen.

She'd keep her maiden name and insist they all carry the Manis name.

Nineteen. Twenty. Twenty-one.

Yeah, that would be awesome.

Twenty-two. Twenty-three. Twenty-four.

Except it wasn't going to happen.

Twenty-five. Twenty-six. Twenty-seven.

It was fucked. Everything was fucked.

He stood up, deciding to cut his workout short and hit the shower. Skye was going to hospital tomorrow and she needed him. She was more important than puny calves.

"Everything okay, Theo?" asked one of the female trainers. She was wearing a name badge, yet every time he'd talked to her he never managed to take in her name. He'd go to look at it and get so distracted he'd forget why he'd lowered his glance in the first place.

"I'm fine, thanks, umm..." He forced his eyes to her badge. "Carly. Just calling it a night."

"Is there something I can help you with?" The flirtation in her voice was as obvious as a hard on at a swimming pool. It was also as inappropriate. His wife had cancer for fuck's sake. Everyone knew. Didn't she?

"Just need to get home," he said. "Everything's fine."

"See you tomorrow." Carly's eyelids batted as if she were a cartoon character.

He smiled.

Everything's fine. Yeah, everything's fine-ally fucked.

That was why he was in mourning. It wasn't Skye's potential death —she'd get through this—it was the certain death of the son he'd always thought he'd have.

43 DAYS BEFORE THE BREAK

George was at the table feeling pleased with his wife and the feast she put in front of him every night. Tonight's dinner featured a few of his favourites. A big plate of lamb kebabs with homemade tzatziki on the side, stuffed peppers for Beth who was going through some kind of freaky vegetarian thing (he really needed to talk to her about that), some spinach pita bread and the finest damn marinated chicken in town.

That was the best part about marrying a Greek girl. Sophie loved her food almost as much as he did. So did their kids. Well, Lukas, anyway. He'd had the appetite of a grown man by the time he was twelve, putting away plates of food almost as big as George's. He'd grown into a strapping young bloke. A little on the chubby side perhaps, but he was only seventeen and still growing. He needed his food. He'd slim out when he got older.

Damn, he was proud of him!

If Skye were able to give Theo that son he'd always wanted she'd probably feed him like a bird. He'd be a skinny, rich kid with slicked back hair and an ego so big it'd be a wonder he could stand up. One of those poofter sorts he saw walking to the train station in their posh blazers.

He grabbed a couple of kebabs by their skewers and put them on his plate.

"Thanks, Soph," he said. "I'm starving."

"You're always starving." She laughed as she slopped a large dollop of tzatziki on her plate.

He took a quick bite of chicken as he reached for some pita. "It's your fault for being such a good cook."

"Too good a cook." She patted her stomach. "I feel so fat lately."

He'd been married long enough to know his cue when he heard it. "You're perfect just the way you are."

The truth was she had put on a little weight over the years, but he didn't mind. Her curves were a sign of the good times they had together. She was still a looker. As much as he liked checking out women like Skye, there was no way he could be married to one of them. He far preferred his blonde goddess. Although, recently she'd reverted to her more natural hair colour of light brown and cropped it into a bob. He preferred it long but, again, he wasn't stupid enough to tell her that.

He leaned over and kissed her on the cheek. "You're gorgeous, Soph."

She rolled her eyes, not as good at taking compliments as she was at cooking.

"It's true." He slipped his hand to her thigh, causing her to turn a nice pink colour. He loved that he could still do that to her after all these years.

"Get a room," said Lukas, stuffing a pepper in his mouth.

"Hey! Mum made them for me." Beth crossed her arms and pouted.

George's hand returned to his cutlery and he took a bite of his lamb.

"They're for everyone," said Sophie. "There's plenty there."

Beth put three peppers on her plate and scowled at her brother.

"Did you talk to Theo today?" asked Sophie.

"Yeah, he's doin' okay, considering," George said between mouthfuls. "Skye's going into hospital tomorrow for her surgery."

"That was fast." Sophie set down her knife and took a sip of water.

"No point mucking around, I suppose." George shrugged.

"Does Skye *still* have cancer?" asked Beth.

"Of course, she does, you idiot," said Lukas.

"Apologise." George pointed his knife at his son. "You do not call your sister an idiot."

"Sorry," mumbled Lukas, his mouth full of food.

"It's so sad." Beth sighed loudly.

"Who cares," said Lukas. "It's not as if we like her or anything."

"Lukas!" This time it was Sophie who reprimanded him. "We do not talk about family like that."

"You do," he said. "I've heard the way you and Dad talk about her."

The colour returned to Sophie's cheeks, although this time for a different reason.

"Enough, Lukas." George eyed his son. It was tough reprimanding your kids when they spoke the truth. He and Sophie needed to be more careful about what they said.

"Maybe they'll put her in the same hospital as her mother," said Beth.

Lukas groaned loudly.

"No darling," said Sophie. "That's a different kind of hospital. Skye's mother has a sickness in her head. Skye's is in her body."

"Lukas showed me a video of Skye's mum dancing," said Beth.

George looked across at his son. "How'd you get a video like that?"

"It's called YouTube, Dad." Lukas rolled his eyes.

"They didn't have YouTube when she was a dancer," said George. "And for the record, I know what it is."

"Yeah, but they had video recorders." Lukas shook his head like it was an effort to tolerate someone as old as his father. "Some fan of hers posted heaps of videos of all the old ballerinas."

"What on earth made you look that up?" asked Sophie.

Lukas shrugged. "Just curious."

"He was checking out the ballerinas." Beth giggled.

"Shut your mouth." Lukas glared at his sister.

"How am I going to eat with my mouth shut?" Beth shoved a piece of pita bread at her tightly closed lips.

"Stop being silly." Sophie waved her hand in Beth's direction. "Eat your dinner."

"Show us the videos," said George. He wouldn't mind seeing what the fuss was all about. People were always raving on about Skye's mother and how brilliant she'd been. From what Theo had described, the day he'd met her she'd been anything but brilliant.

"Not now, George. He's eating," said Sophie.

"All right, all right. Later then." He got up from the table to get another beer.

"Get me a Coke, Dad," called Lukas.

He could hear Sophie protesting, saying something about sugar.

What was the big deal? His son was thirsty. He grabbed him a Coke. Not long now and he'd be able to grab him a beer.

His parents would be so proud if only they were here to see their grandchildren. It wasn't fair they were taken so young. No wonder Theo was so cut up about Skye. If anything ever happened to Sophie, he'd die.

Probably of starvation.

He headed back to the table to start on his second helping.

———

Skye watched Theo tip his glasses to the end of his nose and turn to her in bed.

"I want to come with you tomorrow," he said.

"I already told you that's not necessary," said Skye, doing her best not to get frustrated. "You're in the middle of a trial. Plus, Elle said she'd go with me. I'll be fine. It's just a bit of surgery."

"It's not just a bit of surgery." He reached out and took her hand, squeezing it gently.

"Don't make a big deal out of this, babe." She smiled, willing him to understand. "If you take time off from the trial—which I don't even think is possible—then I'll feel like I really am sick. I need to think of this as just a little bit of surgery."

"Then I think I should be there for your *little bit of surgery*." He removed his glasses and put them on the bedside table. This meant he was serious.

"You hate hospitals," she said. "And needles. Really, I'll be fine with Elle."

Skye shuffled across, closing the gap between them in their king size bed. She often lost him amongst all the pillows their interior designer had laden it with. She had to insist each pillow be covered in white slips to match the rest of the decor. Their variety came from their shape, not colour. There were triangle pillows, square ones, rectangles and some the shape of rolled up towels. She knew it must take Linda an age to arrange each one in its predetermined place. The bedspread was barely visible underneath them all.

"Remind me who Elle is," said Theo, putting an arm around her.

"You've met her before." Skye snuggled into his firm chest. "She was the friend I was having coffee with that day you ran into us in the cafe."

"The brunette?"

"Yes, tall, slim, gorgeous. Don't pretend you don't remember her." She laughed. Theo had never forgotten a beautiful woman in his life.

He let out a sharp breath. "Yeah, all right. I remember her. Where do you know her from again?"

"She's another one of the freelancers." She slapped him playfully. "Honestly, Theo, do you even listen to a word I say?"

He caught her hand and brought it to his lips. "I didn't realise you were that close, that's all."

"What do you mean? She writes stuff on my Facebook page all the time. You must have seen some of her comments?" She ran her finger over his bottom lip, wishing this conversation would hurry up and be over so she could kiss him.

He took her hand and placed it carefully back in her lap like she might break. "Babe, you know I hardly look at Facebook."

She'd often wondered why he even bothered being on there. He'd said it was handy sometimes for finding out things about people. His page was so bare there wasn't much risk of anyone finding out very much about him in return.

"Well, take a look next time and you'll see her there," she said. "I'll tell her to send you a friend request."

"As long as you're sure she'll look after you." He tucked her hair behind her ear and ran his index finger down her cheek.

"Of course, she will," she said, leaning into his touch. "I'll only be in hospital for two or three nights, depending on how things go. You'll hardly notice me missing."

"I doubt that's possible." He leant in for a kiss, lighting all kinds of hope in Skye's belly.

But it was a chaste kiss, the kind a friendly uncle might place on your cheek.

She sighed. Ever since she'd told him about her cancer, he'd barely laid a finger on her.

"What's the matter?" he asked.

"You won't break me." She sat up and lifted her camisole over her head, now wearing only her cream lace Victoria's Secret panties. "I'm still your wife."

"Don't, babe," he protested. "It's okay. Put that back on."

"You don't find me attractive anymore?" She tilted her face and blinked at him.

"Of course, I do. I just want you to get better." He glanced at her breasts, then straight back to her face. "You have a big day tomorrow."

"I know. With plenty of time to lie in a bed and rest. I don't want to rest now." She traced her finger down the line on his chest where his pecs separated. She could feel each muscle through the thin cotton of his tee-shirt and longed to remove the barrier.

"I don't want to hurt you," he said, on a groan.

"It won't hurt a bit." She got to her knees and straddled him, pulling at his shirt until he conceded and allowed her to lift it over his head, revealing his impressive torso. He wasn't a naturally hairy man with only a fine layer fanning out from the central line of his chest. Just enough to make him manly, without looking like a werewolf. If only he could present in court like this. He'd never lose a case.

"My gorgeous man," she purred. "My Kronos, I miss you."

He looked at her with uncertainty and she leant forward, letting her breasts spill over him. This was the one part of her body that contained any curves and she knew how much they turned him on.

She'd had her breasts done not long after she'd fixed her nose.

Before Theo. Before Dean even. Dean had always said she needn't have bothered. He loved her anyway. Theo had never said that. He loved her boobs almost as much as he loved her. Sometimes she wondered if he loved them even more.

She arched her back, teasing one of her hard nipples against his lips.

His warm tongue darted from his mouth and she knew she had him.

———

Skye lay awake in the dark, ignoring the damp mess on the sheets next to her.

Theo was snoring. It was a sound she'd grown used to over the years, just as people living on railway lines grow deaf to trains rattling past.

Dean had never snored, but she didn't want to think about that right now.

Her brain was cluttered with thoughts about Theo and the terrible sex they'd just had. He hadn't fucked her like a bull. More like an echidna, frightened he was going to hurt her with his spike. It was depressing.

At the core of their relationship was the mind-blowing sex. What did they have without that? If the core was pulled out of an apple, would its skin be enough to hold it in shape or would it shrivel and collapse? She wasn't even sure what the skin of their relationship was made from.

She looked at his profile in the shadows and watched the rise and fall of his chest. Was his sudden lack of interest in her due to her illness? It had to be. There was no other explanation.

Unless it was the idea of her infertility that was turning him off. Now that she could no longer provide him with the son he yearned for, she was useless to him. He was probably already lining up his next wife.

She remembered the fears she'd had about Dean when he went on his business trips to Adelaide. She'd been paranoid then, just as she was now.

She didn't want to think about Theo with anybody else. It was hard enough to imagine him married to Rin. Or having sex with Sophie. Not that she could imagine a sixteen-year-old version of her husband had been very impressive between the sheets. His performance with Sophie was probably much like his performance had been tonight.

Uncertain. Cautious. Fearful.

Anything but impressive.

That wasn't her confident husband who lay beside her. Her news had changed him more than she'd expected. It'd robbed him of the arrogant spark that made him so damn attractive. She wouldn't have believed this was possible without seeing it for herself. Never in all the times she'd imagined telling him she had cancer did she expect their sex life would be affected like this.

Wasn't she the one who was supposed to lose her libido at a time like this? Cancer was supposed to rob her of her desire, not turn her back into some kind of horny teenager. But all she wanted was Theo's reassuring hands upon her, making her feel like an attractive woman.

She didn't want him lying next to her snoring like a fifty-year-old heartbroken husband.

He must really care about her. Or no longer care at all.

"My Kronos." She shuffled closer to him, draping her arm across his chest.

If she could hold onto him in his sleep, then perhaps she could hold onto him forever.

42 DAYS BEFORE THE BREAK

Theo excused himself when the court took a short recess and headed to the men's room.

He locked the door in one of the stalls and leant against it, not needing to relieve himself, but desperately wanting a private moment with nobody interrupting him wanting to talk about the trial.

He pulled his phone from his pocket and scanned through his list of missed calls. Nothing from Skye. He'd asked her to call him when she was out of surgery. Maybe she was still under the anaesthetic? Or maybe something had gone wrong?

A pain gripped his chest. He was a terrible husband for not going with her. Any other husband would have. George would never let Sophie have such an important operation without him by her side.

Maybe he should've insisted Sophie be the one to take her into hospital, not this Elle person, whoever she was. She had a nice smile, a nice pair of tits too, but she could be anyone. There was a stranger looking after his wife.

He opened the Facebook app on his phone, wondering if Elle had sent that friend request. It was time to learn more about this mysterious friend.

It took him a few false starts as he clicked on all the wrong buttons.

Damn! He hadn't been on this bloody thing for ages. He found the button that led him to his friend requests and scrolled past a list of names he didn't recognise until he found Elle's. That was one problem with being a high-profile lawyer—everyone wanted to be your friend. Or your enemy.

He accepted Elle's request and clicked on her page. She didn't look exactly as he remembered the brief time he'd met her, but then again did anybody actually look like their profile picture? He knew his own photo was a particularly flattering one. He'd even converted it to black and white to make him appear younger.

He knew he looked good for his age. How else would he have been able to snag a woman like Skye? But he still got self-conscious. Particularly when he was mistaken for her father, as had happened a handful of times. It was these thoughts that motivated him to keep fit and down those revolting green glasses of slime Skye left for him in the fridge each morning. She called him Kronos. Would she still love him if he lost his ability to hold back time?

A large part of his success came from his looks. The better he looked, the more intimidating he could be. He couldn't control getting older, but he could control what shape he kept himself in, what clothes he wore and how he groomed himself.

Skye's followers referred to him as George Clooney. He loved that. Every woman thought George Clooney was hot. Damn, even he thought George Clooney was hot.

He scrolled through Elle's profile. There were a few photos of her on holiday somewhere exotic, drinking cocktails and dancing in clubs. He clicked on her profile photo to make it larger on his screen, his eyes drawn immediately to the tiny green bikini she was wearing. She had one rocking body on her that was for sure.

He clicked away, feeling aroused. Skye had a body like that. He didn't need to look at photos of her friend.

There was a photo of Skye on Elle's page, her mouth stretched across her face in her cute way of smiling without teeth, her sunglasses resting on the top of her head. She was holding out a glass of champagne to the camera.

He read Elle's caption. *I love my beautiful friend to the Skye and back.*

He'd used that line once in a birthday card. Elle wasn't so original.

After several more false clicks, he found where his private messages were stored and sent one to Elle.

Theo Manis 12.08pm
Hi Elle. Thanks for being with Skye today. Any news? Is she out of surgery yet? I'm about to head back into court, but if you could please let me know, I'll check my messages as soon as I'm able. Cheers, Theo.

Maybe he should send George a message and ask him to call in at the hospital to check on her. Then he remembered the crude comment he made about Skye when he visited him just after her diagnosis and decided not to.

He didn't have time, anyway. The judge wasn't going to wait for him.

———

It wasn't until much later in the afternoon when Theo got back to his desk that he had the chance to check his messages again.

Elle Thomas 2.28pm
Hi Theo. Skye's out of surgery. She was so brave!!! All went well. The doctor's confident they got all the cancer and everything went to plan. She should be able to come home on Thursday. She's asleep now, but before she drifted off, she asked me to tell you not to worry. E xx

Elle Thomas 4.59pm
Sorry, me again. Just letting you know Skye woke and ate a sandwich. The nurses are really impressed with how strong she is. She's in good hands. I'm heading home now as she's too tired for visitors and just wants to sleep. E xx

Theo Manis 5.46pm
Hi Elle. Thanks again for looking after Skye. I feel a bit guilty about

not being there so it's nice to know she has you with her. I'll drop by the hospital on my way home.

Elle Thomas 5.47pm

My pleasure. Well, not exactly a pleasure but you know what I mean. I'd do anything for Skye. She's helped me out plenty of times. It's nice to be able to do something for her for a change. I checked with the nurses on my way out and they said you'd be better to wait until tomorrow to see her. She's pretty drugged up and needs to sleep. Plus the visiting hours here are brutal. LOL.

Theo Manis 5.47pm

OK. I'll go past the hospital tomorrow night. Visiting hours won't be a problem. I'll threaten the nurses with legal action if they don't let me in! When you see Skye in the morning, please tell her that I love her and I miss her.

Elle Thomas 5.48pm

Awwww!! You're so sweet. I wish I had a husband like you ;-) Skye's so lucky.

Theo Manis 5.48pm

I'm the lucky one.

Elle Thomas 5.48pm

You're both lucky. You're married to Superwoman and she's married to George Clooney.

Theo Manis 5.48pm

Ha ha. I wish.

Elle Thomas 5.48pm

No need to wish, it's true. You do look like him, you know.

Theo Manis 6.07pm

Sorry, my phone won't stop ringing. Had to take a call. Where were we? George Clooney I think.

Theo Manis 6.08pm
Hello? Elle? Anybody there?

Elle Thomas 6.23pm
Sorry, I was in the shower. It must have been all that George Clooney talk. You don't happen to have a twin brother do you?

Theo Manis 6.24pm
I do actually! Didn't Skye tell you?

Elle Thomas 6.24pm
Very funny.

Theo Manis 6.25pm
No really, it's true. Check my friends list. His name's George.

Elle Thomas 6.25pm
As in George Clooney? Ha ha.

Theo Manis 6.26pm
Seriously, his name is George Manis. Check my list.

Elle Thomas 6.26pm
OK. I'm checking, but pretty sure you're tricking me.

Elle Thomas 6.27pm
OMG!!!! You're not tricking me. Is that for real? He looks exactly like you.

Theo Manis 6.27pm
Not exactly like me, but yeah, we're pretty similar.

Elle Thomas 6.28pm

You're much better looking of course. He's got the George Clooney name. You've got the George Clooney swagger.

Theo Manis 6.28pm
Swagger?

Elle Thomas 6.28pm
Yeah, I loved the way you walked into the café that day. You looked like you owned the place.

Theo Manis 6.29pm
Maybe I do.

Elle Thomas 6.29pm
It wouldn't surprise me.

Theo Manis 6.30pm
I have to run. Have to get some things ready for court tomorrow.

Elle Thomas 6.31pm
Impressive. George Clooney looks and Albert Einstein brains. Skye really is one lucky girl.

Theo Manis 6.31pm
Thanks again for taking care of her for me.

Elle Thomas 6.31pm
No problem. Let me know if you need anything else taken care of ;-)
Happy to help xx

Theo jumped back from his computer like it'd bitten him. What was he doing? Elle was clearly flirting with him. Was he flirting back? He re-read his messages and hit himself on his forehead with the palm of his hand. Yes, he'd been flirting and behaving like a mindless teenager. He'd gotten caught up enjoying the attention of a younger woman. Wasn't Skye enough for him?

He hoped she never saw those messages. He'd have to claim inno-cence if she did and remind her how thick men are. They didn't realise when women were coming onto them. She'd believe that. He didn't actually say anything incriminating. It was more that he didn't put a stop to the things Elle was saying.

Some friend Elle turned out to be, cracking onto her friend's husband like that. He'd have to try to warn Skye to stay away from her. She had enough going on in her life at the moment. She didn't need someone like Elle hanging around.

He picked up the phone and called George's home number.

Sophie answered.

"How's Skye?" she asked, sounding genuinely concerned.

"That's what I'm calling about actually. Are you busy Thursday morning? I was wondering if you could pick her up from hospital for me?" He drummed his fingers on his desk. It wasn't normal for him to ask a favour of Sophie, but nothing about life was exactly normal right now.

"I thought George said her friend was collecting her." There was a hesitation in her voice that made Theo wince. He knew Skye wasn't exactly her favourite person, but he'd thought she might be able to put that aside in a time like this.

"I'd feel better if it was you," he said, trying to sound just a little desperate.

Sophie let out a gentle sigh. "Sure, as long as you think Skye would be happy with that."

"Of course, she will," he said, fairly certain the opposite would be the case, but not caring in the slightest.

He gave her the details, said goodbye and leant back in his chair with his hands behind his head. Skye was better off with Sophie, even if they'd never gotten along particularly well.

He wished George and Sophie had embraced his relationship with Skye like they had when he was with Rin. They'd loved her. Sophie and Rin were still friends. They had a lot in common. Such as the fact he'd screwed them both, and not just in the bedroom.

He knew he'd been a bastard with women in the past. That was just one of the reasons he was so determined to stick by Skye through her illness. He needed to convince the world he was a changed man. Skye had changed him. She'd tamed the wild beast.

He pictured her in a lion tamer's outfit, the buttons of her shirt undone to her waist, her magnificent breasts spilling out of a leopard skin bra as she cracked a whip in the air.

His wife was hot. He saw the way other men looked at her and he liked it. He, himself, had looked at her like that when they first met. It was love at first sight. Lust was a kind of love, wasn't it? He'd had to have her.

All of her.

Finding out she was recently widowed had come as both good news and bad. It meant she was available but might also mean she wouldn't be ready to move on.

As it turned out, she was more than ready. They'd chatted over dinner for hours on their first date. It was possibly the longest conversation they'd ever had. He'd made up some flimsy excuse about wanting to show her the Charles Blackman hanging over his fireplace and found her more than willing to play along.

He never ended up showing her his painting that night. He had other assets he was far more eager to show her and by the way she undid his belt the moment they walked through the front door, it was clear she was just as keen to see them.

Despite the pathetic performance he put on in the bedroom last night, his feelings for her hadn't changed. When he thought of her, he still got turned on, but when she was there in front of him, all he could see was the cancer.

He shook these thoughts from his head and clicked onto the trail of messages he'd sent to Elle.

It was time to get this woman to back off.

Theo Manis 6.40pm
Sorry, Elle. I just spoke to George's wife, Sophie, and she's insisting on picking up Skye on Thursday. She feels bad that she hasn't had any family there with her. Skye will call you when she's settled back in at home. Thanks again for all your help. I appreciate it.

Elle Thomas 6.40pm
I am family! Skye and I are like sisters. Tell Sophie not to worry. I've
already made plans to collect her.

Theo Manis 6.41pm
Really, Elle, there's no need. I'll visit her tomorrow and then Sophie
will be there Thursday morning to bring her home. She wants to do it.
She's not the kind of woman you argue with.

Elle Thomas 6.41pm
Neither am I! LOL

Theo Manis 6.41pm
Sorry, Elle. I really do appreciate your help but I have a lot to do and
can't argue about this. Sophie will collect Skye. Thanks.

There were no replies after that, so he got on with his work,
pleased it would be Sophie collecting Skye and not Elle.

He really did miss his wife. He didn't need the attention of some
chick in a green bikini, no matter how hot she was. He thought about
Skye in a bikini. Then he thought about her not in a bikini and felt a
shot of energy in his groin.

If only he could bottle this feeling and take it home to bed when
Skye got back from hospital.

Maybe he'd feel differently now the cancer had been cut away. But
there was still chemotherapy to come. When she lost her hair, she'd
not only just be sick, but she'd look sick.

"Sorry, old fella," he said, adjusting his crotch. Like it or not, his
cock was going on holiday for a while.

He reminded himself that the best part about going on holiday was
coming home. And when Skye was better, he intended to come home
many times a night.

41 DAYS BEFORE THE BREAK

Rin kissed Sophie on the cheek and slid into the chair on the opposite side of the table.

"I've got exactly thirty-seven minutes before I have to pick up Rory. Start talking."

She knew her hair was a mess and the pathetic attempt she'd made at putting on make-up was sliding down her face, but that was nothing new. She didn't have spare hours to fuss over her appearance like Skye. She considered herself lucky if she got to pee without an audience.

She had very little in common with her ex-husband's new wife, but then again there was just as little to compare between Theo and Jeff. Had their marriage really been that bad they'd both had to go for the complete opposite the second time around?

"I ordered you a coffee to save time," said Sophie.

"You're a saint." Rin blew Sophie a kiss across the table. "Thanks."

"God, it's been ages." Sophie smiled warmly and Rin was struck by how much she loved her ex-sister-in-law. They'd bonded back in the days when Rin was married to Theo. They'd had to, given the amount of time Theo and George spent together. It'd been strange for Rin to begin with, knowing that Sophie had once dated her husband, but when she saw how much she was in love with George she found any feelings of jealousy easy to set aside.

"You look beautiful, Soph." She meant it. Theo should've married her while he had the chance, instead of letting George get his hands on her. Still, she was happy for Sophie. George loved her more than Theo ever would have.

Sophie screwed up her face and ran her hands over her recently cropped hair. "I wish. I swear this haircut's never going to grow out."

"Just be glad you don't have my hair. I don't think Amber's ever going to forgive me for passing it onto her." Rin tried to smooth down her curls only for them to bounce back up.

"Your hair's amazing. Don't you ever say that! Amber's lucky to have it. How is she, by the way?" Sophie sat forward in her chair. "We haven't even talked about what's been happening."

"Isn't it terrible?" Rin shook her head. "I could never have imagined. Poor Skye."

"I know," Sophie agreed.

A silence hung in the air as they let the chatter and hum of the cafe take over. Normally they enjoyed making fun of Skye. It'd become almost a sport as they'd giggle over what nonsense she'd been writing online. The way she wrote about Theo made him sound like some kind of saint. If anyone knew how untrue that was, it was them.

But mocking Skye didn't seem right today. She had cancer. They couldn't pay out on her.

"How bad is it?" asked Rin. She'd only heard snippets about Skye's condition from Amber. Depending on a sixteen-year-old to convey medical information was more than a little unreliable.

"It sounds pretty bad. She's just had both her ovaries removed." Sophie pulled her face into a pained expression. "Theo's asked me if I can pick her up tomorrow."

"You're picking her up? Oh my god." This was surprising. It was no secret Skye and Sophie had never been the best of friends. Rin had always hoped it was due to Sophie's loyalty to her, but suspected it might also have something to do with her own former relationship with Theo. Sophie had been able to accept Rin as Theo's partner because they were friends, but accepting that the man she once loved was with such a bimbo couldn't be easy. She knew that better than anyone.

Theo was a difficult man to let go. It didn't matter how much of a bastard he was, he had that certain something about him that just made you want to be by his side.

Although she loved Jeff, there were days she felt an ache deep in her bones for Theo. Being married to him had been exciting, every day unpredictable and charged with an energy she'd never felt since. On those days she had to remind herself of all the negatives that came with that excitement. The constant disappointment at being let down, the nagging suspicions about what he was doing and who he was doing it with and the never-ending fiery arguments.

Her life with Jeff had none of those things—the plusses or the minuses. Life with Jeff was calm and predictable. He looked at her in a way Theo never had, like she was the most beautiful and fascinating woman in the world. He didn't run out on her when their babies were young. She doubted he'd run out on her when their babies were grown either. That was a better way to live. Wasn't it? At any rate, it didn't matter. She had three kids with Jeff now and wasn't going anywhere.

She snapped back to attention, realising Sophie had been talking about her plans to collect Skye from hospital. She was glad it wasn't her.

"You're a good sister-in-law," said Rin. "Trust me. I know. Skye's very lucky."

"You were the good sister-in-law." Sophie reached for Rin's hand and squeezed it. "You still are. In my mind, nothing's changed. Sisters for life."

The waiter brought two coffees to the table.

"Coffee for the sisters," he said, grinning.

Sophie's family was from the northern part of Greece and her blue eyes and milky skin were an enormous contrast to Rin's dark Mauritian tan.

"You bet we're sisters. I've just spent more time in the sun," said Rin, running her fingers up and down her bare arms.

The waiter looked panicked for a moment, not sure whether he was allowed to laugh at such a comment.

"Coffee smells great," said Sophie, letting him off the hook.

"Enjoy." He backed away from the table and any potential offence.

"Men these days have no balls," said Rin.

Sophie laughed and they both took a sip of their coffee.

"So how is Amber?" asked Sophie. "We got distracted."

Rin was used to having conversations that jumped around like they were taking place on a pogo stick. That was one of the challenges of having children. Quality time for uninterrupted conversation seemed like something that only existed in fantasy novels.

"She's okay, thanks. I mean, she's so busy with school, I don't think it's affected her that much." Rin really hoped this was true. "It's not like she's close to Skye and she knows she can come and hang out with me and the kids if things get too intense."

"It still hurts, doesn't it?" Sophie asked cautiously.

For a moment Rin thought Sophie was asking about her feelings for Theo, but it wouldn't be like her to ask a question like that. Although they liked to criticise him, the topic of any remnants of their feelings for him was one they left alone. It was a topic lined with danger.

"What still hurts?" Rin picked up her teaspoon and scooped up some froth from her coffee, enjoying the sweet taste on her tongue.

"Amber living with Theo," Sophie explained.

Rin breathed a sigh. "Of course, it hurts. Who knows what the hell goes on in that place. But she's a good kid and it's not like I don't see her all the time. What can I do? Her school's practically around the corner from Theo. It doesn't make sense for her to live with me."

"I know." Sophie smiled warmly. "I just can't imagine Lukas or Beth sleeping under another roof."

Rin brushed off the sting of this comment knowing Sophie didn't mean to hurt her. One of the reasons their friendship was so solid was because of how honest they were with each other.

"This is why instead of complaining about our blokes, we go home and cook them dinner," said Rin. "There's no way I'm letting anyone take my kids away from me again. It was hard enough losing one. I'm not losing the other three."

"You love Jeff, though, don't you?" Sophie took a big sip of coffee and patted her lips with a paper napkin.

"Of course, I love him." Rin set down her spoon and looked Sophie in the eye, wanting to be certain she believed her. "What's not to love? He treats me better than anyone ever has. I'd be lost without him."

"I'm glad. He's a good man. I wish George would put Theo's crap aside and just be mates with him." Sophie shook her head and sighed. "It's not like you left Theo. He's the one who did the wrong thing."

"It goes both ways, you know that," said Rin. "Jeff's not too keen on having a friendship with George either. He looks too much like Theo, I suppose."

That's the way it was with them. The women were sisters and the men were strangers. Amber was the only glue that floated between all parties with ease. It was a lot of pressure for a sixteen-year-old.

"Every family has its issues," said Sophie, smiling.

"True." Rin rolled her eyes. "Some are just worse than others."

"Hey, it's not so bad." Sophie's eyes twinkled with mischief. "None of us have killed each other yet."

"Give it time," laughed Rin.

Sophie shook her head. "You're evil."

"Thanks. That's why you love me, isn't it?" Rin tilted her head innocently.

"Actually, it is," said Sophie.

"Shit!" Rin glanced at her watch. "I've only got twenty-three minutes left."

The two unlikely sisters bent their heads together and spent the next twenty-three minutes solving half the world's problems before promising to get together again soon to solve the rest of them.

———

Skye shifted uneasily in the hard bed. She missed her bed at home. Who knew how many people had slept on this mattress? Or died on it. It was a horrible thought.

She was sore, but happy the surgery was over. One more night and she'd be home with Theo.

Her Kronos.

He felt so bad about not being with her at the hospital, but really it was fine. She wasn't one of those wives who just said it was okay then brought it up in an argument five years later. She understood. Theo's job was important. He made the difference between people being able to return to live normal lives with their families or having to spend years behind bars. He was practically a saint.

Assuming his clients were all innocent, of course.

She knew that couldn't be possible but liked to think it was. It was so much more romantic to think of her husband as a knight in shining armour rescuing the innocent than a monster who manipulated the truth to ensure the guilty went free.

Besides, everyone deserved the right to a fair trial whether they were guilty or innocent. If Skye ever found herself charged with a crime, she'd want someone like Theo on her side. She certainly wouldn't want her lawyer running off to visit his wife in hospital in the middle of her trial.

There was plenty of time for Theo to take care of her when she returned home. And she still had all the chemo to come. There was no rush for him to transform himself into Florence Nightingale. She pictured him in an old-fashioned nursing hat and giggled. These painkillers must be stronger than she'd thought.

Maybe she should be the one to put on the nurse's uniform? A bit of dressing up in the bedroom might be just what her bull needed to get him bucking again. If she could dress like somebody else, he might be able to forget for a moment that she was sick.

She knew it was wrong to once again be thinking about sex. But that's how it was between her and Theo. Sex wasn't just about a physical need, it was about power. Her power over him as a younger woman. His power over her as a wealthy man. It equalised them. If she lost her power, then ... She could *not* lose her power. She'd rather die first.

Theo was driving to the hospital feeling pumped after a particularly arduous session at the gym to make up for calling it quits early last time. This time, he'd successfully channelled his anger and frustration at Skye's cancer into the weights, resulting in him doing dozens more reps than he'd usually manage.

The hot water of the shower afterwards had felt good. He was going to be sore tomorrow.

"No pain, no gain," he said aloud, lifting his hands from the steering wheel and pumping his fists in the air.

His mobile phone rang, making him jump as his palms instinctively landed back on the wheel. It was Bruno Martini, the leader of a gang of notorious thugs. Theo had represented him and his associates in court too many times to count.

"Theo Manis speaking," he said, answering the call.

"Mate, it's Bruno."

He could hear noise in the background, male voices, chinking glasses and a TV with some kind of sport being commentated in a droning voice.

"G'day mate, how ya doin'?" Theo always ended up sounding like he lived in the western suburbs when he spoke to Bruno. It didn't happen intentionally, but he didn't try to stop himself either. Clients like that felt more comfortable dealing with people on their own level. If Bruno noticed he didn't speak like that in court, he never said anything.

"I'm at The Commercial. Meet me here." Bruno had an edge to his voice. "It's urgent."

Theo hesitated. Bruno wasn't the sort he'd normally say no to. But how could he let Skye down again? He'd never forgive himself. "Mate, I can't tonight."

"I said it's urgent." Bruno sounded more than a little annoyed. "I wouldn't ask ya otherwise."

"Okay. I'll be there in ten minutes," said Theo, before realising Bruno had already disconnected the call, confident he'd be on his way.

He turned his BMW around, enjoying the way it responded to only the slightest pull on the steering wheel. Most of his peers drove German cars, although they went for the more conservative models, whereas he preferred the sportier look of the M4 coupe. It was red, of course, and able to turn any woman's head at the traffic lights. His car was the epitome of success. He deserved it with all the bullshit he had to put up with when he wasn't driving it.

He dialled Skye's number.

"Hello," she said, her voice a whisper.

"Babe, it's me." His heart was already breaking at the sound of her voice.

"I know." She laughed softly. "How are you?"

"Don't worry about me. How are you?" He frowned. "Why are you whispering?"

"Other patients are resting so I'm just trying to keep it down." Her voice sounded croaky, as in sexy croaky, not like when someone wasn't feeling well. He had to remind himself she was in hospital and probably not up for any pillow talk.

"You don't have your own room?" he asked, horrified at the thought. "I thought you were admitted as a private patient."

"All the single rooms were full," she explained. "It's okay. They're taking good care of me. I can't talk long, though. Are you coming in?"

"That's why I'm calling." He gripped the steering wheel harder, hating what he had to say. "I was on my way to see you, but then Bruno called and..."

"Don't worry," she said quickly. "I understand."

He knew by her voice that she did understand. She was used to him having to dash away at strange hours to represent clients in interviews or meet with them to discuss the current state of their freedom. It was rare for her to get angry with him. Rin would've had a fit if he ditched visiting her in hospital to go and have a beer with Bruno.

"You're the best, most beautiful, most sexy, most amazing wife in the world." He smiled widely.

"Stop it," she giggled. "Save it for when I get home."

"I spoke to Elle." He swallowed down yet more guilt. "She said you'll be home tomorrow."

"Yeah, the doctors are really happy with me," she said, still keeping her voice low.

"Fantastic. Bet they've never had a patient in your kind of shape." He paused, deciding to get the next part of the conversation out of the way. "Listen, I've organised Sophie to pick you up. I hope that's all right?"

"That's fine," she said, sounding genuinely okay about it. "Elle told me."

Relief swept out of Theo's body in a deep sigh. Maybe there was hope for Skye and Sophie, after all. "So, I'll see you tomorrow at home then?"

"Can't wait. Love you."

"Love you, too, babe. I'm sorry again."

"Don't be sorry. Drive safely. Don't drink too much."

"I won't," he promised. "I mean, I won't drink too much. I will drive safely. Bye, babe."

"Bye." She made a kissing sound then disconnected the call.

He felt like a pig for not going into the hospital. Bruno's timing was appalling. But then again, most things about Bruno were appalling. He hadn't gotten so rich by being a nice guy.

He wondered if the same could be said about him.

———

Theo could tell Bruno was stressed out. It wasn't that he looked worried, it was more that he was smiling.

When Bruno smiled it was generally time to be concerned. Usually his smiles were directly connected to one of three things.

1. He'd just made some kind of deal (almost always illegal).

2. The deal had paid off without him getting arrested or murdered.

3. The deal had not paid off and he was facing either arrest or murder.

On the surface, the third reason didn't look like much to smile about, but Bruno had long ago learnt the value of giving the appearance that everything was fine. Better than fine. Everything was great. Fantastic! Nobody wanted to do business with a loser.

If things were going badly, he had to smile all the harder to convince everyone he was okay.

Given the panicked phone call Theo had just received, he thought he could safely assume option number three was at play here.

Great. Just what he felt like doing tonight. Digging Bruno out of a pile of his own stinking shit. He cursed himself for ever getting involved with him. He'd been young and stupid when they first met, his hungry ambition blinkering him to the danger of linking his name to Bruno's.

It was too late now. Once a man like Bruno latches onto you, you're not the one to decide when the bond is broken. Unless you want to end up dead, which Theo most certainly did not. Although he sometimes wondered if his connection to Bruno would cause him to end up dead anyway. It'd happened to plenty of people before him.

"Mate," Bruno called out, spotting him approaching from the other side of the bar.

He was an ordinary looking bloke in his fifties with wispy hair carefully combed over the rapidly increasing dome of his head. He wore a leather jacket he favoured to the point it'd become a uniform, and jeans that hung low on what used to be his waist before it turned into a gelatinous mound of wobbling flesh, poorly disguised under his black t-shirt.

Theo was glad he'd changed into jeans and a Ralph Lauren polo shirt after his workout. It helped him blend in. A bloke in a suit in this grungy pub would be asking for trouble.

Being a weeknight, it was fairly quiet, with only a few regulars scattered about the place, some sitting on their own either by choice or circumstance, others clustered in small groups. They were all men. It wasn't that women weren't allowed in a pub like this, it was just that somehow, they were able to resist the allure of the dim lighting, stained carpet and peeling paint.

"How are ya?" asked Theo, putting out his hand.

"Never better. *Ne-ver* better." Bruno pumped his hand, more forcefully than necessary. It was an action that did little to disguise the fear in his eyes. Whatever shit he'd gotten himself into, it was serious.

Theo took a seat at the bar beside him, pretending not to see the dark marks on the fabric of the stool. Who knew what they were from. If you sprayed some luminol around and turned out the lights, you could turn this place into some kind of disco.

The bartender slid two beers across to them without being asked.

He knew what Bruno liked to drink and it went without saying that whoever was with him would be drinking the same.

Bruno nodded at the bartender who scuttled to the other end of the bar. He was smart for a young guy. Theo wished he could go with him.

"Hope I didn't pull you away from anythin' important," said Bruno, in an unusual gesture of politeness.

Only visiting my sick wife in hospital.

"Nah, it's okay. It's good to see you, mate." Theo knew better than to ask about the reason for his summons. Bruno would get to that in his own time. Sometimes it took him hours, but he always got there eventually.

Hopefully it wasn't hours tonight. He was knackered. It would be nice to get home in time to check up on Amber before she went to bed. That's if she could pull those stupid headphones off her ears and spare five seconds to talk to him.

Bruno handed him a piece of paper. "Have a gawk at this."

It was a printout of an email addressed to Bruno. A short email, although its contents must be bad. Bruno hadn't even bothered with the small talk.

He took a sip of his beer, wishing it was a nice glass of red and began to read.

Bruno. Do you like movies? I came across a most interesting one recently. And you know what? It was starring you as the main character, handing over a big wad of cash to Neville Simmons. Oh, and by the way, you're going to need to hand over another wad of cash. Put $50,000 in a sealed zip-lock bag and leave it in the cistern of the middle toilet in the men's room at The Commercial. Don't worry, I'll make sure it doesn't block the plumbing. Do it by 10pm tomorrow or I'll send the video to the police so they can decide if they want to nominate you for an Academy Award.

Theo glanced to the top of the page. It had yesterday's date. He looked at his watch. It was just after eight. Only two hours until the deadline. No wonder Bruno looked worried.

Theo knew exactly what video the email was referring to. Neville Simmons was a thug who'd been arrested several months ago for murdering one of Bruno's *associates*. The detectives on the case had pushed hard to prove Bruno had paid Neville to carry out the hit. It was their big chance to put him behind bars, only hindered by lack of evidence. Ultimately, they'd had to let him go.

Unbeknown to the police, some grainy but damning video evidence was taken by a security camera at The Commercial. Bruno hadn't even realised it was there.

Theo had.

When the whole Neville Simmons thing started to hit the fan and Bruno was spilling his guts in Theo's chambers, Theo had calmly stood and caught the next available taxi to The Commercial, dragging a confused Bruno with him.

He wasn't confused for long, turning white when Theo requested the footage for the day in question from the manager.

The manager, a reserved man named Chris, knew better than to say no to a request from Bruno's lawyer and handed it over. Theo didn't need to tell him to keep his mouth shut. Bruno took care of that when he asked Chris to give his best to his wife and kids. The fact he knew their names was frightening enough.

Theo had slipped the disc into his suit pocket, telling Bruno he'd destroy it. He did too—after he'd made a copy of it on his home computer. You never knew when having evidence against a man like Bruno could come in handy.

"I thought you destroyed that footage," said Bruno. His voice was level. It wasn't a direct accusation, but Theo felt the threat.

"I did." Theo's heart was pounding but he kept his exterior calm. "Unless there was a backup here at the hotel we didn't know about..."

Bruno nodded, seeming unconvinced.

"What could possibly be in it for me for that footage to get out?" Theo wasn't taking any chances. He needed Bruno to believe he had nothing to do with this.

"Relax." Bruno held up a palm. "I got it. It wasn't you."

"If you go down, I go with you." This wasn't strictly true. Not even loosely true, but it wouldn't hurt for Bruno to believe it.

"Where the fuck's Chris?" Bruno slammed his raised palm down on the bar. "I'm gonna fuckin' kill him."

The young bartender approached. "Is there a problem here?"

"Yeah, there's a fuckin' problem and it's name's Chris." Bruno leaned forward as he sneered. "Tell him to get the fuck out here."

"He's in Thailand." The bartender took a step back, wiping his hands on his jeans.

"Then get him on the fuckin' phone, all right." Bruno turned a shade of purple as a look of fear crept across the bartender's face.

"Jesus, Bruno," said Theo. "He's only a kid. Let it go for a minute."

"Who the fuck are you to tell me to let it go?" Bruno was standing now, his eyes wide with fury.

"I'm your fuckin' lawyer," Theo reminded him. "You know, the bloke who's going to keep you out of jail. Now sit back down and let's talk about this sensibly."

The bartender hovered, unsure as to whether or not he'd been dismissed.

"Just bring us another round, mate, and leave us to it," Theo instructed in what he hoped was a calming tone.

The poor guy couldn't scurry away fast enough.

Bruno sat down. "What the fuck, Theo?"

"The last thing we need here is for you to make a scene." Theo kept his voice down, hoping Bruno would follow suit. "Think about it. Whoever sent you that email is probably watching you right now, waiting for you to head to the bathroom. Let's be smart about this."

They glanced around the room at the dwindling crowd.

"I don't think it's Chris," said Theo, feeling guilty for giving Bruno that impression.

"Why?" Bruno grunted.

"Because for a start, he's in Thailand." Theo shrugged. "Any one of the staff here could've taken that video. If they were going to use it then it makes sense for them to wait until the boss goes overseas."

Chris was a nice guy. A decent bloke working hard to make a living. Theo didn't want Bruno hassling him. He didn't ask to have Bruno as a loyal customer, just like Theo hadn't. Bruno had chosen them, not the other way around.

The bartender placed two beers in front of them and hurriedly returned to the sink to stack some glasses, making the task look much more labour intensive than it was.

Bruno stood again.

"What ya doin' now?" asked Theo.

"I'm going to the fuckin' dunny to stick fifty large in it. Then I'm gonna wait and see what dumb cunt goes in to get it." He patted his pocket, indicating he'd come prepared with the ransom.

"Like they're gonna do it while you're here." Theo swivelled on his chair to face Bruno.

"They might." Bruno stuck out his chin. "Depends on how desperate they need the cash, doesn't it?"

"Nobody's that desperate. It might take them days to pick it up. You gonna to set up camp in there?" Theo raised his brows as he waited for the answer.

"If I hafta." Bruno crossed his arms like a defiant toddler.

"Was there a video attached to the email?" asked Theo. "This whole thing could be a bluff."

Bruno shook his head. "You willin' to bet my freedom on that?"

"Hey mate," Theo called to the bartender. "You got a permanent marker handy?"

The bartender shuffled through a drawer and tossed him a pen.

Theo raised his hand and caught it with ease.

"Come on then," he said to Bruno, heading to the men's room.

There were three filthy toilets in the bathroom with black, plastic seats and brown stained cisterns. The green tiled wall behind them could barely be seen underneath all the graffiti. Theo would have to be dying from dysentery before he'd consider taking a crap here.

The flush button on the cistern was tight, but it undid with a bit of pressure from Theo's right hand. He lifted the lid, revealing the inner workings of the toilet.

Bruno reached in his pocket and pulled out a ziplocked pack of neatly folded notes.

"Put it back in your pocket," said Theo, snapping off the lid to the pen.

"What ya doin'?" asked Bruno.

"Breaking the law. Shh, don't tell the graffiti police." Theo smirked as he wrote a message on the inside of the porcelain lid.

Give me the proof and I'll give you the cash.

"That should do it." He leant back so Bruno could read his message. "Let's *flush* out the truth."

Bruno didn't laugh, so Theo replaced the lid and screwed the button back in place.

"They're bluffing you, mate," he said.

"Yeah, they're fuckin' bluffing me." Bruno pursed his lips and nodded like a chicken pecking for its dinner. "To think I nearly gave them fifty grand. I'll give the prick fifty fuckin' bullets in the chest if I ever find out who it was."

Theo went to the sink and turned on the hot tap. Bruno wasn't joking. If he ever managed to carry out his threat, he doubted he'd be able to save him. Fifty bullets in the chest generally wasn't a crime people got away with.

He squirted soap onto his hands and began to scrub. As disappointed as he was not to have seen Skye tonight, he was glad he came to the hotel. If he hadn't, Bruno would probably have stuck his money in the toilet and killed the next poor unsuspecting bastard who came in to take a dump.

He needed to find a way to extricate himself from Bruno's clutches. And he needed to do it soon.

40 DAYS BEFORE THE BREAK

Sophie approached an amber light and pressed her foot to the accelerator. She was running late. Very late.

Normally, punctuality was her specialty. Hopefully Skye's doctor was also running late on his rounds and she hadn't been discharged yet.

Her phone chimed letting her know she had a text message.

Don't look at it. It's dangerous. Don't look at it. Don't text and drive.

She repeated these words over and over, giving herself the same advice she always gave her kids. Lukas would be getting his licence next year and she wouldn't want him reading a text message while he was driving. It was probably just George asking her if she'd picked up Skye. It couldn't be her kids. They were in school. Unless it was the school calling to say one of them was sick. Maybe she should just have a quick look at who it was from?

No! Don't look at it. It can wait five minutes.

She put on her indicator and swung the car around a corner, hitting the kerb with such force it caused her to slam on her brakes. She jolted violently as the car behind drove straight into the back of her.

"Damn it!" She banged her fists on the steering wheel. George was going to kill her. This was the second time this year someone had rearended her. The first time was her fault, too. Thankfully the insurance company disagreed with her on that point, as they would no doubt this time too. There was only so much damage her ancient CRV would be able to take. It was getting to the point where it may not be worth repairing.

She drove forward and parked her car, stepping out wearing her most apologetic expression, only to see the other driver take off, waving at her with his middle finger.

Her eyes went straight to the back of his car to get his licence plate, only to see it was missing.

"Malaka!" she cried out, realising she'd have no choice but to pay for the accident this time. She'd make sure she reminded George she was doing his brother's wife a favour at the time. That was if she ever made it to the hospital.

She'd have to pay the excess out of the wage she took for running George's plumbing business and hope he didn't notice.

She had a look at the back of her car and cringed at the damage. The bumper bar was hanging on as if frightened for its life. George was going to notice.

"Bloody eff!" She went to kick the bumper before withdrawing her foot, deciding not to push her luck.

She got back into her car and pulled her phone out of her bag, ready to fess up. Better she told him than for him to find out himself.

The text message she'd received earlier was on the screen.

Skye Manis
Hi Sophie. Thanks for offering to collect me today. They let me out early for good behaviour. I'm out the front. No rush. I'm happy to wait. Skye xx

"Shit." She tossed her phone into her bag and pulled out from the kerb. She'd ring George later. Or maybe she wouldn't bother. There was still a chance she'd get away with it.

At least she wouldn't need to worry about parking now. With the luck she was having, she'd probably crash into a pole.

If only Theo wasn't in court, he could've picked Skye up himself and her car would be in one piece sitting outside her house.

She overtook the truck in front of her, smiling as she saw a clear patch of traffic ahead.

It wasn't Theo's fault, she supposed. A lot of people counted on him with his job. He couldn't exactly just stand up in the middle of a trial and tell the judge he needed to go and collect his wife.

His *wife*. She was still getting used to thinking of Skye in that way. She was young enough to be his daughter. The whole thing felt very strange.

She'd been shocked when George told her about Skye's cancer. It was the last thing she expected to hear. How awful. Her heart bled for Theo. He was obsessed with Skye. This must be hurting him a lot. He'd be sick with worry. The poor client he was representing today surely wouldn't be getting the best out of him.

She approached the hospital and spotted Skye almost immediately, sitting on the front steps. She waved at Sophie.

Sophie waved in return and pulled the car over.

Skye walked slowly, holding her stomach with one hand and her expensive overnight bag in the other. Sophie knew she was supposed to be able to tell what designer brand the bag was, but she'd never much cared for these things. No doubt it was worth more than it was going to cost to fix the damage to her bumper.

She climbed out of the car and took the bag from Skye, placing it carefully on the back seat.

"Thanks, Sophie," said Skye, kissing the air several inches away from her face, wincing either from the effort of this token gesture of affection or the pain of her surgery.

Sophie helped her into the car, noticing how bony she'd become. Still, she somehow looked glamorous. Was it the Lorna Jane active wear she was wearing or her anorexic model look? Whatever it was, it wasn't fair that on her worst day she still managed to look better than Sophie on her best. Life could be cruel.

A car tooted for her to move along and she raced around to the driver's side and hopped back into the car. The way Skye was moving, she looked like she was in a fair bit of pain, so Sophie leant across and did up her seatbelt for her.

"Let's get you home," she said, starting the engine. "How are you feeling?"

"Pretty sore. Not as bad as I expected, but that's probably the drugs talking." Skye waved a paper bag in the air and it rattled.

"So, it went well?" Sophie put on her indicator and checked her mirrors.

"Really well. My doctor couldn't be happier."

"That's fantastic." Sophie navigated the car back onto the road and headed in the direction of Malvern. She hated driving on this side of town.

"I'll have to have regular tests of course and the chemo, but at least this bit's out of the way," said Skye.

Sophie nodded, wondering what question she could fill the empty space in the car with next. "When's the chemo?"

"Oh, not for a couple of weeks. I need to heal up from the op first." Skye winced, adjusting the seat belt across her waist.

"I can come with you if you like. You know, be your chemo buddy." She'd never been very close to Skye. Chemo might be a good chance for them to get to know each other better. At the very least, it would make George happy to see her making an effort.

"Thanks, that's so sweet," said Skye. "But my friend, Elle, has her heart set on going with me. It's only a few sessions anyway. I'll be fine."

"No problem." Sophie tried not to feel rejected, but this was what always seemed to happen when she reached out to her sister-in-law.

Skye smiled. Well, it looked like she was smiling. It was always hard to tell, given the way she smiled without her teeth. Perhaps she was just grimacing from the pain.

"I read your blog post," said Sophie. "You've got a lot of people supporting you with this. Quite a big fan base."

"Yes, the more tragedy that strikes me, the more popular I get." She laughed. "Hope I don't die, imagine how popular I'd be then."

Sophie smirked, unable to laugh with her. Dying wasn't something to be joked about. Her mother had died from bowel cancer a few years ago and it was anything but funny. She missed her every day.

"Ouch." Skye squirmed in her seat, her hands pressed to her middle.

"What's the matter?" Sophie slowed down so she could look at

Skye. "Do I need to turn around?"

She did look awfully pale. Maybe she should've talked to her doctor herself before she took her home, instead of just letting her get in the car like that.

"No, no. I'm fine." Skye waved her hands. "It just hurts when I laugh."

"Then no more laughing." Sophie glanced in the rear vision mirror and increased her speed.

"But laughter's the best medicine, isn't it?" asked Skye.

"Not always." Especially when it was about cancer. Maybe that was just Skye's way of trying to cope.

"Then what is the best medicine?" asked Skye.

Sophie thought about it for a moment. What was her best medicine? It would have to be George. With his arms wrapped around her at night she felt safe. Like nothing could possibly go wrong. But she couldn't exactly tell Skye that. She didn't know what kind of relationship she had with Theo when the doors were closed. Did he make her feel safe? Or was it his bank account that made her feel secure?

She scolded herself for being so nasty as she pushed away thoughts of what her own life might have been like if she'd married Theo instead of George. It was a silly thought. He'd never have married her. One look at Skye could tell her that. A familiar pain in her heart nudged her, reminding her it was still there. Some things—some people—were hard to get over.

Theo and Skye may not have a conventional relationship, but they loved each other. Anyone could see that. She remembered the first time Theo brought her around to their house and how inadequate Skye had made her feel, tottering around on those stilettos in her skinny jeans. Sophie had never felt older, fatter or frumpier.

She knew she wasn't too bad looking for her age. George still seemed to be attracted to her and that was the main thing. Still, she wished her hair was a little thicker and her waist a little slimmer. She was only five foot four, part of the reason her weight was such a challenge. If only she had long legs like the set in the passenger seat beside her it'd be so much easier to control her weight.

"Still thinking of an answer?" asked Skye.

"Love. Love's the best medicine." Sophie smiled at Skye, just as a loud clanging noise sounded at the rear of the car.

"What's that?" Skye looked alarmed.

"Probably just my bumper bar. I had an accident on my way here." Sophie kept her voice calm. Calmer than it should be under the circumstances.

"What?" Skye turned to look out the back window. "Are you okay?"

"I'm fine." She smiled reassuringly. "Not sure about the car, though."

"Should we pull over?" Skye turned back to face the front of the car.

"No." Sophie laughed, feeling lightheaded. Maybe it was the shock of the accident catching up with her. Or Skye's cancer. Or was it her broken heart that so stubbornly refused to heal no matter how many years dragged past?

"It sounds kind of serious," said Skye. "Why not pull over?"

Sophie gripped the steering wheel. "Because, Skye, sometimes when life hits you in the arse, your only choice is just to keep on moving."

"True, but in this case, I think your whole arse is about to fall off."

"Wouldn't be a first."

This time they both laughed, Skye with genuine amusement and Sophie as the only way to prevent herself from falling apart.

"Ouch. Don't make me laugh." Skye clutched her stomach.

"Sorry, I didn't mean it." Sophie's eyes widened with concern.

"It's okay. I'm good. Look, I really appreciate the lift, Sophie." A serious expression crossed her perfect face. "It's nice to have you here. With my Mum being ... the way she is ... you're the closest person I have to a mother."

The bumper bar clattered to the road, taking with it the last shreds of Sophie's confidence. That was just what she wanted. To be a mother to her ex-lover's wife.

She decided the only good thing about this day, was that it couldn't get any worse.

———

Skye waved goodbye to Sophie at the front gate and climbed the stairs to her bedroom, letting her fingertips run along the white balustrade. She was a little lightheaded. Time with Sophie could do that to you.

She'd never warmed to her sister-in-law, mainly because Sophie had never warmed to her.

Sophie was suspicious of her the moment she first laid eyes on her. She'd often catch her staring, like she was some kind of turd stuck to the bottom of her shoe. Clearly, she was jealous. She went out with Theo briefly about a million years ago, before Skye had even been born. She was no competition.

It was nice of her to pick her up from hospital, she supposed. She had plenty of time on her hands, though. It wasn't like she had a real job or anything.

Although, she'd been late. She'd had to sit on those hospital steps for ages. Not that Sophie had even apologised for that. She was too busy putting her seatbelt on for her like she was five years old.

She sat down carefully on her bed holding her stomach and smiled as she remembered what she'd said just before she got out of the car.

You're the closest person I have to a mother.

The expression on Sophie's face had been hilarious. She wished she had a photo of it. And to top it off, as soon as she said it, Sophie's bumper bar fell off. It was like the car was giving her a standing ovation.

She knew she was being unkind with all these thoughts, but that was the effect Sophie had on her. And she was certain that whatever Sophie was thinking about her right now would be far from kind. Fair was fair. Some people just weren't born to get along.

She closed her eyes and tried to get comfortable in the nest of pillows. It was nice to be home. It would be even nicer when Theo got home, too.

She reached for her handbag and pulled out her mobile phone.

"Call Theo," she said, feeling too lazy to dial the number herself.

The phone obediently connected her call.

She knew he wouldn't answer. She just wanted to hear his husky voice on his message service.

Hello, you've called Theo Manis. Please leave a message after the tone.

Two short, simple sentences she'd heard a thousand times on a thousand different people's message services, yet somehow on Theo's it sounded like she'd called a sex line. Probably because it was the same voice she heard whispering in her ear as he ran his hand down the curve of her hip when he lay next to her in bed.

"Hi, babe," she said, deciding to leave a message. "I'm home. Sophie just dropped me off. I'm tired and a bit sore, but otherwise feeling pretty good. Can't wait to see you tonight. Love you."

The front door slammed. Amber was home. Linda never slammed the door like that. She knew better than to make such a racket.

How was anybody meant to get any rest? She was going to need to speak to Theo about this.

It'd never bothered Skye that Theo had a daughter. Until she moved in, leaving brightly coloured jackets draped over chairs and sticking tacky posters on her bedroom door.

"She's just a teenager," Theo had said. "Give her some space."

So, Skye had ignored the loud music, and the dirty plates discarded on the coffee table and tried to form a friendship with her. After all, the age gap was only fourteen years. Surely, they could be friends?

She'd tried so hard to make it work, buying Amber concert tickets to see her favourite bands and clothes she thought she might like. She even had her decorator come in and fix up an entire wing of the house on the ground floor especially for Amber, painting it in her favourite colour, purple. Amber had her own living room and bathroom. What kind of teenager had that!

But her attempts at friendship had fallen flat. Amber made it clear she'd have preferred her father to have remained single.

That was when Skye decided to take Theo's advice and give her some space. Amber already had a mother and she wasn't looking for another. She wasn't in need of any more friends either, judging by the amount of time she spent on her phone.

Another door slammed and Skye winced.

Peace and quiet was what she needed to recover, not a moody teenager stomping around. But if she ever had a chance of getting Amber out of her house, it was now.

There were some definite upsides to this whole cancer business.

34 DAYS BEFORE THE BREAK

Theo picked up his phone and smiled, happy to see his ex-wife's name lit up on the screen. This wasn't his usual reaction, but he really needed to talk to her.

"Theo Manis speaking," he said out of habit.

"Hi, Theo. It's Rin." It was late for her to call. She must've just gotten her horde of kids to bed for the night.

"Right. Rin. Hi ... um, thanks for calling back."

He always felt awkward talking to her. He knew it was the guilt for walking out on her all those years ago. He'd been a bastard. He could see that now. Her only crime had been loving him so much she'd suffocated him.

Skye smiled at him from the other side of the kitchen, looking delicate and beautiful in the silk camisole and pyjama pants she liked to wear to bed. Not that they usually stayed on for very long. Often, she'd leave the pants neatly folded in the drawer beside the bed before she hopped under the covers. It saved time.

She didn't like it when he spoke to Rin, but this time was different. This was a conversation she wanted him to have.

"No worries. Is everything all right with Amber?" asked Rin.

It was fair enough for her to assume that was why he called. Amber was the only topic they ever spoke about.

"Yes, she's fine. Great, actually." He sat back in his chair at the breakfast table and drummed his fingers on the glass surface.

"Oh, okay. Um, look Theo, I'm sorry to hear about Skye."

She sounded as awkward as he did. It was sad. Two people who'd once been so mad for each other they could barely make it through the front door without ripping each other's clothes off and now they'd forgotten how to even talk.

"Thanks. Nice of you to say that." He winced at his politeness.

"How is she?" Rin asked. "Sophie said she had surgery last week."

He nodded, not liking how close Rin and Sophie had remained. What else had Sophie told her? "She's not great. That's why I was calling. Her surgery went well—really well actually— but her chemo's about to start soon and ... well ... I was wondering if maybe we could have a chat about Amber's living arrangements."

"You're trying to get rid of her? Come on, Theo!" All politeness was now officially out the window. "You fought me tooth and nail to get hold of her and now it's not convenient you want to send her back? You're unbelievable, you know."

She was upset. Actually, no, she was pissed off and he deserved it. He felt terrible to ask this of her, but it was what Skye needed. As she'd pointed out to him, she had the best chance of recovery if she could do it in peace. Amber was a good kid, but she was still a kid. And kids were noisy creatures by nature. What Skye needed was tranquillity.

"So, you won't take her?" he asked.

"Of course, I'll bloody take her," she spat out. "She's my daughter. I'd love to have her under my roof again. As you'll recall I never wanted her to leave in the first place."

"Then what's the problem?" He drew in a deep breath, trying not to buy into her anger.

"You, Theo. You're the problem. You always have been." Her tone was far colder than he felt he deserved. "How do you think this is going to affect Amber? Have you even thought about that? She hasn't gotten over you rejecting her the first time."

"Hey, now that's not fair." He fought to keep his voice level. "I never rejected her. It was—"

"Me," she said, finishing his sentence in a totally different way than how she used to. "I get it. It was me. Just say it. I can take it."

He winced. "I was going to say it was me."

'*It's not you, it's me*,' she quoted in a sing-song voice. "I think that line's been used somewhere before."

"Listen, can we just talk about Amber please?" he asked, trying to get the conversation back on track.

"Sure. Go ahead," she said, anger still clear in her voice. "What's your plan here? You know we don't have a spare bedroom for her. She's not going to like this."

He'd been to Rin's house a few times to drop off Amber, although he'd never stepped past the front fence. The house actually belonged to her husband, so going inside didn't seem right. He'd never asked but was certain Jeff would feel the same way. It was a small brick bungalow in Burwood, a nice suburb, but far less impressive than the one he lived in. The house looked tiny. It would be lucky if it contained three bedrooms, let alone a second bathroom. The whole thing could fit inside his living room, yet it was home not only to Rin and Jeff, but their three children. Fitting Amber in there would be a struggle. Thankfully, he'd already thought about how to solve that problem.

"Amber's mentioned you have a shed in the backyard," he said. "How about I pay some builders to convert it into a bedroom for her?"

"Is this a joke?" she asked. "Please don't tell me that you're suggesting I stick our daughter in a shed."

"I'll pay some builders to convert it into a bedroom," he quickly explained.

"It's Jeff's shed," she said, still sounding entirely unconvinced. "It's full of his stuff. Where will he put it all?"

"I don't know. Underneath? We can make it two storeys. Amber can have a little apartment in your backyard." His mind whirled with possibilities. "Or we can build Jeff another shed. It'll add a lot of value to your house."

She was quiet, which meant she was thinking about it. It must be a tempting offer for someone on a limited budget like hers. When they'd divorced, he'd only just started working as a lawyer. Giving her sixty percent of everything he owned hadn't been too much of a hardship. He'd barely owned anything. She hadn't seemed to have improved her situation much over the years. Jeff was an accountant on an accountant's salary and Rin had never returned to work, instead increasing the household expenses by having more children. She lived a very different life to him.

"And how will she get to school?" asked Rin, sounding a lot calmer.

"Can't you drive her?" He frowned, aware that she no longer worked.

"And I've got nothing better to do than be a taxi driver," she huffed. "I have three other kids, you know."

"I thought you wanted Amber to live with you? We can drop this whole thing if you like." Years of arguing in a courtroom had taught him it was time to call her bluff. He was being very generous offering to rebuild her shed *and* give her what she'd fought so hard for all those years ago. Amber. She could figure out how to get her to school.

"Fine," she conceded. "I'll talk to Jeff and call you back."

He could hear a child whining in the background. One of Amber's half-siblings. This would be a good chance for her to get to know them better. He was doing the right thing. It would be a win for everyone. Amber could move back in with him next year once Skye's treatment was finished.

"Thanks, Rin," he said, trying to inject some warmth in his tone. "I appreciate it."

"I'm sure you don't."

She disconnected the call, leaving him feeling ill. The conversation had done nothing to ease the guilt of his past sins. It'd only added to it. Maybe this whole thing was a mistake. Amber wasn't that noisy.

Skye came over to stand behind his chair, wrapping her arms around him and feathering his face with tender kisses.

"Thank you, Kronos," she whispered.

"You're so supportive." Her kisses trailed to his neck.

"And loving." She undid the top button of his shirt.

"And sexy." She slid her hand into his shirt and caressed his chest.

He could no longer think. When she was standing behind him like this, he couldn't tell she was sick. He could close his eyes and pretend she was well.

"Your surgery was only last week," he said. "We can't ..."

"There's plenty we can still do." Her hands slid to his stomach and he groaned in response.

Whatever she wanted was all right with him.

———

Jeff watched his wife put down the phone, having just talked to Theo. He noticed a flush creeping up her neck.

He doubted she was the only woman to get nervous around Theo. He was that kind of guy. All suave and debonair with overtones of power and wealth. Still, he wasn't very clever. No man with a brain in his head would leave a woman like Tamarin.

That was one of the reasons Jeff always called her by her full name. Everyone else called her Rin, including Theo. Calling her Tamarin gave him a point of difference. Besides, it was an exotic name. It suited her. When her parents had named her after a picturesque Mauritian surfing town, he'd bet they never expected it to be stripped back to three harsh sounding letters. Theo could call her Rin as much as he liked, she'd always be Tamarin to Jeff.

It was hard not to be jealous of Theo. No woman had ever flushed like that around him.

He reminded himself he should be grateful. Theo had treated Tamarin so poorly she'd practically fallen into his arms. He wasn't sure he could've ended up with a woman so beautiful in any other circumstances.

As she'd had their daughter and two sons, she'd only gotten more beautiful, for now she wasn't just his wife, she was the mother of his children. He had to pinch himself sometimes. He was one very lucky guy.

He'd been listening in to her conversation, his ears pricking up when she said something about his shed. What on earth was that about? Why was his shed any of Theo's business?

Then Rory had started to whine. He was hungry. Rory was always hungry.

"Shh, Rors," he'd said, trying to hush him. "Mummy's on the phone."

There was nothing like a child to kill your ability to eavesdrop.

Tamarin had now moved to the sink to wash some dishes. He'd noticed this was her habit after speaking to Theo—to find the nearest bit of housework and launch herself into it. The flush had reached her chin now, threatening to overtake her whole body.

He was so bloody sick of that arsehole. It seemed divorce wasn't enough to sever him from their lives. Unless Theo got hit by a bus, they'd never be free of him. Maybe if Tamarin hadn't had a child with him, he'd have disappeared for good by now instead of constantly showing up and upsetting her. Or worse, putting that secret smile on her face when she thought nobody was watching. He couldn't help but wonder if she was still in love with him.

He should've been a bus driver instead of an accountant.

"Rory, come quick," Samantha called from the next room. "James is getting a high score."

Rory raced from his side, happy to be included by his older siblings. Usually they got more pleasure from leaving him out. Samantha's timing was unusually brilliant.

"Is Rory okay?" asked Tamarin, seeming to remember a moment ago he'd been whining for something.

"He's fine. Dying of hunger, but I think he'll pull through. What did Theo want?" Jeff tried to sound casual. The look on her face told him he'd failed. It annoyed her when he asked too many questions about Theo.

"He wants us to take Amber back while Skye has her treatment," she said, like this wasn't exactly what she'd always wanted.

"That's fantastic. Isn't it?" he asked, trying to work out why she wasn't happy with this news. She'd been devastated when Amber moved out.

"Of course, it is. You know that's what I want." She dried her hands on a tea towel and leant against the sink. "It's just ... where are we going to put her?"

"She can bunk with Samantha," he suggested.

"Sammy would love that." Tamarin smiled. "Amber not so much."

"Don't tell me he's suggesting we put her in the shed?" he asked, putting together the snippets of conversation he'd overheard.

"Yes." Tamarin raked her hands through her thick hair.

Jeff shook his head. "What the hell is he thinking?"

She bit down on her lip like she did when she was unsure about something. "Actually, it's not such a silly idea."

Jeff knew Theo could be persuasive. He persuaded people for a living, but this was ridiculous. He wasn't going to let Amber sleep in the shed like she was a dog!

"He wants to pay a builder to renovate the shed and turn it into a little apartment for her," said Tamarin.

"But where will I put all of Dad's stuff?" he asked, horrified at the thought of moving it all. Their house had once belonged to his parents, who bought it when they were first married. When Jeff inherited it, a lot of his father's belongings had ended up in the shed.

"He'll build you a new shed as part of the deal." She folded her arms. He could sense a fight brewing if he didn't get on board with this crazy idea.

"And you like the sound of this?" he asked.

She nodded.

She'd lost her marbles. She'd gone completely and absolutely bonkers.

"Think about it," she urged. "We've been craving more space around here. This could be the answer. Amber can live here for a few years—or longer if she likes—and then later we can rent it out or maybe we could use it as an office and start a business or something. It'll add heaps of value to our house and it won't cost us a cent."

That sounded like a line from Theo, but he had to admit it did make a lot of sense when you looked at it that way. He'd always liked the idea of working from home one day and they were living on top of each other in this place. When their kids became teenagers, it was only going to get worse. He hated the idea of Tamarin asking him to move to a bigger house, as she no doubt would. Maybe this was one way to put that off.

But ... sheds are sacred spaces. Every man knows that. And he was supposed to let his wife's first husband mess with his? It would be like a woman asking her husband's ex-wife to give her a leg wax.

"How much control would we have over the plans?" he asked.

"Full control," she said confidently. "Theo will just be paying the bill. It'll still be our shed. *Your* shed."

He sighed, already exhausted at the thought of having to contend with his father's belongings. He'd been avoiding sorting them out for twenty years. He wasn't sure he was ready to do it yet.

"All right." He nodded. "If it means that much to you."

"It does. You know it does." She kissed him on the cheek.

He turned his face and gave her a long kiss on the lips, feeling her respond.

"Mummy. James isn't sharing. It's not faaaaair," came Rory's voice from the living room.

Tamarin pulled away from him. He looked at her neck and noticed the flush she'd had earlier had disappeared, despite the passionate kiss he'd just given her.

"I'll sort the kids out," he said.

"Good luck."

She laughed.

He didn't.

He'd much rather negotiate turns on a Playstation than stay there and think about the implications of Theo being able to raise his wife's pulse rate far higher than he ever could.

33 DAYS BEFORE THE BREAK

Amber snorted when she read the latest comment to pop up in her group.

You're so lucky to have Skye as a stepmother. She's amazing.

What a joke! She was glad to be able to have this conversation with fingertips rather than her mouth. This way, she could at least consider her response before hitting the send button.

She composed some replies in her mind.

You can have her if you like ... Yeah, she's amazing, just ask my dad ... Seen Cinderella lately?

She could say none of this, of course. Being mean about someone with cancer was poor form. Those kinds of diagnoses came with a free pass from being talked badly about.

Her friends were swarming around her. She was the most popular girl in the school. This wouldn't be a problem if they liked her for who she was and not because of who her stepmother was.

The girls at school recited lines out of Skye's articles like they were quotes from the holy bible. Each time a new story was posted online, they'd flock to Amber to try to glean any additional information about their messiah.

It was getting annoying.

"Have you got a second, sweetheart?"

It was her dad, standing at her bedroom door. His hands were on his hips, which meant he was nervous, puffing himself out like some kind of rooster.

"What's wrong?" She swung her chair around to face him.

"I've been talking to your mother—"

"You're trying to get rid of me, aren't you?"

She'd overheard him talking to Skye about it. She wasn't surprised. She knew it would happen eventually. He'd already walked out on her when she was a baby. She'd been almost waiting for him to do it again. She was just wondering when he was going to talk to her about it. It wasn't like that decision affected HER ENTIRE LIFE or anything.

"No, of course I'm not trying to get rid of you." The unusual high pitch to his normally husky voice said the opposite to his words.

"Then what?" She raised a brow and waited for him to continue.

"Like I said, I was talking to your mother and we both think it'd be best for you if you moved back in with her for a while." He coughed as if allergic to his own hurtful words. "Not permanently. Just for a little while until Skye's feeling better."

"What about school?" she asked, not liking the idea of increasing her travel time each day.

"Your mum will drive you." He smiled even though Amber wasn't sure this would even be possible. She'd seen how hectic mornings were in that house getting everyone organised.

"What about my stuff? My bedroom?" She crossed her arms. "There's no room at Mum's."

"That's the cool part..."

She drew in a breath, knowing whatever he said next would be anything but cool.

"I'm paying a builder to redevelop the shed in your mum's back-yard." His face lit up with excitement. "We're converting it to a new pad for you."

The shed? Definitely not cool. She wanted a bedroom, not a shed-room. The girls at school would have a field day with that one. Her popularity was about to take a dive so deep she might have to start wearing a snorkel to school.

"And exactly how is that cool?" she asked.

"Because you'll have a little kitchen in it, a bathroom, a lounge area..." He grinned at her like that made this ridiculous idea sound any less insulting.

"You mean, exactly like I have now, only smaller? And colder? And miles away from school?" She shook her head, unable to believe what she was hearing.

"Don't be like that," he soothed. "It's only for a little while."

"Why can't I just stay here?" She heard the whine in her voice and winced. "It's not like Skye needs to look after me."

"She's really sick, Amber." The smile fell from her father's face. "She needs to be left in peace to recover."

That seemed unfair. It wasn't like she was exactly noisy. Amber couldn't help but feel she was being conveniently moved away.

Cancer or no cancer, at that moment she hated Skye. She hated her for taking away her father and she hated her for forcing her family into the public spotlight. Most of all she hated her for getting cancer. She was behind this shedroom idea, Amber was certain of it. Her father seemed genuinely frightened about her reaction to the idea. Skye would probably chop off his nuts if he didn't get her to agree with it.

"Okay," she said, deciding someone had to be the grownup here.

"Really? It's okay with you?" His eyes lit with relief.

She forced a smile to her lips. "Yeah, whatever."

Maybe it'd be nice to live with people who actually gave a crap about her for a change. Her mother would never send her away. She'd been devastated when she'd asked to move in with her father, only agreeing to it because she could see it was in her best interest. Her mother always put her first. Her father used to as well, before Skye came along.

"Thanks, Amber," he said, rubbing his hands together. "It's only for a little while. I promise. As soon as Skye's better we'll move you straight back in."

She turned back to her computer.

Cancer really sucked.

But right now, her father sucked even more.

———

Theo threw some pillows off the bed to make room for himself. Those bloody things drove him crazy. There was absolutely no point to them. He only needed one to put his head on at night.

"It's done," he said.

"You told her?" Skye smiled with full teeth. He'd seen clients less excited to hear they'd escaped a prison sentence.

He nodded as he lay down on the bed next to her.

"Oh, babe. Thank you." She blinked at him. "You take such good care of me."

Fuck, she was beautiful. Even sick like this, she was still gorgeous. That hair, those big blue eyes, those tits. Man, she was amazing.

"You know I'm not one hundred percent happy about this," he said, wanting to maximise the credit he got for making this decision.

"I know you're not happy. Which makes me love you even more." She kissed him lightly on the cheek. Her lips were warm, and he caught the scent of her perfume. It was the one he'd brought her back from Singapore last year. "Thank you."

"Stop thanking me," he said, pulling back. "It's what you need. Isn't it?"

"Of course, it is." She shuffled over once more. "This gives me the best chance of recovery."

He let out a long breath. He'd done the right thing. Why then did it feel so wrong?

Amber had let him off lightly, he knew that. He'd make it up to her, though. Maybe he could take her with him to Paris next year when Skye was better. He loved Paris and Skye never wanted to go with him. *Anywhere but Paris*, she'd say, which was strange for someone who loved fashion so much. Amber would enjoy it. He could buy her some new clothes, they could go out to breakfast and he could take her to the Louvre.

"What are you thinking about?" asked Skye.

"Nothing." He smiled, glad she couldn't read his mind.

"You know you're the greatest husband to ever walk the earth." She grabbed at his shirt and pulled him closer. Her ample cleavage loomed in front of him, leaving him wondering if the wound from her surgery had healed yet. That hand job she'd given him when he'd asked Rin to take Amber back just hadn't been enough. He missed fucking her when he woke up. Releasing his stress in the shower just wasn't the same.

She sat up and pulled her camisole over her head, revealing her hot pink bra. Another gift he'd brought her from Singapore. He'd bought one cup size too small and her breasts were spilling over the edges, as the lace struggled to hold its load. She didn't normally wear a bra to bed, unless it was for him.

Okay, so maybe it wasn't just her confidence that he'd been attracted to.

He threw his tee-shirt over his head as an urgent need built deep inside him. If it wasn't satisfied, he'd end up in hospital himself. *Death by internal combustion caused by having the hottest wife on the planet.*

"I love you, babe," he breathed.

"I love you more," she said, before taking hold of the fire she'd lit in his groin.

Yep. He'd made the right decision, that much was for sure. Happy wife, happy—oh my fucking god.

26 DAYS BEFORE THE BREAK

"Goodbye, farewell, hasta la vista!"
Skye Manis puts cancer on notice as battle continues.

Well, give me a pair of sparkly red shoes and call me Dorothy. I've officially started following my chemo-bricked road and am on my way to Oz. Soon that Wicked Witch we call cancer will have melted into a puddle on the floor and I'll be clicking my heels together and returning home.

Okay, I'll drop the corny analogy. Cancer does that to you. It makes you regress into your childhood, causing you to think about life in all sorts of weird and wonderful ways.

Chemo wasn't at all like I was expecting. Was it confronting? Sure. Was it painful? Sort of. Was it bubbly green liquid being injected into me by men wearing hazard suits? Not at all.

It was a roomful of people sitting around with needles in their arms, talking, reading magazines or listening to music. It reminded me a bit of giving blood, only this time the nurses were putting things in instead of taking things out. I could feel the poison running through my veins, but somehow managed to distract myself from what was happening. After all, you're not going to cure something as deadly as cancer with a glass of water.

So, all in all, it was confronting, but it wasn't that scary. What was scary was getting home and feeling like I was Sigourney Weaver with an alien about to burst out of my stomach.

Sorry, I broke my promise. See, those movie analogies are hard to pass up once they enter your head. Next I'll be likening my body to the arena in *The Hunger Games* as my cells fight to the death. Let's hope the cancer alliance is the first to get its image projected into the night's sky.

I did it again, didn't I? That was the last one. I promise. I suppose it just helps to think of cancer in those kinds of terms, particularly because we know in stories the good guys always win. Dorothy melts the Wicked Witch with a bucket of water, Katniss survives not one but two Hunger Games and Sigourney finishes the alien queen off with a forklift and an ill-fitting shoe.

Listen up, cancer! You're on notice. I'm evicting you from my body effective immediately. Once I stop throwing up, you're definitely out of here. Goodbye. Farewell. Hasta la vista. Don't let the door hit you on the way out.

Actually, no. Let the door hit you. You deserve it.

Thanks everyone for your continued support. I promise my story will have a happy ending.

Love Skye xx

6.7K people like this
238 shares/980 comments

SuperMama12
Go Skye!!!! Good fo you, able to keep your sense of humor about this. Not sure I could if it was me, U R an insparation to all woman.

CarlyJane
Just remember you can cry too. You don't always have to make us laugh. We love you anyway! Good luck with your recovery.

Julia97g
Always hated that Wicked Witch. Such a bitch. Hope you get to Oz soon.

JoJoGo
You're on your way!! You'll get there soon. I beat ovarian cancer 9 years ago now. Your not alone in this. Don't listen to CarlyJane. Keep laughing. I did and it kept me sane.

CarlyJane
She can laugh. Just saying its important to cry too. No need to get personal. And by the way it's 'you're'...

MarkyJohnpp
Get better soon beautiful.

JoJoGo
Not getting personal?? Just speaking from experience. Better to keep things positive than to give in and cry. Crying tells you're body something is wrong.

MrsHappyNow
You rock Skye!!! Keep us posted as you beat this thing good. Your awesome.

Daisy21
Ummmmm, theres something wrong. She has CANCER. Derr.

BellaSwannnn
It's like a vampire trying to suck the life out of you, only you're stronger than that. Team Skye all the way!!!!

Cait31
I go to school with Amber. We all think you're the best. Cancer has no chance against you xx

JoJoGo
Cancer isn't a death sentence. Just a medical condition that Skye needs to sort out. Watch what you say here. This is her life you're messing with.

Ferzzy
You hot. Friend me.

View more comments

———

Rin stood at her kitchen window and watched the builders work. She hadn't expected them to start almost immediately. Plans normally took far longer than that to go through council, but if anyone knew how to pull strings, it was Theo.

In only a few days the shed had really started to take shape. There was still quite a bit of work to do, but it'd be quite an asset to their home when it was finished.

It would be so good to have Amber home with her again. It wasn't right for a child to sleep under a different roof to her mother.

Every night before she went to sleep, she'd lie awake and picture Amber in her bed in that Malvern mansion. Amber had snuck Rin in there once when Theo and Skye weren't home to show her where she lived. She'd felt like a naughty teenager tiptoeing into the house. A giant marble statue of a goddess stood in the entrance hall. Rin had been certain it was glaring at her. It'd given her the creeps and she'd almost turned back. But Amber had taken her by the hand and led her through the rest of the house. She'd stopped short of going into Theo and Skye's bedroom, though. That was too much of an invasion of privacy. She'd die if she ever found out Theo had been in the bedroom she shared with Jeff.

The house was beautiful. Very white. But beautiful. She couldn't imagine what it must be like to live in a place like that. It was no wonder Amber had wanted to move in. She couldn't deny her that opportunity.

Besides, Amber loved her father. She doted on him in a way he didn't deserve. Jeff had tried so hard to be a good stepfather, yet his efforts always went unnoticed. Amber had been reeled in by Theo's shiny charisma, just as she herself had been in the early days. Sensible Jeff was no competition with his receding hairline and chino pants. Well, no competition in Amber's eyes. He was more than satisfactory competition in her own eyes.

She hadn't had to try to trap him into loving her like she had with Theo. That seemed like another lifetime ago. She was amazed she'd not only thought she could trap Theo by having a baby, but that she'd wanted to trap him at all.

Skye hadn't had to trap Theo. From what Rin knew about their relationship Theo had been the one to trap her.

It was a shock when she first found out he was dating Skye. She'd actually been a fan of hers, following the story of how she'd lost her first husband in that terrible car accident, relating to it not as a widow but as a woman who'd also had her marriage taken from her against her will.

Sometimes she thought having your husband leave you was far more painful than having him die. Both were experiences of loss, yet only one of them came with an overwhelming sense of rejection and betrayal.

She'd read with interest as Skye re-entered the dating scene, again relating to how she'd felt when she'd first started seeing Jeff. Then Skye had gotten more liberal with her details about Theo and things had started to fall into place. The coincidences were too great. Skye was dating her ex-husband.

Once Rin realised that, she stopped considering herself a fan of Skye's and started thinking of herself more as a ... rival? No, rival wasn't quite the right word. That implied they were on the same playing field when they quite clearly weren't. They weren't even playing for the same prize. Arch enemy was probably closer to the truth.

No matter what any woman says, there's no way anyone would be happy for their ex to end up with a woman like Skye. Toothpick legs up to her armpits, boobs the size of rock melons and blonde hair that reached all the way to her choirboy behind.

Loyal Jeff always claimed to find Skye highly unattractive, saying he hoped Theo didn't light a match near her as she'd probably melt. He didn't like plastic women. Rin was never sure if she believed him, yet still these comments made her love him even more.

At least Skye wouldn't be able to have children with Theo now. That had always been a worry of Rin's—that Theo would get the son he'd always wanted and lose interest in Amber, filing his feelings for her away with yesterday's news.

She saw the builders nod to each other, their signal to lay down the tools for lunch.

It was time to put on the kettle. She liked looking after tradesmen who worked on her house. They always did a better job that way. It would be hard to take a shortcut on your work after being fed with coffee and cake all day.

She took an apple cake out of the oven. Amber said Skye loved to bake. She wasn't the only one. She might have exclusivity over Theo, but she didn't have exclusivity over that.

"Would you like a coffee?" she called out the open window.

The builders smiled and gave her a thumbs up.

"Thanks, love," they called out.

"No, thank *you,*" she muttered as she took out three mugs. They were doing a very important job. They were helping her to bring her daughter home where she belonged.

22 DAYS BEFORE THE BREAK

Linda went into the ensuite and grimaced. She hated cleaning other people's bathrooms. It was bad enough having to clean her own.

Not long ago she'd been in Skye's position, spending her days shopping or having coffee with the girls while someone less fortunate cleaned her husband's piss off their toilet seat. But that life was eons ago. It almost felt like it happened to someone else.

She sprayed the surface of the basin with disinfectant and ran the hot tap, staring mindlessly as one of Skye's blonde hairs swirled in the water before escaping down the plughole. She'd been finding a lot of Skye's hair lately. It was strange. Usually it was Theo's dark hair she had to pull from the sink.

There'd been hair on her pillow, in the shower and stuck to the back of the couch. Maybe Skye was sick? She was spending more time in bed than usual and she'd been barely touching her food. And she had gone in for that surgery recently, but surely if it was anything more serious than one of her usual cosmetic procedures, she'd have mentioned it. But then again, maybe she wouldn't.

It would take at least an hour to clean this already clean bathroom. It was four times the size of hers, its gleaming Italian marble tiles teasing her with their opulence. The walk-in double shower could fit a whole football team in there.

She ran her cleaning rag over the basin, removing any signs of anyone having used it any time in the last century. It could be worse, she reminded herself. Skye and Theo were fastidiously neat, which meant she only had to clean, not tidy. She'd hate having to pick up Theo's dirty underpants from the floor. The humiliation would be too much.

If only this house wasn't so damn white, then maybe it would be easier to clean. Every single speck of dirt showed up in this place, making cleaning even more of a chore. Her favourite rooms were Amber's. At least they had some personality.

Her favourite person was Amber, too, now that she thought of it. She was the only person in this place who treated her with any respect.

It was a grand house, even larger than the one she'd once lived in only a few streets away. It took her forty hours a week to keep it sparkling to the kind of standard Skye was happy with. This included doing all the laundry, grocery shopping, cooking and errands such as transporting the never-ending stream of dry cleaning. Cleaning the staircase was her most hated task. It had a wrought iron balustrade (painted white, of course) with intricate patterns that doubled as magnets for dust. She'd lost almost five kilos since taking this job. The white cotton dresses Skye liked her to wear had started hanging off her.

This was Linda's first housekeeping job. Her first of any kind of job in over thirty years.

When she'd met Tony, he promised she'd never have to work again. That was the first of many lies he told her. She didn't mind his lies so much. They were far preferable to his truths, especially when he told her about his affair with Sandra.

She hadn't wanted him to confess. She already knew. She wasn't an idiot. He was the idiot who hadn't realised she was turning a blind eye to his infidelities. She didn't really mind who he slept with, as long as it wasn't her.

Skye reminded her of Sandra. Another bimbo second wife. Actually, bimbo was probably harsh. Skye was a fairly intelligent woman, she just looked like she should be a bimbo. Maybe she'd find herself cleaning houses one day when Theo upgraded her with an even younger model. He might get himself a real bimbo next time.

Linda finished cleaning the basin and wandered out into the master suite, not able to resist poking her head into Skye's dressing room.

One wall was lined with racks of clothes, hanging in their dry-cleaning cling film wrappers. Coats and jackets on the top left rack with pants and skirts hanging below. Dresses in a separate section to the right and shirts located in the middle. All enclosed by mirrored doors to hide the hideous mess of the perfectly pressed and organised clothes.

The other side of the room was dedicated to accessories. There was an enormous shelving unit, housing over a hundred pairs of shoes, drawers filled with neatly folded active wear, lingerie, stockings, silk pyjamas, camisoles, hats and scarves and an entire dresser bursting with velvet-lined trays of jewellery.

In the middle of the room, sitting delicately on the plush white carpet was a white leather chaise longue. Skye would sit there as she fastened her shoes or took a break from the overwhelming exhaustion she must experience at deciding which outfit to wear for the day. Should she wear the Saint Laurent baby doll dress or the Dolce and Gabbana pencil skirt? And would it look better with the Christian Louboutin heels she favoured, or should she mix it up with her Manolo Blahnik pumps? It was a wonder she managed to cope with the stress.

Once, Linda had caught Amber in there and had to pretend she didn't notice, hoping she wouldn't get the blame for whatever it was she was up to. It was no wonder. What teenage girl would be able to resist the treasures and temptations contained within that room? It was like a grown-up woman's Disneyland.

Linda noticed it was unusually messy today. A large pile of leather-bound books was scattered on the floor, the full-length mirrors magnifying the scale of their untidiness.

As curious as she was, she didn't dare touch them. They looked like diaries and Skye was an intensely private person. Linda used to read Skye's articles online until they became as dull as the colour scheme in this house. The diaries were probably just extended versions of that.

She'd not only lost interest in Skye's life, she'd also lost her internet connection when she failed to pay her bill. Going online now required her to make a trip to her local cafe that had free wifi and overpriced coffee. It was a trip she rarely made. She was too exhausted most of the time to even think about such a luxury as sitting in a cafe. Besides, she'd lived without the internet for most of her life. It wouldn't kill her to live without it again.

But as she looked at the diaries now, she couldn't help but wonder if maybe she might feature in any of them. Now *that* would be interesting. A chance to find out what Skye really thought of her.

"Don't be a fool," she told herself. There's no way Skye would write about the hired help. She was no more important to Skye than a t-shirt at a nudist colony.

Linda wished she'd treated her own former housekeepers with more respect. She'd never really stopped to wonder about their lives or the fact that when they went home, they still had their own houses to clean.

That was one of the problems with life. You never really knew how fortunate you were until it was all taken away.

She turned from the dressing room, knowing if she got caught snooping, her job would be lost. This job was the one thing keeping her afloat. Tony had really stitched her up with the divorce settlement and she'd been foolish with the little she'd ended up with. After so many years of not having to worry about money, it took her years to figure out she'd have to paint her nails herself and cancel her overpriced membership at the health club. The money slowly whittled away and with no more coming in, she soon lost her house along with her pride.

Meanwhile, Tony lived a life of luxury with precious Sandra. Even her two adult sons were well-off. She was the only one left destitute by the divorce.

She knew Theo's first wife had also been left destitute. She'd seen her a few times outside the house dropping off Amber in her Corolla, wearing her K-Mart clothes. Theo didn't seem to care. He was just like Tony.

She'd first met Theo a very long time ago at a party, but as he didn't remember her, she kept this information to herself. Nobody wanted a housekeeper who had a connection to their life. Particularly if that connection went by the name of Bruno Martini, who Tony had happened to go to school with. She had a better chance at keeping her job if she just kept her mouth shut.

She screwed up her nose at Skye's photo in a frame next to Theo's side of the bed. She could only just see it poking up above all those pillows that were her morning headache of a jigsaw puzzle. She had to be careful to place each one in exactly the right position if she wanted to avoid another bed-making lesson from Skye.

Skye smiled at her from behind the glass frame. She really was a beautiful almost-bimbo. Perfect teeth, dainty features, eyes the colour of the ocean and a figure like some kind of supermodel. No wonder Theo hadn't been able to resist her. Not many men would be able to. At least he hadn't been married at the time, she supposed.

"Lucky bitch," she said to Skye's photo. "Enjoy it while it lasts."

Her mobile phone buzzed in the pocket of her apron, making her jump. It was a text from Skye.

Skye Manis

Won't be home until late. Forgot to tell you the microwave is filthy. Please clean. Thx.

"Thanks, my arse," muttered Linda.

She paused as she reached the bedroom door and smiled. The microwave could wait. Now she knew Skye wouldn't be home for hours, there was something else she'd much rather do first.

———

Linda sat down in the chaise longue in Skye's dressing room with the leather-bound diaries in a pile at her feet.

She picked one up at random, her foot drumming nervously on the plush carpet. It was wrong to invade Skye's privacy like this, but the temptation was too great. Besides, when you hand-washed someone's underwear there weren't really too many secrets between you. There could be no surprises in here.

She looked at the date on the first entry.

2 May 1989

How strange. That date was far too early for Skye to have been writing diaries. She wouldn't even have been born.

She looked inside the front cover and found a familiar name scrawled in red pen.

Clara Butterford

Skye's mother.

Linda's shoulders slumped. She wasn't interested in reading the diaries of some crazy old bird. Still, it wouldn't hurt to skim through them a little. It sure beat cleaning a microwave.

2 May 1989
I thought when I was appointed as a principal dancer with the Australian Ballet that my life was perfect. Wrong! Wrong! Wrong!!!!!!!! When that happened, I hadn't even known what it was like to be happy. I wasn't even properly a woman. I hadn't met Jacques. Well, actually I had met him. We had all met him. He is the most respected artistic director in town. But now ... now I have really met him. I have met every part of him and he made my body dance in a way it never has before. I accidentally told him that I love him right after we made love. It just slipped out from underneath my happiness. I nearly died with embarrassment in case he didn't love me too, but he tucked my hair behind my ear and said, 'Me too, ma cherie.' I never meant to love him. I mean, he has been with so many women before and I have only been with him. (I refuse to count Troy because he turned out to be gay so anything that happened between us doesn't count.) But to think that with all the women he's had, I am the one he

loves! Me!!!! Hearing those words from him was like a receiving a standing ovation. It was the same buzz. Maybe even a bigger buzz. Jacques loves me! And I love him.
Clara xxxxxx

Linda yawned as she skipped through the next few pages—they were filled with the same kind of gushing phrases and exclamation marks —until she found an entry that held the promise of some drama.

21 July 1989
Jacques has returned to Paris. He didn't even say goodbye. Not a note, not a phone call, not even a message passed on through a friend. Did I mean so little to him? Why did he tell me he loved me if that was his plan? Technically when I think about it, he didn't actually say he loved me. He said, 'Me too.' But still, doesn't that count??? He wasn't talking about the weather, was he? He said it. I didn't imagine it. I even wrote it down in this diary so I wouldn't ever forget. I found out about it at rehearsals today. A group of girls were talking about him and one of them asked me if it had been a teary farewell. I didn't even have a clue what they were talking about. I must have looked like the world's biggest idiot. I had to go to the bathroom to vomit. I haven't stopped vomiting since. I haven't kept anything down for three days now. I have thought about following him to Paris to confront him, but opening night is next week. I would be thrown out of the ballet and I've worked too hard for that. I will not let him ruin my life. Mark my words. I am going to dance and dance and not give that liar another thought. I will show him what he is missing out on. When he comes back to Melbourne, he will be begging me to take him back.
Clara xx

In the next few entries, Clara seemed to be trying to prove to herself that she wasn't thinking about her runaway lover. She wrote about the ballet, other dancers, movies she'd seen and what she ate for breakfast. There was page after page outlining every banal detail of her life. It was no wonder Jacques chose Paris over her company. She was about as interesting as watching television in a blackout.

Things started to get interesting again in October of that year.

3 October 1989

I am in a nightmare. Please, wake me up! I can't believe this is happening. I'm pregnant. Like, actually, properly pregnant. Five months gone and the doctors say it's too late to get rid of it. It is Jacques's (of course). I wish it belonged to anyone else. Even Troy. I would happily have Troy's baby, if it meant it didn't belong to Jacques. No, that's not true. I don't want a baby at all. I never have. I have been drinking raspberry leaf tea by the bucketful. I heard it can bring on a miscarriage. With me, it only seems to be making the pregnancy stronger. It looks like the only way to get rid of this baby would be to kill myself. If only I noticed what was going on earlier. I thought I was vomiting because Jacques left me. I haven't even put on any weight, nor have I had regular periods since I got serious about ballet. And my back has been aching, but I thought it was just because of all the extra rehearsals. The doctor looked at me like I have lost my marbles. I hate it when people do that. I don't know what to do. Jacques still hasn't come back from Paris. I heard someone say that he's staying there for good. They said he's getting married to some French ballerina. That can't be right. He's not the marrying kind. If he was, then he would have married me.
I wish you could tell me what to do.
Clara

Ouch! Linda couldn't image how Skye must have felt reading that. To know that your mother not only hadn't wanted you, but she'd thought about killing herself to get rid of you. That must lodge a pain deep in your soul. It was surprising Skye wasn't even more messed up than she already was.

The way Clara had talked about getting rid of Skye, reminded her of the callous way Tony had severed her from his life, only somehow it seemed far worse. Husbands promised to love you forever, but often that wasn't the case. But mothers ... If you were supposed to be able to count on anything in life, it was your mother's love, wasn't it? Even her own sons, who'd treated her far from well in the past few years, were still the only people in the world she'd throw herself in front of a train for without a second thought. They were her children. She loved them, even if she didn't always like them.

Concerned about the time and wanting to read more, she skipped forward to November.

12 November 1989

I wish people would stop expecting me to be happy about this baby. Who in their right mind would be happy about the end of a career they love? I have worked so hard to be on that stage. I have danced with broken bones, fevers and blisters the size of the Sydney Opera House. I have said no to every dessert and glass of wine ever offered to me and yes to every rehearsal request, interview and photo opportunity. I have missed out on sleep, weekends away with my girlfriends and dates with rich and handsome men. I have turned my body into a machine, able to endure crippling pain while projecting an image of serenity and grace. Nobody realises what sacrifices I have made, unless they are a dancer themselves —and they are too busy celebrating my demise as they rub their hands together thinking about what opportunities that opens up for them. I know, because I have been in their shoes. When Miranda broke her leg all those years ago, I could not have been happier. It was the best thing that ever happened to me. This is the worst. I know I will never dance the same again. I can feel my body crumbling as my stomach begins to expand. It is betraying me in the same way Miranda's leg betrayed her. I wrote to Jacques and told him. I'll copy out his reply here:

No, that isn't a misprint. HE DID NOT REPLY. That's how much he cares. This baby is sucking the life out of me already and it hasn't even been born. Does thinking that make me a bad person?
Clara

Personally, Linda thought it possibly did make Clara a bad person. It wasn't the baby's fault, even if that baby had grown up to be somewhat a bad person herself.

She wondered if she was being harsh. Was Skye really a bad person? She was shallow. And selfish. And rude pretty much all of the time. But it wasn't like she'd robbed any banks or killed anyone. Perhaps she wasn't a *bad* person. Just a bit of a bitch.

She flipped forward to the entry announcing Skye's birth.

17 February 1990
The baby came early, of course. It's a girl. I have called her Skye. I always liked that name. I thought if I gave her a name I like then maybe I will like her too. Besides, Skye suits her. She is everywhere I look, her presence hovering over me

night and day. Sometimes she's sunny and bright and other times she's dark and menacing. It has been six weeks since the birth and my body is a wreck. The actual birth wasn't too much of a problem. The doctor said he has never seen anyone cope with the pain so well. I am told she is a pretty good baby. Makes me wonder what other babies are like. This one cries and poops like she is worried it is about to be outlawed. Maybe she will be a ballerina and can take over my career. She has taken over everything else, she may as well take that too. I am not sure she has the legs for it though. I know she's just a baby, but they are kind of chunky. Perhaps I am just not used to seeing so many rolls of fat on a person. She looks a lot like Jacques. She has his eyes. I still think about him all the time, hoping he'll come back. I sent him a photo of Skye as an enticement, but so far his response has been the same as last time. Nothing. I wonder how many other ballerinas he's knocked up. Skye probably has half siblings all over the world. At least she will know she won't have any siblings courtesy of me. I will never repeat this mistake. Never.
She's crying again. I wish she would stop.
Clara

Linda put the diary down. Oh, how she'd love to take these home and read them properly.

She noticed a diary on the bottom of the pile with a red piece of paper sticking out the top. It must be some kind of special entry.

It wouldn't hurt to read just a little more.

13 March 2015
I am losing all sense of myself. It is like having a loose thread on a favourite sweater and the more you pull at it, the more the sweater begins to unravel. So, you tuck the thread through a loop and tie a knot. Some days the thread manages to remain in place and other days it pulls itself loose, making the hole bigger and bigger, until you are forced to accept it's ruined. My mind is that sweater. I am unravelling and no matter how hard I try to stop it, the damn thread just keeps pulling loose. I don't want to live like this. First, my body was stolen by my child and now my mind is eating itself alive, determined that soon there will be nothing of me left. It frightens me so much that I can no longer sleep at night. Can I keep any part of myself safe? No!!!! I must hand my mind over to the place my body went years ago. It is sitting there in the junkyard next to my career.

I tried to take my own life today. It wasn't the first time. It wasn't even the second. But I just couldn't go through with it, while there is still so much of me here inside my head. I need to wait for the golden moment. That perfect moment in time when I'm insane enough to want to kill myself, yet still sane enough that I know how. I would love to know when that moment will be. If only I could set my alarm and do what I wasn't brave enough to do today.

Life isn't fair. I need to stop expecting it to be. It's not a movie. It's not going to have a happy ending. I know Skye thinks I was a terrible mother. I was. I am still a terrible mother. I wish I hadn't been. Maybe then I could ask for her help to finish me off if I don't manage to do it in time. It's ironic really. I am wishing she loved me more so that she would kill me. As it stands, she hates me far too much to ever possibly consider taking on a task like my murder. Pity. I'm not even sure that's true. She's always wanted my attention. I've been the one unable to give it to her. When her father broke my heart, he broke it for good. Nobody has been able to make it work again. Not even our daughter. Especially not our daughter who looks at me with his eyes. He left without giving me a second thought, leaving me with a souvenir that would keep him in my life every second that I have left. Maybe this dementia will be a blessing. Maybe it is the only way I'll ever be able to forget about Jacques.
Clara

26 September 2015
This will be my last entry. I look at these dairies and I know they are mine, but wreading them is like eavesdrooping on a stranger.
I am forgetting how to write. How to spell. How to wread. It's humiliating.
As my sane mind drawes to a close, so do the entrys in these dairies. My only freinds. My record that I ecisted.
Goodbye.
Clara

Linda wondered if perhaps some lives were best left unrecorded. She felt sick.

Imagine keeping diaries like these hidden in your closet. Skye had obviously been reading them recently. How disturbing.

So much made sense now. Skye must have married Theo as a substitute father figure. And she visited her mother every week still hoping to gain acceptance from her. Or maybe it was to torture her? Maybe she visited her and slipped laxatives into her coffee and thumb-tacks into her bed.

Linda put the diaries back the way she'd found them and went downstairs to clean the microwave, feeling far less resentful about it than she had an hour ago.

20 DAYS BEFORE THE BREAK

Skye liked a lot of things about her job, but in particular she liked that she wasn't expected to make too many appearances in the office. Usually she just dropped in to say hello if she was in town shopping or if a staff meeting was called. She'd hated being tied to a desk all day when she worked at the call centre.

Her boss, Mariana, had never been to her house, but had called the day before to ask if it was all right if she came over for a coffee.

Skye had hesitated. She wasn't sure if she wanted Mariana to see where she lived. It was never a good idea for your superiors to be aware you were doing better financially than they were.

Mariana had the team over for drinks last Christmas and had swanned around like her house was a palace. It was a lovely home, but the almost-actual palace Skye lived in was in a completely different league.

If Mariana saw where Skye lived, she might feel bad about her own home. That wasn't good for Mariana, and it certainly wasn't good for Skye.

"Why don't I come past the office?" Skye had suggested.

"Don't be silly," said Mariana. "It will be easier for you if I come to you. You'll be swamped with people and questions if you come in. Let's keep it low key."

She reluctantly agreed and now found herself waiting in the kitchen, one eye on the video screen of the security camera pointed at the front gate, and the other on the oven, making sure she didn't burn the scones.

Mariana loved scones and Skye loved baking. It was a win-win. She wouldn't eat any of them herself, but the fun was in the making. She could bring any leftovers into the nursing home to share with the other residents

She felt good today. It was nice to be up and out of bed, pottering around her house like normal. It wasn't at all difficult to pretend that nothing was wrong with her.

The doorbell rang at the exact moment the oven bell went off.

"Linda!" she called out of habit, before remembering she'd sent her to the shops with a list a mile long, certain to keep her busy for hours. It was bad enough Mariana was about to see the size of her house. She didn't want her to know she had a housekeeper. She hadn't heard the gardener around today, which was a bonus. Although one look at their grounds would be enough for anyone to figure out they had some help in that department. The lawn was like a golfing green and the garden beds were bursting with flowers and neatly pruned hedges. They were clearly tended to by someone with not just a green thumb, but an entire green hand.

She pressed a button on the security system.

"I'm coming," she called in the cheeriest voice she could muster. She didn't need Mariana's sympathy. There were worse things that could happen to a person than chemo.

She saw Mariana open the gate, cradling a large bunch of flowers in her arms. Skye hastily got the scones out of the oven before they burned. They looked fantastic. Her reputation as the queen of desserts would remain intact. Her colleagues loved it when she brought them sweet treats. She'd already prepared a tray of peppermint slice for Mariana to take back with her.

She set down the scones on the counter and removed her apron, then quickly changed her mind and put it back on. It made her look more homely. Plus, it might protect her eskandar silk shirt dress from the pollen that was no doubt going to fall from the heads of those flowers. She went to the front door, adjusting her knotted headband while she walked. Her hair was patchy, but nothing a wide headband like this one couldn't hide. Soon, she'd have to gather her courage and shave it all off.

"What a house!" cried Mariana when Skye opened the door.

Skye could barely see her behind the flowers she was thrusting towards her as she simultaneously tried to kiss her on each of her cheeks. There were gerberas of every colour imaginable. They were as beautiful as they were inappropriate for Skye's colour scheme.

Mariana wasn't a tall woman, so Skye found herself stooping to catch the kisses. Her loud outfit was a sharp contrast to Skye's soft, rose-coloured dress.

Mariana wore a red suit jacket and black pants. Her bright orange hair should've clashed with the jacket, but somehow on Mariana it seemed to fit. A chunky yellow necklace dangled above her cleavage, the colour a perfect match to the frame of her glasses. All she needed was a pair of brown shoes and she'd look like a tree in autumn.

"What beautiful flowers," Skye said, stepping back from the door so Mariana could enter. "Thank you."

"I can't believe this house." Mariana stepped into the entrance hall and spun around, trying to take in her surroundings, her eyes darting from the sweeping staircase to the enormous French windows and crystal chandelier hanging in the middle of the hall.

She reached out to touch the larger than life sculpture of Athena the goddess of wisdom that sat at the bottom of the stairs. Theo had commissioned this for Skye as a wedding gift. It wasn't just a nod to his Greek heritage, but his way of telling her how smart and beautiful he thought she was. Skye had loved it on first sight. It wasn't one of those gaudy statues adorned with gold but was cut from marble of the purest white. Athena looked as vulnerable as she did wise. It should probably be in a gallery or museum, not her entrance hall.

"Come through to the kitchen. I've just baked some scones," said Skye, trying to divert her attention away from Athena.

"I told you not to go to any trouble." Mariana tore her bulging eyes away to plant them on Skye.

"I'm feeling good today." Skye smiled. "Besides, you know I like baking. I've made a slice for you to take back to the office to share with the others."

"Do I have to share?" Mariana giggled.

Skye laughed politely as she led Mariana through the living room.

"This way," she prompted to hurry her up. She'd stopped to look at the Charles Blackman above the fireplace. Personally, Skye hated that painting and all its colour, but Theo already had it when she moved in and had dug his heels in about keeping it. He claimed to be sentimental, saying that painting was the only way he'd gotten her to come home with him when they met. She reminded him she hadn't even seen the painting that night, but he didn't seem to care. As far as he was concerned, it was staying. If you asked Skye, it was on borrowed time.

"Is this an original?" Mariana's jaw hung in awe.

"Yeah. Theo bought it a long time ago." Skye tried to sound casual but failed. Marina knew her art. She'd know Theo would've paid a small fortune for that painting. Or a large fortune, depending on your perspective.

She knew she'd made a mistake agreeing to Mariana coming here.

"Wow." Mariana's eyes were as wide as a virgin's at a strip club.

Skye cleared her throat. "Scones are getting cold."

"Of course." Mariana tore herself away from the painting and followed her through the dining room, her eyes boggling at the glass table suitable for entertaining thirty guests. At the rate she was going, Mariana was going to need a new prescription for her glasses, her eyes were getting so worn out.

Skye had considered entertaining her in here, but decided she'd feel foolish taking up only one end of such a large table.

The kitchen would be better. They could sit at the stools at the counter and keep things casual.

"You certainly like the colour white," said Mariana, taking in the sparkling kitchen.

Skye looked around trying to see the room through her eyes. It was a large, square shaped kitchen with an enormous alabaster marble island counter in the centre, surrounded by chrome stools with white leather seats. A circular light fitting hung above the counter made from architecturally moulded plastic. The glossy white floor-to-ceiling cabinetry and frosted glass splash-back caught the light making them seem even shinier than they were.

A breakfast room connected to the kitchen with plush white upholstered sofas marking out the borders of the room. A smaller version of the glass table in the dining room sat on a fluffy white rug nestled perfectly in the curve of the large bay window, set off by white Egyptian cotton drapes that hung in sweeping folds, tied back by lush white silk ribbons. There was a china vase on the table with a bunch of long-stemmed iceberg roses. Last week it had held some lilies. Skye's florist sent her a bunch of whatever white flowers were in season two times a week.

There was quite a bit of white, she supposed. But it did look fabulous.

She decided Mariana didn't look like an autumn tree. Now she was inside her house, she looked like more like a circus clown caught in a snow storm.

Mariana took a seat at the kitchen counter while Skye reached into a cupboard and selected a vase for the flowers.

"These are lovely," she said.

"They're from all of us. We've been so worried about you." Mariana shifted on her chair, as if sitting still was a burden. She must be itching to take a look at the rest of the house.

"Oh, don't worry about me." Skye filled the vase with water and began arranging the flowers. "You know I'm a fighter. Always have been."

"Maybe we should've bought white flowers." Mariana laughed, but Skye could sense her hesitation.

"Not at all," she lied. "A bit of colour is nice."

"I'm sorry to be rude, but do you mind if I use your bathroom?" Mariana hopped off her chair like it had a spring in it.

"It's straight down the hall, second door on your left." Skye smiled. Mariana had a bladder made from steel. She didn't need the bathroom.

She just wanted to see more of the house. She'd probably take a selfie of herself sitting on the loo.

Skye finished with the flowers and set them down on the breakfast table, wincing at their brightness as she thought about how far she'd come in her career since her days in that hellhole of a call centre. She'd hated the job and how invisible it made her feel to be one of a hundred people doing exactly the same thing, but it'd helped pay the bills.

She'd dreamt of one day doing something like she was doing now, never imagining she'd become this successful. She hadn't gone to university, only just scraping through high school. Maybe if she'd had more support at home things would've been different. She'd certainly proven now she was capable of much more than D-average marks. The only D-average she had these days was her bra size and she'd had to pay a fortune for that.

"Gorgeous bathroom." Mariana sailed back into the room and balanced on the stool at the counter once more.

"Thanks," said Skye, waiting for her to begin sussing out whether or not she had a cleaner.

Mariana leant forward on the counter. "It must be a lot of work to keep everything so clean."

Yep, there it was.

"It is." This wasn't a lie. It was a lot of work for Linda. If Mariana wanted to know if she had a cleaner, she'd have to ask her directly. She was a trained journalist for goodness sake. Why didn't she just come out with it?

Mariana blinked at Skye. "You must have someone come in to help you with it all."

Bingo! There we go.

"I get a little help," Skye said, throwing her a crumb.

"I must say, you look fantastic," said Mariana, dropping the subject. "I mean, you're awfully thin and a little pale, but otherwise still your gorgeous self. Are you feeling well?"

"I'm pretty good at the moment. Chemo was a week ago, so I get a brief window of feeling good before the next one. I was a mess last week." Skye grimaced at the thought.

"Yet you still managed to send me an article. I loved what you wrote by the way. We've had heaps of comments. Oh, that reminds me ..." She picked up her handbag and shuffled around. It was one of those bags sold at markets, made from pieces of old fabric stitched together in a kind of retro kaleidoscope effect. Who knew where that fabric had been! Mariana could be walking around with the crotch from an old man's pyjamas slung around her neck. The thought made Skye shudder.

Mariana pulled out a small bundle of letters held together by a pink rubber band and handed them to her. "You have some fan mail."

Normally people wrote to Skye electronically, but occasionally she received snail mail at the office. Usually they were cards or letters wishing her well or invitations to events she'd never dream of attending.

The letter on the top caused Skye's breath to catch in her throat. Could it be the letter she'd been waiting over twenty years to receive? No, she was jumping to conclusions. It could be anything. Millions of people lived in Paris.

She placed the letters to one side. "Thanks, I'll take a look at them later."

"Skye, your hands are shaking." Mariana reached for her, but Skye took a step back, folding her arms across her chest.

"Just a side effect from all the medication," she said. "I'm fine thanks. Now, how about those scones?"

"Oh, yes please." Mariana rubbed her hands together.

Skye put the scones onto a serving dish and retrieved a tray from the fridge that she'd arranged with small dishes of cream and jam.

"This looks amazing." Mariana's tongue darted over bottom lip. "But I wish you hadn't gone to all this trouble."

"It's good to keep busy. I feel so useless stuck in this house." Skye flicked a switch on her coffee machine without asking Mariana if she'd like one. Of course, she did. She practically lived on coffee.

"You know if you need to take a break, we'll all support you." Mariana helped herself to a scone, slicing it in half and smearing it with jam.

Skye retrieved two coffee mugs from the cupboard and set one underneath the machine. "I don't need a break but thank you."

"Are you sure?" Mariana added a giant dollop of cream to the scone and smiled. "Maybe some time off would do you good."

"I'm sure," said Skye. "I like working."

"Thank god for that!" Mariana mimed wiping sweat from her brow. "You're the hottest potato in town at the moment. You're on fire! Advertising on our site has gone through the roof. I'd be devastated to lose you. You'll be getting a raise of course. We'll double your rate per published piece. We've even put you on our home page. Have you seen your twitter stats lately? They've gone bananas."

It seemed to Skye that Mariana was the one going bananas. She was salivating over her stats (or was it the scones?) Still, it was great news about the raise. She knew about her twitter followers, of course. The hashtag #ReachForTheSkye had been trending ever since her cancer was announced. She *was* the hottest potato in town. Far preferable to being yesterday's cold soup. Mariana certainly hadn't paid her any home visits back when her stats were shrinking like a pair of testicles in the arctic ocean.

"That's very generous of you," said Skye, wondering if the real reason for Mariana's visit was to ensure she didn't drift over to a competitor's website. Perhaps that was something to think about. After all, people who were on fire generally didn't stand still in the one place.

"I just don't want you to think we're taking advantage of you," said Mariana.

"Take advantage of me. Please!" Skye laughed. "Something good's got to come out of all of this."

She could tell by the look on Mariana's face that was exactly what she intended to do.

And given it was working in her favour, Skye really didn't mind a bit.

———

Skye pushed aside the vase of gerberas. She'd have to send them home with Linda tonight. They were a lovely thought but were starting to hurt her eyes.

There was something else a lot more interesting Mariana had brought with her that had nothing to do with flowers or gossip from the office. It was the bundle of letters, in particular the one on top with the French stamp.

Her stomach clenched as she slipped it from the confines of the rubber band. Her name had been written in sweeping, cursive handwriting—the kind favoured by the older generation. She tried not to get her hopes up. It could be from anyone. She had fans all over the world.

She turned it over, her heart pounding harder and faster as she saw the name of the sender.

Jacques Moubray.

Her father.

He'd responded to her letters at last. It only took him twenty-two years and a little bit of cancer on the side.

Every year since she was eight-years-old Skye wrote him a letter on her birthday. And every year since she was eight-years-old he failed to reply. Until now. There'd been a difference with the last letter she sent. Firstly, it wasn't her birthday and, secondly, she told him she had cancer. He must have responded the moment he'd received her letter. It seemed too good to be true.

Maybe he hadn't received her other letters? Although if he got this one, he must have. The address had to be correct.

On her eighth birthday, her mother had asked her what she'd like as a present and she'd asked for her father's address. Her mother had quietly gone to her bedroom and returned with a piece of paper.

"Good luck," she'd said, half smiling, half crying.

Skye was surprised to actually receive what she'd asked for. The year before she'd asked for a pony and received a Ballerina Barbie.

She could remember sitting down to write that first letter. How she'd painstakingly selected a sheet of her mother's best letter paper, the one with the lavender watermark nestled behind a set of neatly drawn lines.

'Dear Dad,' she'd written, having already thrown away several other drafts beginning with *Dear Father, Dear Papa and Dear Mr Moubray*. She wasn't sure what to write, so she decided to just get to the point.

'*I'm your daughter, Skye. My mother is Clara Butterford, the ballerina. When you come to Melbourne next time can you please come and visit me?*'

She'd paused at that point. Having said what she wanted to say left her wondering what else she could put in there. It looked a bit short. There were still a dozen blank lines left to fill. She should probably tell him a little bit about herself.

'*I am eight years old and I am in grade three. I like cats, watching TV and writing stories about fairies. My best friends are Sarah and Mia.*'

She wondered if she should ask him about himself. That was what you were supposed to do with grown-ups. But she didn't know anything about him to ask after.

'*What do you like to do? Do you still work in the ballet? Do you have children other than me?*'

She decided that should do it. She signed it off with '*Love from Skye,*' drew a picture of a fairy and a cat and put it in an envelope.

Her mother gave her five dollars to post it and said she could keep the change.

It was the best birthday of her life, for it was filled with hope, dreams and a bag of lollies from the milk bar next to the post office.

But her hopes were soon dashed when her daily check of the letterbox failed to turn up a response.

He must have been busy with his other children or working in the ballet. Or maybe he was dead. Her mother had said he was older than her so he must be fairly ancient.

Banking on the chance he was alive, she continued to write to him on her birthday, a tradition she carried on into adulthood. Her letters grew longer as she aged, but the response remained the same. This taught her one more thing about her father—he wasn't a very good pen pal.

She now knew her mother had given her the address for her own selfish reasons. Maybe she could achieve what her mother had failed to do and get her father to respond. She'd looked the address up online and was surprised to discover that her father lived on a farm just over an hour's drive from Paris. That seemed an odd choice for someone who worked in the ballet, but Skye assumed he must be the sort who needed a home life far different to the one he lived at work.

When she went to London with Dean for their honeymoon, she considered visiting him, but ended up avoiding not only Paris, but the whole of France. Her father didn't love her. He didn't want her. He never had. Seeing her wouldn't change that. Her relationship with him consisted of a one-way annual letter. She may as well be writing to a ghost.

But now he'd replied, and she was holding his words in her hands.

Theo had never understood her need to continue writing to him. He'd offered on more than one occasion to have his investigator look into him, but she'd refused, preferring to do things her own way. Her father should be the one to contact her and tell her about this life. Using a private investigator added a whole new level of humiliation to the situation.

That was when she'd started using her work address on her letters. If her father replied, she didn't want Theo getting his hands on the letter. She was certain he'd make a copy and start an investigation without her permission. The thought of him knowing things about her father that she didn't rubbed at her nerves. This was between Skye and her father. Theo needed to stay out of it.

She slit open the envelope to read her father's first words to her.

Dear Skye,

Forgive me. Letter writing is not my strong part. My English is not longer good either. I am a foolish old man with stones in my head where my brains should once be.

I am sorry for a lot of things. I should written you before. I have not known what I am to say back to you. I am sad you have cancer. My mama died from cancer in her ovaries many years ago. I thought you should know that. Your cancer is my fault. I passed it to you and I am frustrating for that.

You ask me lot of questions and I cannot answer all of them so I will answer the ones you ask mostly.

I do have more children. My wife for thirty years Antoinette gave me five sons. From them I have seven grandchildren. Six of them is girls. Antoinette died last year from stroke.

I do not work in ballet anymores. I live on a farm and enjoy quiet life. I have
never been back to Melbourne.
I do not remember your mother well. I'm sorry if this is rude but the time I
knew her was very busy and I met many people. I do remember that she danced
like her ballet slippers were made from the clouds.
I did want to meet with you but my wife did not want. She hid your letters for
me. I think there are many I did not see. I am glad to see your last one as it is an
important one.
You are very beautiful in your heart and face. I pray for you to be healed. I'm
sorry for your cancer and that this letter being slow.
Your Papa

Skye read the letter six times, memorising each line and trying not to correct his grammar. Part of her had always hoped her letters were going to the wrong address and he'd never known she existed. But it was clear that wasn't the case.

She always imagined him as some glamorous artistic director wowing audiences across Paris, not as some farmer with five sons and a nagging wife.

Who would hide the letters a child had written to her father? It was criminal! His wife was probably jealous she hadn't been able to provide him with a daughter. Thank goodness she had that stroke, or Skye might never have heard back from her father. Her *Papa,* as he called himself.

As awful as it sounded, it was also fortunate his mother had died from ovarian cancer. That had really made him sit up and take notice. It was hard to imagine this mythical grandmother. Skye had grandparents on her mother's side. They were still alive, apparently, although it'd been years since she'd seen them. They hadn't approved of her mother having a child out of wedlock, moving to country Victoria as a protest, no doubt afraid of being lumped with child-minding duties. Skye seemed to have that effect on people. Nobody had been happy about her birth.

Her mother had taken her to visit them a handful of times and it was like visiting strangers. They were polite, but lacked any warmth, preferring to pat Skye on the head rather than take her in their arms.

Eventually, her mother stopped bothering. She never told her why and Skye didn't ask, afraid if she did her mother might make plans for another trip. She'd rather pull out her eyelashes one by one than sit at that hideous vinyl kitchen table drinking watered down orange juice while her mother tried to cover up the awkward silence polluting the air.

When her mother moved into the nursing home, she'd called her grandparents to let them know. She was certain they'd want to visit, but this only confirmed how little she knew them.

They told her how sorry they were to hear such dreadful news and quickly explained their pension didn't allow much extra for them to be of any help. They were too frail to make the trip to Melbourne to see her, but would she please pass on their best.

Their *best*.

What the hell was their best? Raising a daughter like polite strangers, then abandoning her when she presented them with a chance of redeeming themselves.

Given that their best sucked, she never bothered to pass it on. Not that her mother would've understood what she was talking about if she tried.

Despite the ovarian cancer gene appearing to have some strength on her father's side, the parenting gene seemed to be just as weak on her mother's.

She had no hope, really.

Except now, a very faint glimmer had begun to shine. Her father had given her reason to think hope was possible. If she could find a way to forgive him then maybe he could be the parent she'd longed for all her life. Someone else to love her, who wasn't her husband.

She shoved the letter back in its envelope, uncertain what to do about it.

Hope was a concept far too dangerous for her to deal with right now.

18 DAYS BEFORE THE BREAK

Amber turned in her chair and smiled to see Linda standing in her doorway. Despite her being the *hired help*, she was the only friend Amber had in the house at the moment. The hot gardener didn't count as he wasn't technically in the house. She wouldn't mind if it he was, though. What was his name again? Probably no point trying to remember. He'd move onto another job soon enough. Gardeners always did.

Not Linda, though. She'd been here for years.

"Darling, have you got a second?" Linda asked.

Amber pulled the headphones from her ears and patted the bed. "Sit down. I haven't seen you for ages. What's happening?"

"Exactly my question." Linda crossed her arms as she perched on the edge of the bed.

She often popped in for a chat, yet never had she seemed so awkward. They got along well, bonded by the fact they were both outsiders under this ridiculously white roof.

"I'm not sure what you mean," said Amber. "What are you asking about?"

"Is Skye sick?" Linda tilted her head.

Amber's jaw fell open. "You mean she hasn't told you?"

Linda shook her head, her lips pursed together as if frightened she might say something she'd regret.

"Oh, well that's a new low, even for Skye." This was unbelievable. Didn't Skye realise you just can't treat people like that? Especially Linda, a perfectly lovely woman who Skye seemed to have no problem handing a list of shitty jobs to do every day. That sucked.

"I knew it. What's wrong with her?" asked Linda.

"Ovarian cancer." Amber winced as she waited for the reaction.

Linda jumped to her feet like the bed had been infested with cockroaches and clutched at her chest. "Oh my god!"

"I know. It's a shock, hey?" Amber shook her head. "Didn't you read about it online?"

Linda ran her hand through her hair. "I stopped reading her blog ages ago."

"I can't believe she didn't tell you," said Amber. "You shouldn't have to read her blog to find out something like that."

"It's none of my business, I suppose." Linda shrugged.

"Yes, it is. I should've told you." Amber stood and gave Linda a hug. "I'm so sorry."

Linda hugged her back. "It's not your job to tell me."

"It's just that we haven't talked for ages." Amber let go of Linda and sat back down on the bed. "Most of the time you're here, I'm at school."

"So how bad is the cancer?" Linda asked.

"Pretty bad." Amber pulled her face into a grimace. "She's started chemo. Her hair's falling out."

Linda nodded. "That's why I asked. I've been finding it all over the place."

The thought of Skye's hair falling out gave Amber the heebie jeebies. She rubbed her bare arms to repress a shiver.

"Does her mother know?" asked Linda.

Amber raised her eyebrows. Linda knew Skye's mother had dementia. Surely, she must realise Clara was beyond retaining such kind of information.

"If she knows, she would've forgotten," said Amber. "She still thinks Skye's married to her first husband. She doesn't even know Dad exists, even though he pays all her bills."

"That poor woman. What a tragedy. To lose your mind at such a young age." Linda shook her head and tutted.

"She's not young." Amber said, puzzled. "She must be in her fifties at least. Sixty maybe. Older than Dad, at least."

"One day you'll get old, too." Linda sighed.

"What would you do if you were like that?" asked Amber.

"If I'm ever like that I want you to visit me and put a pillow over my head, you hear me?" Linda smiled.

"Are you serious?" Amber laughed.

"Of course, I am." Linda sat back down on the bed. "I could think of nothing worse than rotting away in a home like that."

"I know what you mean," said Amber. "It must be awful for her. Awful for Skye too, to have to watch it."

"Life can be so cruel." Linda put a hand on Amber's arm. "Enjoy life while you're young, Amber. Make the most of every minute."

"I don't suppose anyone's told you I'm moving out," said Amber, realising that if nobody told Linda about Skye's cancer, she's unlikely to know about this, either.

"What? No, Amber. No." Linda reached for her hand and held it. "Where are you going?"

"To Mum's." She squeezed Linda's hand. "Dad said Skye needs quiet to recover."

"But you're not noisy." Linda tutted. "You're quieter than a mouse. You look like one too with those silly headphones on all the time."

"Ha ha." She rested her head on Linda's shoulder. She was going to miss her. If only she worked for her mum instead of her dad. Not that her mum could afford a cleaner in a million years. Amber was going to have to clean her own bathroom over there.

"When are you going?" asked Linda.

"Soon. Dad paid some guys to build me a new bedroom in Mum and Jeff's backyard. The builders have already started."

"What will I do without you?" Linda patted Amber's head. "I'll never know what's going on."

"Then you're lucky." Amber sighed. "Sometimes I think it's better not to know. Knowing things just makes you feel like shit."

"Language, Amber," Linda warned.

"Sorry." She smiled. Her dad never pulled her up on her language anymore. He probably didn't notice with the amount of swearing he did. She liked it when Linda treated her like a surrogate daughter. "It's true, though. Why do you think I like my headphones so much? The more things I know around here, the more miserable I feel."

"Smart girl. It took me years to figure that out. Pity my ex-husband didn't agree. He insisted on telling me everything." Linda let go of her hand and stood up.

Amber grinned. "Oh yes, tell me more."

"Enough. These stories aren't for your ears." Linda laughed.

"Oh, come on," she pleaded. "I told you about Skye."

"And I appreciate it. Now, would you like your sheets changed?" Linda fussed with a corner of the bed. "I'm just about to put a load of washing on."

"No thanks." Amber waved her away. "You did them already this week."

"Skye likes hers changed three times a week," said Linda.

"Do I look like Skye?" Amber batted her eyelashes.

"Good point. You're much more beautiful." Linda blew her a kiss. Amber knew she was just saying that, but it was nice to hear someone other than her mother thought she was beautiful. What a shame her father had married Skye, rather than someone like Linda. She could handle having a stepmother if it was someone actually nice.

———

Theo couldn't believe his luck when court was adjourned early. If he moved fast, he could catch Skye while she was still at chemo. It was about time he got over his fear of needles. He'd just have to look into her eyes and pretend everything was normal. If he didn't look at the needles directly, they didn't have to be real. He could do it.

He walked into the hospital like he was eight feet tall. He was a good husband. Skye would see how much he cared. But when the nurse told him she didn't have an appointment for Skye for the afternoon, his eight feet quickly shrunk back to his usual six.

Why hadn't Skye told him plans had changed? Most likely because he'd told her he'd be spending his day locked in a courtroom.

He called her from his car, unsure which direction he should head —to his chambers or home. Was she even at home?

"Hello," she said, picking up the call. She sounded terrible, like she had the flu, gastro and tonsillitis all at the same time.

"Hi. I've just left the hospital looking for you," he said.

"Oh, babe, they changed my appointment to this morning. I've been and gone," she croaked. "I'm back home now."

"You sound awful." He turned left, heading towards home. "How are you?"

"Not great but struggling through." She let out a long sigh. "I'm in bed now."

"I'll be home in ten minutes, okay?" He pressed down on the accelerator. "I'll sit with you."

"You're busy, don't worry," she protested. "Linda can bring me anything I nee—"

He heard her put down the phone and retch, the sound reverberating through the audio system of his BMW like some kind of messed up death metal song.

Poor thing. What a cruel disease this was. Why did it have to happen to her? She was one of the healthiest people he knew. She took such good care of herself. All that yoga and discipline with what she ate. This shouldn't be happening.

"Sorry," she said, coming back on the phone.

"Oh, babe." His heart hurt to hear her like this. "I'll be there as soon as I can. Just hold tight."

"I'm okay," she insisted. "I feel better now to get that out. I'm going to hang up now, though. I need to sleep."

"Sure. I'll be there soon," he promised. "I love you."

She hung up without another word. She really was unwell.

By the time he reached her, she was in a deep sleep, her face so pale she looked like a blonde Snow White. Not that she'd be blonde for much longer. There was so much hair on her pillow. Her arm was tucked up beside her head, with blood seeping through a dressing in the inside of her elbow. A dark bruise was poking out from the bandage.

It must be pretty nasty under that dressing. He shuddered. She was just too damn delicate to be having needles shoved into her body like that.

He went to get a towel and gently placed it under her arm, brushing away the loose strands of hair and adding them to the bucket of putrid vomit next to the bed.

She didn't even stir. His poor angel.

He picked up the bucket, took it downstairs to the laundry and tipped it into the trough.

"I can do that," said Linda from the doorway.

"It's okay." He turned on the tap and watched all signs of Skye's illness wash down the drain. If only he could cleanse her body of the cancer as easily as that. "Where do you keep the disinfectant? Skye might need this bucket again."

Linda walked over to him and smiled. "Move over, I'll do it."

"Thanks," he said, too exhausted to answer. Seeing Skye like this was draining him.

He heard a door slam from the direction of Amber's room. He cringed, hoping she hadn't woken Skye. It was a big house, but the noise of slamming doors had a tendency to weave its way into any room. Particularly any room Skye was in.

Linda held out the clean bucket. "Would you like me to take this up to Skye?"

"No, I'll do it." He took the bucket. "I might lie down with her for a bit."

"Amber told me about her ... illness. I hope you don't mind." Linda shuffled on her feet as she adjusted her crisp, white apron.

"Amber told you?" he asked. "You mean Skye?"

"No. Amber," she said.

"Skye didn't say anything to you?" he asked.

Linda shook her head.

That was odd, even for Skye, although she really didn't like to be fussed over too much—except by him, of course.

"I'm sorry, Linda. She should've told you. Or I should've. I think we just assumed each other had talked to you." That must be it. Skye would've thought he told her.

"It's not a problem," she smiled. "I just would've liked to have been able to help her a bit more. She's been so unwell."

He nodded. "She has. I'm really worried about her."

"She's very thin." Linda wrung her hands together. "She's barely eating, and I've been cooking her favourite meals all week."

"I know. I'll have a talk to her about that. She has to keep her strength up." He took a step towards the door.

"Amber's a good kid, you know." Linda had a nervous tone to her voice. It wasn't like her to speak to him about anything other than how he wanted his socks folded in his drawer or whether he'd like to have his breakfast in his den.

"She's a great kid," he agreed, unsure as to where she was heading with this.

"She told me she's moving out."

Right. So that's where she was heading. He didn't need a guilt trip from his housekeeper right now. He was having no trouble feeling guilty all on his own.

"That's right," he said. "Now, if you don't mind, Skye needs me."

"Yes, of course." Linda picked up the disinfectant and sprayed the trough.

Theo went back upstairs, shaking his head. He liked Linda, but women her age had trouble minding their own business. Just another reason why he'd married a younger woman. Skye never tried to meddle in his life. Well, she had asked him if Amber could move out for a while, but that wasn't meddling, it was a necessary part of her recovery.

"Get better, babe," he said under his breath as he made his way back to the bedroom.

He wanted his life back. No, scratch that. He wasn't greedy. All he wanted was his wife back.

17 DAYS BEFORE THE BREAK

Theo lay by Skye's side all night, waking every time she stirred, ready to call an ambulance if needed.

He eventually slipped into a deep sleep, disturbed only by a strange buzzing sound coming from the ensuite. It wasn't a sound he'd heard before.

It was five o'clock, the time he usually got up to do some work in his den before climbing back into bed to wake Skye. He'd slip his hands inside her camisole and run his thumbs across her nipples, waiting for them to harden at the exact moment she opened her eyes. She was always ready for him. He'd heard enough men complain about their wives to know this wasn't normal. Rin certainly hadn't been like that. Just one more reason to be thankful for being married to a woman like Skye.

Lately though, he'd been letting her sleep. It would be selfish of him to wake her when she so clearly needed her rest.

"What are you doing?" he asked, opening the door to the ensuite, barely able to believe what he was seeing.

Skye was standing in front of the mirror, wearing only her underpants, holding a pair of clippers in her hand with a pile of blonde hair at her feet.

"What does it look like?" she said, sliding the clippers across her scalp. The left side of her head was completely bald. The right side still had patchy clumps of hair hanging on, stubbornly refusing to fall out. "Oh, Theo. I can't stand looking at it any longer. You must've seen how much has been falling out. Better to get it all off in one go. Then I know what I'm dealing with."

He thought she'd start crying, but she didn't. She just kept on with the clippers, turning her head to try to see the back of it. She was just so damn brave. His heart swelled with love.

"Babe," he said, taking the clippers from her. "Here, let me do it."

"Thanks." She offered him a weak smile before bending her head towards him so he could continue what she'd started.

He took a deep breath. This wasn't a job he'd ever expected to have to help her with. Her hair was one of the things he loved about her. How depressing to have to shave it off. But still, it was only hair. It would grow back. The most important thing was that she got better.

He ran the clippers across her head in lines, evening up the patches as long strands dropped to the ground.

Soon the job was done, and he was left staring at the back of her bald head. It reminded him strangely of when Amber was a baby. It made her seem kind of vulnerable. He ran his hand across her scalp, already missing her silky hair.

He looked in the mirror and saw she had her eyes closed.

"It's okay to look. He bent to kiss her bare neck. "You're still beautiful."

She opened her eyes, blinked at her reflection, then turned to bury her head in his chest.

He held her tightly.

"It's okay, koukla," he soothed, using the Greek term for little doll. She was so tiny and loveable. He had to stop himself from squeezing her in half. "You're amazing. You really are amazing."

She wriggled from his arms and pulled him towards their double shower, turning on the water until steam billowed into the room.

When she slipped out of her underwear, he saw the scars from her surgery. Two thin, pink lines, one on each side of her lower abdomen. He was sure he had matching scars on his heart.

"I want you," she whispered in his ear as she tugged at his tee-shirt. "I need you to show me I'm still a woman."

He willed himself to go hard. What was wrong with him? She was still beautiful. She was still his wife.

She slid his shirt over his shoulders and tugged at his boxer shorts, sending them falling to his ankles.

If she noticed the state of affairs in his groin, she didn't say anything. Instead she urged him towards the shower and pressed her naked body to his, her large breasts pushing up against his chest, water pooling in her cleavage.

Although his eyes were glued to her, a more crucial body part below his waist was failing him. Or was it his brain that was failing him? Whatever it was, he wished it would get its act together. He might have a much younger wife, but he prided himself on his ability to keep pace with her.

Stupid old man, he told himself.

She slid down his body, kissing his chest, then his stomach, her lips trailing across his front as warm water caressed him from behind.

He felt a stirring and reached for her, his hands finding the back of her bald head. The stirring disappeared as quickly as it'd arrived.

He closed his eyes and moved his hands to her shoulders, not wanting the humiliation of her mouth on his flaccid penis. Normally he thought of it as his cock, but he couldn't possibly call it that in this pathetic state.

She ignored him, her kisses continuing south as her hands found him, followed quickly by the warmth of her darting tongue.

The stirring returned with force as she took him into her mouth.

He groaned as much with relief as the sheer pleasure of the moment.

His cock was back, crowing proudly from the rooftop as the sun lit the sky.

Cock-a-doodle-doo!

———

Skye found her leather Polo Ralph Lauren skinny jeans were starting to gape at the waist, despite being an already minute US size 0. There was no smaller size she could go down to.

She'd completely lost her appetite. It'd been pulled into a black hole along with her hair and Theo's sex drive. That blow job in the shower had been one of the most embarrassing experiences of her life. It wasn't echidna sex. This time he was more like a turtle with his dick trying to decide whether or not it was safe to poke its head out.

He was making her feel so unattractive.

She went to her wardrobe and opened a large drawer that she'd filled with hats, wigs and scarves. Some of the hats she had before, but she'd recently splurged on some new additions. There was a Burberry beanie for colder days, several Nerida Fraiman turbans and three fedoras by Rag & Bone. She preferred Givenchy when it came to scarves and had ordered several of their new designs to add to her collection, thinking they'd come in handy on warmer days when she didn't feel like wearing a hat or a wig.

She kept her wigs on a shelf above the drawers, draped on mannequin heads like some kind of serial killer's wet dream. They were so realistic, although she'd stopped short at buying the type made from real hair. It seemed so unhygienic to walk around with someone else's hair on your hair. It took finding a hair in your soup to a whole new level.

She'd ordered three different lengths of blonde hair and one with long, dark locks just in case she felt like something different. Or more to the point if Theo felt like something different. Given last night's proceedings, that was looking like a strong possibility at some stage.

She selected the longest of the blonde wigs and added a cream fox fur headband as extra security. The wig wasn't going anywhere with that headband in place. Plus, it looked cute with the cashmere sweater she was wearing.

"Hey babe," said Theo, leaning on the doorframe, wearing his suit.

"Hey, yourself." She walked over to him and tipped her head up for a kiss. "Like my new hair?"

He pressed his lips to hers and she swooned. After all these years, he still made her stomach flip.

"You look beautiful," he said, reaching out to touch her wig. "My little snow bunny."

Her stomach flipped again, and she realised it wasn't Theo making her feel like this. She was going to throw up.

"Just a minute."

She ran to the ensuite with her hand over her mouth, making it to the toilet just in time to retch up its meagre contents.

"You should stay in bed today." Theo handed her some tissues.

"I'm only dropping in on Mum," she said. "Just a short visit to bring in her magazine and the brownies I baked yesterday. I won't stay long."

"You're getting very thin." His eyes swept down her body. "Are you eating enough?"

"I'm eating plenty." She used the tissues to wipe both the lie plus the vomit from her mouth, then leaned over the basin to take several large gulps of water.

"I'm really worried about you," he persisted. "You don't look great."

She felt his hand run tentatively down her back. "I thought you said I looked beautiful a minute ago."

"You did. You do!" His voice went up an octave. "Beautiful, but unwell. *Really* unwell. You're very pale."

"I just threw up. Of course, I'm pale." She stood to face him.

"Let me make you breakfast before I go," he suggested, not seeming to want to leave her like this.

"No. You must be exhausted. You were up half the night watching over me like some kind of bodyguard." She turned to the mirror and adjusted her wig.

"I was worried about you. I still am," he said. "You really should eat something to settle your stomach."

"Linda will make me breakfast. You can call her and check up on me if you like." She poked her tongue out at him, trying to convince him.

"I don't know..." He kissed her on the top of her head. It was the top of her wig actually, which felt fairly strange.

"Stop it, you big worry wart. I'm going to eat breakfast, then see Mum, then I'll come home and rest. I promise." She adjusted the sleeves of her sweater, making sure she looked more put together than she felt.

"Do all cancer patients dress like that?" Theo asked, a frown crossing his face as he took in her outfit. "You only had chemo yesterday."

"Since when have I been like everyone else?" Skye put her hands on her hips. "Just because I have cancer doesn't mean I have to dress like I have cancer. Besides, the side effects usually settle down on day two before kicking in again on day three. I may as well get out of the house now while I still feel okay. And I'd prefer to look as normal as possible. I'm still me, in case you hadn't noticed."

"I kind of noticed that, especially in the shower." He grinned sheepishly. "Thanks for ... umm—"

"Theo!" she chided. "Since when have you ever thanked me for ... that?"

This was getting even more serious than she first thought. What had happened to the man she married?

"Sorry, I ... "

"Get to work." She gave him a quick kiss on the cheek. "Go save the world."

Just as long as he saved her from this awful, awkward conversation, she'd be happy.

"I'm going, I'm going," he said. "I'll call you later, okay?"

She wiped her lip gloss from his cheek. "I'll text you when I get home."

"Bye, babe. Love you." He turned and went to the door.

"Love you too," she called after him, as she reached in the bathroom cabinet for her pills.

Her head was throbbing. This whole cancer business was so much more difficult than she'd imagined.

———

Clara ate her brownies, licking her fingers so the last of the crumbs would stick to them. Her cheeks felt sticky. She'd ask one of the nurses to help her clean her face later.

She opened the ballet magazine on her table. It was nice of that pretty lady with the silly headband to bring it in for her. She'd have to ask her what her name was next time.

A memory bubbled at the front of her mind and she glanced at the photo of Skye on her bedside table. It was a shame her daughter never visited. She was too busy being married to Dean, she supposed.

She sighed. If she were married to Dean, she'd be busy, too. He was one very handsome man.

She knew nobody believed he'd painted her feet with glue, but he had. He really had. She knew it because she could feel it—not the actual glue, which had long ago washed off— but the truth of it having happened weighed on her. It was a nasty thing to do. He must've been trying to make sure she couldn't run away from the nursing home. How disappointing. She was sure he loved her.

Sometimes she dreamt he was sitting by her bed, watching her. She'd try to wake herself up so she could talk to him, but her eyelids were always too heavy.

There was very little she was jealous about when it came to her daughter, but Dean was an exception. Skye was lucky to have him. She'd give anything for Jacques to look at her the way Dean looked at Skye.

She sighed and turned back to her magazine. There was a photo of a ballerina, mid-arabesque. She looked beautiful. Maybe it was a photo of Clara. She'd been a ballerina.

Her hand trailed to the belt of her dressing gown and she undid it, staring down with fascination at the protruding belly in her lap. No, the photo wasn't her. Her slender body had been buried under her dementia along with her mind.

The buttons of her nightgown were straining from the effort of keeping closed. It felt like a boa constrictor was wrapped around her waist. She undid a few buttons and watched her rolls of flesh spill out. That was better. She could breathe at last.

A teenager walked into her room. His face wasn't familiar. Clara didn't like faces that weren't familiar. They made her feel crazy. She wasn't crazy. Definitely not crazy.

He sat next to her bed and stared at her. She stared back.

He was a fat boy. She'd never liked fat boys. Especially boys with little pudgy breasts like this one had. He wore a baseball cap, which was another thing she didn't like. It was disrespectful to wear a hat indoors.

"You have something on your face," he said. "Would you like me to clean it up?"

"Go away." She screwed her face up at him.

He was still staring at her like he was expecting her to do something interesting. Did he think she was going to jump out of bed and perform the dance of the sugar plum fairy? Maybe she should. It'd been ages since she'd done that. She was sure she'd be able to remember all the steps if she tried.

"I'm a big fan of your work," he said.

She poked her tongue out at him, but he only smiled.

"How are you?" he asked.

She was fine. More than fine, but that was none of his business. Why should she tell him how she was?

"Go away, go away, go away!" Her voice took on a high pitch and she felt a scratch at the back of her throat.

"I just wanted to talk." He put his hand on her arm. "I didn't mean to upset you. I think you're a wonderful ballerina, that's all. I've seen your videos on the internet."

She spat and watched her saliva land on the back of his hand.

He moved his chair back a few feet, but remained steady, wiping his hand on the leg of his faded jeans.

"I'm not going to hurt you," he said. "I'm just a big fan."

She started to cry, not sure what was causing the tears. Fans used to visit her all the time. Some of them still wrote to her. The nurses read her the letters sometimes.

Not many fans had visited her in the home. They'd forgotten about her along with the rest of the world. This boy was a novelty. An unwelcome one at that. He was confusing her, reminding her about how many details of her life she was unable to retrieve. She needed him to leave.

"Go away," she said, baring her teeth like a frightened monkey. If he wouldn't go away when asked, she'd have to scare him away. She made a screeching noise to go with the monkey face.

"Are you happy?" he asked, when she paused to take a breath.

Happy! What a strange question to ask. Nobody had asked her that for at least twenty years. What did he care if she was happy?

She continued to screech until he stood up slowly and backed out of the room, staring at her from the safe distance of the doorway. It took some people a while to get the hint. Clearly this wasn't one of her most intelligent fans.

Her stomach groaned and she felt her bowels open, spilling into her pants. The nurses had started putting her into grown-up diapers. She knew how to go to the toilet, the problem was she'd get up to go and halfway to the bathroom she'd forget where she was going, until it was too late. She didn't mind wearing these things. It was better than the puddles that would otherwise end up at her feet.

"Fuck off," she said to the boy, taking things to the next level. She never usually swore. It surprised her she even knew how to. The word had slipped out so easily.

The boy glanced down the hallway, but his feet remained planted.

She reached into her pants and pulled out a handful of liquid shit, flinging it towards him. She missed and it splattered on the carpet in front of him.

That did it. He took off.

She rose from her bed and pulled her nightgown over her head as she walked to her small bathroom, wanting to stand in front of the mirror like she'd done so often in her youth.

She was surprised to see the image staring back at her. Her hips looked wide and her belly sagged down so far she could barely see her diaper. She raised her arms in the air and studied the flaps of skin that hung so loosely they looked like they might slide off her body and fall to the floor.

She stepped closer, wanting a better view of her face. Her hair was grey and greasy. When was the last time the nurses had washed it for her? It'd been months. Years maybe. Her face was wrinkled and a soft pad of skin billowed underneath her chin, making her neck disappear.

Perhaps this mirror wasn't real. It could be one of those circus mirrors. Maybe Dean was playing another trick on her.

Then she caught sight of her eyes, recognising them in an instant. Her eyes hadn't changed. They weren't affected by the mirror. The mirror was real.

The old Clara would have screamed in terror at this realisation, but not the new. The new Clara howled with laughter.

"You're hideous," she said, not caring in the least.

In the muddled, hazy world she lived in, she was offered a brief moment of clarity. Her looks weren't important to her because she was no longer the person she once was. She was different now, as much on the inside as on the outside.

That boy had asked her if she was happy and the truth was that she was. She was happier than she'd ever been. The new Clara may not be beautiful, but she was acutely aware of the preciousness of life and the importance of living in the moment.

And if that moment meant standing naked in front of the mirror laughing at how hideous she'd become, then to hell with it, she was having a great day.

"Come on, Clara," said a voice behind her. "Let's get you cleaned up."

In the mirror, she saw a nurse standing behind her.

"I'm not crazy," she said, uncertain as to why she felt the need to defend herself.

"Of course, not," the nurse said. "You're a ballerina."

Clara frowned, noticing a flash of colour near the door of her room.

It was the boy again. Some people really didn't know how to take a hint.

9 DAYS BEFORE THE BREAK

Amber hadn't realised it was possible for builders to build so fast. It made her wonder how much extra her father had paid them. Her new shedroom had been made ready for her in record time.

Even Jeff had moved quickly to help the project along and he hadn't moved quickly on anything in his life—except marrying her mother and producing three children. Which wasn't so bad she supposed.

She didn't have a problem with Sammy, James or Rory, except for the fact they were her mother's children. They'd make very nice next-door neighbours or cousins. But siblings ... she wasn't too sure about that.

She remembered how nice it was when she was her mother's only child. She felt special and important, not having to fight for attention or space in her heart. She'd occupied all her heart's spaces in those days. Now it was divided into five. One piece for each of her children and another for Jeff. Sometimes Jeff's piece seemed to be the biggest, which was annoying. It wasn't as gross as watching her father with Skye (at least they were the same age), but still it wasn't great.

Jeff followed her mother about with his tongue hanging out like some kind of demented puppy dog. Weirdly, her mother didn't seem to mind. She actually seemed to enjoy it.

Thankfully, none of her siblings looked like their mother. Rory had her voluminous black hair, but his skin was fair like his father's. James had her dark skin, but somehow his eyes had turned out blue. And Samantha hadn't seemed to inherit any of her mother's traits. She looked more like a miniature female version of Jeff. Maybe even a tiny bit like Skye, which was quite funny.

Being the only one to resemble her mother connected them in a way the others weren't.

She decided her powerful father's sperm must be weak. It hadn't seemed to have had any impact on her appearance whatsoever. That must bug a man like him. Not that she'd dare ask him about it. It was kind of ironic that meek and mild Jeff was the one with the super sperm.

Eeew! Gross. The thought of Jeff's sperm made her gag.

She spat out her chewing gum and sprawled out on her new bed, desperate to think about something else.

She looked around her *cool new pad*. It was okay, she supposed. She could never admit that to anyone, of course. Jeff had a new, smaller shed on the other side of the yard. This older, larger shed was unrecognisable from what it'd been before. The outside had been lined with weatherboards and painted in a sunny primrose colour, with pots of flowers sitting on the porch. She'd requested it be painted purple but had been forced to compromise when her mother said she couldn't stand to look at anything so gaudy while she washed her dishes. So, they painted the front door purple instead. The old tiles had been pulled off the roof and replaced with shiny new tin panels. She loved the sound when it rained. The inside had been insulated, then lined with plaster, and a bamboo floor floated on the old concrete slab. Internal walls had been put up to divide the space into a bedroom, bathroom and living room with a small kitchenette off to one side.

It was a lot bigger than she'd expected it to be.

Her father had sent Skye's interior designer around and together they'd filled the space with colour and warmth. Clearly, this was a much more interesting job for the designer than decorating Skye's washed-out house must have been.

She supposed it was nice of Jeff to let the builders come in and make so many changes, all for her. He was a nice stepfather, really. She'd never given him much of her time, figuring she already had a father. Maybe things would be different now. She'd make more of an effort with him.

The whole family had to help sift through Jeff's father's hoarded rubbish that had been carefully carried from the shed and placed in piles in the backyard. She'd watched Jeff with wry amusement picking through the junk, marvelling over each piece of trash as it sparked some precious childhood memory.

Her contribution with the clean-up had been minimal. She'd shuffled a few boxes around from pile to pile to make it look like she was doing something but had given up the pretence when she'd kicked at a carton and four smaller boxes tumbled out almost breaking her toes. She'd left the rest of her family to it.

The whole building project had taken less than a month and the result was kind of breathtaking. She wasn't so sure anymore that she wanted to return home to her father when Skye was better.

Sammy had already asked if she could move in with her and their mother had to steer her away from that idea, telling her she could have it one day when Amber was a grown up and moved away.

Obviously, this was something Sammy was now counting down the days for. Amber promised her she could have the occasional sleepover in the meantime. This had lit her little sister's face with joy.

"No boys allowed, though," Sammy had whispered to her.

"Definitely not," said Amber. As much as she loved James and Rory, they'd destroy this place in about three minutes flat with their wrestling matches and inability to sit still. Rory would drop crumbs everywhere and James would pick up every item she owned and ask her a thousand questions about where it came from.

She smiled at the thought. Maybe the boys could visit occasionally.

Then she reminded herself how upset she was about being evicted from her home by Skye. She was going to have to get up at the crack of dawn to get to school in time from now on. And none of her friends would ever visit her all the way out here in Burwood. Not that they'd visited her much in Malvern either.

She crossed her arms and sat up on the edge of the bed, cursing the day her father had choked on his muesli. If only it was some other woman he'd fallen in love with.

———

Sammy was mad. No, she was madder than mad. There was another word to describe it. She chewed on her bottom lip as she tried to think what it was. It started with F. Not the rude F word (ten year olds weren't allowed to use that word). Another F word. The one that meant really, really mad.

Her big sister, Amber, had moved in. That wasn't the bit that made her mad. She loved her big sister. It was nice to have another girl in the family. One that didn't burp and fart all the time like James and Rory.

It was just that Amber got the new bedroom in the backyard and it wasn't fair. She'd lived here her entire life and Amber had lived here for only a little while years and years ago. If anyone should get the good bedroom it should be her. Or she should at least be able to share it with her—it might be a bit scary to be out there at night all on her own.

It was so pretty and yellow and shiny and new. Her bedroom had cracks in the wall, a cordial stain on the carpet and sometimes when you opened the window it got stuck and wouldn't close properly again.

Her mum bought her a new bedspread, like that was going to make her feel any better. It was just a bedspread. Amber was getting a whole new room. And it had its own living room. It even had a kitchen!

She picked a blade of grass from the back lawn where she was sitting watching the painters finish the final coat on the weatherboards.

It looked so good she wanted to die. It made her furious.

Furious! That was the word she wanted.

She was FURIOUS.

Amber had said she could have sleepovers. She didn't say James and Rory could. Just her. Maybe she could start off doing that once or twice a week, then build up until she lived there permanently. If she did it slowly enough maybe Amber wouldn't notice before it was too late and she had all her stuff in there.

She pulled more grass from the lawn, shredding each blade down the middle with her fingernail.

Amber would notice if she moved in. She was practically a grown-up and grown-ups noticed everything.

Amber's dad must have a lot of money to pay for all of this. She heard her mother telling her friend once that he was loaded. She'd never heard that expression before and had to google it to find out what it meant. It was hard to figure out. The first definition she read said it meant he was drunk.

She knew about drunk. Sometimes her mother got drunk when they went out for dinner and she had too much wine. She'd sit at the table giggling and rubbing her father on the leg and he'd say, '*You're drunk, Tamarin!*' Then they'd both laugh like he'd told some kind of joke.

So, she'd decided loaded must mean he carried around a lot of things, but that didn't sound right either.

The few times she'd seen Amber's father he hadn't been giggling or carrying any big bags on his back. He hadn't even been smiling. He'd sat in his fancy car outside their house frowning like the sight of it scared him or something. Once, she gathered her courage and stuck her tongue out at him from her bedroom window. He didn't notice. Unfortunately, her father had been standing in the doorway and he noticed. She hadn't been allowed to use the Playstation for a week.

Her dad could be strict like that, but she'd still rather have him than Amber's dad. At least her dad was soft and friendly and smiled more than he frowned. Amber's dad seemed more like a movie star than a father. She wondered what Amber talked to him about.

Eventually she asked James what loaded meant. He was always reading books, so he knew a lot of things like that. He told her it meant he was rich. She wondered if that meant Amber was rich.

"You all right, Princess?" asked her father, taking a seat next to her on the lawn and draping one of his arms around her shoulder.

She shrugged. "Yeah."

"Looks good, doesn't it?" He nodded towards Amber's new room.

"Yeah."

"Do you like the yellow?"

"Yeah."

"You're chatty today." He laughed, squeezing her that little bit tighter.

"It's not fair, Dad. Why does Amber get the good bedroom?" She shoved her father's arm from her shoulder and turned to face him.

He sighed. "She's older than you, darling."

"But she's not even your real daughter," she protested.

"Don't say that." He pulled the face he always used when she was in trouble, which sucked because she was only telling the truth.

"But it's true," she wailed.

He reached for her again and she shifted away a little, not ready to give into him just yet. "Well, if you want to look at it that way, her *real* father is paying for it."

"Is Amber rich?" At last, her chance to ask the question.

"Where did that come from?" He looked genuinely shocked.

She shrugged. "I just wondered. So, is she?"

This time he shrugged. "I suppose so."

"Are we rich?" she asked.

He put his finger under her chin and tilted her face upwards. "If you ask me, I'm the richest man in the world."

"You mean you're loaded?" she asked, testing out the word.

"Yep, loaded with love."

She shuffled back across to him, deciding things weren't so bad after all.

8 DAYS BEFORE THE BREAK

Skye hated visiting her mother in the lounge with all the other residents. It was so depressing.

"Hi, Mum," she said, reluctantly taking the vacant seat beside her.

Her mother's eyes lit up, not at the sight of her daughter, but at the brownies she held in her hand.

Skye wanted to tell her how much she'd have liked her mother to have made her desserts when she was a child instead of the constant supply of celery sticks she set down in front of her.

"It's the only food that's calorie-negative," her mother used to say. "You burn more calories digesting celery than you gain by consuming it."

Whether or not that was true, it still didn't make it taste any good. Not to a child anyway. These days, Skye added plenty of them to her green smoothies in the morning, but you could hardly taste them underneath the parsley and mint.

"Would you like a brownie, Mum?" she asked.

Her mother nodded as eagerly as if she were a young girl.

"Then let's go to your room." Skye stood and took her mother's hand. "That way you don't have to share."

She saw the shoulders of the woman next to her slump. There

weren't enough on this plate. Despite being a less than exemplary mother, Skye still didn't think she should miss out on the few pleasures she had left in life.

She watched her mother as they walked to her room at the end of the hall, reminding herself she wasn't actually old, despite the way she shuffled her feet. Her disease had aged her body and regressed her mind, sending them running in opposite directions like two poles of a magnet. She was like a toddler in an elderly person's body when in truth both her body and her mind were somewhere in between.

"I don't like your hat," said her mother, sitting in the only chair, leaving Skye to perch on the edge of the bed.

Skye's hand flew to her head and skipped across the band of her turban. There were women all over London wearing these to accessorise their full heads of hair and nobody was telling them they didn't like it. Her mother really had lost touch with the world of fashion. She had a half wig on underneath the turban to give the appearance of having hair. She couldn't exactly remove the turban, or she'd look like Friar Bloody Tuck.

"How are you, Mum?" She spoke more to the clock behind her mother's head than to her directly, not wanting to see her eat the brownies.

Her mother grunted in response and Skye was glad Theo wasn't here to see her behaving like a farm animal. It was no wonder he only ever visited once, just after they got engaged. She hadn't wanted him to visit at all, preferring to hide her mother away. She'd heard men studied their girlfriend's mother as an indication of how they'd look in the future. She didn't want him thinking she'd be like that. Besides, Theo wasn't all that much younger than her mother. She'd thought he might feel strange about meeting her.

But he'd been very persistent, insisting family was important. He wanted to meet her mother just as he wished she could've met his. She'd relented, taking him with her on one of her regular visits, wishing she had a father she could've introduced him to instead.

He'd turned up with a bunch of flowers and a smile. He left with the same bunch of rejected flowers and a look of sheer horror.

He'd upset her mother so much that they decided it was best for everyone if he stayed away. Instead, he paid for her to be moved to a facility especially set up to care for people with dementia. It was expensive, yet money well spent according to Theo who freely admitted it eased his guilt about his lack of a relationship with his mother-in-law.

She watched her mother put down the brownies and shake out her hands.

"What's wrong with your hands?" asked Skye.

"Numb. Always numb." She picked up the brownies and resumed eating.

"Maybe you're sitting too much," Skye suggested. "You really should make an effort to move around a little more."

Her mother looked at her like she'd suggested she travel to the moon.

"My hair's falling out," said her mother, wiping chocolate from her lips with the back of her hand.

Skye drew in a sharp breath. Of all the ailments for her mother to invent, it had to be that one. Her feet were no longer covered in glue, this time her hair was falling out. She felt like removing her turban and showing her mother what it really looked like when your hair fell out.

Her mother tugged at her hair. A large chunk came free and she waved it in front of her in her fist.

"Oh my god." Skye leapt to her feet and took the hair from her. Her hair really was falling out.

Her mother reached for her head again.

"Stop pulling at your hair! You're making it worse. Don't touch it." She was going to need to talk to the nurse about this. What the hell was happening?

"The doctor is doing tests on me." Her mum smiled proudly.

"What tests?" Skye frowned. "He's testing your hair?"

"No, silly." She laughed. "He took my blood to see why my hair's falling out."

"Right." Why hadn't Skye received a call about any tests? She was supposed to be informed about things like this.

"I used to be a ballerina." Her mother rounded her arms and lifted them above and slightly forward of her head into what Skye recognised as fifth position.

"I'm going to go and find a nurse to speak to." Skye took a step towards the door. "Finish up your brownies, Mum."

"I'm not your mum."

"Okay then, Clara." She sighed. "Eat your brownies. I'll be back in a moment."

"My name is Clara." Her mother let her arms fall and picked up another brownie.

"I know. That's why I called you that."

"I was a ballerina," she said with her mouth full.

"You still are." Skye smiled to hide her concern. She always would be a ballerina to Skye. Not this mad woman who sat before her. Her mother—her formerly sane mother—wouldn't want to live like this. She'd be mortified if she could see herself.

She handed her the latest ballet magazine, squeezed her hand. She'd talk to the nurse and head home. Her mother didn't seem to care today if she visited or not. She had her brownies and her magazine. She was happy, even if her hair was falling out.

———

Skye knocked on the door of the nurses' station.

"Have you got a moment?" she asked.

A plump woman wearing a lanyard around her neck looked up from her computer. The lanyard said her name was Desmona. Her uniform said she was a nurse.

"How can I help you?" She smiled at Skye like she was one of her patients.

Skye cringed. "I've just been to see my mother, Clara Butterford."

"Oh, Clara." Desmona smiled warmly. "I'm only new here, but she's already one of my favourites."

"Really?" Skye tried to hide her surprise. Nobody had talked about her mother like that since her dancing days.

"Yes. She's such a happy soul," Desmond gushed.

Skye coughed, wondering if there could be two Clara Butterfords in residence.

"A wonderful ballerina, too," Desmona continued. "I looked her up on YouTube the other day after that young fan of hers visited. She was wonderful. What a gift!"

So that was why Desmona was so besotted with her mother. She was star-struck. It'd been a while since Skye had met any of her mother's fans, but she knew they were still out there. She'd been very well-known. Occasionally, she'd search for her name on the internet to find people still talking about her

"She was very talented," smiled Skye. "I was j—"

"I've seen you here a few times," Desmona interrupted, not seeming to have the need to take a breath. "You're a good daughter. Sadly, most families choose not to visit. *It's too painful,* they say. You know, I just want to shake them and tell them to stop expecting their loved one to be the same as they were before. If you can think of them as two different people, it's easier to cope with."

Skye thought perhaps that was the problem. They *did* think of them as two different people and that was why they could walk the other way. They didn't love this new person. It was the old person with all their marbles who they loved.

"She was very confused today," said Skye, trying to get to the point. "You see, h—"

"That's to be expected with her condition." Desmona made a strange clucking noise.

Skye inhaled and stretched her lips into a smile. Did this woman ever shut up?

"You can expect some days she'll be more confused than others," continued Desmona.

Nope, this woman never shut up. Skye bet she talked in her sleep.

"Perhaps I could speak to the manager," Skye suggested, deciding not to waste any more of her time.

"Oh, sorry, I have a habit of rambling." The smile fell from Desmona's face. "No need for the manager. How can I help you exactly? What's your specific concern?"

"My mother's hair's falling out. Is that specific enough?" Her tone was colder than a shot of vodka in a Russian ice bar.

Desmona sat up straight in her chair, her mouth finally clamped shut.

"She seems to think the doctor has taken her blood to do tests," said Skye, not caring in the least if she'd offended her. "I would've thought I'd be consulted about such things."

"Let me just check her file to see if the doctor's made any notes." Desmona turned to her computer and began to type, pressing the keys more loudly than necessary, perhaps compensating for her current lack of speech.

Skye noticed an engagement ring flashing on her left hand as she typed. She was engaged! It would be a brave man to marry her. Perhaps he was deaf.

"Oh right," said Desmona, her brow furrowing as she read from her screen. "The doctor's made a note about that. He said he took some blood to test her thyroid function. Most likely alopecia, he says. There's a note here to contact you about it."

"So, why wasn't I contacted?" Skye arched a thinning eyebrow at Desmona.

"The doctor only saw her this morning. We would've called you this afternoon," she quickly explained. "Please, there's nothing for you to be concerned about. Alopecia is more common than you'd think."

"May I have the doctor's contact details please?" There was no point talking to this fool about her mother. Better to talk to someone who could give her real information rather than making it up as she went along.

Desmona picked up a pen, scribbled some details on a notepad and handed her the page.

"Thank you so much for your trouble," said Skye, sarcasm dripping from her lips in such vast quantities she almost needed a bib to catch it.

She turned on her stilettos and left.

3 DAYS BEFORE THE BREAK

Theo scowled at his screen. He'd only just sat down at his desk, preparing to return some phone calls when a message popped up.

Elle Thomas 4.55pm
Hi Theo. Just making sure you're ok? Skye's been doing so well at chemo! She says she's doing well at home too so hopefully that's not just her being brave again. How are you coping?

He knew he should be grateful to Elle, not suspicious, but there was just something about her that was a little off. Not off as in off-putting—her profile picture was still as sexy as hell—just off as in not quite right. He couldn't put his finger on what exactly it was.

He clicked on her photo and let it fill his screen. What a body. She obviously knew it. Why else would she use that photo as her profile pic? Yep, she was so hot he could fry an egg off that flat stomach of hers.

His gaze trailed to her cleavage and he felt his cock shift in his pants. If only it was that easy getting turned on with Skye.

She was so sick most of the time it was surprising she even wanted to be with him. With her bald head and bones protruding from under her skin, he was worried he might snap her in half. It sounded terrible to say, but there really was nothing sexy about cancer.

Elle's green bikini on the other hand ... now that was sexy.

He clicked away from her photo, a fire raging in his pants. What if an associate walked in and he had to stand up? It wasn't a good look.

Theo Manis 4.59pm
Hi Elle. Thanks once again for taking care of Skye. It's good to know she has you there.

He paused, wondering why he was being so polite. He should've insisted Sophie take her to chemo, but Skye had been adamant she'd wanted Elle with her.

Elle had gotten him off the hook. He didn't want to go. He couldn't handle seeing Skye connected to those machines. It was hard enough to cope with her illness without having to witness the treatment first hand. He was lucky he had his work as an excuse.

Elle Thomas 4.59pm
No probs! But you didn't answer my question. How are you coping?

Fuck. Why did she have to ask that? Nobody had asked him how he was coping for ages. They always wanted to know about Skye—as they should, of course.

Theo Manis 5.01pm
I'm good thanks. If Skye's OK, then I am too. Just rushing off to a meeting now. Thanks again for your help.

He couldn't deal with Elle and her green bikini today. He shifted uncomfortably in his seat, unable to quash his arousal.

There was a gentle knock at his door.

Great. He picked up a file, preparing to use it as a shield.

"Come in."

An oddly familiar woman appeared at the doorway. He only saw her face for a moment as she turned to close the door behind her, clicking it locked. Her long, dark hair trailed down her back. Was that Elle? Was that why she looked so familiar?

"What are you doing?" he asked.

"Hello, Kronos." The woman undid her coat and let it slip to the floor, revealing some extremely skimpy green lace lingerie.

It wasn't Elle. It was Skye wearing a wig he'd never seen before. Was she dressing as Elle intentionally? No, it must be a coincidence. Plenty of women had dark hair and green was a common enough colour. He was just seeing what he wanted to see.

Besides, he didn't care what her reasons were. He was more turned on than he'd been in months.

She sat on his desk and swung her legs across to him, placing her high-heeled feet in his lap.

"I want you to fuck me," she said, her eyes wide and blinking as if she'd said the most innocent thing in the world. Skye didn't normally talk to him like this.

He liked it.

A lot.

He grabbed her by the knees, roughly prising them apart, all the time wondering if it was possible to explode with lust.

He tore her underwear from her body, ripping it to shreds as he took her on his desk.

Damn, she felt good. Kronos was back.

2 DAYS BEFORE THE BREAK

George shifted his weight from foot to foot as he waited for Skye to open the front door, wishing it were Theo who'd buzzed him inside the gate. He wasn't sure what to say to her. Theo had told him she no longer had her hair, and for some reason that made George nervous.

The door opened and he tried not to grimace at the shock.

"Hi, Skye. You look ... you look great." He did his best to smile and pulled her into a hug, being careful not to crush her.

"You like my new image?" She ran her hand over her head and smiled.

"All you need are some tatts and you can come and work with me," he said, trying to break the tension he felt building inside him.

She laughed and for a moment he saw the old Skye flash across her face.

He couldn't believe it when Theo first introduced her to him. She looked like some kind of model. It was completely and entirely unfair given that Theo looked like ... him. Did that mean he could score a woman like Skye? That thought had plagued him ever since. He had to sweep it from his mind by reminding himself that Theo had other assets going for him, such as the piles of money he had stacked up underneath his bed. Lucky bastard. Everything always came easy to him.

Not that he was unhappy with his life. He had Sophie and the kids, and he wouldn't swap them for Theo's charmed life. His life was just as charmed, only in other non-financial ways.

Sophie may not have Skye's youth, but he'd loved her since the moment he first laid eyes on her—even if she'd had her tongue shoved down his brother's throat at the time. There was just something special about her that'd hypnotised him. He'd been thrilled when Theo had cast her aside. Normally this would've been a turn off. He didn't do sloppy seconds, but for Sophie he'd made an exception. She'd been hot back then. She still was. She might have rounder hips than she used to and a few wrinkles around her eyes, but when he looked at her, he saw not only the mother of his children, but the sex goddess she was between the sheets. She knew exactly what to do with those hips of hers, not to mention those hands, those lips ... Yep, he still had a hard on for his wife, thank god for that.

"Theo's not home just yet," said Skye, leading him to the kitchen for what would no doubt be several minutes of awkward conversation.

He took a seat at the counter. Damn, these fancy stools were uncomfortable. He could barely get one bum cheek on it properly. What was it with Theo and furniture like this?

"I'll get you a beer." Skye opened the fridge.

He caught sight of a plate of brownies. Theo often complained she only ever made them for her mother these days. He'd kill for one right now.

She reached for a beer and closed the fridge.

"Are those your famous brownies I just saw?" If she wasn't going to offer them, then he'd damn well ask for one. Surely, she could spare one. Her mother didn't need them all.

"They're for Mum. I'll get you something else."

She handed him a beer and he clutched it like a baby with a pacifier.

Damn.

The plate she placed in front of him looked all right if you were into fancy things like cheese with mould growing on it. Personally, he thought the only place to serve mouldy cheese was directly into the bin.

Given it was the only thing she offered him, he shovelled some in his mouth and pointed to a pile of miscellaneous belongings strewn across the counter.

"Doing a clean up?" he asked. It was highly unusual to see anything in this house out of place.

"I lost something, that's all." She opened the largest handbag he'd ever seen in his life and began placing each belonging carefully back in its allotted place.

"Need help looking for it?" he asked.

She gave him an empty smile. "No, it'll turn up. It's nothing important."

He doubted that. People generally didn't turn their bags upside down to find things that weren't important.

"How's your Mum?" he asked.

"Same, same. She's okay."

Uncomfortable silence filled the air. Whatever did Theo talk to her about? Sophie was easy to talk to. They had common interests, mostly due to being the same age. Skye was closer in age to his kids. He tried to remember what he talked to them about, realising he never actually had to *try* with them. Conversation just came naturally.

"Seen any good movies?" he asked, wincing at his pathetic small talk.

Skye's face lit up. "Have you been reading my posts?"

He was confused. Had she started writing movie reviews? He never read anything she wrote, preferring to get Sophie to recap the highlights for him. If they'd had a few drinks, occasionally she'd act out Skye's posts using a high-pitched voice and batting her eyelashes like a crazy woman. They'd stopped doing that since the cancer.

"It's okay," said Skye. "I wrote about my cancer being like a movie. You know, good guys versus bad guys."

"That's right." He vaguely remembered Sophie saying something about that, but he hadn't been listening closely.

Skye reached back into her bag and pulled out some kind of weird looking turban. She stretched it over her head and smoothed out some of the folds of black fabric.

He took a slug of his beer to hide his amusement. That hat looked like something a model would wear in one of those magazines Sophie read, not something you'd see an actual person wear in real life.

Hurry up, Theo. He would've gone to the pub with the boys for a bit if he knew he was going to take this long.

The housekeeper stepped into the room.

"I'm heading off now," she said.

"Thanks, Linda," said Skye with another one of those empty smiles. "Have you got that dry cleaning I need done for Thursday?"

"Yes. I'll drop it off on my way here in the morning."

George caught a look of sheer exhaustion on Linda's face. It must be a hard job cleaning this place. He hoped she had some nice bloke at home to rub her feet.

"Great," said Skye. "See you tomorrow."

Linda nodded and turned to leave. George wished she'd stay. She wasn't a bad looking sort and probably easier to talk to than Skye.

"Where's Sophie?" asked Skye, turning back to him.

"Beth has netball," he said. "Hey, where's Amber tonight?"

In truth, he knew exactly where his niece was. Amber had appeared on his doorstep only the week before, upset about Skye kicking her out of the house. Sophie and Beth had made her hot chocolate and sat up with her for hours consoling her. That was the reason for his visit tonight. Sophie had *suggested* he drop in and find out what the hell Theo was thinking, evicting his own daughter from her home. Of course, it wasn't really a suggestion. More like a command. Still, Sophie was right. He should take more interest in his niece and find out what was up.

"Didn't Theo tell you?" asked Skye. "She's moved in with her mother for a while."

"Oh. Her decision or ... Theo's?" Clearly it was Skye's, but he chickened out from confronting her about it. He'd talk to Theo. Skye had cancer for god's sake. What did Sophie expect him to do? Get her in a headlock until she talked?

"A joint decision." She smiled. "It's only temporary. Truly, it is."

HC MICHAELS

He wasn't buying that for a minute. Now that Skye had Amber out of the house, he'd bet his left one there'd never be a convenient time for her to move back in. This was Skye's dream come true.

"Besides, she visits all the time," said Skye, still trying to convince him. "She was here earlier today picking up some of her stuff. It's not like we've kicked her out or anything. She's welcome anytime."

"Of course." He took another slug of his beer, deciding to let the conversation drop. If Sophie wanted to know more about it, she could ask Skye herself. It was just too damn awkward for him to do it.

"It was nice of Sophie to pick me up from hospital," said Skye, clearly just as keen as him to steer the conversation in a new direction. "Is her car all right?"

"What's wrong with her car?" George set down his beer and frowned.

"Oops. Nothing. Think I just got confused." Skye grimaced. "You know, cancer brain."

"It's in your brain?" He'd thought it was just in her ovaries. "Bloody hell!"

"No!" she quickly corrected. "I just meant I'm not thinking clearly."

"Oh." This conversation was getting more awkward by the moment. He was fairly certain Skye was thinking more than clearly. Certainly, clearly enough to be trying to distract him away from Amber by dropping Sophie into the shit.

"What were you saying about the car?" he asked, determined not to show his frustration with Sophie. They were a team. It would be disloyal to let Skye know he was annoyed with her.

"Maybe you should ask Sophie about that." Skye pushed away from the counter. "I hope I haven't gotten her into trouble. It was just a little accident."

He drew in a deep breath. Sophie must've hidden another crash from him. Why would she do that? He wasn't such an ogre, was he? Still, it did make him mad. She'd already damaged the car a couple of times this year. He wasn't made of money. Unlike Theo.

"Hey, boofhead." Theo walked into the kitchen and slapped him on the back.

He was so happy to see him, he didn't even mind about the boofhead.

Theo kissed Skye on the cheek. "Hi, babe."

George cringed. He hated how Theo called Skye babe like he was trying to be some kind of cool teenager. Didn't he realise it made him sound like a fool? He imagined what would happen if he went home and called Sophie babe. She'd probably laugh so hard she'd fall over.

"Chatting up my wife, were you?" asked Theo, as he chose a bottle of red from his wine fridge.

"You know me. Always waiting in the wings for your scraps." He cursed himself once more. Why had he said that? Sophie wasn't a scrap. She was the best bloody thing that ever happened to him.

"I'm getting out of here." Skye slapped the air in front of him with a tea towel. "Too much testosterone for me."

Thank fuck for that, thought George.

He was relieved to be left alone with Theo. Cancer was far easier to deal with when you didn't have to look it in its skinny, bald face.

———

Skye looked in the mirror, checking her wig was straight. It was still itchy despite the bamboo cap she wore underneath.

She was wearing the shorter blonde one today. It showed off the neckline of her Brunello Cucinelli sweatshirt better. Plus, she wanted to wear her jade Bvlgari necklace today and didn't want to risk her wig getting tangled in the clasp.

She'd prefer not to wear a wig at all but didn't want to upset her mother by turning up at the nursing home bald. She'd clearly disapproved of the turban she wore last time, so, really, she had no alternative but to wear this thing.

She wondered how her mother's hair loss was going. Maybe she should've bought her a wig, too. A two for one special. They could be matchy matchy. The thought made her laugh. If her mother were still sane, the idea would make her wrinkled mouth pull into a grimace. She'd never wanted her daughter to look like her.

She hadn't wanted her to look like her father either. Skye knew how much it bothered her mother that she had her father's eyes. It wasn't like she'd done it on purpose.

Perhaps if her mother looked in the mirror now, she wouldn't mind looking like her daughter so much. Skye doubted she'd had a good look at herself for years.

Anyway, everybody already knew she had cancer, so she didn't know why she was so worried. She hadn't bothered wearing her wig last night when George had dropped around and he didn't seem to care. The way he'd kept staring at her head, he'd seemed to like it. Maybe Sophie should shave her head for him to spice things up in their bedroom.

Men really did like it when you did something different. The dark wig she'd worn to Theo's chambers had certainly done the trick. It was by far the best sex they'd had since she'd told him she had cancer. She was going to have to wear it more often.

She went to the kitchen and sighed. Linda hadn't arrived yet and Theo's dishes were still sitting in the sink from last night. It was still quite early, she supposed.

She picked up the latest ballet magazine she'd left on the counter, afraid if she kept it neatly tucked away on a shelf, she might forget it. She was excited to bring her mother this particular edition. They'd done a centre spread with old photos of their star principal dancers over the years. Her mother's photo was there. Finally, when she pointed to it and asked if it was a photo of her, Skye could say yes.

It was a beautiful shot of her mid-pirouette, one leg bent, her foot gently touching her supporting knee, her arms raised above her head. It wasn't the perfection of the pose that made the photo beautiful, it was the look of serenity on her face. She must've been in extraordinary pain at the time (her feet still looked more like a contorted piece of ginger root than actual feet) yet still she managed to make it look so natural. Her father had been right when he'd said she danced like her ballet slippers were made from clouds.

She opened the fridge to get out the tray of brownies she'd made the day before. The ones she'd had to practically beat George away from. Men were hopeless when it came to baking. Surely Sophie could make brownies for George if he loved them so much. Lukas certainly looked as though he'd had a brownie or two in his time.

She laughed as she imagined a bald Sophie standing in a tight-fitting lace teddy holding a tray of brownies out to George.

The lack of brownies hadn't seemed to have dampened Theo and George's spirits last night. They'd sat up half the night drinking and talking. This wasn't unusual for them. As competitive as they were with each other, their bond was close. It was a strange relationship, but one Skye had come to accept. She'd gone to bed, leaving them to it. She was so tired, and her head had been thumping again.

It was hard at times being married to a twin. Sometimes she felt like she was married to the both of them. She'd noticed the way George looked at her, almost like he was wondering if she was as attracted to him as she was to Theo. It was strange, but she wasn't even the slightest bit attracted to him. They might be identical to everyone else, but to her they couldn't be more dissimilar.

George was so rough around the edges. And it was Theo's polished edges that drew her in. He was like the perfectly cut and polished six carat diamond she wore on her left hand—a work of art.

She opened the fridge to see the brownies were gone. The plate was still there, only now it held a folded piece of paper.

Her hands trembled. The brownies were for her mother. She looked forward to them every week. What had Theo done? Her mother might have dementia, but she had rights too. Those were her brownies!

She slid the note off the plate and opened it.

We're so sorry, Skye. Two evil goblins snuck into the house while you were asleep and demanded we hand over the brownies. Please forgive us. It wasn't our fault. Enclosed is $20 to buy your mother something from the cafe. P.S. They were delicious (so the goblins told us). Love you xxxxxx

She should have hidden the brownies when she saw how George was eyeing them off. The house was full of food! Only one thing she'd asked them not to touch and they couldn't help themselves. Theo had

162 HC MICHAELS

never taken her mother's brownies before. He knew they were the highlight of her week.

Skye ripped the letter in half and washed it down the sink, watching as the garbage disposal gobbled it down. She stuck the twenty dollar note in after it, wishing it would take her frustration with it.

Leaning back on the counter, she slid to the floor and buried her face in her hands. Her wig tilted and she ripped it from her head and flung it aside.

What on earth was she going to do now?

THE DAY BEFORE THE BREAK

Theo wasn't feeling great. Actually, no. Theo felt like crap. Thank goodness he didn't have court today.

He shouldn't have come in. It must've been all that wine he drank with George. Maybe he should call him and see how he was feeling?

Nah, he'd only call him a pussy. George had always been able to drink him under the table. Theo had finished off a bottle of red, while George had downed about a dozen beers. He'd had to get a cab home. Sophie must've dropped him back this morning to get his ute.

He rose from his desk, put on his jacket, shoved his keys into his pocket and looked at his phone. There were three missed calls from Skye. Damn. He'd left it on silent again. He'd call her back from the car. Hopefully everything was okay. Sometimes she liked to call to listen to his voicemail message, so hopefully that was all it was.

"Not feeling great," he said to Jane as he passed her desk. "I'll see you later on."

"Of course," she said, unable to hide her surprise. He'd never gone home sick. "When will you be back?"

"I'll let you know," he replied, unsure how to answer that.

"Get better soon!" she shouted after him, as he continued down the passageway.

He stumbled as he approached the elevator.

"Shit." He wasn't normally the clumsy type. What was wrong with him?

The doors to the elevator opened as soon as he pressed the button. That never happened in a building with as many floors as this one. Perhaps it was a sign of his luck turning. He could go home, rest, and be back at his desk by the afternoon.

The elevator lurched into motion and he resisted the urge to vomit.

No, he wasn't going to be back at his desk by the afternoon. The way he was feeling, he might not even be back tomorrow.

There was no way he could drive like this, either. He'd run off the road and end up dead like that poor bastard Skye had been married to before him. The last thing she needed was two dead husbands with a cancer chaser.

He hit the ground floor button instead of the basement. He'd have to get a cab. Skye had said she was visiting her mother today, otherwise he'd call and ask her to pick him up. She might still be home, though. It was early. No, she was sick. Better not to bother her.

The cab driver didn't look too pleased when he crawled into the back seat, one hand on his stomach, the other hovering near his mouth. He was losing feeling in his feet. This wasn't a normal hangover. He'd polished off a bottle of wine a thousand times before and never felt like this. Maybe he'd picked up that gastro bug that'd been going around? He could go straight to the hospital, he supposed. But plenty of people got gastro all the time and they didn't go to hospital. He was being weak. Maybe he deserved to be called a pussy.

"Where to, mister?" asked the cab driver. He was a young guy, with a heavy accent. Normally Theo would've asked him where he was from. Not today. He couldn't give a fuck where he was from, just as long as he knew how to drive.

The waves of nausea settled, and he gave the driver his home address. His body was getting a grip on whatever this bug was. He was going to be okay.

The cab driver pulled out onto the road and made a sharp u-turn, sending the waves of nausea crashing back with force. The urge to vomit built as the motion of the car increased. It looked like it might be a little while until he was okay.

"Hey mister, you want me to pull over?" asked the driver, glancing in his rear-vision mirror. "You don't look much good."

"I'm fine." He waved his hand in front of him, noticing how numb it still was. "I don't live far."

Thank goodness. He was barely going to make it home at this rate without vomiting. And that was best case scenario. There was always the chance his stomach would explode from the other end.

Skye was going to be so worried. She didn't need this. She was having trouble enough with her own illness without him adding to it.

He felt the bile rise in his throat, spew pouring out of his mouth, spurting through his fingers as he tried to block its path. He could barely feel the wetness on his hands. They felt like rubber mallets dangling from the end of his arms. It was freaking him out. He needed to go to a hospital.

"I told you I could pull over," yelled the cab driver, clearly pissed off.

Theo wiped his hands on his pants, the world's most expensive spew rag designed especially by Tom Ford. No amount of dry-cleaning was going to remove that stench.

There was no way now he was going to ask the driver to change direction and head to the hospital. He'd be lucky if he didn't kick him out on the street.

He reached for his wallet and tried to slide out two fifties. His fingers couldn't seem to grip onto the notes. He tried a few more times, eventually managing to get them out. What the fuck was going on?

He threw the notes into the front seat. "This should cover it."

"Cover it! Man, I'm never going to get this car clean." The driver waved the notes at him.

Theo opened his wallet and wrestled with it until the remaining fifty came free. He threw that into the front seat, too, not having the energy for an argument.

This seemed to placate the driver.

The welcome sight of his house came into view and Theo stumbled from the cab, tripping over his feet and falling on his arse on the pavement. The driver didn't check to see if he needed help, his tyres squealing as he took off down the street.

Theo tried to stand up, but it was difficult. His feet felt like iron blocks. This wasn't normal. He was in serious trouble. Skye was going to need to call him an ambulance.

He crawled to his front gate. Damn his neighbours with their high fences and remote-control gates. Didn't anybody go out on the street anymore? What happened to the days where neighbours waved to each other from their front gardens? Wasn't there anyone who could see him and give him a hand?

He dragged himself to his knees and grabbed the railing of the gate, pulling himself into a stand.

There was no way he was going to be able to coordinate his rubbery fingers to do something that took as much precision as putting a key into the lock. Lucky he was a lawyer, not a brain surgeon.

He pressed the doorbell.

"Theo!" Skye's panicked voice came through the speaker. Even on her tiny video screen she must be able to tell he was unwell.

The gate clicked and he pushed his way through. Stumbling. Falling. The world spinning. His stomach lurching.

Skye came running through the front door and caught him before he hit the ground. He leant on her tiny frame like a crutch as she helped him into the house.

"You need water," she said.

He didn't need water. He needed to lie down. To close his eyes. He was dizzy, the numbness bubbling up around his senses.

Another wave of acid rose up his throat. He vomited again, only this time it was blood. Waves of bright red liquid rushed from his mouth, splattering on the white, marble tiles like a Pro Hart.

He collapsed on the floor at the bottom of the stairs, lying at the feet of Athena the goddess of wisdom, her stony eyes staring at him in lifeless wonderment. When he'd commissioned this statue for Skye, he never imagined it would be the last thing he saw.

He stared up at Athena, calling on her within all the recesses of his mind. But her ears were made from stone and his pleas for help went unheard.

Skye was with him. He could hear her screams and feel her banging on his chest.

He was going to die. He knew it with a force that was threading and weaving its way around his body until he was cocooned.

The world went dark and an image of George filled his mind. He was holding out his hand, beckoning him to go with him towards a bright light.

He never stopped to wonder if it was a good idea. George was his brother. His twin.

They linked hands and, together, they walked to the light.

———

George wasn't feeling great. Actually, no. George felt like crap.

He packed up his tools, mumbled something to his co-workers and climbed into his ute.

He shouldn't have come to the site today. It must've been all that beer he drank with Theo last night. He was sure he only had twelve stubbies, although perhaps he'd lost count. That tended to happen after the sixth or seventh one.

If he felt this shit, then Theo would be practically dead. He could drink him under the table any day.

He should call him and see how he was feeling. Although that pussy only drank one bottle of his yuppy grape juice. He wouldn't have a hangover from that.

He pulled away from the kerb, resisting the urge to vomit.

This was different to how he normally felt after a big night. It wasn't even such a big night. He'd drunk twice as much beer before and only felt half as shit.

Maybe it was gastro, although it didn't feel like that either. He didn't only feel like he was going to chuck, his feet and hands were going numb. It was getting hard to grip the steering wheel.

He should go straight to the hospital. Cabrini wasn't far. He'd passed it after he'd picked up his ute from Theo's house earlier that morning. That would be his best bet. He didn't have time to go anywhere else. They'd probably laugh at him, but still something wasn't right. He might've been bitten by a spider when he was unloading his ute. It could've been a redback. Those things were lethal.

The urge to vomit built. He pulled over and spewed into the gutter.

"Shit," he said, noticing it was pink. Was that blood? He was definitely going to the hospital now. Must've been a fuckin' redback.

He barely made it, pulling into the emergency bay and stumbling out of his ute before falling unconscious in front of the automatic sliding doors.

The world was dark, apart from a bright light shining in the distance. He wanted to go to the light but was afraid. He had Theo by his side when he entered this world. It wouldn't be right for him to leave without his brother.

He'd never really been alone in this world. When he wasn't with Theo, he was with Sophie.

Sophie! He could no more leave Sophie than he could Theo. He had to fight the urge to go to the light. It was calling him, urging him to come closer.

He wanted to walk to it. Hell, he wanted to run to it. But he couldn't. Not yet. It wasn't his time.

He became aware of Theo standing next to him and reached out to see if he was real.

Theo gripped his hand and he felt his energy rise. His brother was giving him strength. He felt it building within him, his chest swelling with love. With his brother by his side, he could do this. The light was nothing to be feared.

Together, they walked towards the light. With each step they took, the strength within him grew.

The light was getting larger and warmer, reeling them in as it pulled them closer.

He hesitated. Soon it would be too late to turn back. Once he stepped inside the light, he'd never be able to return. He saw Sophie and Lukas and Beth calling to him, begging him to return to their sides. They needed him. He needed them.

The link that held him to Theo broke and he felt himself falling, his arms reaching up, trying to grab his brother and pull him down with him. He couldn't get hold of him.

"Theo!" he screamed.

"Goodbye, brother," said Theo, smiling at him so angelically it wouldn't occur to George for weeks that he hadn't called him boofhead.

He would never see his twin again.

———

Skye took almost an hour to call the ambulance. When Theo hit the floor, she knew straight away he was dead. Paramedics were trained to cure all sorts of medical conditions, but curing death wasn't one of them.

Instead, she sat by his side and mourned.

Her mourning was loud, and she howled like a wolf under the full moon. Her husband was dead. Her second husband, just like her first. She was two times a widow at the age of thirty. She already knew how long the grief would last. It would never go away.

Once she called the authorities, it would be chaos. She needed time to sit with Theo and accept what had happened. To say goodbye in a way she hadn't been able to with Dean.

"You said you'd never leave me," she cried. "You promised."

She held her hands to her temples, leaving lines of blood streaking across her face.

"Come back," she said, shaking Theo by the shoulders. "Come back to me."

Her words were useless. Theo wasn't coming back. Not to her. Not to anyone.

She leant forward and rested her head on his chest.

"Kronos, my Kronos."

His eyes were still open, and she tried to close them like she'd seen people do in the movies. It didn't work and she was forced to leave him with that shocked expression on his face. Death had taken him by surprise.

She got up and went to the kitchen for a cloth, dampening it and returning to dab at the blood caking around his mouth. He was a handsome man. He didn't deserve to be left looking like this. Her poor Kronos, her Greek god of time, only now his clock had stopped ticking. His time was up. *Their* time was up. She was on her own once more.

He looked better without the blood on his face.

She kissed him on the cheek, aware as her lips reached his face that he was no longer there. This was his shell only. The body that had once held the man she loved.

"Goodbye, my darling."

She went to the phone and called the emergency number.

"Police, fire or ambulance?" asked the operator.

"I think I need them all," she said, clutching the phone with shaking hands. "My husband is dead."

She gave her address and ended the call, aware the operator was still talking, but she didn't care. There was nothing she could say to bring Theo back.

Theo's mobile phone rang, vibrating in the pocket of his suit jacket.

"Leave him alone," she said, fishing it out.

It was probably George checking up on him. He always seemed to know when there was something wrong with him.

It was Rin's number on the screen. Was Theo psychically connected to his ex-wife, too?

"Hello," she said, deciding to take the call.

"Oh, Skye. Umm, hello. It's Rin." There was an awkward pause. "Can I speak to Theo please?"

"No, you can't," said Skye.

"Is he busy?" Rin asked.

"He's dead," she said, unable to sugar-coat the words. Besides, it didn't matter how she told her, the effect would be the same. Telling her nicely didn't make him any less dead.

"He's what? Skye, what are you saying?" Rin's voice was high-pitched. Was she crying?

"You need to tell Amber." Skye was aware of feeling like she was outside her body while she was talking. Almost as if she was dead, too.

"Tell Amber what? What happened?" Rin was practically screeching now. "How did he die?"

"I'm not sure." She looked at her beautiful dead husband lying on the floor. "He just came home and ... died."

She heard sirens approaching the house. More than one. How many ambulances had the operator sent?

She ended the call without saying goodbye.

The silence of the house was in sharp contrast to Rin, who'd been screaming in her ear.

She pressed the button on her security system to open the front gate, wishing Linda was here to answer the door. She'd gone to the shops for groceries and was taking an awfully long time to return.

She glanced at Theo, not wanting to go near his body again. She couldn't cope with it.

The security system's screen lit up and she saw two ambulance officers rushing through the gate. She'd told them there was no hurry. Still, she supposed they couldn't take her word for that. Two police officers followed them through.

Everyone travelled in pairs. It was almost like they were rubbing it in, that she was the only one alone.

She opened the front door, smiling out of habit, then realising how inappropriate it was. Her husband was dead. There was nothing to smile about.

"He's right here." She pointed behind her.

The ambulance officers raced ahead, their only interest in the person it was too late to save.

The police however, seemed interested only in one person.

Skye.

Rin had called Theo to see if he knew why Amber hadn't turned up at school, not expecting Skye to answer. When she had, she hadn't expected her to say that Theo was dead.

Dead.

Theo was dead.

She'd heard sirens in the background. Clearly whatever had happened it'd been happening while she was calling.

How odd that Skye had answered the phone at a time like that.

This wasn't possible. Theo was tough. He'd shown her just how tough when he'd left her with a newborn baby.

He couldn't be dead. She didn't even know how he'd died.

Skye had ended the call without answering any of her questions.

Rin stood at her kitchen sink wondering what was wrong with that woman. Apart from cancer, of course. Was she in shock?

"Mummy," said Rory, tugging on the leg of her pants. "I'm hungry."

"Not now, Rory." Rin wiped the tears from her cheeks. "Mummy's busy."

Her other two children were at school, thankfully. It was hard enough to think with only one of them here demanding she put on her waitressing hat and serve him food.

"I'm hungry!" Rory wailed.

Rin went to the pantry and retrieved a packet of chips, opening it and handing it over.

Rory smiled. Chips were *sometimes food* saved for special occasions.

"Party!" he hollered, running into the living room with his bounty before his mother could change her mind.

Rin leant on the kitchen counter, resting her head in her hands.

Theo was dead.

Dead, dead, dead.

The word echoed in her mind, yet she was unable to attach it to Theo.

It had to be true. Skye wouldn't make up something like that. People didn't joke about those kinds of things.

Amber was going to be devastated when she eventually answered her bloody phone. Where the hell was she?

And what the hell had happened to Theo?

Amber climbed out of the car and heaved her school bag over her shoulder. "Thanks, Jeff. See you later."

"Bye," he called after her. "Sorry again about making you late."

She shook her head. "Don't stress."

Jeff had to drop off some papers to a client on the way to school and they'd gotten stuck in traffic, making her even later than usual.

So far, since living with her mum, she'd only managed to get to school on time once. Her teachers' patience would've worn very thin by now if she weren't the stepdaughter of the great and wonderful Skye-Manis-who-had-cancer.

She walked into the school grounds. They were quiet, devoid of the usual hordes of gossiping girls in their push-up bras. It reminded her of a ghost town. There were definite plusses to arriving at this time.

Her phone buzzed in her bag and she ignored it, distracted by a poster fluttering on a pole near the office. She grimaced when she saw what it was.

Pray for Skye, it said. There was a picture of Skye overlaid on a background of blue sky with clouds. Very original.

She tore it down and scrunched it into a ball, wishing there was at least one place in the world she could go without Skye dominating her life.

She had the urge to run away and spend the day somewhere without anyone asking about her stepmother.

Without giving it much thought, her feet turned around and she walked out of the school gates, heading towards Armadale Station. Maybe she could go into the city and walk around for a bit or catch a movie.

Just as she turned onto High Street, a car tooted at her. She jumped, thinking it was Jeff. It pulled to the kerb in front of her and she recognised it as Aunt Sophie's CRV.

Great. She couldn't even wag school without her family finding out about it. All she'd wanted was a bit of space. She hadn't been planning to rob a bank. Sophie didn't even live on this side of town.

"Get in," Sophie yelled out her window.

She obeyed, wondering how much trouble she'd be in when her parents heard about this. The way she felt at the moment, she didn't even care.

She'd barely closed the car door when Sophie stepped down on the accelerator.

"Why aren't you at school today?" she asked, driving at a far too ambitious speed.

"I forgot it was a day off today." Amber checked her seatbelt was plugged in properly. "Silly me."

She smacked herself on the forehead for extra effect, but soon realised she needn't have bothered. Sophie was in some kind of trance, changing lanes and beeping at other cars to get out of her way.

"What's going on?" asked Amber. "Aunt Sophie, where are we going?"

They were very close to her father's house. Surely, they weren't going there?

"Cabrini Hospital." Sophie's eyes didn't leave the road. "I saw you. Thought you should come."

That didn't make sense. Something big must be happening.

"Is Skye sick?" So much for a stepmother-free day.

"No. George. Hospital called. Poison." Sophie beeped at the car in front of her to drive faster. "They think he's been poisoned."

"Poisoned!" Amber's gut dropped, almost like she'd been poisoned herself. "But how could that happen?"

"Dunno," said Sophie, not even glancing at her. "He was at your Dad's last night. Maybe he knows."

Amber reached into her bag and started tapping on a phone.

"Don't put it on Facebook!" screamed Sophie, piercing Amber's eardrum.

"I wasn't." Amber resisted the urge to roll her eyes. "I just wanted to make sure I have your mobile number in my phone in case we get separated at the hospital. What is it again?"

Sophie recited her number before blasting her horn at the car in front of her again.

The hospital came into sight. Sophie pulled into the emergency bay and threw the keys at Amber. "Park this and meet me inside."

"But I don't know how to drive!" Amber protested.

"Figure it out." Sophie disappeared, running towards the sliding doors of the entrance without a backwards glance.

Amber crawled over to the driver's seat and gripped the wheel. What if the cops caught her driving without a licence? She didn't want any trouble. She was only a kid.

She put the keys in the ignition and slowly drove out of the emergency bay. Thank goodness the car was an automatic. It was kind of just like a big go-kart. She could do this.

She followed the signs to the visitors' car park, her heart pounding when the car behind her gave her a frustrated honk. She was driving too slowly. She made a silent vow when she was old enough to get her licence, she'd be patient with other drivers. Who knew what stress they were under to make them drive like that? They could be an underage driver, trying to park a car in an emergency for heaven's sake.

She managed to negotiate her way through the boom gates and followed the ramp down into the car park. Parking the car was a little trickier. Once she found an available spot, she realised she had no idea how to actually fit the car inside that tiny rectangle.

After half a dozen attempts, including scraping the car on the adjacent pole, she got it in. Surely Aunt Sophie wouldn't care about minor damage like that? Uncle George said she was always damaging her car. After the way she'd been driving today, it was no wonder. What was one more scrape?

Uncle George. She felt sick once more. Was he going to be all right? He had to be all right. He was one of the best people Amber knew.

Her phone rang and she reached into her bag, expecting it to be Sophie.

It wasn't. It was her mum. The school must've called her.

"I can explain everything," said Amber.

"Darling. Thank god you're okay." Her mother sighed. "Your school called and said you didn't show up. I've been trying to call you all morning. Why haven't you been answering your phone?"

"I didn't hear it," she said. "I'm at the hospital."

"Hospital? But your father never made it to the hospital," her mother said. "How did you hear?"

"Aunt Sophie saw me as she was driving here," she explained. "She picked me up. Is Dad on his way?"

"Hold on," said her mother. "What are you doing at the hospital? I think we're talking about two different things."

"Uncle George's been poisoned. What are you talking about?" Amber fought back tears. "Is Dad okay?"

"Oh, my darling girl," her mum sobbed. "No, your dad's not okay. He ... your dad's dead."

Amber dropped the phone like it had given her an electric shock and screamed.

———

Sophie ran towards the information desk, her chest aching with stress and exertion. She had to get to George. He'd fight if he knew she was there. He couldn't leave her.

George had been working at a site on this side of town. She'd dropped him off at Theo's place earlier this morning and had only just made it home again when the hospital called. Why couldn't he have been closer to home? She'd have been at the hospital ages ago in that case.

None of this made any sense. People like George didn't get poisoned. He had the constitution of an ox. No, stronger than that. His stomach was like that of a bloody T-rex. Nothing made him sick.

It couldn't have been anything he ate, and it wasn't like a few beers would put him in hospital. If that were the case, they'd need to set aside a permanent bed for him.

The nurse who called had explained they thought it was more serious than a hangover or a stomach bug. Apparently, they'd called the police. The police! This must have something to do with Theo. People were always trying to get back at him in his line of work. Maybe it was a case of mistaken identity? He did hang around with that thug, Bruno Martini. Nothing good could come from that. She'd told George to talk to Theo about him a million times.

She reached the desk and explained who she was.

The woman on duty smiled at her and tapped something into her computer. Her smile was momentarily replaced by a frown, a slip she immediately tried to cover up with another smile, this one more forced than the last.

"He's in ICU," she said. "First floor of the theatre block."

"What does that mean?" Sophie clutched the cool timber of the desk in front of her.

"I'll take you." The woman glanced at her co-worker who nodded in response.

"Thank you," said Sophie, hoping she'd move faster than the cars on the road that morning. The woman's grey hair didn't inspire much confidence.

"My name's Bree," she said, marching down the hallway at an impressive pace. Looks could be deceiving.

"Is it far?" asked Sophie, not having time for introductions. George could be dying right now. ICU was serious, wasn't it? *Intensive. Care. Unit.* Those three words screamed at her, repeating themselves inside her head.

She could hear her phone ringing in her bag. What had possessed her to set the song *Happy* by Pharrell Williams as her ringtone? It couldn't be more inappropriate. It wasn't possible to answer the call. She couldn't tell anyone what was going on right now. She didn't even know herself.

She followed Bree's marching legs like her life depended on it. In many ways it did. Her life depended on George and the way to get to him was to follow those legs.

Her phone rang again, distracting her. What if it rang in the ICU? Especially with that ringtone. She needed to turn it off.

She reached into her bag and pulled out the phone. There were several missed calls and text messages on the screen, but only one that caught her attention. It was from a blocked caller.

Prussian Blue is the antidote for Thallium poisoning.

"Bree," she called out. "Prussian Blue. We need to get George some Prussian Blue."

Bree stopped to read the text message and nodded at Sophie.

"I'll deal with this," she said.

Sophie let out a breath. George would be all right.

He had to be.

THE BREAK

Detective Hooke sat in the interview room across from Skye Manis. His lower back was killing him, causing him to shift in his seat at regular intervals.

Skye was an attractive woman. Nice figure, big blue eyes and long blonde hair that shone, despite the dull light overhead. He figured that must be the famous wig he'd read about online.

He'd expected her to be beautiful. After all, she'd been married to Theo, who Detective Hooke had the pleasure (or perhaps displeasure) of meeting several times over the years when Theo was defending people he'd been trying to put behind bars. Theo had been annoyingly good at his job. Thanks to him there were far too many criminals roaming freely on the streets, instead of pacing up and down in exercise yards. The name Bruno Martini was the first to come to mind.

"Do you have a lawyer?" he asked.

She shook her head. "No. Do I need one?"

"That depends on what you have to tell me."

She smiled at him in a strange way without parting her perfectly made-up lips and he wondered how Theo had managed to kiss her with all that paint on her face. Poor Theo. It was both easy and hard to believe he'd been murdered. It was always strange when someone you knew died, although in Theo's case there were many people out there who'd be happy to see him dead. Perhaps that's why he could relate to him.

The list of suspects for Theo's murder was long. As usual they were starting with the spouse. Sadly, far too often that was also where they ended. It was depressing to think the person who was supposed to love you the most could end up being the one to kill you. It was just as well he was no longer married. Unless he counted his job—it was the last thing he thought of when he fell asleep at night and the first thing to plague his thoughts when he woke in the morning, it had a habit of calling to nag him whenever he sat down to watch the footy and somehow it ended up being where he spent all his special occasions, including Christmas and birthdays. Yep, he was one big cliché. A detective married to his job. It didn't exactly keep him warm at night, but in a strange way it satisfied him.

He looked at the frail woman sitting across from him. He knew nothing about fashion, but it was obvious her clothes were the expensive kind. For someone so unwell, she was extraordinarily well put together. Even in his prime, he couldn't have attracted a woman like her.

"Well, if you're sure you don't want a lawyer, we'll get started in just a minute," he said.

She nodded, wringing her hands together in her lap. Was that a nervous tick? Was she guilty? He decided to stall a bit longer and let the tension build. This was one of his favourite tactics. People hated silence. It primed the suspect, so by the time they finally broke the silence, they'd be ready to spill their guts—anything just to fill the air with words.

Skye didn't look like she had murder in her. She had cancer, for goodness sake. He could usually pick a killer from a mile away and his gut told him it wasn't her. Still, he couldn't let her go just because of his ever-expanding gut.

He'd taken on the case given how high profile it was going to be. It hadn't taken the media long to arrive at the scene and start reporting on a crime they knew nothing about. Not only was Theo a well-known identity in Melbourne, but his wife was the poster girl of every woman in the country. That looked set to change. Murder charges didn't normally do much for popularity.

"Well then?" said Skye, stretching her hands out in front of her and tapping her manicured fingertips on the table.

"Just a moment." He shuffled his papers, taking his time.

She shifted in her seat and he hid a satisfied smile. It was working. The tension was building nicely. Just a little longer and he'd start.

He glanced down at the medical report in his file. Theo had been poisoned with thallium, traces of which had been found on a plate of brownie crumbs on the kitchen counter. Brownies that had been baked by Skye and fed not only to her husband, but to his twin brother. He was fairly certain they'd also been fed to her mother. She'd had blood tests taken recently when her nursing home staff noticed her hair had been falling out. He'd put a rush on the results yesterday when he visited Skye's mother for a chat.

The poor old woman didn't seem to know what was going on. Although, she was certainly exhibiting enough symptoms of thallium poisoning. Not only was her hair falling out, but her extremities were numb and her carers had reported several recent incidences of vomiting. He was toying with the theory that Skye had been trying to poison her mother with the brownies and Theo and George had eaten them by mistake. Except George had been very clear about the fact Skye had offered them the brownies, insisting they eat them.

Maybe she'd been poisoning her mother, then decided things were going so well she'd branch out and bump off her husband and his brother while she was at it. That didn't feel right either. Theo was a bull of a man next to Skye's mother. It was strange the poison had been enough to kill him and not her. Just another mystery to add to the case.

George had gotten to hospital in time to be saved thanks to a text message from a mobile phone paid for in cash, then switched off. The message had gone to his wife instructing her to tell the doctors to give him Prussian Blue, the antidote for thallium. Finding that phone was a major part of the investigation, but so far, they'd turned up nothing. It was probably sitting on the bottom of the Yarra River.

He flipped through the pages in his file, looking for his notes on thallium. It was an unusual poison these days, due to its difficulty to obtain. Back in the 1950s it was readily available as rat poison and had been the housewife's murder weapon of choice, earning the nickname *inheritance powder.* It was odourless, colourless and tasteless. The perfect poison indeed. He could only hope it wasn't making a comeback. Where on earth had Skye obtained such a thing?

This should be an open and shut case, yet all his years of experience nagged at him. He was missing something. If Skye was the killer, why would she leave the plate of brownie crumbs on the counter? It was too obvious. Someone must be setting her up. But who? There might be a long line of people wanting to bump off Theo, but who would want to kill Skye's mother? What possible motive could anyone have for killing a harmless woman in a nursing home? The fees to keep her in the home were chicken feed to someone like Skye and it wasn't like she'd be hankering after any measly inheritance. He hadn't looked into it yet, but he doubted Clara Butterford had more than a few dollars to her name.

"You think I killed him, don't you?" said Skye, unwilling to let the silence continue.

"Did you?" He set down his papers and glanced at the recording device to make sure it was working. He could almost taste the beer he'd have later at the pub with the boys to celebrate breaking this case.

"Everyone thinks I did it." She wrung her hands in her lap once more, then put them to her head, threading her fingers through her long hair. Despite knowing it was a wig, he was surprised at what he saw underneath when she pulled it from her head. She wasn't completely bald as he expected. She had a full head of shortly cropped hair. More hair than he had in fact.

It was amazing how the wig had transformed her appearance.

"Feel better?" he asked, wondering why she'd chosen to remove her wig now.

She made a small noise as if swallowing some words that had begun to escape from her lips.

"What is it, Mrs Manis?" he prompted.

"Oh ... I just ..." She patted the wig sitting in her lap.

"You just what?" he asked. "You know there's no point lying to me, don't you? The truth's all going to come out. It always does."

She inhaled, threw her shoulders back, but still said nothing.

"Come on, Mrs Manis." He sat forward in his chair. "It's time to tell the truth."

"Fine. Look, it's no big deal. Really, it's not." She looked up from the wig to stare him in the eye. "There's just something I thought you should know. Just in case it makes me look bad ..."

There she was trailing off again.

"Yes, Mrs Manis. What is it?" he asked.

"See how my hair's growing back?" She ran a hand over her head.

"I do." He frowned, trying to connect the dots.

"Do you know why it's growing back?" she asked.

He shrugged, waiting for her to explain.

"It's growing back because it never fell out in the first place." She coughed, nervously. "I shaved it off."

"Okay, but what does this have to do with Theo's death?" He was struggling to make the connection here.

"I don't have cancer," she said, her trailing to a whisper. "I made it all up."

He sat up straight in his chair. "You made it up?"

She nodded, locking eyes with him as if trying to drag his thoughts from his mind.

How could she make up such a horrendous lie? He'd heard a lot of fibs in his time, but this one took the cake. She lied about... cancer?

She leant in closer. "I'm worried when people find out, they'll think I'm also lying about killing Theo. But I didn't kill him. I didn't. I loved Theo."

"Let me just get this straight," said the detective. "You told the world that you have cancer when you're actually perfectly healthy?"

She nodded.

"And you're also saying that you're telling the truth about not poisoning your husband, despite the fact you baked those brownies?"

She nodded again.

Oh, boy! Well, this changed everything. It also went to prove his theory. You never could know what lurked beneath life's murky depths.

The surface of this case hadn't just broken, it had shattered into a million fragments.

"Why don't we take a step back and go through this again?" He sat forward and pushed all thoughts of a beer from his mind. Getting to the bottom of this stinking pond was going to take all night.

AFTER THE BREAK

Skye twisted her hands in her lap, determined not to be the first to speak.

Dr Addison also seemed in no hurry to start the session, just like that frustrating detective. Did all these people really have so much time on their hands? He sat forward in his chair, his face as blank as the desk in the corner of the room.

Skye wondered if that particular facial expression was taught in psychology school. Or counselling school. Or whatever school it was this strange man had attended.

He coughed and stretched his lips across his face into a thin smile. She realised they had something in common already. He didn't like his teeth either.

He was older than her—maybe Theo's age, but certainly not cut from the same cloth. Where Theo was sexy, Dr Addison was geriatric. Where Theo was brash and confident, this man was dull and staid.

Her lawyer thought it would look good for her if she saw a shrink. If things didn't go well with the police, she was going to need a psychological assessment, so better to get talking to someone now.

She'd balked at the idea initially, just as she'd resisted the idea of getting a lawyer. Although, after being married to Theo, she knew she'd be foolish not to have someone on her side who knew the law.

She ended up opting for Carlos Tagliatori, not because his name sounded like a pasta dish, but because Theo hadn't liked him. She was aware that a large proportion of people Theo disliked were those he was intimidated by. An intimidating lawyer seemed like a good choice.

She'd known within five minutes of her first appointment she was right. Carlos was ten years younger than Theo and outrageously good-looking. It was no wonder Theo had been intimidated. He was the Brad Pitt to Theo's George Clooney—a smooth talker with a head of blond hair so full it was incredible that all those individual strands were able to find a free bit of scalp to grow out of.

He said he referred all his clients to Dr Addison as he was the best of the best.

"So, what brings you here?" Dr Addison asked, making Skye jump.

"Carlos Tagliatori." She smirked, not ready to give into the process just yet.

"And what did he want you to talk with me about?" He crossed his legs and rested his face on the palm of his hand, giving the impression he had all day to wait for her to give him a serious answer. Would he sit there for the full session in silence if she decided not to speak? There wasn't much point in that, she supposed.

So, why was she here? A simple question with an exceptionally complicated answer.

"I told a lie," she said, deciding to dive straight into the heart of the issue.

Dr Addison nodded and rubbed one of his bony fingers on his chin. It made a scratching sound on the grey bristles bursting at the surface of his skin.

"Go on," he encouraged, raising his eyebrows.

She remained silent.

"Perhaps you could tell me what the lie was," he suggested.

She nodded, despite the feeling he already knew exactly what her lie had been. She was all over the newspapers, being called every awful name in the dictionary—and many that were far too crude to warrant a place in such a book.

"I lied about having ovarian cancer." She crossed her arms and analysed his reaction.

His face remained non-judgemental, although she'd bet his mind was anything else. *Everybody* had judged her, friends and strangers alike. What made this man so special he was immune to passing judgement?

"Would you like to tell me about that?" he asked.

"I don't know where to start," she replied, trying to buy some time.

"It can be hard to untangle the beginning of a story, but I'd like for you to give it a go if you can. Take all the time you need." He smiled again, trying to encourage her to talk.

Her eyelids fluttered closed as she tried to decide when it began. It all depended on how you looked at it. Did it begin when her father rejected the idea of her? Or when her mother rejected the reality of her? Perhaps it began when Dean died? Or when her first article was published online? It was too hard to tell. Every single moment of her life had led up to her lie.

"Perhaps you might like to tell me about the first time you told the lie, and we can work backwards or forwards from there?" Dr Addison prompted.

"I told Theo first. He's my husband. *Was.* He was my husband." She winced, hating referring to him in the past tense. "Before he died."

Dr Addison wrote something on a small notepad.

She tried to make out his words, but his writing was either deliberately illegible or written in some kind of shorthand.

"And what did you say to him?" he asked.

"It wasn't easy to lie to him."

It seemed important to convey her lie had been as difficult for her to tell as it had been for Theo to hear. She wasn't the monster the press were making her out to be. She'd needed to tell the lie. She didn't do it for fun.

"It's not usually easy to tell a lie," said Dr Addison, using his smile again. "In fact, often it's quite difficult."

Skye drew in a deep breath of lavender-scented air and got comfortable in the high-backed armchair, resting her feet on a small stool. If he really wanted to hear the story, they were going to be there for a while.

She'd worn her Victoria Beckham tuxedo trousers for the occasion, anticipating she'd be lying down. They looked perfect with her Chloe ruffle crepe top and Salvatore Ferragamo loafers. Casual sophistication had seemed the appropriate dress code.

"I practised all day in front of the mirror trying to find the words," she said. "I knew I had to tell him in just the right way. Theo was a lawyer, you see. A criminal lawyer. He listened to lies for a living."

And told a few of them himself, she thought. Not to her, of course. Their marriage had been solid, but he'd admitted to her that deception was an important part of his job. He never told direct lies—he'd be thrown off the bar for that—but he frequently stretched and moulded the truth as if it were a piece of clay in his hands.

"He was very sharp," she said. "Nobody could get anything past him. He prided himself on being able to spot a player from a hundred paces."

Except for her.

Although, she had a clear advantage over the strangers who'd tried to deceive him in a courtroom. Her lies could be delivered with the touch of a hand or the gentle warmth of her breath on his neck and he'd become so distracted he wouldn't know what she was saying. Despite men's balls being located outside their bodies, they sure didn't know how to think without them.

"My plan was to plant enough clues to make him suspicious," she explained. "So he'd believe me when I told him."

"What clues?" Dr Addison's pen was poised over his notepad. She wondered if what she was about to say would be interesting enough for him to make a note of it.

"One night I faked falling asleep with an ovarian cancer website open on my laptop. I'm not even sure if he saw the notes I wrote in my notepad. Treatment plans and names of specialists, all scribbled in different colours. Then there were all those doctors' invoices on our joint credit card. I was beginning to wonder if he ever looked at our statements. I ended up having to set up a phoney email address from the bank, asking him to check our accounts. I think that was what must have hooked him in the end." She took a deep breath, surprised at how easily these words had fallen from her lips. It felt good to say all of this aloud.

"And was it just you and Theo in the house?" Dr Addison paused his pen. "Or did anybody else live with you?"

"Only Amber," she said. "She's Theo's daughter." Skye always referred to Amber that way. *Theo's daughter.* Never as her stepdaughter. The thought of calling her that made her shudder.

"And what's your relationship with Amber like?" he asked.

"I tried so hard with her," said Skye, thinking about the concert tickets she'd bought that had the added bonus of getting Amber out of the house for the night. And there was that fabulous white Valentino leather jacket and matching boots, that would at least blend into the house a little when she left them lying around. She'd even had a whole wing of the house decorated for her, so she'd never need to bother them again. "But when it wasn't reciprocated, after a while I just gave up. You can't force someone to like you."

"Why do you think she doesn't like you?" Dr Addison gave her one of his thin-lipped smiles.

"Jealousy. She was so competitive when it came to her father." Skye knew it wasn't a fair competition. Amber may have been Theo's blood, but it was her flesh he craved when he woke each morning rock hard and wanting the taste of her before he headed into court for another stressful day.

"Did you ever want children of your own?" he asked.

She shook her head. Who in their right mind would opt of their own free will to have a person live inside you for nine whole months, giving you stretch marks and varicose veins? And that was only the pregnancy part of it. The way babies exited their free ride into exis- tence was positively barbaric. There was no way she was going to let herself be torn in two by the head of a small person destined to make her life hell. Apart from the absolute fortune they cost to raise, chil- dren were sticky, messy, grubby humans whose noses and bums needed to be wiped far more times than she was prepared to—which for the record was zero.

But she wasn't foolish enough to tell Dr Addison the extent of her feelings.

He added a few more scribbles to his notepad. "Do you think the lack of desire to have your own child has anything to do with your experiences with Amber?"

"Why all these questions about Amber?" She frowned. She'd finally gotten that spoilt brat out of her life and now all Dr Addison seemed to want to talk about was her.

"I'm just trying to understand your family unit," he said, waving his pen.

"She's not my family." Skye's words contained more venom than intended and she smiled to disguise it. "My family unit is me and Theo. *Was* me and Theo. That was the way I liked it. He was a lot older than me and as he already had a child, I thought he wouldn't be too worried about having more. That was exactly why he'd seemed my perfect match. He was such a catch. And to think I hadn't even known I was fishing."

She laughed, not surprised to find Dr Addison with a forced smile on his face. He was a tough crowd. Perhaps he'd seen through her. She'd absolutely known she was fishing. She'd had her line cast in the water for a long time when she met Theo. He wasn't the first to proposition her. Far from it. He was just the first who ticked all her boxes. As a result, she'd let him tick her box, so to speak.

"He was besotted with me when we met," she continued. "He was a sworn bachelor when he first saw me on television. Apparently, he stood up and announced he'd just seen the woman he wanted to spend the rest of his life with. I wrote articles about our romance. It was like a fairy tale. The public loved it."

She remembered how carefully she'd crafted those articles, taking great care to show Dean proper respect by giving the stories the angle of finding love when your heart is broken. She explained to the readers that Dean would've wanted her to get on with her life and find happiness once more. If she looked like she'd moved on too quickly she'd lose the public's respect, which would no doubt lead to the loss of followers.

She obviously found the right tone as the public embraced her new relationship and she'd been showered with messages wishing her well and telling her how strong she was.

"Approval can be a heady feeling, can't it?" said Dr Addison, nodding. He wasn't even looking at his notepad while he made his next scribble.

"I loved it," she said. "It was like a drug. Afterwards, I tried writing articles on more general topics, but they never created much interest. It was my personal life the public liked reading about and once there wasn't much else going on, they lost interest in me. They moved on to people who wrote about their children, divorces or health scares. It wasn't fair. I couldn't write about any of those topics."

"You must've enjoyed writing about having cancer then?" he asked, keeping his voice level.

"Believe me, it wasn't easy," she explained. "They were the most difficult stories I've ever written. I had to be so careful with what I said. You know, the right balance of information and emotion. I cried when I wrote them."

"Why do you think that was?" He tilted his head, seeming genuinely interested in her response.

"It was sort of like watching a sad movie," she said. "I got swept up in the emotion, believing the story was real, despite knowing it wasn't."

He nodded. "Interesting."

"So, to answer the first question you asked me," she said as the situation crystallised in her mind. "That was exactly how my lie began. If life hands you lemonade, you can always find a way to extract the lemons."

Dr Addison's face screwed up like she'd just handed him one of her lemons to suck on. He caught himself and quickly fashioned his expression back into a smile.

He needn't have bothered. She was smiling enough for the both of them. She wasn't a bad person. She'd just been entirely misunderstood.

"Why don't you tell me a little more about the rest of your family?" suggested Dr Addison, seeming to be trying to move the conversation to a less acidic topic.

"There's no rest of my family," she said, disappointed. This wasn't a topic she was keen to discuss. She'd thought he'd want to hear more about Theo. He'd just died! Didn't he want to talk about her grief?

"Nobody at all?" he asked.

"Just my mother, but she doesn't count."

She'd bet he already knew about her mother. Anybody who knew anything about her case knew Clara had been poisoned alongside Theo and George. Her mother had become famous all over again.

"Tell me about her." Dr Addison leant forward to show he was listening.

"She was a ballerina."

Skye had used this simple sentence thousands of times over the years to describe her mother. It was like ballet hadn't been just something she did, it was who she was. She wasn't a woman who did ballet. She was a ballerina who also happened to be a woman.

"What kind of a mother was she?" asked Dr Addison.

Frustration brewed in Skye's stomach. She took a deep breath trying to stem the flow of words that bubbled up as she reminded herself where she was. There was no need to stop her words or sugarcoat them. She could tell the truth in a way she'd never been able to before.

"Imagine growing up knowing your mother wished you never existed," Skye bit out. "I was resented with the same amount of passion she once put into her dancing. It was the one constant I had growing up—the knowledge I ruined her life."

"Hmm. That kind of environment would have a significant impact on a person," he said, seeming to ignore her pent-up anger spilling into the room.

"It did. It was chaotic. Mum was in some kind of trance most of the time and the house was a pigsty. Everywhere I looked there was mess. It was out of control. Except for my bedroom, of course. Mum wasn't allowed in there."

"Your room was tidy?" he asked.

She nodded. "It was my only sanctuary from her filth. It was my coping mechanism, I suppose." Now she was sounding like a shrink. Maybe she should let him do the shrinking while she did the talking.

"That does sound like an effective coping mechanism. Do you think you've carried it on over into adulthood?" He tapped at his chin.

She smiled. "You should see my house. Everything in its place, clean and white. I love it. I feel so at peace there."

That must've been worthy of a note as he scribbled madly. "What does the colour white mean to you?"

"It's my favourite colour. It doesn't hide anything. It can't. I mean, if something's white then you can really tell if it's dirty. The only way for it to look clean is if it actually is." Skye craned her neck, trying to catch a glimpse of Dr Addison's notes. "Do you think I like the colour white because of my childhood?"

"It's very likely." He moved his hand to cover his writing. "It sounds like it gives you a sense of control over your life. What do you think?"

"Maybe." She raised her eyebrows, never having thought about it like that before.

"Is it working for you?" he asked.

"Maybe."

He looked at her, waiting for her to go on.

"No, it's not." She thew out her hands. "Look, I do my best. I thought I was doing okay, but lately ... I just have no control with everything that's going on. This isn't how I wanted things to turn out."

"I can't imagine it is. Tell me, Skye, are you taking any medications?" he asked.

She shook her head. "I hate medicine. I mean, before all this happened, I was taking diet pills, so I'd look sick. And some Ipecac syrup to make me vomit, but other than that, I never take anything stronger than a headache tablet. I don't even drink alcohol. Never touch the stuff."

"Why do you think that is?" He tapped his chin again, like he could release the answers.

She paused. "Same reason as the white. I like to feel in control."

"It's starting to make some sense now, isn't it?" He smiled.

"A little, I guess."

It was. The more she talked to Dr Addison, the more she was understanding about herself. She'd never given some of these quirks to her personality much thought before.

"So where did your father fit into your chaotic childhood?" he asked.

"I don't have a father." She adjusted her hat as it scratched at her scalp. "Well, I mean, of course I have a father, it's just that I don't know him."

"You know nothing of him?" Dr Addison seemed surprised.

"He went back to France before I was born." She worked at holding back her tears. "You know, I could never understand why he didn't want to meet me. I'm his daughter. His own flesh and blood."

"Sadly, it does happen." Dr Addison blinked, kindly. "So, you've never heard from him at all?"

"I did get a letter from him recently. The first time I've ever heard from him in my life." She crossed her arms, still feeling the pain of him rejecting her as a child.

"That sounds significant. Your first contact with your father." He nodded as he waited for her to elaborate.

"He lives on a farm in France, has five sons and was married to a selfish woman who hid most of the letters I sent him. She's dead now, which is why he decided to write back. He said he was sorry to hear about my cancer. That was basically it."

Dr Addison made a humming sound. "He knew about your cancer?"

"Doesn't everyone?" She didn't want to admit she'd been the one to tell him. Let Dr Addison think he found out some other way. "It doesn't matter now. I don't need him. I never did."

Dr Addison wrote something down, leading Skye to suspect he wasn't done asking about her father. Not that there'd be much point in that.

Fathers were even more overrated than mothers. Children could live without them. She'd turned out just fine with no father and only half a mother. She knew people gossiped about her when she married Theo, saying she was looking for a father figure. She'd read their comments online and they were upsetting, mainly because they were wrong.

"Do you still see your mother?" he asked.

She sighed. He knew the answer to this. She was being accused of attempting to murder her by bringing her poison brownies each week. Of course, she still saw her.

"As you're probably aware, she has dementia." Skye gave Dr Addison a tight-lipped smile. "I visit her nursing home every week. Well, I did, before all this happened."

"And what was your relationship with her like in recent years?" he asked.

"Good. Better than good. It was fantastic!" Skye sighed. "She finally saw me for who I was. She even seemed to love me. She told me I was gorgeous once. If I can be honest ..."

"Please Skye, you must be honest." His eyes opened wide in anticipation of what she was about to say.

"I never loved her more than when she had dementia." Skye sat forward in her chair. "That's why I didn't try to kill her. Why would I do that?"

He looked at her with a forced blank expression. He thought she was guilty. It was as obvious as if he'd come out and said it.

"Do you think your mother has anything to do with you not wanting children?" he asked.

"Are you kidding me?" Skye threw out her hands. "Why do you keep asking me about this? I thought we covered it earlier. You think I don't want to have children because I'm like my mother?"

She fought the urge to stand and run from the room.

"I didn't say that—"

"I'm nothing like my mother. She didn't want a child because she didn't want to ruin her precious career. Or her figure. I don't want one because ... well, because it's far better not to have a child at all than to have one and treat them the way my mother treated me. Children don't ask to be born, so if their parents are stupid enough to have them then they should at least love them." She sat back, surprised she'd been as honest as this. But maybe it needed to be said.

He scratched at his chin again. "You're worried you'd raise a child in the way you were raised?"

"No! Because I'm not having one." Her feet planted on the floor as she prepared to stand. "That's my whole point. And anyway, what I don't get is why it's so wrong not to want to procreate? Who made the rule saying it's compulsory for every woman to want to have a baby? I should receive a bloody medal for my attitude, not your disapproval. And just for the record, my mother didn't raise me. I raised myself."

"Skye, please. I'm not judging your actions. I'm just trying to understand them. There's a difference." He held up his palm, trying to calm her.

"I think I've had enough today. Are we done?" No longer able to resist the urge, she stood. She didn't have to explain herself to anyone. She was paying Dr Addison. It was her decision what she spoke about, not his.

Dr Addison looked at the clock on his wall. "Yes, I think that's enough for today. Although, I'd like to discuss your grief over losing your husband a little more next time. We've barely touched on that. We've covered a lot of ground today."

They had. Her head was bursting with things she wanted to go home and think about, starting with Theo and how much she missed him. Why would she kill the only person in this world she actually loved?

———

Skye smiled to find her house quiet. It was always quiet these days. Thank goodness Amber had moved out before Theo died. She couldn't imagine having to live in the same house as her without Theo as a buffer.

She went straight to the library. Really, it was more of a study, but she preferred to call it a library. Rich people in the movies always had libraries.

She had a stand-up desk in front of the bay window where she did most of her work. She liked looking out at the front garden. Except in autumn when the mess the trees made would irritate her so much she'd need to close the blinds until the gardener was able to clean it all up.

Before she'd moved in, the bookshelves were filled with fake books, the sort that have spines, but nothing inside. She'd gotten rid of them immediately, filling the shelves with a variety of books she selected based on their colour of their covers—white, of course. There was everything from Charles Dickens to Maeve Binchy to Tim Winton.

The books were arranged in groups according to the colour of the writing on the spine, yellows and pale blues near the top and the bolder colours at the bottom. She was glad Dr Addison couldn't see them. He'd get so excited, he'd probably wet his pants.

The police had taken away her laptop. That was even more irritating than the trees losing their leaves. It was a complete invasion of privacy. If she didn't get it back soon, she was going to have to ask Mariana to courier her a replacement. As soon as the police finished their investigation and realised she was innocent she'd need to write something to set the record straight. She hadn't done anything wrong. Well, except for the cancer thing. But people would get over that. Hopefully.

Theo's computer was also missing from his den. He didn't like to call it a study, either. They both seemed to be allergic to that word. She hadn't been in there since the police turned it upside-down.

She'd closed the door after they left, and it'd stayed that way. It was too depressing to go in there and know she'd never see Theo sitting behind his large, dark oak desk again.

She opened the top drawer of her filing cabinet and found her cheque book. She hardly ever wrote cheques anymore. It was a shame. She liked the feeling it gave her when she scribbled her signature across the bottom and tore it from the book.

Sophie had been leaving her messages about Theo's funeral arrangements. Typical of George to get his wife to do his dirty work. Although, he had just gotten out of hospital, she supposed.

Theo had once said he wanted a service in the Greek church he went to as a kid. She wished she'd paid more attention. She couldn't even remember where it was. George would know. It'd be better if he organised it. At least he'd get the details right.

How much did funerals cost anyway? They were expensive no doubt. They had to be. Would ten grand be enough? Twenty maybe? It was hard to know.

She wrote a cheque for fifty thousand dollars in George's name and put it in an envelope. Better to err on the side of being over generous. It wouldn't be right for Theo to have a budget funeral.

This thought sent tears rolling down Skye's cheeks. Theo hated hospitals. She hated funerals. She'd thought the day Dean died would be the worst day of her life, but she was wrong. His funeral was far worse because that was when it hit her that he was gone forever. And forever is a bloody long time. She'd fainted twice during his service and had to be carried from the church by Dean's brother.

She had no desire to repeat that experience. Who would carry her from the church this time? If she fainted at Theo's funeral, George would probably take the opportunity to kick her in the ribs. No doubt his whole family thought she was responsible for Theo's death. Greeks weren't exactly known for their subtlety.

Then there was the whole cancer issue. She'd have the yia-yias in their black veils trying to hit her over the head with their handbags every chance they got.

No, she couldn't stand to be there. She wasn't going to go. She'd do her grieving in private. No doubt everyone would take this as a further sign of her guilt, but she'd long ago given up caring what Theo's family thought of her.

She guessed George would have Theo buried at Fawkner cemetery next to their parents. She couldn't think of a more depressing place to spend the rest of eternity. It wasn't one of those pretty cemeteries with trees and rolling hills. This was a large piece of flat ground out in the suburbs with miles of marble headstones reaching out from the ground like something you'd see in a horror movie.

She wouldn't visit his grave, either. If she lay in their bed, she could still smell his scent. That was the place to talk to him and shed her tears, not in some field of marble.

Theo would understand. He always had.

What she couldn't understand was why the police had started asking her questions about Dean's death. That all happened years ago. Why would they ask now? It was almost as if they were insinuating she'd reached across the car and pulled on the steering wheel to crash him into the pole. They'd decided she killed Theo and were trying to turn her into some kind of serial killer. It was offensive. Not to mention damaging for her reputation. And... okay, it was scary as well.

They even asked her once if she thought it was possible Dean was still alive. Apparently, they'd spoken to her mother who insisted he still visited her at the nursing home. They either didn't understand very much about dementia or they were getting desperate for answers.

She just hoped that whatever answers they came up with, they did it quickly. As long as they were the right answers, of course.

She'd already come clean about everything she'd done. All her secrets were out in the open now, flapping in the breeze like sheets on the line. The problem was that everyone had it in for her. They wanted to believe she killed Theo. It didn't matter she'd already fallen from grace. The public wanted her to fall further.

"Oh, Theo," she said, collapsing to her knees and burying her face in her hands. Sobs shook her body and she gasped for air. How could she go on like this?

She'd wanted some drama in her life, but she never wanted this.

———

Skye settled into Dr Addison's chair and picked absentmindedly at a loose thread on the label of her hat while she waited for him to indicate he was ready to begin.

Despite the way her first session had ended, she'd enjoyed it a lot more than she thought she would. It felt good to talk to someone. It didn't matter that Dr Addison didn't seem to like what she was telling him. He couldn't call her a bitch or a murderer like the rest of the world seemed to enjoy doing. He had to just sit there, take her money and listen. It was a pretty cushy job. Maybe she should've become a psychologist?

No.

She'd always liked talking more than she liked listening.

"I'm pleased to see you again," said Dr Addison, indicating the session had started. "Would you like to talk about why you seemed so upset when we finished up last time?"

"If I wanted to talk about it, then I would've talked about it last time." She crossed her arms.

"Right." He shifted uncomfortably in his chair. "Then perhaps we should leave the topic of your mother and get back to Theo today. You told me how you lied to him about your cancer. I'd like to continue on from there. Did he ask to go to any medical appointments with you?"

"He did, but I told him it wasn't necessary. He was in the middle of a big trial. He couldn't get away from court, so I told him not to worry. Although, he was really insistent when I had my surgery." Skye's eyes welled with tears at the memory of how concerned Theo had been.

"Just to be clear, did this surgery actually happen?" He wrote something down on his notepad.

"Of course, it did. I'm not that much of a liar," Skye huffed. "It just wasn't the surgery he thought I was having. I had a cyst on my right ovary, you see. While they had me on the table, they took a close look at my left ovary, too. I didn't want Theo to come with me to the hospital. It would take him all of about five seconds to figure out what kind of surgery it was."

"So, you used this cyst as part of your plan?" Dr Addison scribbled madly in his book, not even looking up at her to ask his question.

"It was the cyst that gave me the idea." Skye shrugged. "Nobody wants to read about ovarian cysts. But ovarian cancer ... that's a different story."

"And Theo never tried to visit you in hospital?" he asked. "Even in the evenings after work?"

"He tried to once, but thankfully I had the foresight to put an obstacle in his path." Skye tapped a temple, proud of her ability to think ahead.

"An obstacle?" Dr Addison's brows shot up. "Would you like to elaborate on that?"

"Not particularly," said Skye, toying with him.

He sighed. "Skye, if you're going to hide things from me, then I'm not sure how much help I can be to you."

Skye waved a hand in front of her. "I sent an anonymous email to his most notorious client blackmailing him in exchange for not releasing an incriminating video to the media. I never intended to do it, of course, but the threat would be enough to keep Theo busy for a while. I knew his client would freak. And when he freaks, the first person he calls is Theo."

"That sounds fairly...extreme." Dr Addison scratched at his chin. "So, Theo was happy to leave you in hospital on your own?"

"I wouldn't exactly say happy, but I wasn't on my own. I had Elle looking after me." Skye smiled widely, not caring if her teeth showed.

"You haven't mentioned Elle before. Is she a friend?" he asked.

She nodded. "She was my support person throughout this. Theo was a bit unsure as he only met her once briefly, but she sent him a friend request on Facebook and they bonded that way."

"And Elle knew the truth about your cancer?" He wrote down another note while he waited for her answer.

Skye shook her head. "Nobody knew the truth. I took myself to hospital. It was only day surgery. Then I stayed two days at a hotel to make it look like I was gone for longer."

"Sorry, I thought you said Theo spoke to Elle online." Dr Addison's grey eyebrows pulled together as he tried to figure this out. "Weren't you worried she might tell him she wasn't going to the hospital with you?"

"This is where it gets a little complicated," Skye said. "I had to be one step ahead of Theo, which as you can imagine wasn't easy. The only way I was able to do it was with Elle. She was my secret weapon."

"You mean you manipulated her?" he asked.

"Manipulated? No! I *invented* her." Skye sat back in her chair and laughed at her own genius. "That's the best bit about all of this. Elle doesn't even exist. I made her up."

"I'm not sure I understand." Dr Addison's brows were drawn together so tightly now they looked like a single unit.

"I thought if I made up a friend who Theo thought was supporting me through this then he'd be more comfortable leaving me to it. The last thing I needed was him pulling out of his court case somehow." She smiled, proud her plan had worked so successfully.

"Right." Dr Addison let his brows relax at last as the penny dropped.

"I got the idea when I ran into Theo in the city when I was on a coffee run with one of our interns. Luckily for me she had certain assets that made her memorable to a man like Theo. All I needed to do was create an online profile for her." Skye pointed towards the computer sitting on the otherwise bare desk.

Dr Addison's jaw fell open. "You stole her identity?"

"It's not like I used her real name. I didn't even use her real photo." Skye rolled her eyes. "I just created an account as Elle Thomas, then trawled the internet to find the right images for her profile. It's amazing how many people on social media don't have their settings locked down. You can just go in and copy any photo you like."

She'd made several photo albums for Elle, selecting pictures of hot brunettes mostly wearing sunglasses and cowboy hats. They could easily pass as the same person. Then she selected her favourite as the profile picture. It was of a girl in South America wearing a bright green bikini. She was gorgeous, her body so hot Theo was extremely unlikely to look too closely at what was visible of her face. Elle had quite the convincing account.

"Then I sent out hundreds of friend requests to complete strangers. You wouldn't believe how many of them were accepted. These desperadoes started posting comments on some of the photos and I posted comments on theirs in return. I then logged on to my own account and left comments on Elle's page to show what good friends we were. Theo had no idea the page was a fake."

Dr Addison nodded, so she continued.

"I bought a second phone, paid for with cash and accessed the page with that. If Theo had met Elle and seen us interacting online then he was sure to believe she was real. He would never think to doubt it. It worked brilliantly ... until I lost the bloody phone. I turned the house upside down looking for it and it never turned up. I still don't know where it is."

"Do you think Theo found it?" he asked.

She shook her head. "Even if he did, it wouldn't have mattered. It had a passcode on it. I reckon our housekeeper probably took it. It's the only thing that makes any kind of sense. Sometimes I noticed some of my clothes going missing, too. I know it was her. I mean, she was the only other one who ever went into my dressing room, so it had to be her. I let it go, though. Most of the stuff she took was last season stuff and would only have ended up going to charity anyway. This just cut out the middle man. Pathetic, hey?"

Skye lay back in her chair, aware her eyes were wide, and her heart was racing. She was enjoying telling this story. If only she could write a blog about it. Maybe she could write a book one day...

"So, getting back to Elle," said Dr Addison. "When you said Theo was messaging her online, he was actually messaging you?"

"I know, it's crazy." Skye shook her head, laughing at the absurdity of it all. "I thought it'd be fun to talk to him as another woman. It's always the ones you least suspect who are running around behind your back. I knew all his buttons to push and he bit back each time. I was surprised. Then I pushed too far, and he backed right off."

"What happened?" Dr Addison was hanging on her every word, making Skye wonder how much of this was therapy and how much was his own curiosity.

"Disaster happened," she said. "Well, near disaster. Theo proved himself to be a faithful husband, but in the process blew my plan to pieces. He organised for his brother's wife to pick me up from hospital and told Elle not to bother. I was already in the hotel by this stage and was freaking out, until I decided to text Sophie first thing Thursday morning saying I was discharged early. I met her out the front of the hospital. I figured she wouldn't question me too much. It wouldn't be right to interrogate someone with cancer."

"You don't get along with her?" He wrote something in his notepad.

"She doesn't get along with me," Skye corrected. "I'm sure she was only picking me up as a favour to George. Or maybe she wanted a mention on my blog."

"I read one of your posts last night," said Dr Addison.

"Really? Are you allowed to do that?" Now it was her turn to be surprised.

He laughed, although it sounded more like a cough. "Of course. It's in the public domain. It was the one with all the movie parallels. Can you tell me what it felt like to write?"

"I tried to make it a light-hearted piece about a serious topic." Skye smoothed out a crease in her trousers. "Nobody wants to read anything written by a whinger. They want to hear from brave people they can turn into heroes. It also meant I could avoid going into too much detail about my treatment. That's how people get caught out. Best to keep it light and assume people know enough about cancer these days to be able to fill in the blanks for themselves."

"And was it a successful post for you?" he asked.

"Within a minute there were already over a dozen comments. Hundreds more followed." Skye flushed with pride at the memory. "They were all positive comments too, attacking each other and not me."

Dr Addison nodded slowly. "What did Theo think of it?"

"He was busy. I'm not sure he ever read much of what I wrote very closely. You know, he was so disappointed my chemo sessions always seemed to clash with his court appearances. It almost made me feel guilty."

Apart from his lack of sexual desire in the last months of their marriage, Theo had been the perfect husband. Leaving her alone when she requested it and holding her hand when she needed it most. She was glad he'd never find out about her lie. She couldn't even imagine how he would've reacted. A man as black and white as Theo would either laugh it off and forgive her, or never talk to her again. She couldn't decide which way he would've gone.

"Would you like to talk about how you lost your hair?" asked Dr Addison, noticing her fidgeting with her hat.

"Theo found me in the bathroom clipping it off. I'd been snipping off clumps all week and leaving them around the house, wanting him to think it was the chemo. Once he caught me with the clippers, I had no choice but to ask him to shave my hair off for me and hope he didn't notice how thick it really was." She removed her hat and ran her hand through her short hair.

"And how did it feel to see all your hair gone?" he asked.

"To be honest, I thought I looked amazing. Better than Britney Spears when she shaved her head. It was hot. I had to bury my head in Theo's chest, so he couldn't see me smiling."

She remembered how turned on she'd been seeing her hair like that. She'd felt a tingle run through her body as she pulled Theo towards the shower. She'd wanted to prove to him she was still a sexual being. For him to see the hot goddess she'd seen in the mirror.

She'd undressed him only to find him completely soft.

So, she'd slid down his body, kissing his chest, then his stomach, her lips trailing across his front, getting closer to her target. Closer and closer until slowly she felt him begin to respond.

Then he'd grabbed the back of her head and just like she'd stuck a pin in his dick, he deflated. She'd never felt less attractive.

"Skye, are you with me?" Dr Addison was staring at her, tapping his pen on his notepad.

"Sorry," she said, crossing and uncrossing her legs, trying to shift the warm discomfort pooling in her groin. "Can I use your bathroom for a moment?"

She left the room, headed down the small hallway and pushed on the blue door to the toilets, wincing as the smell of cheap air freshener assaulted her nostrils.

The tap turned on faster than she intended and cold water splashed onto the floor. She reduced the pressure and held her hands under the flow, wishing she could scoop the water onto her face. But she didn't want to ruin her make-up, even if she wasn't wearing as much as usual today. Only a light smattering of foundation, her mascara and some lip gloss. Enough that if the press decided to take her photo, she'd look good, but not enough to make it look like she'd gone to too much effort. Widows didn't normally go to great lengths with their appearance and she didn't need the press attacking her any further than they already were.

Besides, perhaps it was better she presented herself to the world in exactly the way she felt.

Like shit.

The memory of seducing Theo in the shower had messed her up. She missed his cock almost as much as she missed him. The shower wasn't the last time they had sex. There'd been one last magnificent time on Theo's desk, even if she'd had to pretend she was Elle to get him in the mood.

She'd messaged him from his lobby as Elle, knowing exactly what he'd find a turn on—a hot woman in a bikini asking after his welfare.

Theo's assistant didn't recognise her in the dark wig and Burberry trench coat, and she had to tell her who she was before she asked to go through to Theo's chambers.

Theo didn't recognise her at first either. Well, not until she slid off her coat and revealed other more familiar parts of her body.

Damn, he'd felt good.

When would she ever have sex again? Especially if she ended up in prison.

She shuddered at the thought of losing her freedom, then quickly pulling herself together, she returned to the armchair in Dr Addison's office and sat back down.

"Sorry," she said. "It's been a rough week."

"You were talking about Theo," he prompted. "And how you kept him away from the hospital. How did all those lies make you feel about yourself?"

"Well, they weren't really lies," she said. "More like distraction techniques."

He wrote something down. "What kind of distractions?"

Like straddling him and putting her tits in his face? Men couldn't fuck and talk, let alone fuck and think. But she couldn't tell Dr Addison about that.

"Once, court was adjourned early and he went to the hospital, calling me when the nurses couldn't find my appointment. So, I told him they'd rushed me through with a morning treatment and I'd returned home. That kind of thing."

"And you don't see that as a lie?" he asked.

She thought about the way she'd put down the phone that day and hurried into the kitchen to find the meat tenderiser and repeatedly bashed the inside of her elbow to create a bruise, before twisting a steak knife into her skin to create a puncture wound. It'd hurt like hell, but the result was so graphic she knew Theo would never think to doubt her. She'd then run into the bathroom and wrapped her arm in a bandage and shaved a few chunks of hair from her head to scatter on her pillow. After applying some foundation so pale it made her look like a geisha, she'd crawled into bed, took some Ipecac and vomited into a bucket.

"Well, I was genuinely exhausted that day," she said. "So, being asleep in bed wasn't really a lie. If only I could've rested properly, but when Amber returned home from school, it was like she was having some kind of rave party downstairs. The only reason I could cope with it was because Theo had already suggested that Amber should move in with her mum."

"You felt like things were falling into place for you?" Dr Addison made the humming sound he favoured.

Skye nodded. "I had a gain in popularity with a public who adored me. I had a husband who treated me like a queen. A mother who saw me for the first time in her life. A father who'd come out of hiding. And my husband's daughter was finally going to get the hell out of my house. It was perfection on a to-do list."

He wrote something down on his notepad. Perhaps he was making his own to-do list. "How are you coping with the public's reaction to all of this?"

"You mean being shoved away and scorned? Treated like a liar and a murderer?" She tried to keep the anger out of her voice, suspecting she'd failed badly.

"And you don't feel you deserve to be treated like that?" he asked.

She raised her eyebrows.

"I'm not saying that's what I think," he clarified. "I'm asking if *you* think you deserve it."

Skye huffed, no longer concerned about hiding her anger. "I may not have been completely honest, but I sure as hell didn't kill anyone, especially not Theo."

"And how does it make you feel not to be believed?" he asked.

"Let me see ... Not only might I be about to be charged with murder, but my career has gone down the toilet, I'm unable to visit my mother and Amber's probably going to inherit Theo's entire estate, move into *my* house and redecorate it from top to bottom in purple. Plus, my husband is dead. How do you think that makes me feel?" She directed her gaze at him, feeling him retreat into a safe space within his head. How dare he sit there like that asking her how it made her feel that nobody believed a word she said.

She stood and leant before him, her face inches from his.

"How the fuck do you think it makes me feel?" she hissed.

Dr Addison nodded, appearing unfazed, yet the fear in his eyes betrayed him.

"That's why I decided to tell the police the truth about my cancer," she said, taking a step back. "It's all going to come out anyway when I'm arrested. If I ask for bail on the grounds of medical reasons, a judge will want proof of my cancer. Proof I can't provide. If I go to jail, the prison doctors will figure out the state of my health quickly enough. Either way the truth is going to emerge. It looks better for me if I admit it now. At least that way I have an ounce of control over the situation. My cancer game was up the moment Theo died."

She walked to the door.

"All I did was bend the truth a little. I'm not a liar like you're making me out to be. None of this makes me a murderer. End of story. I have nothing more to say to you today."

She walked out, throwing the secretary a sarcastic grin as she left.

Okay, perhaps she'd done a little more than bend the truth. But lies were only words. How did that children's nursery rhyme go? Sticks and stones may break my bones, but words will never hurt me.

See, only words. No sticks, no stones. And definitely no poison.

She wanted to go home.

She wanted her husband.

She wanted to turn back the clock.

Skye was getting nervous. The police questioning was hotting up.

She lay back in the spa bath in her ensuite as if washing the filth of the accusations from her body could cleanse them from her mind.

Pouring some bath gel onto her loofa, she rubbed it down her arms, wishing Theo were here to wash her back. Not to say that ever lasted for long. There were far too many of her other body parts he was more interested in washing.

The accusations were ridiculous. She hadn't killed Theo, nor had she tried to kill George or her mother. She didn't want any of them dead.

She loved Theo. *Adored* him.

She didn't exactly love George, but she had no reason to want him dead.

As for her mother ... why would she kill her when for the first time in her life she was feeling her love? Dementia made her a better person, not worse. With dementia she was happy to see her. She gave her compliments and held her hand. The state of her mind was a blessing as far as she was concerned. It was no reason to kill her. It was reason to keep her alive.

So, who had tried to kill her? And had they been trying to kill Theo or was that a mistake? Why the hell did he have to eat those bloody brownies?

She sank into the warm water, dipping her head back. It felt strange without her long hair. She had a nice, thick coverage of hair growing back, but it would take ages for it to return to the length it was before.

She thought of Samson, relating to how he must have felt when Delilah cut his hair, robbing him of his strength. When Theo found her in the bathroom that day, her own life had fallen to the floor along with her hair.

Whoever the killer was, they had to be someone who could get access to her house. Someone close to her. If she ever found out who it was, she might prove the police correct and become a murderer herself. How dare anybody rip Theo from her arms like that! And framing her for it in the process. She wasn't sure what she felt more acutely—her anger or her grief.

Maybe it was Amber? No, that couldn't be right. She didn't even know Skye's mother and she loved Theo too much to want him dead.

It could be George. He was at their house all the time, including the night Theo ate the brownies. He'd always been jealous of him. Perhaps he'd decided to bump him off so he could be the triumphant twin at last. But why would he hurt her mother and almost kill himself in the process? That didn't make any sense. Although, the police had hinted at the fact he'd told them she'd offered him the brownies when she'd done the complete opposite. That part made no sense, either. If only she'd kept the note Theo had left her in the fridge.

She rubbed at her temples. She was getting a headache.

Maybe Sophie was guilty. A scorned lover getting back at Theo for dumping her all those years ago and trying to inflict pain on her by killing her mother. That was possible. Sophie could've sent herself that message about the Prussian Blue when she realised she'd accidentally poisoned her husband. Or maybe she intentionally poisoned him to throw the police off her track, always meaning to save him at the last moment. Or perhaps their marriage wasn't so picture perfect after all and she'd meant to kill George, too.

Skye stood up in the bath as if the water had been infested with leeches and reached for her towel.

That must be it.

It was Sophie.

That fat bitch had killed her husband. Somehow, she'd gotten a key to their house and messed with her brownies. She needed to call Detective Hooke and tell him.

She dried herself and went to her bedroom to look for her phone.

Unless it was Rin...

She was a good possibility, too. Her motive would be identical to Sophie's. Yet another one of Theo's scorned lovers who not only still held a candle for him but had a grudge against him. She had an even stronger motive than Sophie. With Theo out of the picture, she'd have sole custody and control of Amber, just like she'd always wanted.

She could have easily used Amber's key to get into their house.

Yes, that must be it. It all fit so perfectly. She'd never trusted that woman.

It was definitely Rin.

Where was her bloody phone? Skye spilled the contents of her bag onto the bed, certain she'd left it in there.

Rin could be covering her tracks right now. They needed to hurry up and arrest her. No doubt her boring husband was in on the whole plan, too. The way he looked at Rin was enough to make you sick.

Maybe he committed the crime for her, and she knew nothing about it. The ultimate gift for his wife—a dead ex-husband.

They were definitely dodgy.

She wondered what would happen to Amber if the police arrested Rin and Jeff. She'd have to go and live with George and Sophie. There was no way in hell that spoilt brat was going to live with her.

She found her phone in a side pocket of the bag and scrolled through for Detective Hooke's number.

He answered on the second ring.

"Detective Hooke speaking."

"It's Skye Manis calling. I have some information for you." She was shaking. Why hadn't she thought to tell him this earlier? She'd been too busy trying to deal with her grief, she supposed.

"Go ahead," said the detective.

"It was Theo's ex-wife. I've got it all figured out." Skye drew in a breath, trying not to rush her words. "Rin had motive and opportunity. Think about it. With Theo gone, she could have their daughter all to herself. And she wasn't exactly his greatest fan."

"Where's the proof?" asked the detective.

"Isn't that your job?" Skye screwed up her face. "It's not my job to find you proof."

"Actually, Mrs Manis, we already have quite a bit of proof."

"That's fantastic." Maybe she'd been wrong about this detective.

"But I'm afraid the proof doesn't point to Theo's ex-wife."

Skye's stomach dropped, fully aware of exactly who it pointed at.

"And besides," he continued. "What's her motive for trying to kill your mother?"

Shit. She hadn't thought of that. This was what happened when your mind went over the speed limit. It forgot to consider the facts.

"Maybe she was framing me?" she suggested.

"I'll be in touch, Mrs Manis."

Skye disconnected the call, looking across at her belongings strewn across her bed. She'd made a mess. She could feel her pulse rising just at the sight of it.

She tried to still her shaking hands as she placed her purse neatly back in her bag next to her make up case and returned her phone to the side pocket.

Her hand brushed against a piece of paper she'd hidden in the bottom of the pocket several months ago now, not wanting Theo to see it.

She smoothed the paper out on her bare thigh. There was no need to hide it now that Theo wasn't here to read it.

She scanned through the letter almost as if there was a possibility it had changed while sitting in her bag.

No, the result was still the same.

Earlier in the year she'd decided to go ahead with the genetic testing her doctor had recommended to see if she carried the mutation linked to early onset Alzheimer's disease. She knew she should've told Dr Addison about the test. The result had been a large part of the reason she'd lied about her cancer.

It just seemed too personal. Let him think she'd lied to get attention. Granted, that had been a very positive side effect to her lie, but it wasn't how it started. Her test result had been a far more effective catalyst.

As part of the process, she'd had to see a genetic counsellor who was extremely concerned about her decision to face this news alone. Normally people had a support person come with them.

She didn't want Theo there. She couldn't cope with it. She needed to sit with the result on her own first. If she had the mutation she'd be robbed of her mind. If she didn't, she'd be robbed of her body, forced to birth a child she didn't want.

Either way the result was going to be challenging and she hadn't been at all sure how she was going to deal with it. She was going to need time to come up with a plan without Theo whispering his ideas in her ear. He only had one plan. He wanted a son. He wanted it so badly he'd probably go ahead and have a baby with a crazy lady, making her do IVF to ensure the gene wasn't passed on. She'd be poked and jabbed and examined until all shreds of her dignity were erased. One of the freelancers at work had written about her experiences with IVF and it sounded like a horror movie with the only prize at the end being a screaming child.

So, against the counsellor's advice she'd turned up for her result alone. The news was private. It was hers to deal with. She could handle it.

When the counsellor explained the result was negative, she'd sat very still in her chair, holding her breath as she tried to work out if that meant she was negative for the gene or if she was simply saying the news was bad.

It wasn't until the counsellor pointed at the result on the sheet she now held in her hand and said she didn't have the mutation that she exhaled in a deep sigh. Her mother's future was not her own.

The blissful relief sliding though her body was quickly replaced by sheer terror, knowing she no longer had an excuse for putting off having children.

Which left her with the problem of what to tell Theo.

It was strange really, the way it worked out in the end. She'd only just decided to tell Theo the truth—the whole truth—when her doctor requested she go for an ultrasound to check out some pain in her left ovary, most likely due to a cyst.

As she'd been having her scan, pretending she was anywhere other than lying on a table while a complete stranger had his hand between her legs, the solution came to her.

What if it wasn't a cyst causing her pain? What if it was cancer? What if her ovaries needed to be removed, leaving her unable to have children?

By the time the sonographer confirmed it was indeed a cyst, her imagination had arrived at a completely different destination.

The answer was cancer.

It sounded like a line from a movie trailer. She'd turned the words over in her mind, enjoying the way they rhymed.

The answer was cancer.

As she'd gotten changed back into her clothes in the cubical at the clinic, she had to fight back tears. She could finally see the future in the way she'd always wanted.

With Theo.

Without dementia.

Without children.

The memory of the emotion of that moment affected her even now and tears flooded her eyes.

She'd gotten two out of her three wishes, only the one she'd been robbed of was the one she'd wanted most of all.

Theo.

She hunched into the foetal position, her wet towel slipping undone, leaving her naked.

She'd give anything to have Theo back with her. *Anything*. She'd even have a child for him. She missed him so much.

BELOW THE SURFACE

Dr Addison retrieved his laptop from the drawer of his desk, preparing to type up his notes from his sessions with Skye. He didn't normally like making too many notes while his clients were talking. He found it made them too self-conscious. Better for them to think they were just having a casual chat. They were more likely to talk freely that way.

With Skye he'd had no choice but to take a copious amount of notes. She was such a complex person and he had to be certain he paid attention to what she was telling him and not what he'd read about her in the media.

It wasn't often he had a client with a profile as high as Skye Manis. His brain had to work overtime during their sessions to keep himself from asking questions he wanted to know personally, rather than what he needed to ask professionally.

What a mess her life was. Given the clients Carlos Tagliatori had referred to him in the past, that was saying something. Here was a woman who had every opportunity in life, and she'd pissed them all up against the wall. She was wealthy, attractive *and* intelligent. She had the trifecta, for Christ's sake!

He thought of his own daughter, Maddy, who was almost the same age. She wasn't as wealthy as Skye (not even close), not as attractive (although, still beautiful to him) and not as intelligent (he'd had to face that fact long ago when she told him she dreamed of visiting Rome so she could see the Eiffel Tower). Yet, Maddy was far more successful than Skye in so many ways. She loved her job in that clothing store, had a terrific husband, a mad passion for yoga and was surrounded by hordes of giggling friends who dragged her all over town.

If success was defined on a scale of happiness, rather than money, then Maddy was top of the list. He was proud of her. She'd taken what she'd been given in life and made the best of it.

Skye had made the worst of it.

He'd enjoyed listening to her talk, even if she'd disturbed him a few times. It was so much more interesting than the usual drivel he had to listen to—couples bickering over who should put the bins out, bored housewives frustrated with not having found their purpose in life, middle-aged men lamenting their lost youth. Usually his job was Boring with a capital B. He'd heard it all before. That was why he liked his referrals from Carlos and was happy to give him a larger kickback than usually considered normal. Carlos's clients were rarely boring.

Skye had said things to him he'd never heard before. He didn't know where to start with his notes.

First, there was the issue of her lying about her cancer. That was a whole thesis in itself. Her warped childhood had a lot to do with it. It was a classic case of attention seeking. She definitely showed signs of narcissistic personality disorder. Having been given no attention as a child, this cancer was her ticket to a whole world of being noticed. It made her somebody.

The death of her first husband had given her a taste of it. She'd even admitted the public's attention was like a drug.

But the problem with drugs is they eventually they wear off, leaving you craving another hit. Hits of attention and sympathy are hard to score when you're a healthy woman in the prime of your life, happily married to a wealthy man. It was no wonder the letdown had started making her nauseous.

It seemed there was more to her lie than just pure attention seeking. There was a certain convenience with it being in her ovaries, leaving her unable to have children. And it had led to her stepdaughter moving out of her house. Plus, her father had contacted her for the first time. Like she'd said, it was perfection on a to-do list. She had a lot to gain from the cancer and nothing to lose—unless she was found out, which of course she was. Telling a lie like that would be hard enough to pull off, but not ever being found out would be like some kind of miracle.

Whether or not Theo died, the truth would have surfaced eventually.

These were all very complex issues and he needed more time to think them through before he'd be able to prepare the psychological assessment Carlos had asked him for.

He wasn't required to comment on her guilt or innocence, but always liked to decide this for himself. He couldn't say with any certainty he thought she was innocent, although he couldn't find any reason why she'd want to kill Theo. She seemed to genuinely have loved him.

In his experience, pathological liars were certainly capable of far worse crimes than making up stories. Murder included.

But killing Theo didn't fit with Skye's plan. Why bump him off if she was already faking the cancer? She would've gotten plenty of attention with the cancer alone. She hadn't needed to kill him. Unless she'd wanted him dead for other reasons.

Maybe this was an issue of self-control. Once she got started with her lies, she couldn't stop. She wanted more attention, then more and more. She couldn't get enough, and her plans became increasingly elaborate.

No. He still didn't buy it. It was likely she'd tried to kill her mother —if what Skye said about her was true then who wouldn't want to finish her off—but he doubted she'd tried to kill Theo or his brother. It just didn't fit.

Her problem was going to be convincing anybody to believe her.

If she was arrested, which seemed a likely scenario, then he was glad not to be on the jury for her trial. She'd made it impossible for anyone to be able to tell if she was innocent.

Carlos had his hands full with this one. Which reminded him, he really needed to send him that cheque for all the referrals he'd sent him this month. And perhaps a bonus for sending him Skye.

Carlos sure knew how to inject some excitement into an old man's life. Skye had given him so much to think about, he doubted he'd ever sleep again.

———

Skye was stuck at the police station in another never-ending interview. The detective had brought her something to eat and left her alone with Carlos Tagliatori and his impressive hair for a few minutes.

"I'm just popping out for a quick ciggie," said Carlos, miming smoking with his fingers as if she didn't know what he meant.

"Aren't you supposed to give me a pep talk or something?" she asked, pursing her lips. Lawyers didn't leave their clients for a smoke on *Law and Order*.

"You're doing fine, Skye." He reached over and patted her hand.

"They're going to arrest me, aren't they?" she asked, pulling away.

"I'll get you bail. It'll be okay." He stood and went to the door.

"So, they are going to arrest me?" Ice ran down her spine. This couldn't be happening! What was the point of a lawyer if they couldn't stop you from going to jail?

"Most likely. Look, I'll be back in a minute. Don't worry. I've got you." He flashed her one of his thousand-dollar-an-hour smiles and left.

She poked at the plastic-wrapped ham and cheese sandwich the detective had placed in front of her, with no intention of eating it. It was full of calories. It was probably full of salmonella, too. Revolting. She felt sorry for the pig that had given its life to make this pathetic lunch.

She felt exactly like that pig right now. When the detective returned, she needed to prove to him she was innocent. She couldn't go to jail! The thought of it sent chills through her body. The problem was the detective hadn't believed a word she said ever since she told him about faking her cancer.

What was so bad about that? Everyone was so bloody sensitive these days. People lied about medical conditions all the time. She'd love to have a dollar every time someone said they had the flu when really it was just a cold, or they had a migraine that was technically only a headache. Their reasons for stretching the truth were no different to her own. You didn't get half as much attention for a cold, headache or an ovarian cyst compared to the flu, a migraine or cancer.

Seriously, what was all the fuss about?

The worst part about all of this was while the police were convinced she was responsible, the real killer was loose and their trail was getting cold. That bastard was getting away with it!

Detective Hooke came back into the room and sat before her, turning on the recording device as he folded his large hands on the table.

"Not hungry?" He pointed to her unopened sandwich.

"Not *that* hungry." He pulled a face.

He smiled with just a hint of sarcasm. "Sorry it's not the standard you're used to."

She ignored his comment.

"Are you ready to confess?" he asked.

Carlos chose that moment to walk back in the room.

"What the hell's going on?" he asked, his face turning pink.

"Relax. We haven't started yet," said the detective.

Carlos turned to Skye for confirmation.

"It's okay," she said. "He's only interrogating me about my sandwich at this stage."

The detective sighed as Carlos took a seat next to her.

"I told you not to say a word without me here," Carlos hissed in her ear.

"I didn't say anything," she hissed back.

He shot her a stern look.

"Are we ready?" asked the detective, pulling an evidence bag from his jacket pocket and placing it on the table.

"Recognise this?" he asked.

"My phone," said Skye, reaching for it. She'd looked everywhere for that. Where on earth had he found it?

The detective moved it out of her reach and Carlos glared at her.

"My client has no way of telling if this is her phone," he said. "That was not an admission."

"What's my phone have to do with any of this?" she asked.

"Skye," warned Carlos.

"We found it in your front garden," said the detective. "It's the same phone used to tell Sophie Manis her husband had been poisoned with thallium."

The door opened and two uniformed police officers appeared.

"Skye Manis," said the detective. "I'm placing you under arrest for the murder of your husband Theo Manis and the attempted murder of both George Manis and Clara Butterford. You're not obliged to say or do anything unless you wish to do so, but whatever you say or do may be used in evidence. Do you understand?"

Skye nodded, not hearing another word the detective said.

All she heard was blood rushing to her brain, adrenaline coursing through her veins and the meagre contents of her stomach retching their way up her throat.

"Carlos! Do something." She fought against the police officers as they lifted her to her feet and clipped handcuffs to her wrists.

"Relax," said Carlos. "I'll get you out of this."

"Why don't you believe me?" she screeched at the detective. "You won't listen to a word I say."

She thought she heard one of the officers stifle a laugh and she knew she'd been wrong to lie about her cancer.

It was a lie that was about to send her to jail for a crime she didn't do.

———

Clara didn't understand what all the fuss was about. There was more than the usual number of strange faces popping in and out of her room. She was hungry, too, certain that normally on a Tuesday she ate something tastier than the bland nursing home food. She just couldn't remember what it was.

She did remember a policeman had visited her. A doctor, too.

People were treating her so nicely, acting like she was very important. Nobody had treated her like that since her days on the stage.

She asked the policeman if he was here to talk about the glue on her feet, but he hadn't known what she was talking about. It was strange. She couldn't think what else he could be there for.

He said he had reason to believe she might've been poisoned. That made her laugh, but she wasn't sure why. It just sounded funny. Nobody would try to poison her. Except maybe Skye and she hadn't visited her for years.

Her stomach groaned and she wondered again what food her stomach was missing. At least she had the feeling back in her hands and feet. That tingling was starting to get annoying.

Brownies! That's what it was. She licked her lips. That pretty lady with the blonde hair always brought her brownies on a Tuesday. The same lady who sometimes pretended she was Skye.

Maybe she'd visit later today.

She smoothed out a wrinkle in her nightdress, proud she'd managed to solve the mystery of the missing food herself. She wasn't mad. Everyone else was.

———

George knew that bitch had killed Theo. She'd been nothing but trouble since the first time he saw her. What was Theo thinking marrying a woman like her?

Even Theo hadn't trusted her. He'd had her investigated before he married her. Not that Skye knew that. Disappointingly, the investigation hadn't turned up much. She seemed to be who she said she was— the daughter of a ballerina with a mysterious father who lived in France somewhere. Theo had checked if the letters Skye sent him each year were being delivered to his house. They were, which meant one thing. That old French dude was one smart bastard. He knew crazy when he saw it and was keeping well away.

Theo had made him swear never to tell Skye what he knew. He said he didn't want to crush her hopes or something like that. She was better off thinking the letters weren't reaching him.

While the investigator had been at it, he'd looked into the death of Skye's first husband. She'd mentioned once she thought he might have been having an affair with some chick in Adelaide. Theo had gone off on some loopy tangent saying maybe he'd faked his own death and was alive and well, screwing his way around the city of churches. As it turned out, he wasn't. He was dead in his grave with a bunch of worms feasting on his charred remains.

Now Theo was dead too, gone to join their parents in heaven.

Their mum would've been waiting for him, a spanakopita in one hand and a tray of baklava in the other.

"You too skinny," she'd have yelled at him, while looking for a place to put down the food so she could free her hands to pinch his cheeks.

"Leave him alone," their father would've said, pulling him into an embrace and slapping him on the back.

It made George sad to think of this reunion happening without him. It'd always been the four of them when he was growing up. Now he was the only one left alive.

At least he'd been able to give Theo a proper burial. It was a great comfort to know he was at Fawkner with their parents. Skye hadn't been to the grave. Nor had she gone to the funeral. She couldn't even be bothered to pretend to care he was dead. What a bitch!

How could Theo possibly be dead? It wasn't meant to be like this. He didn't know how to live without his twin.

He hadn't told anyone yet, but when he'd collapsed outside the hospital, he'd seen something. To be more precise, he'd seen Theo. They'd linked hands and walked together before George had felt himself being pulled away. It must've been what people called a near death experience. He'd seen something on TV about that once and thought it was a load of crap. Maybe he'd tell Sophie about it one day. Or maybe he'd keep this one to himself. It felt too private to share, even with his wife.

He blinked back tears and took a swig of his can of Coke. He couldn't stomach the thought of a beer at the moment. His stomach groaned at the idea of alcohol, leaving him drinking this lolly water crap. It was going to take him a while to get back to normal. Whatever normal was without Theo.

The tears stung his eyes, determined to force their way out.

"Oh, fuck it," he mumbled, letting them roll down his cheeks as he gasped for air.

He was pretty sure he knew how everything had gone down. Skye was sick of visiting her deranged mother so had been trying to kill her off with those fucking brownies he and Theo had eaten. Which as far as he was concerned made her as guilty of murdering Theo as if she'd stuck a knife directly into his heart. A jury probably wouldn't see it that way, though. The bitch would probably get away with it and be given a couple of years for manslaughter. That wasn't enough. She deserved to rot in jail for life. She'd taken his twin away from him.

The scale of her evil was hard to comprehend. Not only had she murdered Theo, but she'd lied about her cancer. Who the hell lied about having cancer? She was like the scum that sat at the bottom of the ocean. Did scum even sit at the bottom of the ocean? Well, if it did then that was her. Actually, no. That was too nice. She was like the shit that got stuck to a dog's arsehole. Yep, that was a better description, despite it being cruel to animals.

He'd never hated anyone in his life, but he hated her. He despised her. The feeling was crawling on his skin and eating him from the inside. Or was that the poison she'd fed him? It was hard to tell the difference.

Evil bitch. But he'd fixed her. That detective had loved it when he told him how Skye had insisted he and Theo eat some of her brownies. He'd gobbled up that story like it was one of those fucking brownies itself.

Yep, he was going to make sure Skye stayed behind bars until she was old and grey. He owed it to Theo to make sure of that.

———

Sophie decided she was the only person in the world capable of thinking clearly, yet nothing made sense even to her.

Skye had poisoned the brownies. That much was clear. It couldn't have been anyone else.

But she remembered George laughing when he'd rolled home

drunk that fateful night, saying he and Theo had eaten the precious brownies Skye had baked for her mother. She'd apparently banned them from eating them and he was laughing like a naughty schoolboy.

So, it must've been her mother she'd been trying to kill. Not Theo or George. Surely the police could figure that out, yet they'd charged her with Theo's murder and the attempted murder of George and Clara.

She was certain Skye was guilty of only one of those crimes.

She was also guilty of being a bitch. George was right about that. Anyone twisted enough to lie about having cancer deserved everything they got. She hadn't even turned up to the funeral. Theo was her husband! Who didn't go to their husband's funeral?

She'd had to organise the whole thing under George's instructions. He was far too sick to do it himself. At least Skye had the decency to pay for it, she supposed. Not that George was grateful for that. He said it was Theo's money anyway, so it didn't count.

Poor George hadn't taken any of this well. She'd never seen him cry before this. Not even when his parents died. She would have to keep a close eye on him to make sure he didn't do anything stupid. It was going to take him a long time to learn there was a place in this world for him without his twin. He was still her husband and a father to Lukas and Beth. They needed him.

Skye's absence at the funeral demonstrated exactly how much she'd needed Theo. What a low act.

That was why Sophie decided to keep her questions to herself.

She'd overheard George giving a statement to the police from his hospital bed saying Skye had offered him and Theo the brownies. He said she put them on the counter and told them to help themselves.

Sophie wasn't sure if it was the quantity of alcohol he'd drunk that night that'd clouded his memory or if he was just running with a version of events that suited him. A better, albeit fictitious, version of events.

If she corrected him then some of the charges against Skye might be dropped or downgraded to manslaughter. Then what? Amber might lose her inheritance to Skye. She couldn't stand by and watch that happen. Amber deserved that money more than Skye did. She might even give some to Rin. She could sure use some extra cash with her houseful of children.

Besides, George might get in trouble for lying and he was already going through enough stress. The poor man had almost died.

If Skye was such a fan of bending the truth for her own gain, then let it bend in the other direction for a change.

Whatever that evil woman had been up to, she'd nearly killed George, leaving Lukas and Beth without a father. And she'd killed Theo—the first man Sophie had ever loved.

As for poor Clara ... imagine your own daughter trying to bump you off. They all knew for certain Skye had at the very least done that.

The part that made her really sick was she'd done all of this while lying to the world about having cancer.

A shudder ran through Sophie's body as she thought of her own mother succumbing to bowel cancer a few years ago. What gave Skye the right to lie about something like that? Nothing did. Cancer wasn't something to mess with. What she'd done had insulted every true cancer sufferer whether they'd beaten the disease or not. It was unforgivable.

Let her rot in jail.

———

Jacques Moubray sat at his late wife's writing bureau and opened the folder his son had left with him.

He'd asked Claude if he could search the internet for any information about his long lost, great-niece who lived in Australia. Thankfully Claude hadn't asked too many questions. Antoinette would come back to haunt him if he told his sons they had a sister. She'd never been pleased with that idea, very clearly demonstrated by the way she threw him out when he'd received Skye's first letter.

He'd had to beg and plead until she let him back in their house. Then he'd had to stoop to grovelling before she let him back in their bed. Claude had been conceived that night, so the grovelling was worthwhile at least.

He hadn't known what to do with Skye's letter. Antoinette had decided for him and burnt it before he had a chance to respond. He had to wait an entire year before she wrote again. She sounded like such a sweet little girl talking about fairies and cats. She even drew him some pictures. He didn't know what he could say to her in return if he had the chance to write back. She wouldn't be interested in hearing about his sons or his farm. She certainly wouldn't be interested in hearing about his wife.

From the way she wrote, it sounded like she believed he still lived a glamorous life working in the ballet. It would be cruel to tell her the truth. Nobody wanted an old, fat French farmer for a father.

He missed his life in the ballet, but Antoinette had been very clear with him. It was the ballet or her. She'd also been very clear that she came with the farm she'd inherited from her parents. She couldn't bear to live anywhere else.

How different his life would've been if he'd chosen another cafe to buy his breakfast on that cold winter morning in Paris. He'd fallen in love with Antoinette the moment his eyes fell upon her soft curves. She was so different to the slender ballerinas he'd been wasting his time on before. There was something so real about her, with her hips and breasts and rounded thighs.

People thought he was crazy. They said she was plain and frumpy. Someone even called her plump. He didn't care if their eyes were blind to her beauty. They didn't need to see it. He saw it enough for everyone.

His beautiful Antoinette. He missed her with an ache deep in his bones.

He could barely remember Skye's mother. There'd been a lot of women in those days and he certainly enjoyed them, but he hadn't loved any of them, Clara included.

It would be a lie if he said he hadn't known about Clara's pregnancy. He'd received her letter at the boarding house he was staying at, but by then his head was so full of Antoinette he found it easier to pretend she didn't exist. That was the good thing about Australia. It was so far away he could easily convince himself it wasn't there.

He'd assumed Clara would've had an abortion, so receiving a letter years later from his daughter had come as a shock. Not an unpleasant shock, if he was honest. Apart from Antoinette's reaction. That rede-fined the word unpleasant.

Skye had sent her letter directly to the farm. Someone at the ballet must have passed the address onto Clara. She'd been fairly determined to keep in touch with him in those early days so it shouldn't have been a surprise she'd managed to track him to the farm.

As happy as he'd been to receive Skye's letter, it just wasn't possible to have a relationship with her. Not if he wanted a relationship with Antoinette, which he most certainly did.

Then he'd received her most recent letter telling him she had cancer. It was a hard blow to take. He'd waited all these years and now it might be too late. He knew how cruel ovarian cancer could be. His mother had died an awful death. To think he'd passed this onto his daughter was devastating, especially as it was the only thing he seemed to have given her.

He opened Claude's folder and winced at what he saw. It was a newspaper article, featuring a photograph of a woman who was unmis-takably his daughter. The caption said she'd been arrested for her husband's murder.

He swallowed as bile rose to the back of his throat.

This couldn't be true. The sweet girl who wrote him a letter on her birthdays couldn't possibly be a murderer. He must go to Australia and help her. He hadn't been a father her whole life, but that didn't mean he couldn't start now.

His poor girl.

He began to read the article.

Skye Manis has been arrested for the murder of her husband, Theo Manis, as well as the attempted murder of her mother, Clara Butterford and her husband's twin brother, George Manis. This development comes shortly after the startling revelation that she faked a battle with ovarian cancer.

Jacques closed the folder and clutched at his throat as his breath came in short gasps. She faked her cancer!

This wasn't his poor girl. He didn't even know this woman. She might share his blood, but she wasn't his daughter. It was too much to take! He'd had enough tragedy in his life lately. He didn't need this.

What kind of a person would fake having cancer? It was inconceivable. If she was capable of that, she was almost certainly capable of murdering her husband, too. He couldn't stand behind someone like that. His mother must be shaking her head from heaven to think her granddaughter would make such a mockery of the disease that took her life.

It was time once again to pretend Australia didn't exist.

Life as a simple farmer wasn't so bad after all.

Rin barely had a chance to think about the death of her ex-husband. She was far too worried about her daughter.

Amber had taken the news badly.

She'd locked herself in her bedroom and wouldn't talk to anyone. She hadn't even logged into any of her social media accounts. That in itself was a sign she wasn't coping—a big, flashing warning sign with yellow lights and a siren.

Rin had made the mistake of pointing out to Amber that she was going to be rich. Skye couldn't possibly profit from the crime of killing Theo, which meant Amber would get all of his inheritance.

"I don't want his money!" Amber had screamed back at her. "I want my dad. Give it to charity for all I care."

Rin would never do that. She'd always struggled with money and her lack of it. Her daughter was set. She'd get over her father one day, but that money would last a lifetime.

Amber could travel the world, drive a reliable car and eat in fancy restaurants. She wouldn't have to lose sleep wondering how she was going to pay the electricity bill or stand in line at the supermarket praying she had enough to cover what was in the trolley.

It was a relief to know her daughter's life would be so much easier than her own. If only she could be certain her other children would be able to enjoy such stress-free lives. The way they were tracking at the moment, her kids wouldn't have much of a head start on what she'd had when she first moved out of home.

She knew it was horrible to think of Theo's death as a blessing for Amber, but when there was that amount of money at stake, it was hard not to give it a little bit of thought.

There were advantages for her also. Never again would she have to negotiate her way around Theo when it came to Amber. She was the sole parent now. He couldn't take her daughter away from her or choose her school or decide what parties she could attend. Finally, she could finish raising Amber the way she wanted to.

Still, it was sad Theo had died. Murdered by his own wife.

If he hadn't left her all those years ago, he'd still be alive. She wouldn't have killed him. Well, she was fairly certain she wouldn't have. He was the kind of man you did want to strangle sometimes. Or jump into bed with.

At least now she didn't have to decide which way her feelings fell. He was neither strangleable or jumpintobedable anymore.

His funeral had been torturous. It brought back memories of his parents' funerals at the same church. Two hours of sitting on a hard, wooden bench listening to two old men chanting in Greek, their off-key voices rising and falling in unison with George's howling.

He didn't look well, all thin and pale with huge bags under his eyes.

Poor guy. He was never going to get over this. For all the competitive banter that existed between the twins, they really had loved each other.

Tears sprang to Rin's eyes and she blinked them away. She'd lost Theo once before and she'd coped. She could cope with losing him again. She had Jeff now.

Besides, Theo was so much more likeable now he was dead. All her bad memories of him were rapidly fading into the depths of her mind as the good ones rose to the surface.

He hadn't been such a bad person. He was smart, ambitious, inventive...

She shook her head and pounced on the pile of washing spilling out of the laundry. Time to do some housework. If she could clear this lot of washing, she'd be able to get to her vacuum cleaner.

She took the washing basket into her room and tipped the clean clothes onto the bed, folding them into six neat piles, one for each member of her family. She ignored the tears that insisted on spilling down her cheeks.

She didn't need Theo. She never had.

Then why did it feel like the glue was falling out of all the cracks in her heart she'd so carefully repaired?

"Oh, Theo," she said, wiping her tears with a pair of Jeff's underpants.

She'd never be free of his hold, not even in death.

———

Jeff couldn't exactly say he was sorry Theo was dead. Not that he'd admit it to anyone. He'd look like a real bastard if he said that.

If anything, it was a relief he was gone. Never again would he have to watch that rash crawl up Tamarin's neck when she spoke to him on the phone. Never again would he have to wipe away her tears when Theo forced her into a decision about Amber. Never again would he have to wonder if she harboured secret hopes of getting back together with him.

Finally, after all these years, he felt Tamarin belonged to him and only him. The third person in their marriage had left their lives for good.

He'd been so carefully watching for her reaction, he'd hardly noticed how devastated Amber was. It wasn't until Tamarin said something about her that he realised she hadn't come out of her bedroom since she'd heard the news. She just needed time. Teenagers were selfish—particularly teenagers like Amber. She'd be back posting selfies on Facebook in no time.

He knew he was being harsh. It was just hard to imagine anyone being that upset about Theo dying. He really hadn't been a very nice person. He'd left his wife with a newborn baby for goodness sake, and now people were talking about him like he'd been a saint.

Thankfully, so far Tamarin hadn't seemed that affected by the news. He'd even seen glimmers of her being happy about it. Amber wouldn't be able to move back in with her father now. And she'd be wealthy.

These were all unkind thoughts, but they were contained within the privacy of his head, so he figured he was allowed to think them.

If he were as unkind in his actions as he was in his thoughts, he would've killed Theo himself. The truth was that he hadn't. He may have fantasised about it a couple of times, but murder wasn't something he'd ever considered adding to his to-do list for real. Although, if he had such a list, then Theo most definitely would've been on top.

He appeared to have been on the top of Skye's list, too. What a heartless woman to kill her husband like that. Personally, he'd never trusted her motives. Plastic women were always up to something. That was why he'd married a real woman. There was nothing plastic about Tamarin. Theo really had been a dickhead leaving her. She never would have done that to him.

Maybe it was just as well the poor bastard had died before he found out about Skye faking her cancer. That news in itself might have killed him. It would certainly have killed his career.

Or maybe he did know? Maybe he was in on it. Perhaps Skye had told him she was going to come clean about it and he'd killed himself to escape the shame. That seemed believable for a man as gutless as him.

However it had happened, the result was the same. Theo was dead.

Tamarin came up behind him and slipped her arms around his waist.

"The kids are asleep," she said.

He turned to embrace her.

"What are you thinking about?" she asked.

"You," he said. "Always you."

He scooped her up into his arms and carried her from the room.

"What are you doing?" She shrieked with laughter. "You'll break your back."

He threw her down on their bed, kicked the door closed and made love to her in the only way he knew how.

Slowly. Softly. Gently.

Theo had never made love like that in his life. And now he never would.

————

Sammy slammed her bedroom door and leant against it, sobbing as loudly as she could manage.

It was no use. Her mother couldn't hear her. She hadn't heard anything she'd said for the past week. It was like her ears had stopped working. She walked around the house like some kind of zombie.

Her dad's ears were still working, but he was always at the office. He couldn't hear her all the way from there.

Amber's dad was dead. He wouldn't hear anything Amber said ever again, unless heaven was real and he was sitting on a cloud somewhere watching everything that was going on.

Amber had locked herself in her bedroom and hadn't let anyone in for ages. So much for the sleepovers.

But that wasn't why Sammy was crying. She was crying because everyone was treating her like a little kid. Nobody would tell her how the dying bit had happened. She'd seen people die on television, usually from heart attacks or bullets, but her dad said it hadn't been like that with Amber's dad. He went all white when he said it, then tried to change the subject, like he did when he didn't want to talk about something.

It was so *frustrating*. She thought about that word for a moment. It reminded her of when she'd been *furious*.

All the best, most powerful words started with an F. That must be why she heard people talk about the F-word.

————

"Fucking prick!"

Bruno shoved his hands into the pockets of his leather jacket and glared at the front cover of the newspaper on display outside the milk bar.

Why did that bastard have to go and get himself murdered? Who was going to bail him out when he got in trouble now?

Theo's hot little piece of *meow meow* was on the cover. Man, what he wouldn't do to get in her pants and have himself some of that. She was single now. Maybe he should have a crack.

Nah, he had some standards. Bros didn't do that to each other. There was a code when it came to things like that.

Anyway, he wished she wasn't single. That would mean Theo wasn't dead.

Prick.

If what the newspapers said was true, then she did it.

Death by chocolate, screamed the headline.

Not a bad headline, he supposed.

The one they'd used for him a few years ago was better. Someone had taken pot shots with an AK-47 through his bedroom window while he slept. The newspapers had been real clever with that one.

Bruno Martini: Shaken not stirred.

So, they reckoned Theo's wife did it. That sounded like bullshit to him.

Not that it really mattered who did it. The result was the same.

The pigs had better not try to pin it on him. He'd never baked a fuckin' brownie in his life. Or a fuckin' anything.

He kicked the pile of newspapers at his feet and watched them spill onto the footpath, the loose pages fluttering in the breeze.

The shopkeeper glanced up from behind the counter and looked away.

Smart guy. He knew better than to pick a fight with Bruno Martini. Nobody won a fight against The Great Bruno Martini.

He threw his shoulders back and continued down Sydney Road. What he needed was one of those Lebo pizzas. The sort with the mincemeat on top. He could sit down and eat it while he thought about who the fuck was going to represent him in court next time he needed it, which would probably be soon. It always was. He'd racked up frequent flyers at that courthouse. Too bad he couldn't cash them in.

He'd invested heavily in Theo over the years. Not just in a financial way. He'd raised him like he was his fuckin' mother. He'd practically breastfed that cunt. When they first met, he was so green he looked like Kermit the fuckin' frog.

But Bruno had seen his potential. He had a knack for things like that. He knew Theo would never let him down. He never did either. Loyal up until the day he died. He'd have laid down in front of a freight train if Bruno asked him to.

Maybe he'd have had a better chance in front of a train than he had with that brownie.

Poor bastard. What a piss weak way to go.

He thought about how he'd like to go one day. The words *blaze of glory* sprang to mind. That'd be sweet.

He saw himself with his arms outstretched, police bullets flying everywhere, a hot chick in a tight red dress screaming for him to save himself.

Tell my mother I love her, he'd call out, as he sank to his knees. Only, nobody would hear him over the cries of the hot chick as a bullet went straight to his heart, killing him instantly.

He shivered as he pulled his right hand from his pocket and made the sign of the cross.

Now that his lawyer was dead, this scenario seemed a little less fantasy and a little more possibility.

Why did Theo have to die?

Fucking prick.

———

Linda was at the drycleaner when Theo died. She'd arrived at the house to find the street swarming with police, reporters and ambulances. There was even a firetruck.

She knew immediately it had something to do with Theo. Maybe someone had come to even a score. People who associated with the likes of Bruno Martini didn't usually live to get their telegram from the Queen. Thank goodness her connection to Bruno had been severed along with her marriage.

She'd parked the car, unable to get anywhere close to the house, and sat staring at the commotion.

He was dead. He had to be. There couldn't possibly be this much fuss for any other reason. Unless it was Skye. Maybe she had a bad reaction to her medication. It would seem odd though. She'd looked well enough when she saw her that morning. Better than she'd looked earlier in the week anyway.

A man with a camera had walked past and Linda had quickly slipped out of her car to talk to him.

"What's going on in there?" she asked.

"Theo Manis died," he said, barely glancing at her as he weighed up his photo opportunities.

Despite having already figured this out, it came as a shock. Linda had only seen him the night before, coming through the front door as she was leaving. It was extraordinary to think that was the last night of his life. She wished she'd said something more significant to him other than goodbye.

"Who killed him?" she asked.

"Now, isn't that the million dollar question."

She realised she'd just assumed Theo was murdered. People died from natural causes all the time.

"Did you know him?" asked the photographer.

"No."

He gave her some kind of half-nod and walked away, clearly deciding she wasn't worth wasting any more of his time on.

She locked her car. It wasn't a lie. She didn't know him. She knew what brand of toothpaste Theo used, what size pants he wore and how he liked his steak cooked, but really she knew nothing about him at all.

His death barely made a mark on her. The only sadness she felt was for Amber. That girl loved her father. He hadn't deserved her love with the way he treated her, especially towards the end.

Poor Amber would be really messed up over this. She'd have to look out for her. She was the closest thing to a daughter she'd ever had. In the last few years, she'd had more conversations with her than with her own sons.

Linda had pushed through the crowd, explaining to a police officer who she was before being allowed through the front gate.

"Hey, wait!" called the photographer, who only five minutes ago had decided she wasn't worth talking to.

She ignored him and continued on towards the house.

A female police office with more freckles than bare skin led her to the side entrance and asked her to wait downstairs in the library.

It never occurred to Linda she could be a suspect until the detective arrived and started firing questions at her. He grunted at her answers, writing furiously in his notebook. Nothing she told him seemed to satisfy him. Nor did anything she said in the many interviews that followed in the days to come.

His reaction to her made her nervous and she had to remind herself she was innocent. The police just had a way of making you feel guilty, even when you weren't.

There was just one thing troubling her, but to tell the police about it would be dangerous. She was left feeling like she had a bomb strapped to her back. To tell them would mean instant detonation. Her life would explode and nothing would ever be the same. She'd had enough explosions in her life to see her through to her dying days. She didn't need any more.

No, she was not going to get involved. She'd answer any questions the police asked and she'd do it honestly. It wasn't her fault if they were failing to ask her the one question that had the potential to blow this case wide apart. It was probably nothing anyway. She was making a big deal over absolutely nothing.

Did she see Skye making brownies the day before Theo died? *Yes, she did.*

Did she see Skye offer the brownies to Theo or George? *No, George was eating cheese when she left for the day.*

Did she hear Skye tell George not to touch the brownies? *No, she didn't.*

Had she ever made brownies herself? *No, Skye liked to make all the sweets.*

Had she ever seen Amber bringing brownies into the house?

Well, they never thought to ask her that.

———

Amber was gutted. It was her fault. All of it. She'd thought she was doing the right thing and now her father was dead.

Her father! She loved him so much. How could this have happened?

She thought back to when this whole mess began.

It was those stupid diaries Clara wrote.

She'd found them one day on a shelf in Skye's dressing room. One of her friends at school had needed something to wear to a party and Amber had bragged she could swipe one of Skye's designer-label dresses without her noticing. She had so many clothes. Amber often stole them and just as she predicted, Skye never noticed. Her step-mother may not have cancer, but she sure was blind. Or maybe she was showing signs of early dementia like her mother.

She knew Skye believed she never went near her precious master bedroom, but the truth was she was a regular, often sifting through Skye's belongings when she wasn't home. It always paid to know as much as possible about your enemies. Besides, she was certain Skye went into her room when she wasn't home so all she was really doing was evening the score.

She came across the leather-bound diaries in Skye's dressing room, poorly hidden behind a pile of thousand-dollar sweaters.

All thoughts of her friend's wardrobe crisis fled her mind as she sat on the plush carpet and flicked through them.

Most of the diaries were in fairly good condition, apart from the one written at the time of Skye's birth, which had become dog-eared and ragged, falling open at certain entries as if it'd been read a thousand times.

Amber read these particular entries with great interest, devouring their every word. Finally, she'd found someone who could see Skye for who she was. Everyone else loved her. Even Jeff and her mother never spoke badly about her, although she was certain they must think nasty thoughts.

She felt like she had an ally in the most unlikely of corners. Clara seemed to hate and resent Skye almost as much as she did.

She felt a real connection to her.

She'd put the diaries back behind the sweaters, deciding it'd be less obvious if she borrowed only one at a time than to swipe the entire pile. They were a lot more interesting than the Jane Austen she was being made to read at school. Although, a lot of the themes were similar—love, betrayal, heartbreak ... it even had a Mr Darcy, with the equally as alluring name of Jacques Moubray. He sounded hot.

Over the following week she read them all (skipping the boring parts about ballet). In the final diary, the entries started to become as jumbled as Clara's dementia-addled mind. It was tragic. She wrote about her attempts to take her own life, always failing as her desire to live out the remainder of her clear-headed days won out. She was stuck in the ultimate Catch-22.

It was devastating.

Amber's dreams became haunted by Clara's pleas for help. She even visited her once pretending to be a fan, which was kind of true. She *was* a fan—those diaries were brilliantly written. She'd tucked her hair into a cap and worn her baggy jeans in case the nurses tried to describe her to Skye, who definitely wouldn't have approved of her being there.

The visit had been beyond awful. When she'd walked in, Clara had her nightdress half unbuttoned and chocolate smeared all over her face. Then she'd started behaving like some kind of demented ape, spitting at her and screeching, telling her to go away.

The horror of it had frozen Amber's brain and she found herself only able to operate in slow motion, not being able to snap herself back into action until Clara reached into her pants and flung a handful of shit at her.

She went to get a nurse and when they returned, Clara was standing naked in her bathroom, laughing when there was absolutely nothing worth laughing about.

It was frightening. The Clara she knew from the diaries would be horrified if she could see herself. No wonder she wanted to end her life before it came to this. She barely seemed human anymore.

Presumably Skye had also read the diaries. Why hadn't she helped her mother out of her misery and done what she was unable to do for herself? She was probably petrified she'd go to jail. Skye never did have much courage.

That was when Amber decided to go through with the plan that she'd been formulating.

Skye didn't have the guts to give her mother her wish, but she did. It was the least she could do. It was cruel to let anyone live like that. Even Linda agreed with her when she'd asked her about it.

And if she did it right, she could make sure Skye got the blame for it, thereby solving two problems at once. Clara would get the peaceful end she wished for and Skye would be in jail, far away from her for the rest of her days. There was no way her father would stand by a murderer. Especially not in his profession. It didn't matter how big Skye's boobs were.

Amber had sat at the kitchen counter with her headphones on watching Skye make her weekly batch of brownies so many times she knew the recipe by heart. All she'd have to do would be to wait until Skye went to bed for the night and mimic the recipe, baking a new batch (with a little bit of poison added in) and get rid of Skye's batch.

That was one advantage of such a large house. When Skye went to bed, she had no idea what was going on downstairs. Amber could never get away with something like that in her mother's minuscule house.

She tested out her plan a few times without the poison to see if it would work. Eating Skye's brownies was the best way to dispose of them. They were delicious, although didn't exactly do wonders for her waistline. She figured she could always lose the weight later once Skye was in jail.

Skye never once noticed the brownie switch. It probably helped that she didn't actually eat them herself. Far too many calories in a brownie for an anorexic bimbo to possibly consider consuming them.

It was a perfect plan, except for one very important part—the poison. Or lack thereof.

Amber did a few internet searches using Skye's laptop, and got very disheartened. It seemed this wouldn't be as easy as she'd thought.

It wasn't until the Great Shedroom Renovation that everything clicked into place. Ironic really, that it was actually Skye who solved the problem for her by convincing her father to kick her out of the house.

She'd been helping Jeff sort the rubbish from the old shed when she received a sign from the gods. An omen. Only recently she'd read *The Alchemist* by Paulo Coelho and he'd talked non-stop about the importance of listening to omens.

A carton had split open and four small but heavy boxes had fallen out, right on top of Amber's left foot.

She'd sat down on the grass to wriggle her toes and make sure they weren't broken, when she noticed exactly what it was that had nearly severed her toes.

There she was looking for the perfect poison and it had literally landed at her feet, practically begging her to use it. If that wasn't an omen, she didn't know what was.

The boxes were labelled as *Thall-Rat,* a product she'd read about in one of her many internet searches. It hadn't been sold in Australia since the 1950s, where it was once popular as an effective rat poison. The problem with it was that it was also an effective people poison with a spate of murders and accidental deaths so prolific that it had to be withdrawn from sale.

It was perfect.

She'd shoved the boxes into her backpack and fossicked through the junk looking for more. She didn't know how much she was going to need. Were four boxes enough? She soon realised they were going to have to be. They were the only ones there.

She decided to wait until she moved out until she started adding the poison to the brownies. Better to remove herself from the scene of the crime. She didn't want to end up as a suspect herself. She could bake them in her kitchenette in her shedroom and take them to Malvern to switch them. She just needed to make sure she kept a key.

It was nerve-racking the first time. She was paranoid about accidentally licking her fingers with that delicious, chocolaty mixture, but managed to successfully bake and make the switch.

It was the first of many switches she made. Linda saw her doing it once, but she was busy and it didn't seem like she'd paid any attention. Besides, even if she had noticed, she wouldn't say anything to get

Amber in trouble. They had an understanding. Linda had often said she was the only person in the house who ever treated her with any decency. She wouldn't tell on her, especially since she'd been the one to give her the idea with all that talk of putting pillows over her head if ever she got like Clara. So really, she was implicated as well. There was no way she was going to talk.

She started with a small quantity of thallium, but another visit to Clara after the second batch told her she was suffering. Her hair was falling out and her extremities were going numb. Classic signs of thallium poisoning. She didn't want her to be in pain. She had to speed it up and get it over with. It would be cruel otherwise.

So, Amber decided to make a super batch. The kind that would finish anyone off.

And of all the batches her father and Uncle George had decided to eat, it had to be the Super Batch. They could have eaten any other batch and nothing would've happened other than a few minor side effects.

Now Clara was still alive, and her father was dead.

Uncle George would be, too, if it weren't for the stroke of luck (another omen, perhaps) that Amber had stolen Skye's spare phone and had it in her school bag the day Sophie picked her up on her way to the hospital.

She'd found the phone tucked in the pocket of Skye's jacket when she'd been returning one of the diaries. She'd typed in Skye's password (the same one she used on all her devices—7593, the numbers on a phone's keypad corresponding to the letters of her name). It seemed she was using the phone to impersonate a woman called Elle to flirt with Amber's father. It was obviously one of those sick fantasy games married people played. She'd nearly vomited on Skye's carpet.

Knowing it would drive Skye crazy if she thought she'd lost the phone, she decided to swipe it. She could have a great laugh with the girls at school over some of those messages Skye had sent as Elle.

When she realised Uncle George had been poisoned, she'd pulled Skye's dodgy phone from her bag and quickly sent a message to Sophie, hoping to save him in time. It was the only way she could think to tell her about Prussian Blue without incriminating herself.

She'd had to plant the phone on Skye later. She knew exactly which section of the front fence was in a blind spot of the security cameras and threw it over into the garden for the police to find. Thankfully they had. She was worried the gardener might run it over with his mower.

She had no idea when she'd been texting Sophie that her father had eaten the brownies, too. She just assumed George had snuck one off the plate in the fridge when Skye wasn't looking. Her father *never* ate those brownies. Skye had been very clear with him not to touch them.

The only good thing to come out of this mess was that Skye had been arrested and was likely to spend at least the next twenty years in jail. There was so much evidence against her. Internet searches for thallium on her laptop. The empty boxes of Thall-Rat hidden in her garage. The mobile phone in her garden. The brownie crumbs in her kitchen.

Skye had also helped enormously by ruining her reputation with the fake cancer. Now that she'd lied about something as huge as that nobody believed a word she said. She must be a murderer. She clearly had issues. Why would they look at a teenager when they had a full-blown psychopath in their clutches? She hadn't even called an ambulance for at least an hour after her husband died. What kind of normal person would do that?

No normal person.

Maybe if she had called an ambulance sooner they would've been able to get him some Prussian Blue in time.

Now, according to her mother, Amber was set to inherit her father's estate. It would be held in trust for her until she turned eighteen.

But she'd forego all the money (she'd even forego seeing Skye in jail) if only she could have her father back. It was a mess.

She'd committed both the most perfect crime and the most imperfect one. She'd gotten away with murder. The problem was, she'd murdered the wrong person.

———

Detective Hooke sipped on his beer. It tasted even better now he'd had to wait so long for it.

It'd been an arduous week at the station. The other guys had gone straight home to their families, exhausted. Hopefully their wives hadn't baked them any brownies to welcome them. As he didn't have a wife to go home to, he headed to the pub to have that beer he'd been dreaming of all week. It didn't matter he was alone. After the day he'd had, alone suited him just fine.

That Skye Manis was one twisted piece of work.

He'd really thought she was going to crack and confess, but she'd held firm, seeming genuinely perplexed as to why nobody believed her story. She wouldn't even admit to trying to poison her mother. Nobody else would've done that. He might have been prepared to accept her poisoning of Theo was accidental if only she'd admitted to that.

Screw her. If she was going to lie about cancer, then about poisoning her mother, as far as he was concerned she was lying about everything. He felt sorry for Theo having been married to a psycho like her.

Death had changed his perspective on his former rival. It was hard to hate someone who could no longer breathe. All the poor bastard had wanted was to get laid, not poisoned to death with dessert. She could've at least screwed him to death. It might've been worth it then.

He ordered a second beer, watching the bartender pull on the tap sending cloudy liquid swirling into the glass before it settled to an amber colour when the oxygen escaped.

It was strange the way something as transparent as air could change the colour of a liquid. It was no different to people. Usually it was the ones you least expected who had the ability to completely change your world.

He liked that analogy better than the one of the pond, not because it was necessarily better at explaining people, but simply because it involved beer.

The bartender slid the glass across to him, leaving him with his thoughts.

He raised his drink in the air, lifting his eyes to the ceiling.

"This one's for you, mate," he said to Theo, certain that wherever he was he could hear him.

As the cool liquid ran down this throat, he ignored the feeling it left in his gut. Skye was as guilty as she was cancer-free. The case was closed.

12 MONTHS AFTER THE BREAK

Skye pulled at the bright green fabric of her polyester tracksuit pants. They were hideous. Although, they were quite comfortable. So was the baggy green tee-shirt she wore them with. If she closed her eyes, she could almost pretend she was naked.

Screw comfortable. She'd happily swap these shapeless sacks for her MaxMara pants with the seams that dug into her legs and her Dolce and Gabbana shirt with the label that itched the back of her neck.

Not to mention her shoes. Oh, how she missed her beautiful shoes. These flat, rubber clogs made her look like a clown. She'd give anything to see her Christian Louboutins one more time. She wondered where they were now. She'd been stuck in this wretched place for a year. They could be anywhere. As long as they weren't attached to Amber's feet. That would just about kill her. Thankfully Amber's giant hooves would never fit into them.

It was these kinds of thoughts that plagued Skye. She wished she didn't have so much time to think. Prison had robbed her of her freedom, handing her the curse of time in its place.

There was just so much time in here, hovering in the halls like a dark presence, creeping under the door of her cell, snaking its way into her dreams reminding her it was there.

How long was it until lunchtime, exercise time, shower time, library time? How much time had the judge given her? How much time did she have left? What time was she locked in for the night? What time was she woken in the morning?

Time ruled her life, with the ticking of the clock of equal importance to the beating of her heart. Perhaps that's why jail sentences were referred to as hard time. There was nothing easy about the way the clock ticked in here, each seemingly interminable hour stretching impossibly longer than the one to have passed before it.

She thought about all the time she used to spend putting together outfits in the morning or carefully applying her make up. There was no more of that. Nor was there any more having her nails painted, legs waxed, eyebrows threaded or skin peeled. No more laser treatments, massages, spray-on tans or botox.

Not to mention all the time she used to spend at the hairdresser having cuts, colours, blow waves and treatments. Her poor hair was serving a prison sentence all of its own. It'd grown back now in a mousy brown colour she hadn't seen since she was a child. It hung around her neck in greasy strands. There was no way she was going to visit the hairdresser at the prison. Her fellow inmates were a walking advertisement of exactly what damage they could do. No, she'd wait until she got out of this place and have her hair done in a proper salon. It could grow to her ankles for all she cared.

Long gone were the days spent trawling through her favourite online stores or walking the length of Chapel Street with bags of shopping hanging from her arms, replaced by days spent unwinding cords from airline headphones. She thought this was a particularly cruel job to offer prisoners. It was a very effective way of rubbing it in that out in the world people were flying to exotic destinations without so much as a thought spared for the women behind bars ensuring their auditory pleasure was taken care of during their journey.

The more headphones she untangled, the more her grief wound itself around her soul.

She missed Theo. She missed him like she'd miss breathing if the world ran out of air. She half expected him to turn up on visiting days and had to remind herself he was dead.

He'd be outraged if he could see how she was being treated in here as if she were some kind of number. It was like being back in the call centre, only on steroids. She had all individuality stripped of her. She wore the same ugly clothes as the other inmates, ate the same awful food, slept on the same hard beds and washed in the same dirty showers. She'd been treated with a bit of celebrity fascination when she first arrived, but that hadn't lasted long. People's memories were short.

Her father's memory was one of them. Since all this happened, he'd forgotten all about her. She'd sent him several letters, but he hadn't replied. That hurt. To think she came so close to having him in her life only to have it torn away by this ridiculous misunderstanding. All she'd ever wanted was to get to know him. If only he'd give her the opportunity to explain things.

She hadn't bothered to try to explain herself to the other women in here, having quickly learnt it was far better for them to think of her as dangerous. If they knew how harmless she really was she could become a target.

They all called her Manis. She liked that. It helped her pretend she was a different person. Skye didn't belong in prison. It also reminded her of Theo. He might've been torn from her side, but his name stayed with her. The last remaining symbol of the love they'd once shared.

She'd been given a life sentence, found guilty of Theo's murder as well as attempting to murder George and her mother. The prosecution had successfully convinced a jury she'd been slowly poisoning her mother and the power had gone to her head, so she decided to get rid of both Theo and George—Theo for his money and George because she'd never liked him.

It was ridiculous! Theo was worth far more to her alive. As for George, she'd never liked him, but she had no reason to want him dead. There were plenty of people far higher up on her hit list than him if she were that kind of person (which she most definitely was not).

George had actually stood on the stand, sworn on the bible and said she offered him the brownies. He'd cried every time he said Theo's name. One of the jurors looked like she was about to start crying, too.

How could he sleep at night? She'd distinctly told him not to touch those stupid brownies. She remembered saying it. Once again, she cursed herself for destroying the note that proved it.

The police claimed the history on her laptop was littered with searches for effective poisons, including thallium. She'd never searched for any such thing. Clearly, they were making that up to support their case. It wasn't unheard of for police to do things like that. She'd watched a whole series on Netflix about that once.

Even Dr Addison had turned on her with the report he submitted to the court. It was strange listening to his assessment of her. Words were fired, hitting her like rubber bullets, bouncing off and leaving bruises all over her body.

Disrupted moral development as a result of childhood neglect. Smack!

Lack of remorse coupled with limited understanding of the impact of her actions. Wham!

Limited ability to empathise with others. Pow!

Egocentric with elements of narcissism and psychopathy. Boom!

Dr Addison did say she had no apparent motivation for killing Theo, stating she had nothing to gain by his death, but these words were lost amongst all the defamatory statements he made upfront. The jury had already convicted her in their heads before they even got to hear that part of the report.

He also said he believed her grief was real and her lie about having cancer was a separate issue and should be treated as such.

This was an impossible request. The jury could no more separate her from her lie than they could the stars from the sky. She'd become her lie and was wearing it draped around her shoulders like a neon shawl. It was the only thing people could see when they looked at her.

Why would they believe her word over what George had to say? She was a narcissist with disrupted moral development. Of course, she'd offered George and Theo the brownies. George had no reason to lie. So, why had he?

He was the one person who knew for certain she hadn't done it. The only thing she could think of was he believed she'd been trying to poison her mother and therefore blamed her for Theo's death. If that was the case, he'd be determined to see her behind bars for as long as possible.

Unless he was covering up for someone.

But who?

As much as she wanted it to be Rin or Sophie, she now knew it wasn't. The brownies had been found in her own kitchen. It couldn't have been either of them.

It could only have been Linda or Amber.

Amber was far too young and stupid to be able to carry off such a crime. She'd never made a brownie in her life.

Which left Linda. She was the only other person with access to the kitchen. And she knew how to cook.

She was also the only one she allowed in her dressing room. She must have found the diaries and read them. She knew her mother wanted to die. She probably thought she was being humane putting her out of her misery. Or maybe she was setting her up so she could get her hands on Theo. She'd seen the way she looked at him.

Maybe a younger housekeeper might have been a better idea after all. Or at least one who had references she could've checked.

If she kept turning the facts over in her mind, agitating them and sifting through them, everything would become clear eventually.

The thing about the truth is it always rises to the surface.

All she had to do was wait.

THE END

Want more?

Check out The Girl Who Never by HC Michaels now

MORE BY HC MICHAELS

What would you do if your DNA linked you to a crime you didn't commit?

Elvira has a heartbreaking secret. Tessa is more connected to the family she works for than she realises. Kosta has more to hide than all of them.

When this fractured family is brought together by a tragic death, they must travel to a tropical island to organise the funeral. They're about to discover they're not the only ones harbouring explosive truths.

A string of violent crimes follows them, and nobody can figure out the connection. When a member of this troubled family becomes the next victim, the suspicion grows. Key evidence suggests one of them is a serial killer. But how do you prove your innocence when everything is pointing to you?

As the case blows wide open, Elvira, Tessa and Kosta are about to discover if blood really is thicker than water.

Fans of Gone Girl, The Woman in the Window, and The Girl on the Train will love by the twists in this psychological thriller by HC Michaels.

Grab your copy now!

ABOUT THE AUTHOR

HC Michaels lives in Melbourne, Australia. When not writing, she teaches public relations at an online university, and lives with her husband and two sons. She doesn't enjoy cooking but has been known to threaten people with making brownies...

HC Michaels also writes award-winning dystopian and fantasy novels under the name Heidi Catherine. You can find out more at www.heidicatherine.com

(dis)ABILITIES

and the GOSPEL

How to
Bring People
with
SPECIAL NEEDS
Closer to CHRIST

Danyelle Ferguson & Lynn Parsons, M.S.

CFI
Springville, Utah

ISBN 13: 978-1-59955-820-2

Published by CFI, an imprint of Cedar Fort, Inc., 2373 W. 700 S., Springville, UT 84663
Distributed by Cedar Fort, Inc., www.cedarfort.com

LIBRARY OF CONGRESS CATALOGING-IN-PUBLICATION DATA

Ferguson, Danyelle, author.
  (dis)abilities and the gospel : how to bring people with special needs closer to Christ /
Danyelle Ferguson and Lynn Parsons.
    p. cm.
  Includes bibliographical references.
  ISBN 978-1-59955-820-2
  1. Disabilities--Religious aspects. 2. Parents of children with
disabilities--Religious aspects. 3. Children with disabilities--Family
relationships. 4. Church of Jesus Christ of Latter-day Saints. I. Parsons,
Lynn (Lynn D.), author. II. Title.
  BT741.3.F47 2011
  259'.4--dc22

                              2011000418

Cover design by Danie Romrell
Cover design © 2011 by Lyle Mortimer
Edited and typeset by Kelley Konzak

Printed in the United States of America

10 9 8 7 6 5 4 3 2 1

Printed on acid-free paper

I would like to dedicate this book to two very special people. First, to my son Isaac. I am grateful Heavenly Father sent you to be a part of my life. I love you very much and am proud of who you are, inside and out. Second, to my husband, John. Thank you for being my best friend. You have encouraged me through some very difficult times. Thank you for always making me laugh, standing by my side, and loving me each and every day. I'm so blessed to share this journey through life with you. I love you, sweetie. I'd also like to send lots of love and hugs to my other munchkins—MJ, Rob, and Anna. Each of you makes my day brighter and happier.

—*Danyelle Ferguson*

This book is dedicated to my family. Earl, you are a wonderful husband who encourages me to follow my dreams while making your own dinner, doing the laundry, and postponing plans so I can write. Cassie, Tami, John, Earl Ryan, Heather, and Melanie, your cheerleading keeps me going over and through all obstacles. I am proud to be your mother (and mother-in-law). James and William, you inspire your grandmother to keep on working to improve the lives of others.

—*Lynn Parsons*

Contents

ACKNOWLEDGMENTS

In the course of writing *(dis)Abilities and the Gospel*, many people have encouraged and helped us along the way, and therefore we have a slew of thank-yous to send out.

First, we would like to thank our Father in Heaven. He inspired us to write this book and then stood by our sides as we outlined, researched, wrote, and rewrote each chapter. When we were stuck, He answered our prayers through promptings and by sending individuals into our lives with the answers we needed. We truly feel the title and byline for this book should be *"(dis)Abilities and the Gospel* by Heavenly Father, with the helping hands of Danyelle Ferguson and Lynn Parsons." We hope He is as happy with the finished result as we are.

Next, we would like to thank our own children with special needs and all the kids and adults with disabilities with whom we've worked over the years. Our love for each of you and our desire to share Heavenly Father's love for you was what kept our fingers glued to the keyboard. Our greatest wish is that each of you will always remember that you are a precious child of God and that He loves you.

Many parents, siblings, teachers, church leaders, and professionals contributed stories, feedback, tips, and insights. A great big thank-you to Jill Hessler, Julie Presley, Julie Newbry, Tom Knowlton, Roselyn Marble Baird, Teri Fronk, Christopher Phillips, Brenda Winegar, Karen Fairchild, Megan Heath, Kimberly Job, Johanna Wilkin, Kimberly Daley, Sandra Cooper, JaNae Hakes, Lori McIlwain of *The National Autism Association*, and Katie Steed from Brigham Young University.

Some contributors wished to remain anonymous. You know who you are. *Merci beaucoup!*

We would like to send a special thank-you to Doug Hind and Brent Meisinger from the Curriculum Department of The Church of Jesus Christ of Latter-day Saints. They answered many questions, gave excellent feedback, and stepped in to help during copyright approvals. We are tremendously grateful for your support. Speaking of copyrights, thank you to everyone who responded and worked with us for copyright permissions—Ruth Ann Johnson from the Intellectual Property Office of The Church of Jesus Christ of Latter-day Saints, Pat Williams from Deseret Book, Peggy Stack from the *Salt Lake Tribune*, and Rick Hall from *Deseret News*.

We'd like to send a huge shout-out to our cheerleaders—SuperEdits group, AuthorsIncognito, LDS Storymakers, Lisa Mangum from Deseret Book, Kathy Jenkins from Covenant Communications, and everyone who continually emailed and asked when the book would be available. Behind each project, there's a support team encouraging and cheering the writers on. We'd love to send our team lots of Hershey's chocolate kisses and hugs, but we were afraid they'd all melt in the mail.

Before any book is complete and ready to send to a publisher, it goes through several rounds of readers who nitpick and tear it to shreds—all to make the book shine! Thank you to everyone who made our manuscript bleed with red ink—Heather Justesen, Christine Bryant, Rebecca Talley, Lisa Swinton, Regina Sirois, Keisha Hansen, John Ferguson, and Tristi Pinkston.

Of course, this book wouldn't be in your hands right now without Cedar Fort and their confidence in our project. Thank you to Jennifer Fielding; Lyle Mortimer; our editor, Kelley Konzak; and our awesome cover designer, Danie Romrell. This valuable resource would not have been successful without your support.

An extra special thank-you goes to our spouses—John (Danyelle's sweetie) and Earl (Lynn's main squeeze). Thank you for picking up the slack when the sinks filled with dishes and dirty clothes accumulated into mountains. We are grateful that when times got tough—including hospital stays and computer meltdowns right before our deadline—you not only called off work and jumped in to help but also prayed for us and kept telling us over and over that it would all work out. And you were right. Thank you for being our rocks.

If there is just one thing we have learned during this journey, it is that when Heavenly Father has a work for you to do, He also creates opportunities for you to discover and choose along the way. Because we live in different states, we didn't meet until the book was completed. At the beginning of our coauthorship, we struggled with sending documents through email and keeping track of which document was the most current edit. We were grateful when Danyelle's husband introduced us to a (then) new online tool. Google Docs made collaborating a breeze! So thank you, thank you to Google. Your awesome program made it a joy to work together!

And finally, we would like to thank Heavenly Father for putting us together. It's a rather interesting and inspiring tale about how we met online. We were surprised at how our personalities, experiences, and ideas complemented each other so well and helped us forge a strong respect and friendship with each other. Who would have ever thought that two women—living in different states and at very different points of their lives—would meet on a Yahoo LDS Autism group and decide to work together on a book to help families and church leaders teach the gospel to individuals with special needs. Our friendship is just one more unexpected blessing Heavenly Father planted in our lives.

INTRODUCTION

Danyelle Ferguson

When my husband and I were newlyweds, I was asked to teach the three-year-old Sunday School class. My response was, "Who, me?" I joined the Church as a teenager and, quite honestly, never thought about what the younger kids did on Sundays.

During those first few years, I taught children with a variety of personalities. Some were sweet while others were rambunctious bouncers who sapped all my energy. I looked forward to being released as a teacher . . . only to find myself asked to serve as the children's music leader. It wasn't until our oldest son was diagnosed with autism that the most basic Christian truth finally sank deep into my soul—each of us is a precious child of God who is dearly loved.

By the time my son reached his ninth birthday, my husband and I had encountered the challenges of intense therapies, destructive behaviors, communication gaps, social awareness, and endless education meetings. We had also shared triumphs—our son's first sentence, the first prayer he said on his own, and his first Special Olympics medal. We've celebrated each step forward, developed eternal family relationships, and leaned on our Father in Heaven for direction and inspiration all along the way.

While *(dis)Abilities and the Gospel* began as a guide to help families and Church leaders from my own church (The Church of Jesus Christ of Latter-day Saints), it quickly became apparent that these strategies were applicable to any denomination and classroom setting. *(dis)Abilities and*

I

the Gospel will help families and church leaders teach the gospel of Jesus Christ to individuals with mental disabilities such as autism, Down syndrome, ADD, ADHD, traumatic brain injury, and more.

If you are a church teacher working with individuals with special needs, it can be overwhelming—especially if you have little or no experience in this area. The "General Information" and "Teaching Strategies" sections contain information and guidance adaptable to any age or class, such as communication between the teacher and parents, adapting lessons, and supporting positive behavior.

If you are a parent of a child with special needs, your life is filled with school meetings, therapists, and doctors, accompanied by the stress of wondering if you are doing everything you can for your child. Church can be especially stressful. Normally we associate going to church with comforting spiritual experiences. For a family with children with special needs, the experience can be quite different. Sometimes, just staying through the first twenty minutes is a major accomplishment. In the "Family" section, you will find tips for making it through meetings as well as chapters covering topics such as teaching prayer, developing sibling relationships, keeping your marriage strong, and surviving the holidays.

Families and leaders from The Church of Jesus Christ of Latter-day Saints may have a difficult time answering questions about baptism, priesthood advancement, temple attendance, and marriage. In the "Primary," "Young Men & Young Women," and "Adults" sections, you will find chapters with LDS-specific questions, answers, and inspiring stories from families, siblings, and Church teachers.

The very last section, "I Am a Child of God," is a compilation of stories sent to us from families and church leaders, talking about their relationships with the special spirits in their lives. These stories are filled with love and lessons learned. You will definitely want a box of tissues nearby.

Lynn and I both desire that families and church leaders understand that they are not alone. There are many people struggling with these issues. We hope this book will help, guide, and encourage you as you teach the gospel of Jesus Christ, regardless of religious denomination, to all special spirits, young and old.

GLOSSARY OF LDS TERMS

Achievement Days: An organization for girls eight through eleven years of age.

Articles of Faith: The thirteen fundamental beliefs of The Church of Jesus Christ of Latter-day Saints.

Bishop: Leader of a local congregation, called a ward.

Bishopric: The leadership of a local congregation, consisting of three men: the bishop and two counselors.

Calling: A volunteer job at church, such as Sunday School teacher.

CTR: An abbreviation that reminds us to "Choose the Right."

Family Home Evening: A family meeting usually held on Monday nights.

General Conference: A twice-yearly gathering of members of The Church of Jesus Christ of Latter-day Saints that is broadcast worldwide.

Home Teachers: Priesthood holders who visit families monthly.

Joseph Smith, Jr.: The first modern-day prophet of The Church of Jesus Christ of Latter-day Saints.

Junior Primary: Sunday School classes and music time for children ages three to seven.

Mutual: The weekly activity night for young men and young women ages twelve to eighteen.

Nursery: Sunday School class for children ages eighteen months to three years.

Priesthood: A power given to worthy males ages twelve years and older that allows them different levels of authority to care for the Church.

Relief Society: An organization for women ages eighteen and above that includes Sunday lessons and other activities.

Sacrament: The partaking of bread and water in remembrance of Jesus Christ.

Sacrament Meeting: The general meeting for the entire congregation in which the sacrament is blessed and passed.

Seminary: A scripture study class for teens, often held at six o'clock in the morning during the school year.

Senior Primary: Sunday School classes and music time for children ages eight through eleven.

Sharing Time: The general gathering of Primary children to sing songs and be taught a group lesson, held on Sunday.

Stake: A collection of wards or branches ranging from five to twelve in number and run by the stake presidency (president and two counselors).

Sunbeams: Sunday School class for children age three.

Visiting Teacher: A member of Relief Society who visits two or three other female members each month.

Ward: A congregation of The Church of Jesus Christ of Latter-day Saints, usually of three hundred members or more. Fewer members are normally formed into a branch.

Young Men: Sunday School–type organization for boys ages twelve to eighteen.

Young Women: Sunday School–type organization for girls ages twelve to eighteen.

General Information

GOSPEL VIEWS ON CHILDREN WITH SPECIAL NEEDS

by Lynn Parsons

When I was first diagnosed with rheumatoid arthritis, my visiting teacher asked me what I had done to make God curse me. Many members of the Church have this type of misconception. They erroneously believe that if you keep all the commandments, you will have protection from all of life's difficulties. This is not the case. In fact, "Blessed is the man whom thou chastenest, O Lord" (Psalms 94:12). Our General Authorities have provided us with guidance and direction regarding those with disabilities.

Many church leaders have sought to understand and address the challenges of parents of children with special needs, answer questions about why these difficulties occur, give words of comfort to those concerned about the future of their children, and try to help other ward members understand the challenges of having a child with a disability. Most importantly, they have given the teachers and leaders of those with disabilities a challenge to help these children reach their full potential.

Difficulties

It is easy to feel that no one understands the complexities of your unique situation. However, our leaders can and do have compassion for the daily struggles experienced by persons with disabilities and their families. This includes the initial shock of learning that a loved one is not as we anticipated, learning to cope with lost dreams, and dealing with the daily challenges that arise.

President Thomas S. Monson said,

"In our lives, sickness comes to loved ones, accidents leave their

cruel marks of remembrance, and tiny legs that once ran are imprisoned in a wheelchair. Mothers and fathers who anxiously await the arrival of a precious child sometimes learn that all is not well with this tiny infant. A missing limb, sightless eyes, a damaged brain, or the term 'Down syndrome' greets the parents, leaving them baffled, filled with sorrow, and reaching out for hope."[1]

President Monson continues to describe the self-recrimination that can lead to an unproductive downward spiritual spiral.

> There follows the inevitable blaming of oneself, the condemnation of a careless action, and the perennial questions: "Why such a tragedy in our family?" "Why didn't I keep her home?" "If only he hadn't gone to that party." "How did this happen?" "Where was God?" "Where was a protecting angel?"
>
> *If, why, where, how*—those recurring words—do not bring back the lost son, the perfect body, the plans of parents, or the dreams of youth. Self-pity, personal withdrawal, or deep despair will not bring the peace, the assurance, or help which are needed. Rather, we must go forward, look upward, move onward, and rise heavenward.
>
> It is imperative that we recognize that whatever has happened to us has happened to others. They have coped and so must we. We are not alone. Heavenly Father's help is near.[2]

President Boyd K. Packer has explained that the antidote to this is an eternal perspective. When we concentrate on present problems, they can seem overwhelming and never-ending. He points out that we need to focus on the fact that we are indeed our Heavenly Father's children and the struggles of this life are temporary. President Packer has observed that while it may be difficult to pull our thoughts away from the current crisis, a more heavenly view will strengthen us, provide comfort, and allow us to concentrate on those things that are truly important.[3]

As difficult as it may be to pull back from the problems of today and try to focus on eternity, it is this very change in perspective that will provide us with the spiritual strength, comfort, and focus we need to endure to the end.

Why

When something tragic occurs, it is natural for those involved to ask "Why?" We want to make sense of our lives and look for ways to prevent future mishaps. Sometimes we must accept that we may not

understand the "why" during our mortal probation. President Boyd K. Packer addresses this question.

> I must first, and with emphasis, clarify this point: It is natural for parents with handicapped children to ask themselves, "What did we do wrong?" The idea that *all* suffering is somehow the direct result of sin has been taught since ancient times. It is false doctrine. That notion was even accepted by some of the early disciples until the Lord corrected them.
>
> "As Jesus passed by, he saw a man which was blind from his birth.
>
> "And his disciples asked him, saying, Master, who did sin, this man, or his parents, that he was born blind?
>
> "Jesus answered, Neither hath this man sinned, nor his parents: but that the works of God should be made manifest in him." (John 9:1–3)
>
> There is little room for feelings of guilt in connection with handicaps. Some handicaps may result from carelessness or abuse, and some through addiction of parents. But most of them do not. Afflictions come to the innocent.[4]

Comfort

Perhaps the best words of comfort come from our knowledge of the plan of salvation. President Boyd K. Packer tells us that all spirits had perfect forms while in premortality and that current deformities are purely physical.[5]

President Monson also reminds us of the glories of eternal life that we will experience in addition to our physical healing.

> There will surely come that day, even the fulfillment of the precious promise from the Book of Mormon:
>
> "The soul shall be restored to the body, and the body to the soul; yea, and every limb and joint shall be restored to its body; yea, even a hair of the head shall not be lost; but all things shall be restored to their proper and perfect frame. . . .
>
> "And then shall the righteous shine forth in the kingdom of God." (Alma 40:23, 25)[6]

Empathy

It is indeed difficult to comprehend the challenges faced by families who care for those with special needs. While complete understanding

may not be possible unless you have "walked a mile in their shoes," we can still achieve some common feeling. We must look for common ground, learn to listen with compassion, and teach our children empathy.

Efforts to find common ground do not have to be onerous. It can be as simple as a remark. A small girl ran headlong into my husband in the airport. He was hurt slightly, but he recognized the exhaustion in her young mother. As this harried parent apologized, he replied, "That's okay. We have four of our own." He could feel her gratitude for his appreciation of her struggles. If you find it hard to relate to those with disabilities, remember that most people will struggle with physical or mental handicaps at some point in their lives.

As you develop and express these feelings of empathy, please remember to teach them to your children. You may choose to teach similarities rather than differences during family home evening or as you encounter others in your daily life. Show your children how to look at the spirit beneath the outward appearance. Encourage kindness and service toward those with disabilities, and you will discover one day that your children have learned to appreciate people for their diversity.

Challenges

In addition to everyday physical, emotional, and social challenges, the families of those with disabilities face the challenge of teaching their children what they need to know in order to help them follow God's plan. We must remember that individuals with disabilities bear some responsibility for their own salvation. We are all accountable before God and will be judged according to the understanding and abilities we have been given.

Finding the balance between sympathetic assistance and teaching responsibility is difficult. Do not let yourself be so overcome with sympathy that you remove opportunities for your family member to learn and grow by accepting responsibility or focus so much on achieving goals that you forget to accommodate disabilities. This challenge varies from family to family and should be considered carefully, prayed for often, and done with the guidance of the Spirit.

Each teacher and leader within the Church has been given a sacred responsibility from our Heavenly Father. Inherent in our callings are challenges. In addition to the responsibilities outlined in our manuals,

we are to love those we serve, understand our learners, and do all we can to serve those with disabilities.

As a first step, we must truly learn to love all our students, not just the "teacher pleasers" or those who are our friends. We must exhibit true charity to all our students, which will enable both teacher and learner to be more sensitive to spiritual promptings. It has been my experience that those who are the most difficult to have in class need to participate the most and will ultimately be my favorite students and the most rewarding to teach.

Understanding any group as individuals is not easy, but it is essential to good teaching. Before we can instruct anyone, we need to recognize the gospel experience of each class member, his or her background, and how that person relates to others. When we strive to learn about each of Heavenly Father's children, we become more like Him. We are better able to meet their needs and help them feel the Spirit and reach their potential.

Some teachers may be afraid that students with disabilities will not be able to learn the curriculum. While these students may learn in a different manner and progress at a different speed, our efforts are worth it, no matter how small the gain seems to be. Slight improvement is still progress. I'm sure the angels rejoice just as much over a little one who has learned a simple prayer as those who can quote long memorized passages of scripture.

Even if all that child learns is that his teacher loves him, he is accepted by his classmates, and he can feel the Spirit, those lessons may be all he needs at that particular time. Please be understanding of any learning disabilities, cognitive challenges, or physical problems class members may face. But remember that the important things are our similarities. We all need love, acceptance, gospel instruction, spiritual opportunities, group membership, and the chance to perform service.

Above all, we must remember that Heavenly Father knows us better than we know ourselves and that we are uniquely placed in the world. Teachers, leaders, and congregation members are put where they are for a reason. We need to be mindful of Heavenly Father's plan and conscious of the lessons He has for us. These may be things we can learn in no other way.

Church leaders have frequently encouraged us to bear each other's burdens. This may include helping out with extra bills, showing

appreciation to leaders and teachers who serve those with disabilities, giving time for respite care, or seeking other ways to ease the load these families face constantly.

We should always remember the words of our leaders and seek to serve our brothers and sisters in the gospel. We must remember that disability can come to anyone at any time and that we will not be exalted if we seek only to save ourselves. Then will we experience truly charitable feelings toward these spirits and become more like Jesus Christ in the process. This is indeed a great blessing.

Notes

1. Thomas S. Monson, "Miracles of Faith," *Ensign*, Jul. 2004, 2.
2. Ibid., 3.
3. Boyd K. Packer, "The Moving of the Water," *Ensign*, May 1991, 7.
4. Monson, "Miracles of Faith," 7.
5. Packer, "The Moving of the Water," 7.
6. Monson, "Miracles of Faith," 7.

Getting to Know You

A Portfolio to Introduce Your Child to Teachers, Aides, and Church Leaders

by Danyelle Ferguson

Each year, new teachers, aides, or church leaders have an opportunity to work with your child. From year to year, your child progresses and changes. Sometimes what worked one year doesn't work the next year. An effective way to introduce your child is to create a small portfolio or document all about him. Below is an example from a parent who sent me one of her portfolios from when her son was five years old.

Dear Sister (insert name) and Primary Leaders,

My son has a high-functioning form of autism. When he was little, he had a hard time learning that objects have names and that he needed to indicate his wants and needs to others. He also had to be taught how to play with toys appropriately and be reminded to look at other people. He has made tremendous progress! Yet, he still has autism. He doesn't look different than other children, but he still needs a lot of support to be able to keep up with his same-age peers.

Some things you should know about him that will help him in Primary:

Even though he now talks well and has a big vocabulary, his understanding is still several years behind. It helps to speak in shorter, simpler sentences and make sure he understands before expecting him to follow through.

Sometimes his speech can be very repetitive and seem entirely out of context. This is common when he is parroting something he just

heard. He is easily redirected by asking him to say something else, like "Primary is fun!"

He has made a lot of progress with being interested in other children, but he still sometimes has a hard time interacting with them. Sometimes he will completely avoid contact with other kids. Other times he will try to join in, but he may do something kind of odd to initiate the interaction (ex. asking if he can hug someone's elbow or kissing someone's shoe).

My son is easily overstimulated by certain environments. The noise, commotion, and even the lights in Primary may bother him. He usually responds to this by trying to leave or going to sleep. He may also have a hard time staying on task and not getting really distracted. He may need some prompting to stay "tuned in." Taking him out into the hallway or to get a drink of water will help him calm himself down.

He is not yet potty trained, nor is he consistent in being able to tell someone if he needs to be changed. If in doubt, you can come find us!

He is on a very restrictive diet right now to see if it will help him improve. Please check with me before letting him eat anything. If you let me know, I will gladly send an alternate snack for him so he won't feel left out.

Another thing that will require your attention is that he is still prone to putting inedible things in his mouth. He eats paper, crayons, paint, Wite-Out, chalk, and so on if he is given an opportunity. He can be reminded not to do this by saying, "no mouth," although you may have to remind him several times.

Finally, *please* wait for us to come get him after Primary because he would have a lot of difficulty finding us after church.

If you have any questions or something comes up, please don't hesitate to ask!

Thanks!

I love how this parent wrote about her child's needs in a positive and easy-to-understand manner. When you write your child's portfolio, be sure to include realistic information about how he is currently doing at church, beginning with sacrament meeting and continuing throughout other classes. Also, think of the things that help him outside of church. Many times our son's Primary teachers have done research and then come to us with an idea only to find out he was already doing

it at school—we just hadn't generalized it to everyday life yet. Below I've listed some topics and questions for you to consider. Don't feel restricted to only these questions. On the other hand, don't feel you have to include each of the topics. Choose the ones you feel need to be addressed for your child. The great thing about putting together a portfolio is that it can be as unique as your child.

Portfolio Topics

Behavior

When he's displaying good behavior
- What does he do?
- How does he act?
- Should he receive any reinforcements during this time? Examples include praise or a sticker chart.
- Is there anything specific you can do to help him stay in this mode?

When he's displaying bad behavior
- What does he do?
- How does he act?
- What are specific things (including prompts, hand signals, and so on) that help him calm down?
- What would you like the teacher to do when your child is struggling? (Note: I would make this at least a three-step strategy, with the last step being coming to get you for help. Be sure to emphasize the need for the teacher and leaders to work with him first and to come get you as the last resort after trying the other suggestions, with the exception of certain circumstances, such as violent behavior.)
- Are there any habitual behaviors the teacher should be aware of, such as biting, kicking, hitting, screaming, and so forth?
- Are there signs the teacher can watch for that signal these behaviors will follow if he isn't helped or calmed down soon?

Likes and Dislikes
- What are his favorite and least favorite parts of church?
- What are his likes and dislikes outside of church (home, school, day care, and so on)?

- What types of people attract your child's attention?
- Is there a physical characteristic or personality style that your son dislikes?

You may think these last two questions are odd, but my husband and I found that from a young age until he was out of preschool, our son naturally gravitated to people with blond or red hair. He also had a fear of people with gray hair and would cry if they talked to him or tried to touch him. When Grandma and Grandpa came to visit, it would take him several days to warm up to them before he would hug them and let them read him stories. If you've noticed anything like this with your child, you may want to include that information in his portfolio.

- What are his favorite reinforcers? (A reinforcer is something that motivates your child and is used as a reward when he does a good job with something that is normally a struggle. It can be a puzzle, a toy at the end of church, Smarties, or as simple as a hug or high five.)
- How does he like to participate in class (for example, holding pictures, choosing songs, or saying prayers)?
- Is there anything he doesn't like to do or is shy about doing in class (for example, singing songs, saying prayers, reading, or being singled out for questions)?

Strengths and Challenges

- What are your child's strengths and challenges? A strength can also be a challenge! Our son had great motor skills and really enjoyed sports, which was a wonderful strength. But it was also a challenge because he didn't understand when it was appropriate to play tag versus sit in a chair, or run versus walk.
- Does he like to color, read, or write?
- Is he musical or athletic?
- How are his motor skills?
- Does he communicate well? Does he need to use PECS (see the chapter titled "A Picture Is Worth a Thousand Words") or perhaps have things explained to him in a simpler way?
- How are his social skills? How does he interact with his peers?
- What's the best way to give your child directions? Does he need

to be instructed one step at a time, or can he be told three or four steps at once?

- What's the best way to ask your child a question? Does it help to ask a multiple choice question or to have pictures for him to choose from that illustrate the answers? Does he need prompts, or can he answer questions independently?

Diet or Allergies

- Include some general information if your child is on a special diet or has allergies. If he has severe reactions, be sure to let the teacher and leaders know what they are and what steps to take if an allergic reaction occurs. Also, provide a list of some easy ideas for classroom snacks the teacher can purchase at the grocery store. Outside of those snacks, ask to be contacted for help with recipes or to substitute snacks for your child.

Contact Information

- What classes do you or your husband attend or teach? Where are they located?
- Do you carry a cell phone with you at church? My husband and I have found that the most effective way for our son's teacher or leaders to contact us is for them to either call or send a simple text message with the word "help" and their location to our cell phones. My husband and I keep our phones on vibrate. This way we know if someone needs us, but we're not interrupting the class we're in. If our son's teacher calls, we sometimes don't answer the phone. We just leave and go directly to the Primary room or classroom. Thus far, the teachers have liked this system because they can stay in one location rather than finding someone to get us or trying to search for us and deal with behavior issues at the same time.

As this information is put together, parents and church leaders will become more comfortable asking each other questions and reporting the outcome of each Sunday. Good communication will lead to parents feeling at ease sending their child to class and teachers better prepared to serve and meet that child's needs.

Demystifying the Diagnosis

by Lynn Parsons

Marlee Matlin, an award-winning actress who is deaf, once said, "It was ability that mattered, not disability, which is a word I'm not crazy about using."[1]

While it's important to have a basic understanding of each person's *disability*, it's more important to focus on their *abilities*. Every child of God has a tremendous future. Parents and church leaders have the responsibility to help everyone reach his or her potential. This chapter explains the most common disabilities while noting ways in which these differences can bless lives.

As you review each section, it's important to remember that the adaptations you make to benefit one person may also help others. For example, one Primary helper drew pictures on a small whiteboard during the lesson to help a child with autism. These drawings also helped another boy with ADHD to focus and get more from the lesson. Children and teens without apparent learning difficulties may also benefit from the new techniques you try. Professional teachers refer to this practice when they say, "Good teaching is good teaching." In other words, using a variety of teaching methods gets your message across better, helps every student, and makes you a better instructor overall.

The number of adaptations listed below may seem overwhelming. They're recommendations that have been used successfully with those specific disabilities. You don't have to use each technique with every child. Good teachers try a method, look at what happened, and then either continue using it or try another. Select one, pray about it, and

try it out. The chapter titled "Teaching the Spirits" has instructions for each method.

Regardless of what you may learn in this book or from other resources, please remember that each special spirit is unique. They may not fit perfectly into the descriptions found below. See the chapter titled "Getting to Know You" for a list of questions to ask parents and how to organize the information you gather.

ADD/ADHD

Attention deficit disorder (ADD) and attention deficit/hyperactivity disorder (ADHD) include trouble concentrating. With ADD, there may be fear, anxiety, low brain energy, slow cognitive thinking, daydreaming, avoidance, procrastination, mental confusion, and poor memory retrieval. Those with ADHD may be inattentive, impulsive, and hyperactive. This affects five of every one hundred school children in the United States, and boys are three times more likely to be diagnosed with ADD/ADHD than girls. Many professionals believe this is caused by a lack of neurotransmitters, or brain chemicals.

Characteristics

This disorder begins before the age of seven years but may not be noticed until later in life. ADD/ADHD makes it hard to sit still, control behavior, and pay attention. One young boy with ADD moved from seat to seat in Primary and played with anything he found on the floor during sharing time. ADD or ADHD may cause individuals to act or speak impulsively, be disorganized, and lose things. Starting, following through, or completing tasks can be challenging. Details may escape the attention of those with this disability. Children diagnosed with ADHD may also be overly active. On the other hand, those with ADD or ADHD can pay attention to many things simultaneously, are aware of most things in their environment, and have plenty of energy.

Classroom Impact

A child with ADD or ADHD will have trouble remaining in a seat and might run around or climb on objects. He or she may play loudly, talk too much, and blurt out answers. Waiting for a turn is hard, so he or she may join a game without permission. Social skills in individuals with ADD or ADHD are usually less developed than others their age.

Adaptations

Post classroom rules and schedules where they can be seen. Prepare the children for a change in activity or schedule with a warning and reminder of what comes next. Provide as many opportunities as possible for physical activity. Make sure your instructions are given step-by-step so the children don't have to remember a long list of directions. Divide more complex projects into smaller, more manageable parts, a process known as "chunking." Keep your expectations realistic in light of this disability. You may also want to use a signal when a child is being too loud or active. For example, pull your ear to tell a child to be quiet without embarrassing him in front of the class.

Autism Spectrum Disorders

Autism spectrum disorders include autism, Asperger's syndrome, pervasive developmental disorder, not otherwise specified (PDD-NOS), and other disorders. Children must show difficulties in at least six of twelve criteria across the areas of communication, social skills, and behavior to be diagnosed on the autism spectrum.

Children who meet the criteria but have intelligence in the average range and do not show language delays, may be diagnosed with Asperger's syndrome. Those who are diagnosed but do not show symptoms in all areas or show symptoms that are not as severe are considered to have PDD-NOS. Intelligence level, skills, abilities, and talents are not determined by the diagnosis. For example, a child with a diagnosis of autism can be higher functioning than a child diagnosed with PDD-NOS, and vice versa. It's not the diagnosis that indicates functioning level; rather, it indicates the areas in which the individual had difficulties at the time of his testing. Youth in each of these areas will not exhibit all symptoms and will have a wide variety of talents, skills, abilities, and intelligence.

Characteristics

Those on the autism spectrum have problems with communication, social skills, and behavior. They may have no spoken language, repeat phrases or conversations, or sound like a robot. Some will stick to a few preferred topics of conversation. Idioms and other abstract language forms are difficult for them to understand.

Other problems include difficulty relating to people, objects, or events. They struggle to join groups and make friends—sometimes

because they can't understand social cues or the point of view of others. One young lady with autism would approach other youth and ask if they liked a particular video. She didn't understand that most youth don't watch cartoons.

Eye contact may be either too long or nonexistent. You may see unusual play with toys (spinning wheels or lining up objects) or repetitive body movements, such as flapping hands or running in circles. Some have strong reactions to sensory stimulation, which may come from loud noises, flickering lights, or the textures of food or fabrics.

These children are very honest and are happy to share their observations of others. They are generally experts on their preferred topics and may show great talent in one specific area such as math, music, or art. You will see consistent reactions and expectations—they are very "rule bound." These special spirits are also generally strong visual learners. If they see it, they've got it.

Classroom Impact

Individuals with autism may either fail to make eye contact or appear to be staring. They take idioms literally (one child looked for a stampede of pets when he heard it was "raining cats and dogs").

Communication problems may keep them from making their wants and needs known or from solving problems. Their emotional reactions may seem to be out of proportion to what has happened. One young woman was sure that every time someone bumped her in the hall, it was deliberate, and she became angry as a result. Another laughed inappropriately at sad stories because she was tired. These special spirits can't generally read facial expressions and appear aloof because they don't understand how to fit in with others. They may have poor hygiene and few self-help skills.

Adaptations

To ease stress, post the schedule and class rules. This communicates your expectations. Give warnings before making a transition and try to be consistent. Consider using PECS for communication or scheduling (see the chapter titled "A Picture Is Worth a Thousand Words"). Have class members role-play to teach classroom behavior or to prepare for activities such as baptism for the dead. Give very specific instructions one at a time, with frequent praise. Have a friend work alongside

the individual with autism for support. Use their preferred topic as a reward. For example, "After the lesson, you can tell me three things about Spider-Man." Please use visuals to teach these children whenever possible.

Behavioral Difficulties

Individuals who have behavior difficulties can't build or maintain good relationships with peers and teachers. They may show inappropriate behaviors or feelings under normal circumstances, have a general mood of unhappiness or depression, or show a tendency to develop physical symptoms or fears. This may be caused by heredity, a brain disorder, poor diet, stress, or family functioning. This is different from teen moodiness, which may last from a few hours to several weeks. Behavioral disturbances will happen at least several times a week for years.

Characteristics

These children have inappropriate behaviors that can't be explained any other way. Usually, their feelings don't match the situation. They may have a long-standing mood of unhappiness or depression along with physical symptoms or fears. One young man tried to explain his depressed feelings by imagining others were trying to hurt him. Some of these individuals may be more sympathetic to others, very aware of their own feelings, and extra sensitive to their surroundings.

Classroom Impact

In the classroom, you may see hyperactivity, a short attention span, or impulsiveness. Children with behavior problems may be aggressive, try to hurt themselves, act out, or fight. Others may be withdrawn, have excessive fears, or feel a lot of anxiety. These individuals sometimes appear immature, cry or laugh inappropriately, have temper outbursts, or show poor coping skills.

Adaptations

Encourage the behaviors you want with praise or positive behavior supports (see the chapter titled "Teaching the Spirits"). Model how to act appropriately, such as not talking when the class needs to be reverent. Get class members to give positive feedback. Try to establish a positive relationship with these special spirits.

Bipolar Disorder

Bipolar disorder is a brain disorder that causes unusual highs and lows in mood, energy, and activity levels and the ability to function. For some, it may not appear until the late teens or early adulthood. It can be caused by genetics, brain structure, or a disorder in cognitive functioning.

Characteristics

Youth with bipolar disorder will have manic (high) and depressive (low) moments. During a high period, they may be overly happy, agitated, irritable, or jumpy. They might talk fast, experience racing thoughts, be easily distracted or impulsive, or feel restless and sleep very little. In extreme states, they could have unrealistic ideas, such as being able to fly.

During a low period, they may feel empty, worried, or tired. They may lose interest in normal activities. Problems with concentration, memory, and decision-making are common. They may also feel restless or irritable and have a change in habits. If the depression continues untreated, they may have thoughts of death or suicide.

Classroom Impact

Youth with bipolar disorder may have trouble concentrating, worry about what others think, or act out in inappropriate ways.

Adaptations

These individuals need expressions of love and comfort. Listen carefully as they describe how they feel. Try to use positive reinforcers. Most important, be aware of behaviors linked to high and low periods, and report dangerous or impulsive statements to the family.

Down Syndrome

Down syndrome has three causes:

1)   In trisomy 21, there are three copies of chromosome 21 rather than the usual two.

2)   Those with an extra copy of chromosome 21 in some cells are considered to have mosaic Down syndrome.

3)   Translocation Down syndrome happens when part of chromosome 21 is attached, or translocated, onto another chromosome. It usually occurs when the mother is over thirty-five years of age, but generally not more than once in a family.

There are several physical characteristics common to individuals with Down syndrome: They may also have mental retardation, communication challenges, and problems with self-help, social, and motor skills.

Characteristics

Children with Down syndrome have unique physical characteristics, including broad feet with short toes; a flat bridge of the nose; short, low-set ears; a short neck; a small head and mouth; and short stature. They develop physically and intellectually at a slower rate. Some may get sick more easily and have breathing problems, vision or hearing loss, and speech problems. Heart defects, stomach problems, and vertebral misalignment may also be present. These individuals are generally happy and friendly and have a very sweet nature. They are a delight to have in class. One boy with Down syndrome greeted everyone in his class each day and made sure to tell his teacher how pretty she looked. Everyone was blessed to associate with him.

Classroom Impact

These children have a variety of abilities. Some may struggle with communication, need help with hygiene, or have delayed social skills. If they have spinal problems, you may need to make sure they don't participate in rough physical activities. Others may need very little help.

Adaptations

Check with parents before doing any strenuous physical activity with a child who has Down syndrome. Allow for more processing and wait time when you ask questions. Give step-by-step directions. Break activities into smaller parts and give directions one piece at a time. Give concrete examples when you teach concepts. Preteach answers for the next week so your special spirit can participate in class discussions.

Intellectual Disability

Intellectual disabilities are described as low intellectual functioning combined with problems in daily living, communication, or social skills. They are caused by genetics, complications during pregnancy or birth, or other health problems and diseases. Intellectual disabilities occur in three out of one hundred people in the United States.

Characteristics

Individuals with an intellectual disability need more time to learn. They may have slower physical development and speech problems. Problems with short- or long-term memory, social skills, and self-care are also common. Some may not be able to understand that consequences are the result of their actions. Problem solving and logic happen at a slower rate. They can be very sweet, friendly, cooperative, and willing to work hard.

Classroom Impact

Individuals with an intellectual disability may be physically slower than classmates, have problems remembering, and need extra time to think or do tasks. They will need a visual reminder of rules, frequent repetition of information, and a model. A model is a classmate with appropriate behavior to observe and copy.

Adaptations

Give them a specific job to do, like passing out papers, holding a picture, or helping someone. Use concrete objects and hands-on learning whenever possible. Divide larger projects into smaller parts. Give them frequent and immediate feedback so they know they are on the right track. Show what you expect, rather than telling, whenever possible. Recruit classmates to help these special spirits with behavior and activities.

Mental Illness

Mental illnesses affect a person's mood, thinking, and behavior. This disability also disrupts his or her ability to function. There are over two hundred types of mental illness, including schizophrenia and depression.

Characteristics

Individuals with mental illness have many physical problems that can't be explained. This includes pain in various places, trouble digesting food, rapid heart rate, dizziness, dry mouth, sweating, headache, and rapid weight gain or loss. These special spirits experience feelings of sadness, depression, fatigue, and confusion. They may have excessive worries and fears, delusions or hallucinations, and odd eating or sleeping patterns. Those with mental illness are at risk for more anger,

hostility, violence, and substance abuse. They may be unable to cope with average problems and stress and have suicidal thoughts. Those with this disorder may be more sensitive to the feelings of others and more aware of their environment than the rest of us.

Classroom Impact

These children may have problems focusing, make inappropriate comments, and overreact to others. They may isolate themselves, have outbursts, and lack motivation to succeed.

Adaptations

Visit with the family to learn the warning signs of an outburst. Try to convey a nonjudgmental attitude, express love and support, and offer many opportunities for success. Use the positive behavior supports in the chapter titled "Teaching the Spirits" and give signals to stop behavior so the child is not embarrassed in front of peers.

Conclusion

Prayer and the influence of the Holy Ghost will be your most useful tools in determining how best to help your particular special spirit. As you consider the suggestions made above, remember that each person is unique. Some may need a few short-term supports, while others may need help for the rest of their lives.

Note

1. Marlee Matlin, quoted at *Effective Presentations*, http://www .effectivepresentations.com/resources/info/quotes-about-ability.

SITTING, RUNNING, AND HUMMING

A Chapter on Behaviors

by Lynn Parsons

Behavioral problems are possibly the most difficult disability to understand. Youth with behavioral challenges may look just like everyone else. Behaviors may appear inconsistently. The things you try may work one week and fail the next. Solving these challenges begins with an analysis of the trigger, the behavior itself, and the consequences that follow. Then a system of positive teaching methods and supports can be put in place.

Antecedent Analysis

The first step is to figure out what triggered the undesirable behavior. This is done through observation. While it is nearly impossible for a teacher to see everything that happens—especially in a large class—this is still your most reliable source of information. A youth with a disability may not be able to tell you what happened or may be unaware of the specific problem that upset him or her. When watching is not enough, ask the other class members, others nearby, and the individual's parents for help.

Common triggers include interactions with peers, changes in routine, sensory issues, differences in eating or sleeping routines, illness, modified medication, desired escape, and avoidance. The child may have arrived in a bad mood and had been looking for a reason to justify his emotions. Was there teasing, bullying, or another negative exchange with other youth? Has his routine been interrupted? Were class members particularly noisy that day? Had he been eating junk food and staying up late? Did he have a fever or other signs of illness? Had there

been a change in medications or dosages? Was he trying to get out of doing something he doesn't like, such as sitting still? Was he trying to avoid a task or experience?

As you consider possible triggers, look for solutions. Bad moods happen—life isn't perfect for anyone. Try to plan something the individual enjoys, such as an activity, joke, or fun responsibility, and encourage him to participate. Be alert for signs of bullying and teasing and inform the class that these activities have no place in the house of the Lord. Changes in routine are sometimes unavoidable, so try to prepare your special spirit for the changes you can anticipate, such as a change in the Primary schedule to practice for the sacrament meeting program.

Also request that the family keep you informed of any medical changes and possible side effects. For children with sensory issues, you may try turning off the lights or having the class whisper. If the child is looking to escape, you may need to let them "opt out" of an undesirable activity. In cases of avoidance, a motivator of a preferred activity or privilege may solve the problem.

Behavior Analysis

After discovering and dealing with triggers, look at the specific behavior to make sure it isn't filling a need. One boy with autism learned that if he made noise in church, his parents got out the snacks to keep him quiet. His behavior filled his need. One young man with autism purposely made himself upset because being angry made him "feel powerful, like the Incredible Hulk." Others will reenact past conversations as they try to find a resolution to a problem. Some will parrot television shows because they are comforted by knowing the outcome. Discovering these needs will help you find better alternatives to problem behaviors.

Some youth on the autism spectrum may engage in behaviors such as hand flapping, climbing on adults, or running in circles to mentally stimulate themselves. To reduce hand flapping, you can try a squeeze or textured ball in the pocket. The climbers need additional pressure, which you can provide by pressing down firmly on their shoulders. A lap pad filled with rice may keep a runner in his or her seat. His need to run may be caused by a desire for muscle pressure, and the weight will provide that without additional movement. Visit www.autismspeaks.org to find other substitute behaviors that are less disruptive and more socially acceptable.

Negative emotions, including anger, fear, and low self-esteem, may cause a child to act out so they can receive negative reactions that are familiar. This helps them justify the emotions they already feel. A child may say to himself, "I'm angry because the teacher told me to stop making noises." This is easier to deal with than not knowing why he is upset. At special-needs.families.com, you can discover ways to teach your special spirit to relieve stress. Other children will recall disturbing conversations and events and attempt to reenact them repeatedly. This may require professional counseling to deal with the traumatic situation.

Consequence Analysis

Finally, take a look at the consequence. What does the youth get out of his behavior? You may need to limit the action, remove the reward, or find another way to provide that outcome.

Limiting the behavior requires some negotiation. For example, one young woman with autism frequently left class during seminary to wander the halls. This helped her reorganize her central nervous system. She didn't do it during every class, just during certain stressful days. This young lady didn't leave the building, and she returned within a reasonable amount of time. By doing this, she was able to get the break she needed and attend class, and so it was permitted.

Removing the reward is generally a relatively simple solution. Every ward has children who act up during sacrament meeting so they can play with their parents in the hall—essentially a reward for poor behavior. My children were forced to sit either on my lap or next to me on the couch in the foyer, with no distractions and no fun. This was not always easy to arrange, but they learned that being in the meeting was better than being in the hall.

Positive Teaching Methods

When problem behaviors occur, it's easy to move into a negative thought pattern. "Stop it!" "Why are you doing that?" "Knock it off!" When you make the effort to move toward a positive teaching method, you focus on love, persistence, and being proactive.

Begin by greeting your special spirit by name each time you see him or her, whether at church or in the grocery store. Look for ways to compliment him during class. Remember and recognize things about

his life. As you analyze antecedents, behaviors, and consequences, you will begin to see things from the perspective of the child. The more you understand him, the more your love and support will increase. This positive relationship will go a long way toward decreasing poor behavior.

Proactive positive behavior support includes the following:

- Preteach how you expect them to behave, such as how to get ready for prayer.
- Give frequent reminders, like "Let's be quiet and get ready to go to class." Don't point out what he or she is doing wrong.
- Be sure your requests are clear and limited to one thing at a time.
- Always use a quiet voice (unless there is a safety issue).
- Post no more than three to five classroom rules. Make sure they are clear—"be nice" is hard to understand.
- Point out those with good behavior.
- Praise your special spirit when he does the right thing.
- Use peers as models and to help the child see what you want.
- Use appropriate humor. Say things like, "Do I stand on my head during class?" to teach reverence.
- Don't engage in arguments—this drives out the Spirit. Repeat instructions or deal with the problem in the hall. A child who persistently makes noise can be encouraged to help classmates by setting a good example.
- Make sure you give each child a fresh start daily. For example, don't say, "Bobby is never reverent."
- In more difficult or longer-lasting situations, set up a token economy to reward good behavior—ideas can be found at www.proteacher.org.
- Set up a safe room where the child can calm down if extremely upset. This is a quiet location that feels comforting to the child with special needs.
- Only remove the child from class if there is a safety problem or extreme disruption. The child sees this as a personal rejection.

Persistence and consistency are probably the most important things to consider. Keep trying different methods until something works. You probably only see your special spirit once a week, so it may take at least

three weeks of consistent effort to see any progress. Experienced teachers work by using a method for several class sessions, reflecting on its results, and then looking for a new technique if necessary. Remember, nothing works forever, so be flexible and willing to make a change. Sometimes the behaviors you are trying to modify seem to make no sense at all, especially when you are dealing with a child with emotional disturbance. Through love and prayer, you can learn how best to help your special spirit and receive the encouragement you need to never give up.

Teaching Strategies

TEACHING THE SPIRITS

by Lynn Parsons

Thre are many teaching tips and techniques that have been proven successful for those with special needs. We will review a few here, along with ideas for how to use them to teach the gospel more effectively.

In the Beginning . . .

Your first meeting with your special spirit can set the tone for your relationship. First, find out all you can by interviewing the parents. See the chapter titled "Getting to Know You" for more information on this process.

After gathering all the information possible, you can prepare for your first meeting. If they have a special interest, be ready to introduce it as a topic of conversation. You may want to have some questions ready to encourage conversation.

Some people may be more comfortable meeting in their home for the first time, but it will be more appropriate to introduce yourself to others at church. If you are meeting a child or member in a wheelchair, either sit or crouch to be on the same level. Speak directly to the person, even if you are having help understanding his or her speech or method of communication. Remember to keep your sentences short and simple; keep to familiar, positive topics; and express how glad you are for the chance to spend time with him or her.

Alternative Activities

Some of the activities you plan might be too difficult for children

with special needs. For example, one Primary class was learning about repentance. Each child told the teacher their personal definition of repentance, but a child with autism couldn't articulate his opinion. He was able to copy the word onto a small whiteboard and say "Sorry." This was acknowledged and praised just like the other children's thoughts. We need to be sure we consider the needs of all the children as we plan and look for ways they can be successful.

Begin with the End in Mind

Each time we seek to teach the gospel, we need to have an objective. What is the most important thing we want our class to take away from the lesson? For example, if we are talking about tithing, do we want them to understand how to calculate it? When to pay? The blessings received? The one we choose is where we need to put our time and effort. After much consideration and prayer, select your objective and then look for stories and activities that support it. If you find a great story they will love, but it detracts from your point, choose something else. For example, we tried using puppets in seminary. The few students who gave the puppet show loved it, but the rest of the class paid no attention. A few begged repeatedly for more puppets, but I left them in the closet because they didn't benefit the class as a whole. On the other hand, when we made videos, the entire class participated, and they learned much more as they experienced the stories for themselves. As you have more experience with your class, you will be able to choose appropriate activities that will achieve your objective.

Channel Physical Activity

Children with ADHD and many other disorders struggle to remain still because of their excess energy. Instead of fighting it, use it! Have them pass out supplies, run errands, go down the hall for a drink, help other students, get scriptures from the library, or set up the room. Asking them to do small tasks to help the teacher increases their self-esteem and builds a more positive relationship. You can also take stretch breaks and incorporate opportunities to move during the lesson. One young man with ADHD whom I taught in seminary would get things from other parts of the building, pass out materials, and do any other task I gave him that required movement. This made him feel like a valuable part of the class and helped him focus. Younger children could benefit by taking a "field trip" down the hall to see where the tithing

slips are located, walking to the board to choose a picture, looking for hidden objects in the room, or changing seats during the lesson.

Chunking

Many children with learning disabilities find complex activities overwhelming. These individuals may do better if you chunk the activities into smaller steps. For example, if you are working on third-year camp certification for the Young Women, one of the requirements is to both learn how to use a compass and do some orienteering. Rather than giving the young woman the whole task, break it up into smaller, more manageable pieces. For example, use the compass to find north. Then locate which direction she would have to walk to reach various landmarks. The orienteering activity should also be presented as small, individual parts. This way, she can focus on one thing at a time and won't feel overwhelmed and frustrated. I've used this method to teach everything from Scripture Mastery verses to the steps of prayer.

Consistency

Our world is full of inconsistencies. For example, slang is appropriate to use among teens but usually not with adults. Cub Scouts may have belching contests, but that is not considered polite in the school lunchroom. It's much easier for most children with disabilities to deal with a consistent environment. This means that class rules must apply to all. Routines should remain largely the same from week to week, and behavior expectations should be clear and consistent. This makes young people with disabilities feel safe and comfortable.

For example, my seminary class had a strict "no cell phone" rule. One sneaky young woman was able to text under the table without getting caught, so her classmate with autism thought she could text during class. She was not as discreet, and both were caught. Their parents had to retrieve their cell phones after class, and neither did it again. If I hadn't treated the first young woman the same as her less tricky friend, the importance of paying attention to the lesson would not have been reinforced.

Concrete Teaching

Abstract concepts are hard for many special students to understand. Using object lessons, such as coloring water to represent a sin-filled soul and then using bleach to remove the color to show repentance, will help

children and adults understand gospel principles. These methods are attention-getting and help all youth to remember the lesson.

Frequent and Immediate Feedback

Individuals with autism may struggle to read facial expressions. They might ask you repeatedly if you are mad, if they are doing things correctly, or for constant assistance. Giving frequent positive feedback helps them to know that they're on the right track, meeting your expectations, and not in trouble. This makes them feel more comfortable and more open to the Spirit. When doing group or individual activities, I try to do "flybys." I walk around the room, check their work, and offer encouragement and support. This lets them know immediately how things are going. I also make a point of commenting on those who are doing well. This helps everyone in the class, including those with other disabilities.

Gaining Attention

Many church leaders and teachers dive right into the lesson without ensuring their class is paying attention. Using words coupled with visual aids and hands-on activities is a better way of making sure your message is getting across. Eye contact with each class member is another way to check his or her attention span. Having everyone stand up or move is another. Put up a collection of objects and ask your students to guess how the things relate to the lesson. Another idea is to take someone into the hall and have him enter the room doing a strange motion, then let the class guess the point of the activity. It's important to make sure that everyone is looking at you before you start to speak. Individuals with autism may not comprehend up to 60 percent of what you say. A great class activity to see how this feels is to take a general conference talk and mark out 60 percent of the words. How much do you understand now?

Hands-on Learning

Imagine a little girl coming home from Achievement Days. "What did you do today?" her mother asks. "We watched Sister Davidson bake cookies," she replies. Picture this same scene, but the child says, "We made cookies!" Which one sounds more fun? More engaging? More educational?

One of my seminary students with ADD really understood what it was like to be Moroni after we had our "Nephite Hunt." I had

different-colored headbands to separate the Nephites from the Lamanites. The Nephites hid around the gym behind furniture and other obstacles I had created, and after five minutes, I turned the Lamanites loose to capture them. After all were caught, they switched teams. This activity helped this student experience being hunted and being all alone. Even though his life wasn't in danger, he had a better appreciation for Moroni's trials. So did the rest of the group. Activities with movement are great for kinesthetic learners of all ages.

Modeling

"Be thou an example of the believers, in word, in conversation, in charity, in spirit, in faith, in purity" (1 Timothy 4:12). Showing a child with developmental disabilities how to fold his arms and bow his head is much better than giving a description. Just as you can't teach a principle you don't live, you can't expect better behavior than you demonstrate.

Some wards will choose a reverent child to stand with his or her arms folded at the front of the Primary room as the children enter. This not only sets a good example but also encourages others to be reverent so they can be chosen the following week. I had a friend who said she would teach Relief Society just like she taught Primary. "Look, Sister Williams is being quiet! She gets a cracker." This may seem a little silly, but even adults like to be recognized for the good things they do. As you point out models of good behavior, those who are struggling will want to follow along.

A Nonjudgmental Attitude

"Judge not according to the appearance, but judge righteous judgment" (John 7:24). When others struggle with problems we don't understand, it's easy to pass judgment. One mother of two children on the autism spectrum frequently gets calls from ward members who "know" how she can "fix" her children. Their lack of empathy is emotionally painful, and their possibly well-intentioned advice is not useful. Youth are especially sensitive to those who are passing judgment. Do not assume you fully understand their struggles—this attitude damages relationships and drives out the Holy Ghost. Sometimes all you can do is accept the situation and pray for ways you can provide comfort or help. As you try to understand their situation, you will be filled with love for these special spirits and see them as your brothers and

sisters. Please remember that the best way to demonstrate this is to give each class member a fresh start every time you see them. One challenging young lady frequently ran away from her teachers and refused to comply with requests. Her teacher started a program of praise for every little thing the girl did right. This child learned it was more fun to behave than to act out.

Opportunities for Success

Everyone likes to feel special. Children with disabilities often spend a lot of time struggling. Having success raises self-esteem and makes it easier to endure the difficult times. That's why so many children with ADHD love skateboarding, soccer, and other physical activities. As you learn about those you serve, you will discover their strengths. If you make an effort to recognize their abilities, they will feel more a part of the group. How can they believe that a Being they can't see values them if their teacher doesn't? This is especially important for those with behavior problems. One Young Woman with a disability had a hard time being accepted among her peers until she sang in sacrament meeting. Her ability to do what terrified the rest of them raised her status in their eyes.

Peer Support

Don't feel you have to jump in every time your special spirit needs help. Allow others in the class to help. You can ask another class member to be a "buddy" at first. You may find that everyone in the class is competing to be a helper! There are many blessings for these peers. Working together builds the helper's empathy, raises self-esteem, and creates friendships. The child being assisted will feel as though he or she is working equally with the partner. One young boy's classmate in Primary is a girl with physical disabilities. He has decided to make sure she has a place to sit and that everything is within her reach. Another exceptional boy translates for a peer with a speech impediment so her teacher can understand. In these situations, everyone benefits from this Christlike behavior.

Positive Behavior Supports

Creating a positive classroom atmosphere goes a long way toward preventing behavior problems. Begin by greeting each class member by name. Recognize something personal about each child—does Susie

have a new dress? Juwan a new baby brother? Encourage everyone to say something positive about others in the class. Recognize even wrong answers as a good attempt. Express appreciation for those who help. Try to "catch" them being good. This shifts your focus from poor behavior to good, and theirs will change too! For more information on positive behavior supports, see "Sitting, Running, and Humming."

Posting Rules and Schedule

Clear expectations are important to children with special needs. If you choose to post a list of class rules, make them specific. "Respect each other" is too vague for most Primary children to understand. "Raise your hand to speak" is more plain. School teachers also list consequences, but that gives a negative focus that is not appropriate for church. You can also try to answer requests with a positive spin. For example, say, "You can get a drink of water on the way to the Primary room," instead of "Not right now."

A schedule can be made by writing on the board or creating one from word strips or pictures. (For more information, see the chapter titled "A Picture Is Worth a Thousand Words.") We all follow the program during sacrament meeting, and this gives our class the same sense of continuity and direction. This is especially soothing for class members with disabilities and is helpful when there is a change, such as a substitute.

Preferential Seating

Preferential seating is done differently depending on the disability. A child with ADHD needs to sit near the teacher. Some youth with autism have sensitive ears, so they can't sit near the piano or organ. As you visit with the parents, you can review the physical setup of the room and make the decision that best suits your special spirit.

Preferred Topics

Youth on the autism spectrum may have a preferred topic of conversation. If they want to talk about their superhero during the lesson, you can set a limit or use it as a reward. Tell him he can tell you one thing each Sunday or talk for three minutes about his subject. Be sure to show genuine interest in what he's saying, or he may feel the need to repeat himself. This allows him to fill his need and for you to teach your subject. One young man loved to talk about Japanese anime. His

leaders were able to use this as a reward for good behavior—a win-win situation all around.

Preteaching

Children who need additional time to process questions and answers can be pretaught. As you prepare your lesson, you can call the student or parent and either let them know one or two of the questions you will ask or preteach them the answers. This allows the special spirit to participate fully with the class. Sending home an outline, a scripture verse, or an answer allows the teen to participate with the rest of the class. You may give the parents an outline of your lesson (or the reference to look it up online) so they can review it during the week. This helps your student become familiar with the topic so they can prepare appropriate comments.

Processing or Wait Time

Some children will require more than a few seconds to process their answers. Instruct the group to wait and to think. Count slowly to yourself for at least five seconds. Tell the class you will give a signal when it's time to respond. Do not call on those who raise their hands before the wait time is over. This gives everyone a chance to think of an answer or even get a little help, and it levels the playing field.

Proximity Control

Many behaviors can be controlled by the presence of the teacher. Sitting or standing nearby may be all that's necessary. You may want to have class members who struggle to sit still at the front of the class where you can intervene before things get out of hand. This allows the teacher to give out a small squeeze ball, have the child walk to the drinking fountain, or pass a picture to hold before the entire lesson is disrupted. When I had overly chatty ADHD seminary students, I would stand between their desks while giving directions, interrupting their flow of conversation long enough to get the class going.

Quiet Environments

The chaos of a loud Primary activity or ward dinner may be overwhelming for those on the autism spectrum or with ADD. You may have to put more emphasis on reverence or change class locations for these special students to be able to hear. They may also need a quiet place

to calm down before returning to the action. This might be an empty room, the meetinghouse library, the kitchen, or another quiet area.

Realistic Expectations

Many years ago, I was responsible for the nursery as a member of the Primary presidency. One child had recently arrived from France and spoke no English. Another had largely unintelligible speech because of a physical disability. Two came from Spanish-speaking homes. The final child was barely eighteen months old and too shy to talk. On top of all that, we had a new nursery leader. At the end of her first class, I went in for a visit. She was very frustrated and said, "All I did was ask them their names! No one answered me!" I again explained their backgrounds. She replied, "All I did was ask them their names!" Her expectations were unrealistic for this particular group at that point in time. She could have sung "Here We Are Together" and pointed at herself and each child as she sang their names. Mentioning names frequently (for example, "Pablo, can you pass this drink to Tina?") helps all the children get to know each other better.

A few years ago, I had a young man in seminary who did not do his reading. His mother said that because he had ADD, he could only do a little at a time. I relaxed my standards (big mistake!), and he quit reading. He had to delay going on a mission because he hadn't read the entire Book of Mormon. I learned that day to encourage my youth to work to the best of their abilities. Fortunately, this young man rose to the challenge, read the Book of Mormon from cover to cover, and served a successful mission.

In the first situation, the nursery leader's expectations were set too high. Each of those children had much better communication in a few months, but they needed some time to grow and develop. On the other hand, the young man's family had their expectations set too low. This is common for a lot of children with learning disabilities. How do you determine a realistic expectation? Visit with the family, speak to your priesthood leaders, and pray for guidance.

Role-Playing

Teaching class members with special needs how to apply what they learn is sometimes difficult. One method is to have a few skit ideas to help them practice making good choices. For example, a youth

lesson on honesty could include several different scenarios. Ask the group to demonstrate their reactions to the following: a friend asks to copy homework, someone they might want to avoid calls them on the phone, or someone gives them a gift they don't like. Having experience making these decisions helps them see how gospel principles apply to real life. Teens especially love this activity. One young lady with autism would frequently tell me how she taught the principles she learned from seminary role-plays to her friends at school. She was especially good at explaining why the prophet has taught us to delay dating until the age of sixteen.

Specific Jobs

Children with more severe disabilities have a hard time feeling part of the group because they're not asked to contribute. Ask them to pass out supplies, set up chairs, and other small tasks. This gives you a chance to praise them and point out their strengths to the rest. This raises their value in their own eyes and in the group as a whole.

Step-by-Step Directions

Don't assume that children with disabilities will be able to complete something with multiple steps. It's difficult to focus on what you're doing now while remembering what comes next. For example, if you're teaching the steps of prayer, have a poster with words or pictures of each step. Then, after they complete the opening, they can look to see that thanking is next. This reduces stress during the learning process. Not all directions can use a poster, though. When completing a hands-on project, such as cooking, place ingredients in the order they will be used. Other directions may need to be more personal, such as how to greet residents of a nursing home, and should be on a 3x5 card or another discreet reminder. If, during the lesson, you ask the class to participate, break down the steps or continue with extra prompts for the children who need smaller steps. This varies from chunking because when you chunk an assignment or project, the directions aren't necessarily reviewed for each step.

Signals

Children with a variety of disabilities may need reminders. If a girl with ADHD is getting too loud, a touch on the shoulder will remind her to be quiet without embarrassing her in front of the class. A boy

with autism sees a hand signal that tells him it's almost time to go to class. The teacher folding her arms can be a signal for the class to get ready for a prayer. Work out the signal prior to class and remind the child during the week. Talk to parents to see what signals they may use at home to prompt certain actions or to correct behaviors. If there isn't one already in place, come up with something simple and ask the parents to use it at home so the individual has exposure to it more often than once a week.

It's difficult for many children with disabilities to move between activities, especially if they're having fun. Using a schedule will prepare them for changes. Some children may require a five-minute warning. This can be done verbally or through a signal like flashing lights or a sound. Peer models can demonstrate good behaviors. You may need to offer a choice—"Do you want to sit next to Juan or Talia during singing time?" Songs work well for younger children. Picture schedules also help prepare youth for transitions because they can look ahead and see what activity is coming next. You can learn more about picture schedules in the chapter titled "A Picture Is Worth a Thousand Words."

Conclusion

Most of these methods are simple to use. They are tried and true techniques that will help not only your class members with special needs, but also all those you serve. I know that as you prayerfully consider your students, you will find a way to meet their needs as you help them learn those things Heavenly Father has prepared.

Lead Me, Guide Me, Walk beside Me

Helpers and Aides in Primary

by Lynn Parsons

As Heavenly Father's children, we all have an open invitation to be with Him again after we pass through the veil. In 3 Nephi 9:14, we read, "Yea, verily I say unto you, if ye will come unto me ye shall have eternal life. Behold, mine arm of mercy is extended towards you, and whosoever will come, him will I receive; and blessed are those who come unto me." Fortunately, this blessing isn't reserved for the physically and psychologically perfect, or none of us would make it!

I hope Primary leaders feel the need to welcome all children to Primary. We read in the Bible the account of Jesus teaching the Pharisees,

> And they brought young children to him, that he should touch them: and his disciples rebuked those that brought them.
>
> But when Jesus saw it, he was much displeased, and said unto them, Suffer the little children to come unto me, and forbid them not: for of such is the kingdom of God. (Mark 10:13–14)

I look to this example and hope others will follow.

I firmly believe that most children with disabilities can be included in Primary with additional supports. These resources are not unique, difficult to find, or expensive. One ward member can be called as a helper, aide, or shadow. This person can work one-on-one with the child with special needs.

I know from working with Primary helpers that this calling may seem overwhelming. There is no specific manual, and most people have no previous experience with disabilities. Review the information in the

chapter titled "Teaching the Spirits" for classroom management techniques and teaching tips. The Church website also has additional information on dealing with disabilities at disabilities.lds.org.

What if you still feel inadequate after reviewing these resources? "Be strong and of a good courage, fear not, nor be afraid . . . for the Lord thy God . . . will not fail thee, nor forsake thee" (Deuteronomy 31:6). Rely on Heavenly Father to inspire and bless you with patience and insight to take care of His precious children. Now is the time to focus on Christlike teaching, which includes clear communication, planning, love, and problem-solving techniques.

Christlike Teaching

"But the Lord said unto Samuel, Look not on his countenance, or on the height of his stature . . . for the Lord seeth not as man seeth; for man looketh on the outward appearance, but the Lord looketh on the heart" (1 Samuel 16:7).

When I see people as Heavenly Father's children, I learn to love their spirits and overlook their challenges. "Remember the worth of souls is great in the sight of God" (D&C 18:10). Remind yourself often that Heavenly Father loves this child and that every worker in the Church can see others as He does. Look for the light inside, no matter how severe the handicaps might be, and you will find it. Once you glimpse that precious spirit, you can develop the true love of Christ for that individual, which helps you endure trials. There may be times when you don't see as much progress as you may wish or you feel your hard work is unappreciated. If you have charity—the pure love of Christ—you will feel sustained and supported in difficult situations.

As a teacher in the Church, your priority is to help your class members become the best children of God possible. Remember that these special spirits are beloved by Heavenly Father and Jesus Christ. We have a responsibility to cherish them and give them the experiences they need to learn and grow. Try to recall that we are all siblings with individual talents, and we can learn from anyone. Change the question from "What do I do with this child?" to "What does this child need today?" This will open your mind to inspiration as you serve our young brothers and sisters. Inclusion is not the easiest way to teach a child with disabilities, but it is the best. Christ included everyone, from Pharisees and sinners to lepers and others with physical handicaps. By following

His example, our own testimonies will be strengthened, and we will be blessed in unimaginable ways.

One child greeted his shadow with "Yay" each time they met. Some people believed this was because he was glad to see her. But we soon realized that wasn't the case. His helper said "Yay" in response to his accomplishments and then gave him a treat, and this was his way of asking for a snack. She still saw his greeting as progress, and this encouraged her to keep working with him.

Communication

Heavenly Father values communication. When Moses was concerned about leading Israel because he was "slow of speech," he was told, "Now therefore go, and I will be with thy mouth, and teach thee what thou shalt say" (Exodus 4:12). If we, as leaders, encourage good communication with parents, between Church teachers, and with the children, Heavenly Father will guide us.

After prayerful consideration, the helper may become the major contact with the family. Primary leaders need to give the aide any information available about teaching the child with special needs but try not to overwhelm him or her. This is a careful balancing act. Leaders should encourage helpers to meet with the parents. This is not a time to be shy! Above all, pray for the shadow. He or she will need a great deal of inspiration from the Holy Ghost in this new situation. This calling is as sacred as any other, for "if it so be that you should labor all your days in crying repentance unto this people, and bring, save it be one soul unto me, how great shall be your joy with him in the kingdom of my Father!"(D&C 18:15).

Leaders may also wish to consider sharing information about special needs with the other children in Primary. Ask the bishopric and parents if you may conduct a sharing time about disabilities or the special challenges of any child. Consider having the parents participate so that you don't violate the child's confidentiality. With their permission, you may also ask the bishopric to approve a guest speaker, such as a special education teacher or other professional. See the chapter titled "Every Star Is Different" for more information about teaching children about disabilities and for sharing time ideas. The Boy Scouts also have many resources about disability awareness. These are listed in the chapter on Scouting. You may also look for information at the websites mentioned below.

- The Access Center for Independent Living has information about how to speak about disabilities (http://www.acils.com).
- The Center on Human Policy has lessons about various aspects of being disabled (http://www.disabilitystudiesforteachers .org).
- Education World has lesson plans about disabilities (http:// www.educationworld.com).

You may also struggle to communicate with the child. It isn't always possible to tell what gets through when you teach. One child with a disability repeated lines from children's movies when stressed. Sometimes every remark or response she made during the day was a quote from a movie. When we asked her about the lesson later, we were surprised to discover that she did learn an amazing amount even though we were often unsure if she had heard what we were teaching.

Planning

"And thus I grant unto this people a privilege of organizing themselves according to my laws" (D&C 51:15). Church leaders can work with the teacher, family, and helper to develop a plan, which does not need to be formal or even written. As you consider what needs to happen, choose goals. Younger children may have one, while older ones may have up to five.

Goals for this child may be far different from the others in Primary. What is the child going to accomplish?

- Sitting quietly during the meeting?
- Adjusting to the routine of church?
- Learning how to behave by observing other children?
- Feeling the Spirit?

Start with one priority. Don't worry if these children aren't learning everything taught that day or if they complete each activity. These little ones will be learning life-changing behavioral, social, and spiritual lessons. If they can feel the Spirit and know they are loved in Primary, this will affect how they feel about the Church, possibly for the rest of their lives.

Next, develop an action plan to achieve the selected goal(s). Work with the helper to choose positive reinforcement methods and to track progress. This can be shared with new teachers or substitutes and will be

inspiring and reassuring to the parents, child, and workers. One helper found these records very comforting on bad days. Meet with priesthood leaders to determine what safety rules are necessary. For example, men are not allowed to teach Primary classes alone. Many stakes and wards have rules about taking children to the bathroom or out in the hall. Follow these directives as you consider the suggestions made in this chapter.

The child you serve may need special teaching techniques, like those in the chapter titled "Teaching the Spirits." This may seem like a lot of extra work for "just one" child, but no one will be slighted through the use of these additional teaching methods, and the whole class may benefit. One shadow for a child with autism found that the extra pictures she prepared during the week helped the whole class learn.

Bad Days

> And behold, I tell you these things that ye may learn wisdom; that ye may learn that when ye are in the service of your fellow beings ye are only in the service of your God.
>
> Behold, ye have called me your king; and if I, whom ye call your king, do labor to serve you, then ought not ye to labor to serve one another? (Mosiah 2:17–18)

Everyone has bad days. Children may come to church already stressed, not feeling well, or with other challenges. Try not to become upset with the child. Consider taking the child out into the hall if necessary, but try to do as much as you can on your own. Remember that the parents struggle all week, so do everything in your power to allow them to attend their meetings as you help their child.

Love

"Beloved, let us love one another: for love is of God; and every one that loveth is born of God, and knoweth God. He that loveth not knoweth not God; for God is love" (1 John 4:7–8).

Our first priority in any church service is to love those whom we serve as Christ loves us. It can be hard to love someone who looks or acts differently, and we need to seek the Lord through prayer and fasting.

One teacher struggled with a child who was defiant and refused to cooperate. She found that prayer and fasting softened her heart and allowed her to yield her will to Heavenly Father's. The Spirit then

brought her peace, understanding, and limitless insight. Please focus on this goal for each teacher and leader.

The most important time to focus on love is when the child appears to be "backsliding." Many of my students do great one day but struggle the next. One young man with autism started to act out more frequently. His teachers learned he suffered from allergies to pollen, which made him feel terrible and act out of control. Until he felt better physically, the leaders had to be more patient and loving. After the pollen died down, he behaved much better.

I've worked in Primary as a helper for a child with special needs and also trained other helpers. On good days, I encouraged the Primary workers to pat themselves on the back mentally for how much progress the child had made. On bad days, I told them to remember how far he or she had come—for example, from rolling around on the floor and screaming to sitting quietly for most of the meeting. This helped everyone feel appreciated and that what the helper did was important, and it also increased their love for this special spirit.

Supporting the Aide

Support is not a one-time thing. It begins with your first meeting, continues at least once each month, and doesn't stop until the aide is released. From the first time you visit with the helper, set a positive tone. Explain how important the aide will be in the life of this special spirit. Set clear expectations and offer as many resources and as much help as you can. Remind this helper that he or she will allow this child to take their first "gospel steps" independent of their parents. By expressing love, guiding the youngster, and serving consistently, the aide can have a profound impact on this child's testimony, possibly even more than the Primary teacher. You should also review an emergency plan in case of meltdowns or medical emergencies, or for times when a substitute is needed.

The aide should be given a monthly calendar, showing the class lesson schedule and which presidency member will do sharing time each Sunday. After choosing the sharing time topic, communicate it with the helper so they can prepare pictures or other visuals for their special spirit. Either give the aide the appropriate Primary lesson manual or the information he or she needs to access it online. This will give him or her a chance to create materials, modify teaching methods, or perhaps find resources to help the teacher.

This can be a lonely calling, so be sure to express your appreciation, concern, support, and love frequently for this wonderful servant of God. We all have felt tired and lonely at some point in our lives. Do anything you can to assist the aide. Think outside the box—if he or she wishes to spend time with their special spirit during the week, perhaps a member of the presidency can babysit the helper's children during that time. Get to know the youngster better yourself so you can give tips and encouragement when needed. I have known aides who have felt forgotten. They may serve for years with little appreciation and are sometimes given additional callings without release from Primary. Remember this Primary worker frequently in your prayers and you will be inspired to give them what they need and be in a position to prevent burnout, for "ye also helping together by prayer for us" (2 Corinthians 1:11). Parents should also express their appreciation often and tell the aide how he or she is helping the child, the improvement they've seen, and how his or her service helps the parents be more patient and use better parenting skills during the week. This keeps the aide from feeling like a free babysitting service.

Conclusion

Above all, keep focused on progress and goals. Remember that progress will not be steady and may not be visible at times. If you concentrate on what you are trying to help your special spirit achieve, it will be easier to persist in your teaching. I've personally seen miracles in the lives of these children. They learn an astonishing amount of gospel principles, show great empathy, make comments that are clear and insightful, and are prepared to love everyone. Associating with these special spirits is a blessing.

A Picture Is Worth
a Thousand Words

by Danyelle Ferguson

The Picture Exchange Communication System (PECS, pronounced "pecks") was developed by Lori Frost and Andrew Bondy. This system is often used at school as a communication tool between students and teachers. It's also used to create a visual schedule of the day for children to understand and prepare for what's happening next. In this chapter, you will learn how to use PECS in the following situations:

- As a communication tool for individuals who have speech delay or can't speak at all.
- As a tool to help individuals with comprehension disabilities.
- As a way to teach children the routine of church, as well as a way to help older individuals know and follow a schedule.

PECS as a Communication Tool

Speech Communication

Children who have communication difficulties are often frustrated when others can't understand what they want to tell them. This frustration can lead to undesirable behaviors, such as yelling and crying. The PECS program can ease those frustrations by using pictures as a tool of communication. When a child uses the PECS program, he hands an adult a picture or series of pictures to express what he desires. This form of communication has been very successful when used not only with children who are nonverbal, but also with those who have

speech delay or other speech complications.

If you are working with a child who uses PECS as their total form of communication, it's helpful to understand the steps of the program. Please remember it is not your responsibility to initiate teaching PECS to a child if it's not already being used at school or home. PECS is a very intense program, and it's necessary to use it everywhere the child goes in order to be successful, which is why it's important for teachers to be aware of the program but not to be the ones who try to start it.

The other ways of using the PECS program covered in this chapter—for comprehension or as a schedule—can be implemented and used with any child, whether they are using a similar program at school and home or not.

There are six steps to implementing the PECS program for communication. Below, you will find a story using fictional characters— Brother and Sister Brown (Primary teachers) and Katie (child with special needs)—to illustrate how each step would occur in a church setting.

Two years ago, Katie's speech delay caused many problems at church. She spoke less than a dozen words, and only her parents could understand her. She routinely threw tantrums in class. To resolve the tantrums, her teachers called her parents to figure out what she wanted. Many times, even her parents couldn't solve the problem. Brother and Sister Brown, her Sunbeam teachers, felt helpless and often talked about their concerns as they drove home from church. Katie's parents tried to be helpful, but the constant frustrations at church and home made their emotions raw as they watched their beautiful four-year-old daughter struggle.

One day, Katie's parents had a meeting with Brother and Sister Brown to talk to them about a new communication tool Katie was learning at school called the PECS program. Katie's parents explained the program to them and then asked Brother and Sister Brown if they'd help Katie use the system at church too. They agreed and met a few more times with Katie's parents for additional training.

During step one of the program, Brother Brown taught the Primary lessons while Sister Brown sat next to Katie in class. Sister Brown held a binder with some church-related pictures, such as crayons. During class, whenever Katie reached for something, Sister Brown prompted her to choose the picture from the binder of what she wanted and then hand

it to Brother Brown. Brother Brown then acknowledged her request by saying, "Katie, would you like some crayons?" Katie then nodded, and Brother Brown gave her the crayons.

Sometimes, Katie became frustrated and wanted to grab what she wanted. When this happened, Sister Brown would return the item to Brother Brown. Sister Brown would then hold Katie's hand, help her choose the picture she needed, and hand it to Brother Brown. He then said, "Thank you for asking, Katie," and gave her the items she requested.

As Katie became more accustomed to asking for items by using the PECS program, Sister Brown prompted her less and less. Eventually, Katie learned how to request items using her PECS cards all by herself.

Then Brother and Sister Brown started step two of the PECS program. Katie's parents explained that the goal of this step was for Katie to use the PECS program on her own without prompts from her teachers. During this stage, Brother and Sister Brown returned to alternating teaching the lessons each week, while the other sat with the kids in their class—but not next to Katie. This allowed Katie the opportunity to be even more independent in making her requests. Brother and Sister Brown also prompted Katie to use her PECS program to ask her class members to share items—such as pencils or paper—during the class activity time.

For step three, Katie's parents began to add more pictures to the PECS binder, such as pictures of Jesus, the prophet, the scriptures, a drinking fountain, and the bathroom. Soon Katie had a variety of pictures from which to choose and many ways to communicate her thoughts and needs. At this stage, Katie was able to answer questions from her teachers during class, such as, "Katie, who is being baptized in this picture?" She could look through her binder, find the picture of Jesus, and show it to her class. This was an important step for Katie to become an active participant during the lesson.

The last three steps of the program were the most fun for Brother and Sister Brown as they watched Katie master them. Katie's parents added word strips to her binder so she could turn her pictures from thoughts into sentences. The first word strip was "I want." At first, Katie had a hard time remembering to put her word strip and picture together on the Velcro pieces in her binder, but with some extra prompting

from Brother and Sister Brown, she remembered her new step. She was excited when Sister Brown pointed to her sentence and said, "Look, Brother Brown! Katie said, 'I want a drink'!"

Once Katie consistently created sentences with the "I want" word strip, new words began appearing in her binder, such as "please," "thank you," and "you're welcome." Then new sentence strips were added—"I see," "I hear," "I feel," and "I smell." By the end of the last step, Katie was forming sentences for class prayer, which one of her teachers or a class member voiced for her.

Comprehension

Another part of communication is comprehension. Some children with mental disabilities have a hard time understanding a particular word or set of directions. For example, a child with comprehension difficulties may not understand the word "scriptures" but would recognize them if handed to him. In this case, a teacher would tell the class, "It's time to get out your scriptures" and then hand the child with comprehension difficulties a picture of scriptures. This is the child's cue to open his scriptures. When the teacher is consistent with using pictures, the child will begin to recognize the word and directions. Then the teacher can begin to fade out the use of the picture. For more about how to fade out the system, please see the chapter called, "Putting It All Together."

If a child at church is already using either of these systems at home and school, ask the parents to teach you how to use it as well. Once you understand the basics, you can begin to communicate more effectively with the child you are serving.

PECS as a Schedule

PECS is also frequently used to help children understand a routine. When used for this purpose, pictures are created to represent the various activities that occur during a certain time period. The pictures are displayed vertically, and then the child starts at the top and removes the pictures as each activity is completed. This helps the child to visualize what is going to happen next, learn the routine, and know when that step is finished.

Here is one example of how you can create a PECS schedule. When we put together our son's schedule for church, we started with a file folder.

First, you lay the closed folder on a table, with the fold on the left-hand side like a book. Next, you measure and cut the folder so it's six inches wide, being sure to leave the length so the folder is tall, but skinny. Then the folder will need to be laminated for durability. Be sure to laminate it so you can open and close the folder. (I accidentally laminated mine closed the first time!)

The next step is to put together the PECS pictures. Black and white pictures are available on our author websites for your use (www.Danyelle Ferguson.com or www.LynnDParsons.com) or, if you prefer, you can create your own pictures. Either way, the pictures should be two by two inches and laminated.

Once you have your folder and pictures ready, you will need Velcro tabs to attach the pictures to the folder. I suggest not using heavy-duty Velcro because it's very noisy and can be strong enough that it's difficult for the child to remove the pictures. We found it worked best to have the harder, bumpy side of the Velcro attached to the folder, with the fuzzy side of the Velcro attached to the picture. On the inside of the folder, you should be able to create two columns of pictures on each side. As you create the columns, it's helpful to have both sides of the Velcro stuck together and attached to the pictures, with the side that is to be attached to the folder facing down to be sure you have the correct spacing. This also helps you to have the correct side of the Velcro attached to the folder so the pictures will stick. Then close the folder and use the pictures to add more Velcro backs down the front of the folder too. When you are finished, you can place all your church pictures back inside the folder. Now you have a portable PECS binder.

We used our church PECS folder like this:

Before church on Sunday morning, my husband sat down with our son and put the pictures for sacrament meeting on the front of the folder. We had certain times during the meeting when our son was allowed to choose incentives such as taking a walk, going to the water fountain, getting a snack, and so forth. Our son chose which incentives he wanted during sacrament meeting. The schedule ended with a picture of our son's Primary aide, which was his cue that it was time for Primary. Then during sacrament meeting, our son would take each picture off and hand it to his dad after each event took place. For example, he handed his dad the picture for the opening prayer after we said, "Amen."

When sacrament meeting was over, our son saw the picture of his Primary aide and would go with his dad to meet the aide in the foyer. Once there, the aide sat down with our son to put together the schedule for sharing time, including our son's break choices (file folder games, puzzles, and so forth). During sharing time, the aide prompted our son as each part of the schedule was completed. He always scheduled a break before the end of sharing time so he and our son could sit in the foyer again and prepare the schedule for class time with new incentives. The last picture after class time was of our family, which was our son's cue that it was time to meet us to go home.

During the week, we kept the pictures stored in the church PECS folder in our church bags, so it was never forgotten. If you'd like to use this system for multiple situations, I suggest creating more than one PECS folder and labeling them for the different activities. We had folders for riding the bus to and from school, family home evening, and so on. Another fun way to differentiate which folder is which is to make each folder a different color.

PECS for Everyone

Keep in mind, PECS can be beneficial for everyone. A member of the Primary presidency could use the system in sharing time by making larger pictures for the whole group to follow. PECS has been used in Junior Primary as a schedule board, where picture items are taken off as various activities—such as singing time, talks, and prayers—are completed. This allows all the children to see how the time is being used rather than just sitting for an hour. Pictures can be posted on a whiteboard or Velcro can be added to the backs of the picture to be hung on a fabric wall. Reverent children can then be selected to take the symbols down as they start or finish a section of opening exercises.

Likewise, a teacher can use it in a similar manner to show prayer, lesson time, activities through the lesson, singing, a trip to the bathroom, or a drink break.

For youth in Young Men and Young Women, smaller, more discrete schedules can be made by creating a small paper form that can be copied each week. The teenager can cross off activities as they are completed. We began something similar during sacrament meeting when our son was eight and have used it ever since. Each week, we pick up an extra sacrament meeting program just for him. Then my husband draws

a musical note next to the songs, a "P" next to the prayers, smiley faces next to each talk or ward business, and a cup for the sacrament. During the meeting, our son goes through and puts a check mark next to each as they occur. This is a great way to let the individual be independent and aware of his church schedule.

Power Card Strategies

by Danyelle Ferguson

Individuals with special needs are often very attached to a few strong interests. These interests could include a TV show, a movie, toy characters, and so on. Power cards are visual aids that use this special interest to encourage a certain behavior or better social choices.

Power cards are usually the size of a trading card—2.5 inches by 3.5 inches. It's best to use card stock and then laminate the card for durability. On the front of the power card, place a picture of the interest, such as the logo from a TV show or a picture of the character. Images can be easily found online. On the back of the card, place a one- or two-part script:

- A brief scenario describing how the hero solves the behavior you are targeting.
- A recap of how the individual can use the same strategy or a short sentence or two showing that the favorite character approves when the individual acts a certain way.

For example, let's pretend you have a child with special needs in your Cub Scout den. This child loves anything to do with Spider-Man. He also has a difficult time with good sportsmanship when playing games at den meetings. In this case, you could create a power card with a picture of Spider-Man on the front and the two-step script, targeting good sportsmanship, on the back. The script might read like this:

> Spider-Man likes to play games. Sometimes he wins the game.
> When he wins, Spider-Man feels happy. He might smile, give a high

five, or say "All right!" But sometimes he loses the game. When he loses, Spider-Man might not feel happy. He might take a deep breath, say "good job" to his friend, or say, "maybe next time."

Spider-Man wants everyone to have fun playing games. He wants me to remember these three things when playing games the Spider-Man way:

- Games should be fun for everyone.
- If I win a game, I can: smile, give a high five, or say, "All right!"
- If I lose a game I can: take a deep breath and say, "good job!" to my friend, or say "maybe next time."

For an example using the one-step script, let's say there's a girl named Anna who runs through the halls during Primary. Anna loves the movie "High School Musical." On her power card, you would put a picture from the movie on the front. Then on the back, write a simple statement, targeting the desired behavior, such as, "The cast from *High School Musical* likes it when Anna walks in the halls."

Point of View

Individuals with special needs identify themselves differently in written form. Some do well with first-person point of view (I, me, you), and others do better with third-person (their first name, such as Anna). It's most effective to write the power card whichever way they understand best.

Listen to how the individual talks about himself. Our son still uses his first name. So rather than telling someone, "I like hot dogs," he says, "Isaac likes hot dogs." If I were writing a power card for my son, I would use third-person (his first name).

When to Use a Power Card

Read the power card before you do an activity that would result in the behavior you're targeting.

Using the examples above, I would give the boy in Cub Scouts his power card and read it with him two or three times before we began a game. I would also let him keep the card throughout the game as a reminder. He can refer back to it if he has a hard time deciding how to react. During the game, be sure to compliment the Scout when he's using good sportsmanship and remind him that Spider-Man is proud of him too.

In Anna's case, I would give her the power card before going into church. We would read it together two or three times and then have her keep it in her hand or pocket for reference, as in the example above. If she needs to go to the bathroom during sacrament meeting, review the card before letting her get up. She should continue to review it throughout her stay at church. When she meets up with her Primary teacher or aide, it would be helpful for her if they expressed excitement about the power card, such as, "Hi, Anna! I'm so glad to see you! Did you bring your 'High School Musical' card with you today? All right! I know how much the cast likes being with you when you walk in the halls at church."

This may seem childish, but individuals with special needs generally have a hard time differentiating between what's real and imaginary. So to them, the characters they love aren't just cartoons or actors—they are real people with real lives. Even though it's just a picture on the power card, to them it may be more real, evoking a memory of the show or of their own imagination reinforcing the behavior they are trying to perform. It's this connection to their special interest that makes using power cards both effective and rewarding.

Eventually, as the behavior improves, you'll read the card less often. You might only read it once before the individual puts it in his pocket, or he may read it on his own. Gradually, as he masters the behavior, you'll put less emphasis on the card until it is phased out and no longer needed. When you get to this point, you may want to try not using the card a few times and see how he reacts. He may be fine without it. If so, keep it on hand in case he ever asks for it. If he prefers to have the card each week, that's fine as well. You can also keep the cards in a small photo album to celebrate the progress he's made.

ONCE UPON A TIME

Using Narrative Stories to Learn Routine

by Danyelle Ferguson

Children constantly learn and grow. Most children learn by watching others and following their example. Some children with special needs have a difficult time learning socially, and therefore miss the cues that signal a transition. This makes learning how church works very difficult. Routines make things more predictable and less frustrating for both the child and you. As the teacher or aide, you will need to have extra patience as the individual you're teaching learns his church schedule. It may take quite a while, but eventually he will get it.

Narrative Stories

One technique that helps the child to visualize a routine is using narrative stories. A narrative story is simply taking the child's routine, breaking it down into simple steps, and turning it into a story format. This story would then be read to the child at least once before beginning the activity. Be sure to make multiple copies of the story so parents and other church leaders who work with the child are able to use this tool as well.

Let's create a narrative story for Tommy, who is in the Primary CTR 5 class. Tommy attends church with his family, and his dad usually takes him to Primary. His teacher is Sister Joy, and his aide is Brother Clark. First, we'll create a detailed outline, which is basically his Primary routine broken into small steps. When you finish compiling the outline, take it to church the following week and see if there are any steps you may have missed or that need to be changed.

As you will see, the outline is very detailed. Depending on the

individual, you may need to start by stating each step he will go through during the narrative story. For example, you may need to be very detailed and say it's time for prayer—now we fold our arms, bow our heads, and be very quiet while we listen to the prayer. This is especially beneficial for young children or individuals who forget details easily and need reminders more often. If the individual has a better memory, then you can combine some sections together. For example, instead of listing the opening song, scripture, and prayer separately with their own individual pictures, combine them together in one sentence with one general picture. There's a variety of ways to create the steps. For your first attempt, use your best judgment as to what you think the individual needs. Then make adjustments—adding more or combining steps—about every three weeks, if needed. If the story is working, then don't change it until the individual is very secure in his routine and is ready to advance to a shortened story. For some, that may be a matter of a few months. For others, it could be years before they are ready to go on to the next step. There is no right or wrong amount of time for progress. Some teenagers and adults continue to use a detailed narrative story because that's what works best for them.

Detailed Outline:

- After sacrament meeting, Tommy's dad takes him to meet Brother Clark in the foyer.
- Brother Clark and Tommy read the narrative story.
- Tommy walks reverently to sharing time.
- He sits with the class. When he sits in his chair, he keeps his feet on the floor and his chair still.
- First is an opening song.
- A child reads a scripture and then says a prayer.
- Another child gives a talk.
- Then it's time for music.
- After music time, Brother Clark takes Tommy for a short walk and activity. Then they go back to sharing time.
- The Primary president teaches a gospel principle.
- Classes are dismissed to their classrooms.
- Before going to class, Brother Clark and Tommy go for a walk in the hall, visit the bathroom, and get a drink from the fountain near the Primary room.

- In class, Sister Joy sits next to the chalkboard. The children in the class sit in chairs around Sister Joy.
- A child says the opening prayer.
- Sister Joy teaches the lesson.
- Sister Joy usually has an activity after the lesson.
- A child gives the closing prayer.
- Brother Clark takes Tommy to meet his family in the foyer.

Remember that before you begin writing, you'll need to decide what point of view to use for the story. You can figure this out by how the child refers to himself. Does he say, "I like cars" or "Tommy likes cars?" In this case, Tommy refers to himself by using his name.

You may want to consider drawing a picture next to some of the sentences. Don't worry if you're not a great artist—kids love to color stick figures! You can also use some of the PECS symbols found on our author websites or find free black-and-white-outline clip art on the Internet. Then each Sunday, your child can color them while he reads the story.

Another idea is to take pictures of the child throughout his day at church to illustrate the story. This is really fun to do if you choose to have your story look like a children's picture book. I've seen this style of narrative story created extravagantly in a small scrapbook binder complete with cute backgrounds and stickers. While it's very cute, it can potentially distract the individual, who may focus more on the stickers than the pictures and story. You can create a simple storybook by dividing pages in half. If you are doing this on your computer, you can put a guideline down the middle of landscape-oriented pages. If not, then start by cutting paper in half. Each half page will have one section of text, such as, "On Sundays, Tommy goes to church with his family." A picture of Tommy and his family in church dress is then put in above the text. To make the book less bulky, it's a good idea to use both the front and the back of each page. Don't forget to create a title page, such as, "Tommy's Day at Church." You can either laminate the pages and staple them for durability or three-hole punch the pages and add them to a simple binder.

Now that we have made the outline, have decided which point of view to use, and know how we want the book to appear, we can begin to write the actual story.

Tommy's Day at Church

On Sundays, Tommy goes to church with his family.	picture of church
After sacrament meeting, Tommy's dad takes him to meet Brother Clark. Brother Clark and Tommy read a story about his day in Primary.	picture of book
Then they walk reverently to sharing time.	picture of shoes
In sharing time, Tommy sits with his class. He tries to keep his feet on the ground and his chair still.	picture of chair
The music leader helps them sing an opening song.	picture of musical notes
Then a Primary child reads a scripture, followed by the opening prayer.	picture of child with arms crossed
Another Primary child gives a short talk.	picture of child at the podium
After the talk, the children have music time. Tommy gets to sing lots of fun Primary songs!	picture of musical notes
When music time is finished, Brother Clark and Tommy go for a walk in the halls. Sometimes they do an activity too.	picture of shoes
When they get back to sharing time, usually someone from the Primary presidency is telling a story or playing a game with the kids. When she is finished, she calls out the names of classes. When she calls Tommy's class, "CTR 5!," he quietly walks with his class out of the room.	picture with "CTR 5"

Before going to class, Brother Clark and Tommy go for a walk in the halls, visit the bathroom, and get a drink from the water fountain near the Primary room.	picture of shoes
In Tommy's classroom, Sister Joy sits near the chalkboard. The rest of the kids sit in chairs in front of her.	picture of chairs
One of the class members says an opening prayer.	picture of prayer
Then Sister Joy tells Tommy and the class about her lesson. Usually after her lesson, Sister Joy has an activity for Tommy and the other kids.	picture of crayons
Before class is over, another class member says the closing prayer.	picture of prayer
Then Brother Clark and Tommy walk together to meet Tommy's family in the foyer. When Tommy is with his family again, it's time to go home.	picture of parents

As you can see, narrative stories are simple and easy to write. The important thing is to include the steps of the individual's day. The story can also be broken up into smaller stories for individuals of any age and read in sections before church, when arriving at sacrament meeting, before Sunday School, before priesthood, and after priesthood. This is good for youth and adults with short memories. When the individual is more comfortable with his church routine, you'll want to shorten the story and fade it out. At this point, you may want to keep a copy of the story on hand for use after extended vacations or conferences. Reading through the story can help an individual with special needs transition back into the church routine.

Putting It All Together

PECS, Power Cards, and Narrative Stories

by Danyelle Ferguson

In the last three chapters, we learned about the Picture Exchange Communication System (PECS), power cards, and narrative stories. Now we are going to talk about how to use these techniques together.

To begin, let's talk about some guidelines and tips.

Introduce one technique at a time. Give the individual the opportunity to learn and become familiar with one technique (about six weeks of church) before introducing another.

Be consistent. Once you introduce a technique, be sure to use it the same way each week. It also helps if others know and refer to it in a similar manner.

Be patient. It takes time to learn the church routine. Teachers may feel as though the individual takes two steps forward and then one step back. Even so, he is still making progress. Often, teachers at school see their students struggle to learn a concept for an extended period. About the time the teacher starts thinking he needs to try something else or that the student just isn't getting it, the student will suddenly make a big jump in progress.

Occasionally, you may introduce a technique and then, after six weeks, find it's still not working and the individual is rejecting it. In this case, take a break. Stop using that technique and try another. Some teachers find that if they do this and then reintroduce the first technique at a later time, the individual will accept it. This could occur for many different reasons, such as if the individual wasn't ready for that

technique or if he was going through a stubborn phase.

Keep a progress journal. Each week, write down how the individual did and include both successes and difficulties. About every six months, go back and read through it. You'll be surprised by the progress he has made. Journals are a great tool to help leaders and parents see progress more clearly.

Using Techniques Together

Find out if the individual is already using any techniques at school or at home. If one is being used and the technique is successful, generalize it to church. For example, if the individual is using a PECS schedule at school to plan out his day, then it's a technique he already knows, and he will understand it more quickly when it's introduced at church. If none of these techniques are currently being used outside of church, then have a meeting with church leaders, parents, and possibly the individual with special needs. Talk about the different options together and choose a starting point.

If you begin by using a PECS schedule and then later introduce a narrative story, look to see if any of the pictures from the schedule can be used to illustrate the story. The individual has already associated the schedule pictures with prayer, scriptures, music, and so on. So if Tommy (the example from the chapter on narrative stories) reads the part in his story that says, "A child reads a scripture and then says an opening prayer" and sees the same prayer picture from his PECS schedule next to the sentence, he comprehends the sentence and routine more quickly.

Power cards are easy to introduce and use with any of the other techniques because they are targeting one specific behavior, such as walking in the halls. For example, let's say you're reading a narrative story with a young boy, and you're to the part where you are going to walk to the drinking fountain for a break from sharing time. You would then hand the boy his power card and briefly review it together. He can hold it in his hand or put it in his pocket for easy reference while he's in the halls. You can do the same thing if you're using a PECS schedule. When you get to the break picture, you would hand the boy his power card, review it, and then go for your break.

If you begin with a narrative story and use PECS pictures as illustrations, then it's very easy to transition from the narrative story to

a simpler PECS schedule with brief narrations when the instructions are needed most. For example, let's say you have a young woman who spends too much time in the bathroom between the Sunday School and Young Women break. Her schedule could have a small narrative following the break picture that reads, "After Sunday School, I can visit the bathroom, get a drink from the fountain, and then go to my Young Women class." It can be helpful to read the expectation rather than have it all bundled into one break symbol.

As you can see, the PECS schedule, narrative stories, and power cards can be used alone or in any combination. The key is to find a technique or combination that works well for the individual. Then be consistent and use it the same way each week.

Fading Out Techniques

Once the individual has a good grasp of his routine at church or has learned the concept you were trying to teach (such as with power cards), then you will fade out the use of that technique. The goal is not to use them forever but to use them as stepping stones to help him attend church classes as independently as possible.

Power cards are the simplest to fade out. You can congratulate the individual for mastering the concept and then retire the card to a binder with clear baseball card protector sheets. This is important because 1) you may need the card again and 2) it's fun to let him look through it and see everything he's accomplished. And since the cards have pictures of his favorite interests on them, he enjoys looking through the binder as well.

There are two ways to fade out a narrative story. You can tell the individual you think he's doing a great job and you'd like to try not reading the story. Then simply put it away in a place where you can easily access it, if needed. Or you can choose to write a shorter, more general story to ease the transition. For example, "I go to church with my family. After sacrament meeting, I meet my class in the Primary room. First, I have sharing time, where I sing and learn from the Primary presidency. Then I go to class with my teacher, Sister Joy. She teaches us a lesson, and we have an activity. After class, I meet my family in the foyer, and we go home." Once this shorter story is mastered, you can put it away with the expanded story.

There are several ways to fade out the PECS schedule. It may take

a few stages before it's completely faded out. Some individuals do well transitioning from having the schedule in their hands all the time, to looking at it briefly to remind them what is next, until finally fading it out. If he has a very detailed schedule and is pulling off pictures as each activity happens, you will want to make the schedule simpler by combining activities. For example, instead of having scripture, prayer, and opening song pictured separately, combine them into one picture with the words on the bottom. Continue doing this over time until the schedule is faded out.

Conclusion

When you fade out a technique, be sure to keep the materials stored where they can be easily accessed. Individuals with special needs may require help reorienting to their church routine after extended periods away (illness, vacations, conferences, and so forth). They may also need the reassurance of their routine when they change classes each year. Even though the routine is the same, a new class teacher or even a substitute teacher may throw a kink in their perception of routine. Also, any major life change, such as moving or changes in relationships at home or with friends can cause regression. It's reassuring and comforting for the individual to have their routine "helpers" available during these times.

Primary

EVERY STAR IS DIFFERENT

Teaching Children about Disabilities

by Danyelle Ferguson

Every child is unique, and that uniqueness should be treasured. Young children are typically very accepting and loving as they come into contact with other children. As they grow older, sometimes the things that make other children unique seem different, strange, or scary. They may ask their parents about a child with special needs. Some parents aren't sure how to answer their questions. Others may try to be politically correct and answer that there isn't anything wrong with the child in question. Many times, children come away even more confused.

In this situation, what the child needs is an honest, simple, clear answer. At the time the question is asked, the reply may be, "Sweetie, I don't know. But I could call his mommy and ask her about it. Would that be okay with you?" This gives the parent the opportunity to become more informed and to figure out the best way to answer the child's question. At the same time, the child feels that his concern was heard, was validated, and will be answered.

Primary leaders can help children understand the concept that even though we are not all the same, we are all children of God. We each have different strengths and talents. While it's okay to want to be like others or to admire their talents, we should never think Heavenly Father values one child more than another. Likewise, when we meet children who have a difficult time with things that are easy for us, we should remember they are loved by Heavenly Father too. By being kind and a good friend, we can help everyone feel important, valued, and loved.

Sharing Time Activities

To help reinforce these concepts, I have compiled several sharing time activities that help teach about differences or disabilities.

Jesus Loved Everyone

Preparation: On the Church website, find, print, and read "My Friend Aaron" (Alma J. Yates, "My Friend Aaron," *Friend*, Feb. 1994, 2).

Lesson: Share stories about how Jesus loved and showed kindness to others, especially those who were sick or crippled. Talk about how He reached out and cared for them all. Paraphrase the story *My Friend Aaron*. Emphasize that because Benjamin was willing to sit with Aaron and be his friend, many of the other kids at school were less afraid of Aaron and became his friends too. Ask the children if what Benjamin did was an example of trying to be like Jesus. Encourage them to try to be like Jesus. Then challenge them to help someone and tell you about it the following week.

Who's Like Me? Graph

Preparation: Cut out several squares of paper. Make a list of talents, hobbies, and favorite foods (examples: soccer, pizza, food allergies, dancing, singing, writing, reading, camping, playing a musical instrument). Write one of the topics on the back of each square. Use magnets to place the squares on a blackboard, the blank side facing the class. You will also need a large piece of butcher paper to make the graph. Placing the paper in landscape orientation, write numbers on the left-hand side. Zero should be at the bottom, and then go up by multiples of ten to the top of the paper. You will also need to make a column for each topic. Do not label the columns until Sunday, when the kids choose a topic. You will also need markers or crayons to color the columns.

Lesson: Choose one child at a time to pick out a square on the board. Read the topic to the children and then ask the kids to raise their hands to see how many have that talent or interest. Keep track by coloring each column up to the number of hands raised. At the end of the activity, refer to the graph and comment on how it shows many different talents, hobbies, and so on—but that it also shows how they all have something in common with each member of Primary.

Send Me a Letter

Preparation: you will need three sheets of blank paper, three

envelopes, a blindfold, a pair of mittens, and a box.

Lesson: Invite three children to help put letters into envelopes. Once they are up front, have one child put on mittens, have another put on a blindfold, and leave the third alone. All three need to pick up a sheet of paper, put it in an envelope, seal it, and then place it in the box. Time each of them. Usually, the child without any obstacles will finish first. Afterward, ask the children watching why it took the others longer to finish. Then tell about something that's hard for you (such as art or a sport) and that for you, it's like the child who had to wear mittens. Ask the children to share "mitten" experiences they've had. Explain that for some kids, walking, reading, or making friends can be difficult, just like the child who wore the blindfold or used mittens to put the letter in the envelope.

Mini Spotlights

Preparation: Call parents and invite them to come to speak to the Primary.

Lesson: Invite three parents to talk about their children in sharing time. One of the parents could have a child with special needs. Ask each of the parents to share things that are difficult for their child, as well as things they enjoy or do really well. They can bring pictures or other props to represent challenges and talents. Then have a member of the presidency spotlight another member of the presidency and share things that were difficult for her growing up and things she enjoys, and so on. Talk about how we each have things we enjoy and also things that are challenging, but Heavenly Father loves us all. Sing the song, "I'll Walk with You" (Children's Songbook #140). Share your testimony.

Guest Speaker

Preparation: Ask a ward member with disabilities to come speak to the kids in Primary. If there isn't anyone available in your ward, you will need to get permission from the bishop to invite a guest speaker.

Lesson: Ask your guest to share things that make him different from others—some related to his disability and some that are not—as well as things he enjoys. The guest should share stories of how others helped him feel loved and included, as well as inspirational stories and his testimony. You may want to sing some of his favorite Primary songs and play a fun game together.

Conclusion

As the Primary children participate in these types of activities, their understanding and compassion for others will increase. Then, no matter where they are—home, school, or church—they will receive their own promptings from the Holy Ghost to be kind and loving to anyone they meet.

THE BAPTISM DILEMMA

by Danyelle Ferguson

B aptism is a subject parents either are eager to find out about or aren't ready to consider yet. Whichever group parents fall in, they typically experience the same feelings—fear, anxiety, and sadness. *Will my child be baptized? What if he isn't? What if he's afraid to go in the water? What if I feel he's not quite ready yet?* No matter what the child's functioning level, parents wonder what their child's place in Heavenly Father's kingdom is at this tender age when their peers are preparing for that ultimate goal in Primary: baptism.

When our son turned seven years old, we decided to focus on baptism for the majority of our family home evenings until he turned eight. Our hope was that by doing this, he would have a good understanding of baptism principles and be excited to get baptized. A few months before his birthday, we started asking him if he'd like to be baptized when he turned eight. The answer was always "no" or "I don't know." The closer his birthday came, the more anxious and sad I felt. One part of me felt he understood baptism and had a fairly good grasp on the covenants he would make. This part of me wanted to set a baptism date and hope for the best. But the Spirit kept whispering, "Be still."

As I prayed and asked for guidance, memories of my own baptism at age sixteen resurfaced with more frequency. I thought about learning the gospel, my feelings, and the promptings that led me to know baptism was the right thing for me—and not just to be baptized, but to be a member of The Church of Jesus Christ of Latter-day Saints. I also thought about many of my growing-up experiences. Some were

wonderful and others weren't. But as I thought about how they affected my personality and choices, I realized that each experience helped me grow into the young woman I was when the missionaries taught me, and I found joy in their message. For quite a while, all of this tumbled around in my head. Then one day it finally hit me. I wanted our son to have the same experience I did. I wanted him to *want* to be baptized— not because he was eight years old or because of his parents' wishes, but because he had the *desire*. I knew we had taught him all he needed to know and that he had a sufficient understanding to make the decision when he was ready. So I let the decision go from my hands to my son's hands . . . and I finally felt peace.

I know each family will have a different experience with different questions, concerns, and circumstances. But the wonderful thing about baptism is that there's no right or wrong decision. Some families will find the answer easily, and others will have to feel their way. But I do know that through prayer, the Holy Ghost will send promptings to guide you along that path until you, your spouse, and your child find peace.

What are your choices when it comes to baptism? Basically, there are three options:

- Baptism at age eight
- Delaying baptism
- Unaccountability

Baptism at Age Eight

This option is fairly self-explanatory. If your child has a desire to be baptized when he turns eight years old and your bishop feels he's ready, then you would make an appointment for a baptism interview and proceed as usual.

Delaying Baptism

Does your son or daughter need some more time to learn about baptism? Has he said, "I want to get baptized"? Have you felt that he needs more time to develop or to become a little more mature before making a decision? There are a variety of reasons parents choose to delay. Often, parents feel pressure or stress about having their child baptized as soon as he or she turns eight years old. If your child's

birthday is approaching and you're not certain what to do, then make an appointment with your bishop.

My husband and I found it very helpful to talk with our bishop about our concerns. We talked about the wonderful things our son was accomplishing at church, school, and home, as well as the areas where we felt he still needed help. Our bishop reminded us that every child grows and understands gospel principles at a different rate. He also expressed that sometimes it's not how much a child knows about baptism that counts; rather, it's his desire to follow the Savior's example that matters.

Try to remember that every day, converts of all ages are baptized as members of the Church. The important thing is not the age but that your child's testimony and knowledge of the Savior is growing. It's perfectly fine to delay your child's baptism. In fact, it's a great opportunity for him not only to develop his understanding but also to increase his desire to become a member of The Church of Jesus Christ of Latter-day Saints.

Unaccountability

If your child doesn't understand baptism, the basics of the plan of salvation, *and* isn't likely to gain that intelligence in this life, you may decide not to baptize him. In that case, his records would be marked "unaccountable." Essentially, it means he will remain pure and innocent no matter his behavior or the choices he makes here on earth. Here are two beautiful scriptures that illustrate unaccountability:

"Yea, and I know that good and evil have come before all men; he that knoweth not good from evil is blameless" (Alma 29:5).

"Wherefore, little children are whole, for they are not capable of committing sin" (Moroni 8:8).

Choosing to mark your child's records "unaccountable" is not a once-in-a-lifetime decision and isn't set in stone. Your child may grow and choose to be baptized later. After all, who knows what blessings and miracles are in store for your son or daughter?

Which Path Should Be Chosen?

The next question may be, "Which option is right for my child?" That decision is best made in consultation with priesthood leaders and your child. The path to your answer may be easy, but it may require extra time to ponder and pray before you reach the right decision. We

are promised in D&C 18:18, "Ask the Father in my name, in faith believing that you shall receive, and you shall have the Holy Ghost, which manifesteth all things which are expedient." To help you along the pathway, we've included

- several scriptures,
- answers to frequently asked questions, and
- stories from families sharing their experiences in making this decision

Through studying these additional helps, parents and priesthood leaders can gain a better understanding of the baptism requirements and how to gauge your child's readiness.

Scriptures about Baptism

Moroni 8:8, 9–12, 15 "Wherefore, little children are whole, for they are not capable of committing sin. . . .

"And after this manner did the Holy Ghost manifest the word of God unto me; wherefore, my beloved son, I know that it is solemn mockery before God, that ye should baptize little children.

"Behold I say unto you that this thing shall ye teach—repentance and baptism unto those who are accountable and capable of committing sin; yea, teach parents that they must repent and be baptized, and humble themselves as their little children, and they shall all be saved with their little children.

"And their little children need no repentance, neither baptism. Behold, baptism is unto repentance to the fulfilling the commandments unto the remission of sins.

"But little children are alive in Christ, even from the foundation of the world; if not so, God is a partial God, and also a changeable God, and a respecter to persons; for how many little children have died without baptism! . . .

"For awful is the wickedness to suppose that God saveth one child because of baptism, and the other must perish because he hath no baptism."

D&C 20:71 "No one can be received into the church of Christ unless he has arrived unto the years of accountability before God, and is capable of repentance."

D&C 29:46–50 "But behold, I say unto you, that little children are redeemed from the foundation of the world through mine Only Begotten;

"Wherefore, they cannot sin, for power is not given unto Satan to tempt little children, until they begin to become accountable before me;

"For it is given unto them even as I will, according to mine own pleasure, that great things may be required at the hand of their fathers.

"And, again, I say unto you, that whoso having knowledge, have I not commanded to repent?

"And he that hath no understanding, it remaineth in me to do according as it is written. And now I declare no more unto you at this time. Amen."

For more scriptures, search for "baptism" and "accountability" in the Topical Guide and Bible Dictionary.

Frequently Asked Questions

Q. If my child chooses to be baptized, is he fully accountable like other children, or is he only accountable for what he understands?

A. First, we need to differentiate between the two definitions of accountability: the *age* of accountability and the *principle* of accountability.

When I searched for "age of accountability" in the Guide to the Scriptures, I found the following quote: "The age of accountability is the age at which children are considered to be responsible for their actions and capable of committing sin and repenting."[1] From the scriptures, we know the age of accountability is eight years old (see D&C 68:27), but for a child with special needs, the actual age at which he becomes accountable may be after his eighth birthday.

Accountability is knowing the difference between right and wrong and being able to make choices based on that knowledge. For every child, the process of becoming accountable is gradual. Each child learns, understands, and grows at different rates. For example, we are accountable for tithing to the degree that we are able to obtain and understand that principle. Heavenly Father loves our children, understands their hearts and desires, and has great compassion as they learn and grow. He won't hold His children fully accountable for things they are still learning, but He will test them and help them grow in their understanding

throughout their lives, just as He does with each of us.

Q. Do we have to participate in a group baptism? Do we need to follow a certain program outline?

A. If your stake normally schedules group baptisms on a certain day each month, then you would need to talk to your bishop to request a private baptism. You may need to explain why you would like a quieter service. Some bishops anticipate your needs and bring up the subject before you even need to ask. Your child's baptism may still be on the same day as the group baptisms, but possibly later in the day after the other wards are finished using the font and other rooms.

As for the program, that is completely flexible. The only things that need to be done in an exact way are the baptism and the confirmation. For example, you could skip the talks and sing several favorite Primary songs before and after the baptism, or you could just walk in, have an opening prayer, perform the baptism, change clothes, perform the confirmation, have a closing prayer, and then go home.

Note: You may want to think ahead about how many people you should invite to the baptism. If a large group would be too distracting, then only invite those who are closest to your child. Generally, your family, friends, and ward members will understand. You could include them by asking that they send your child a note with their testimony for a scrapbook. Be sure to ask your child if there's someone special he would like to invite.

Q. If my child isn't baptized, can he or she hold callings?

A. Yes, your child can receive callings the bishop feels inspired to extend. There are certain callings that require the holder to be a baptized and confirmed member of the Church, such as a member of the bishopric. There are other callings for which baptism is not required, such as Relief Society music leader or Primary birthday specialist. You can work with your bishop to talk about what strengths your son or daughter has, and then the bishop can go to the Lord in prayer to find the right place where your child should serve.

Q. If my child is not baptized, do his baptism and other ordinances need to be done after he dies, or are his circumstances similar to those of someone who died before age eight?

A. If your child chose not to be baptized at age eight, then when

he dies, his baptism and other ordinances would be performed by a family member at the temple, just as you would perform ordinances for ancestors in your genealogy. At this time, your child will have a clear and intelligent intellect and will be able to fully accept the covenants he wasn't ready to make while living here on earth.

Q. What can I do to prepare my child for his baptism day and the actual ordinance?

A. There are several things that can help your son or daughter get ready. Books, pamphlets, and videos are available through your meetinghouse library, the distribution center, and other LDS sources.

An important step is to have your child practice being baptized at home. Whoever is performing the ordinance should practice often with your child.

Have the priesthood leader and your child stand in the living room and pretend it's the baptismal font. Practice how to stand, how to hold her arms, what the prayer will be, how to take a deep breath and plug her nose, how to bend her knees and keep her feet underwater (the priesthood leader should help by placing his leg in front of hers or his foot on her feet so they don't slip and come up), dipping "under water," and of course, coming back up!

Teach your child that the priesthood leader is saying a prayer. When he's speaking, it's okay for her to close her eyes. When he says "Amen," she can open them again, and he'll help her get ready to go under the water.

A note to the priesthood leader: There's no time limit or rush. Take a moment to help her get ready, prompt her to take a breath and plug her nose, put your leg in front or foot on top of hers, and *then* dip. By taking that moment to prepare, the chances are much higher of having the baptism be successful the first time it's performed.

Q. What if my child doesn't want to be baptized even though I think he's ready?

A. Remember, the person being baptized is your child, and ultimately it's his choice. If he's afraid of water or the ordinance, that's okay. If he isn't ready to be baptized, try not to push the subject. Instead, be loving and supportive as he continues to learn and grow in the gospel. He may change his mind one day or he may never be baptized. Remember that Heavenly Father knows his heart and understands his challenges.

What can you do to encourage him without being pushy? Take the opportunity to attend his friends' baptisms. If there's a fear factor, this may help to reduce it. You could occasionally ask if he'd like to be baptized—just remember, no nagging! And no matter his choice, hug him frequently and let him know that you and Heavenly Father love him.

Family Stories

Before you read these beautiful stories, we'd like to say thank you to the families who took the time to share their experiences, which addressed many of the feelings had by parents who are currently faced with the "baptism question." Each story has a different outcome, but each shows Heavenly Father's love for His children.

Brayden

This turned out to be more of an explanation of how Brayden's spirit doesn't need to be tested rather than our decision about baptism. We just didn't have a big decision to make because he's nowhere near the point of understanding baptism—it would be like baptizing a baby. His deficits have been noticeable since birth. We just always assumed he was one of those special souls sent to earth who didn't need to be tested and tried like the rest of us.

As parents, it's a little disappointing that he won't celebrate this milestone as his siblings have. But we've come to realize his milestones are measured differently than ours. He has already surpassed us in understanding the gospel. Our family feels he was allowed to come to earth to receive a body and to teach others. We cannot wait until we can converse with him on the other side—it motivates us to live the very best we can so we can return to live with Heavenly Father and see Brayden as our Heavenly Father sees him.

The other day, our bishop commented that we are so lucky to have such a special spirit in our family and that we'll know him as a perfect being in the celestial kingdom. We chose to focus on reaching for that blessing, so our disappointment that he wasn't baptized is very minimal. We feel blessed to have such a special spirit in our family. Brayden is so innocent and loving. His spirit is at a point that he doesn't need to enter the waters of baptism—he's perfect just as he is.

Amy

Defining Amy and her disability isn't easy, because there's still no

clear diagnosis for her. Her older brother had recently been diagnosed with autism when Amy was a baby, so our antennae were already tuned to the something-isn't-right-here setting. A breakthrough came at age five, when a severe hearing impairment was confirmed. Her ability to express or understand language is still at a two-year-old level. However, her intellect is normal—it's just trapped inside a body that can't express itself. Today we see Amy as both a normal eight-year-old with a future similar to that of her peers and also a very unusual eight-year-old whose future is a mysterious unknown. The decision of whether to baptize Amy at the age of eight always seemed far off until it was upon us. As Amy approached her birthday, I half-expected a long and tearful conversation with our bishop, but it never happened. We will ever be grateful for a wise and sensitive bishop who took casual opportunity from time to time to share inspired gems of wisdom with us. Two things he said put our minds at ease and helped us to make appropriate decisions.

The first gave us the assurance to trust our instincts: "When the time is right, you will know it." That confidence helped me to relax and not panic about a deadline. I was relieved to be reminded that inspiration would come to us and not to someone else. Our bishop also told us, "When she *wants* to be baptized, you'll know she's ready." I had been in the mind-set that Amy wouldn't be ready until she knew, understood, and verbalized the doctrines of faith and repentance. I realized she didn't need words to know in her heart that she has a Father in Heaven and He loves her. Her understanding of faith would be evident simply by desiring to be baptized.

The second piece of wisdom shared by our bishop was inspiration to us: "The scriptures don't teach us to baptize our children when they *are* accountable, but when they *begin* to become accountable" (see D&C 29:46–47). I don't believe I had previously thought Amy would just wake up one morning and suddenly be accountable for her behaviors. But it was a great comfort to know the process would be gradual and when that process begins, she will have the protection of the Atonement as she continues to develop her language and understanding of gospel principles. Because of our confidence to trust our intuition and the inspiration the Lord grants us, we know that process hasn't started for Amy yet, but we can feel it is very close. Our experience has reenergized our efforts to teach our children gospel principles at family home evening. We have switched gears to "Amy level" and have made our topics

simple: faith and repentance. Amy does know who Jesus is, and she feels His love for her. Like all children, Amy continues to grow and develop, only at a unique pace. And like all parents, we know God is mindful of our efforts and loves our children even more than we have capacity to love. He will help us to know when the time is right—and so will Amy.

Matthew

Long before Matthew turned eight years old, my husband and I realized he might not be ready for baptism right on time. At the age of eight, he seemed to understand many things, but because his ability to talk was so limited, we had no way of knowing what he actually understood. We took the time to read what the scriptures and Church leaders said about baptism for those with mental limitations. We also talked to friends who had older children with disabilities to see what they chose to do. Some people believed he shouldn't be baptized because he would become accountable for all his actions. This didn't make sense to us because we believed the Lord wouldn't hold someone to a level of accountability beyond their ability. Our understanding was that although it wasn't *necessary* for Matthew to be baptized, it was possible to have him baptized—possibly at a later time as his understanding increased.

In the end, Matthew actually made the decision. Matthew wasn't—and still isn't—very conversational, but when he has something he really wants to say, he says it. Several months before his eighth birthday, he came to me and said, "When I am eight, I will be baptized." He was very happy. We wondered if somehow he learned this in our home, although he seldom stayed in the room for more than a few minutes of family home evening. He possibly learned it in Primary, although he never talked about it or gave any indication that he learned or heard anything there. The only thing we knew he learned at Primary were the songs, which he sang all the time.

We approached our bishop, and without hesitation, he told us if this was Matthew's desire, then he should definitely be baptized when he turned eight. We soon experienced several small miracles—the kind Matthew frequently brings into our lives. We had been planning a trip to visit my parents in Nauvoo, Illinois, but then we realized we would miss Matthew's scheduled stake baptism date. We considered postponing it until we realized he could be baptized in Nauvoo.

The next small miracle happened during his baptism interview. We worried that the bishop might ask questions beyond Matthew's ability to understand or word his questions in a way that would frustrate him. We also worried that Matthew wouldn't respond to the questions he was asked. Our worries were soon gone. The bishop asked his questions in a very simple way that Matthew could answer "yes" or "no." Matthew gave the bishop his complete attention and answered each question appropriately. It was truly amazing. Another small miracle happened as we were traveling to Nauvoo. I asked my other children what songs we should sing at Matthew's baptism service. I didn't expect Matthew to be a part of this decision, so I didn't make any attempt to get his attention or simplify my language. I had no idea he was listening or comprehended what we were discussing. We all stopped short when he clearly suggested "The Still Small Voice." It was perfect!

The day came, and Matthew acted appropriately all day, at a time when his behavior was still very inconsistent. He literally beamed before, during, and after the service. The Spirit was strong, and we knew the Lord was pleased with the decision Matthew had made.

John

As John approached his eighth birthday, I wondered whether we should have him baptized. As he is the youngest of five children, I wanted him to experience as many of the same life markers as our other children and as his peers. Yet I wondered if baptism was appropriate for a child with less emotional and mental maturity than his peer group. Being a single mother at that time, I felt particularly alone as I pondered this decision. After consulting with the bishop and expressing my desire that John be baptized, we decided to go ahead with the event.

Much effort went into preparing him for baptism. John is slow to learn and picks up only a small part of what is presented in a formal classroom situation. Thus extra effort was put into teaching at home.

An unusual physical aspect we needed to consider was John's limited swallowing ability. Up to that day, John had never had his head under water. He can't close his mouth tightly enough to prevent water from entering, nor does he use his mouth for eating. He's totally fed with a feeding tube, only taking a few drops of water every Sunday at church during the sacrament and partaking of the bread by touching it

to his tongue. My fear of putting him under water was great, but I felt determined to proceed.

John's oldest brother had just become an elder and was soon leaving for his mission. John's next oldest brother had just become a priest. Together, the two boys went into the waters of baptism with their little brother, giving him support and holding the priesthood authority needed for John to follow the Savior's example and do all the Father commands. There was a wonderful spirit there as John was baptized and received the gift of the Holy Ghost. For our family, it was a matter of faith and obedience as we participated in those sacred ordinances.

Becca

Becca has Down syndrome and desired to take the first step toward the glorious reward that awaits those who are faithful to the commandments—baptism day! Becca had talked about being baptized for years, and our bishop was behind us all the way. She memorized four articles of faith and understood some of the importance of this day—enough to make her worthy of this ordinance. She knew by heart the Primary songs that help prepare for baptism.

Her brother, Eric, baptized her. He was excited, and she was so happy to have him perform the ordinance. Her friend Laura was baptized with her, and it made for a beautiful afternoon. There were no dry eyes in the congregation as family and friends listened, watched, and felt the beautiful spirit in attendance. Becca's father confirmed her as a member of The Church of Jesus Christ of Latter-day Saints. Those in attendance witnessed a powerful outpouring of the Spirit.

Since that time, Becca has gone on to receive her patriarchal blessing, which promises great blessings if she will obey the commandments. She earned her Young Women Service Award and her medallion. She has filled a service mission at the MTC in the mail room. She received her endowments at the Provo Temple and now works there in the laundry every Monday. She has been so blessed. And it all started with her baptism and being included in activities and ordinances in the Church.

Conclusion

It's my hope that this chapter has answered many of your questions and given you hope and a sense of peace. I know that as you pray to

Heavenly Father and ask for His guidance, you will be led toward the path that is right for your child. No matter what your journey may be, always remember your child is precious and loved dearly by Heavenly Father.

Note

1. The Guide to the Scriptures, www.lds.org.

Girls Just Want to Have Fun

A Guide for Achievement Days Leaders

by Lynn Parsons

Achievement Days is designed to allow girls ages eight through eleven to participate in wholesome activities. This program encourages social growth, creativity, physical development, cultural learning, and service. Blessings from program participation extend for many years. One teen with autism credits the friendships she made during Achievement Days with her motivation to attend Mutual.

Planning

Before making plans, you need to learn about any child with special needs who may be in your group. Talk to the parents and find out all you can about her disability. For more information on what to ask, see the chapter called "Getting to Know You." Start with these questions and follow up with any you feel inspired to add.

- What is her disability?
- How does this affect her participation in Primary?
- Are there any medications, food allergies, or other health concerns?
- Are there behavior triggers that should be avoided (noises, bright lights, and so forth)?
- What teaching methods work best at home?
- What ideas are successful for school?
- What is the best way for parents and teachers to communicate?

The last question is designed to help you start working closely with her parents. If you explain that this is a partnership for the benefit of

their daughter, you set a tone that will help you collaborate to solve future challenges rather than working against each other.

After you've learned all you can from the parents, do some research on your own. Some places to start include

- www.disabilityinfo.gov
- www.nichcy.org
- www.ced.gov

These websites will give you teaching ideas that can help you choose and modify activities. You can also ask the family for suggestions.

An agenda is a great way to plan your meetings. You may want to have a gathering activity, a song, a prayer, announcements, an activity, another song, and a closing prayer. If you are consistent (you can even post the agenda), your special child will feel more safe and comfortable. An agenda on the wall helps the child with special needs to follow along, prepare for what's next, and see how many things there are to do before the meeting is over. It also helps the leader remember what comes next. To learn how to use the PECS system and create an agenda, see "A Picture Is Worth a Thousand Words."

As you look over your different plans, see what you need to modify for your special girl. You may need to break down harder tasks into individual steps and allow extra time. Tools with special grips or picture instructions can help with crafts. If she is still struggling, consider having another girl help her or getting an adult helper.

Achievement Days Meetings

When a new girl joins the group, you may wish to introduce her to the other members. This can be done before or during her first meeting. Point out her talents and similarities to the others. Encourage interaction by asking others to help her do tasks and start conversations.

One mother described her daughter's experience: "Achievement Days was difficult for my daughter. She worked with her older sister, or I would demonstrate what to do. This gave her a model and showed her the steps. She asked family members for help when needed. I also had her sing the Articles of Faith because she could sing anything as long as there was music playing."

Your special spirit may only be able to participate in part of the meeting. Staying with the group for the whole time could be too overwhelming. Don't take this as a rejection of you or the program. Instead,

look on it as a baby step toward her future Church activity. If she can't stay the entire time, give her parents the instructions for any games or activities and the supplies she'll need for craft projects. Then she can do the same things as the other girls, just in a different way. It may take her a while to get to the same place, but if you remember where you started, it will be easier to see and appreciate progress.

If problems come up during the meeting, do what you need to do to keep everything in order, but save behavior discussions for later. Use whatever correction techniques you learned from the parents.

Faith in God Award

The Faith in God award is based on the principle that children learn by doing. This program encourages children to live gospel standards, participate in meaningful activities, and earn recognition. By learning to live gospel standards and keep the covenants they made at baptism, children set important patterns for the rest of their lives. Those who have not been baptized will achieve a lasting benefit by learning to make good, Christ-centered choices. Meaningful activities help children learn and live the gospel, serve others, develop talents, and prepare for the future. By earning recognition, special spirits feel valued by their peers, leaders, family, and Heavenly Father. Working toward this award encourages them to keep setting goals and provides positive feedback about their efforts. It also reinforces righteous gospel teachings learned at home and therefore strengthens the family. For example, in one Achievement Days group there was a girl with autism who disliked writing. One week, her group decorated journals, and she became more excited to record the events of her life.

When a girl with special challenges struggles to meet one of the requirements, look for an alternative way for her to accomplish something similar. For example, if she is physically unable to plan, prepare, and serve a nutritious meal, have her plan and do as much as she can. Then her family can assist with the rest. Another option is to ask her to identify the healthiest foods from a group. One class worked together to help a girl with a disability assemble a first aid kit. Everyone was proud of this young lady and her accomplishment.

Considering Functional Level

If your child is low-to-moderate functioning, it will take special efforts to include her in the group and the activities. Have all class

members make an effort to greet her as she arrives and include her in conversations throughout the meeting. Comments such as "Tabitha, what a pretty pink dress. Sarah, isn't pink your favorite color?" will draw the girls closer together. Parents may choose to have a girl with special needs attend only on certain weeks, depending on the topic. Her parents may also attend each meeting to help with communication. For example, if the group is talking about sports, a young lady in a wheelchair can recall her participation in Special Olympics or a time when she watched a sporting event with her family.

Conclusion

Achievement Days leaders should plan lessons and activities to meet the needs of all the children in their group. This is in addition to making sure the children are actively involved and that they enjoy themselves. As you look for ways to meet the needs of your special spirit, please try the following:

- After getting permission from the parents, speak to the group before your special spirit joins. Tell them ways to interact with their new friend.
- Visit with the girl and her parents. Communicate clear expectations for behavior and ask how you can best serve them.
- Welcome the new child and share positive information about her with the group.
- Let the child with a disability participate as much as possible. Step back and try to help rather than doing things for this special spirit.
- Find out all strengths and look for things she can share with the group or ways she can help others.
- Give opportunities for service.
- Reward with lots of praise.

As you prayerfully look for ways to help the girl get the most she can from Achievement Days, Heavenly Father will bless you with wisdom, knowledge, and a love for this girl. You will learn to enjoy and appreciate her many talents and see how she inspires and blesses the other members of the group.

We'll Be Loyal Scouts

by Lynn Parsons

I've had a long relationship with the Boy Scouts of America. My husband and two sons are Eagle Scouts, and I've served as a den leader, Cubmaster, district day camp director, and assistant district commissioner. I have seen this program have a positive impact on the lives of many boys and their families. These sentiments have been echoed by several General Authorities. Brother Charles W. Dahlquist II said,

> I love Scouting and the way it helps us as youth leaders retain and strengthen our boys—and help them develop timeless character traits as well as vital life skills. I love the look of confidence in the eye of a boy at a court of honor, or at a pinewood derby, or when he has completed a merit badge. Scouting helps us build men who truly believe that they can make a difference in the world and in their communities. And I am continually impressed with the strength and goodness of our Aaronic Priesthood and Scouting leaders—particularly as they use the purposes of the Aaronic Priesthood and the aims of Scouting to strengthen the Davids, the Johns, and the Tommys they serve.[1]

History

The Church of Jesus Christ of Latter-day Saints was the first church in the United States to adopt Scouting as an official part of their program. This relationship has continued since 1913 and is the longest between the Boy Scouts of America (BSA) and any chartering organization. "The Young Men General Presidency emphasizes that

Scouting continues to play a strong role in fulfilling the Aaronic Priest-hood objectives of preparing young men for full-time missions, temple blessings, and righteous manhood."[2] A website (www.ldsbsa.org) has been established to promote the relationship between the Boy Scouts of America and the Church, which sponsors 17 percent of the BSA units.

Disabilities and Scouting

The Americans with Disabilities Act (ADA) considers a person to have a disability if he or she

- has a physical or mental impairment that substantially limits one or more major life activity such as seeing, hearing, speaking, walking, breathing, performing manual tasks, learning, caring for oneself, or working.
- has a record of such an impairment, or
- is regarded as having such impairment.[3]

The BSA applies the same ideas in its policy. It should be noted that the boy needs to be regarded as having an impairment by professionals, not Scout leaders.

BSA, as an organization, has a long history of working with disabili-ties. From the time of Dr. James E. West, the first Chief Scout Executive, BSA has tried to accommodate every disability so that as many boys as possible may participate. BSA has developed good working relationships with many agencies who work on behalf of those with disabilities. They also have modified materials (available at www.scouting.org) and special programs to both increase awareness and include those with disabilities to the fullest extent possible.

Some of the programs include handicap awareness. Leaders are trained to understand and make accommodations for disabilities. Boy Scouts can wear a patch identifying them as a sign language interpreter (signing strip) or earn the disabilities awareness badge. Cub Scouts can participate in many handicap awareness activities. In addition, BSA's "Learning for Life" program, handicap awareness trails, modified outdoor facilities, handi-camporees, and jamborettes support Scouts with disabilities. District day camp facilities are inspected prior to camp for easy access, and many camp facilities have been modified to meet special needs.

"Learning for Life" is a set of seven different age-based programs that help children with disabilities build character and prepare for a

career. It's run through schools by teachers and parent volunteers. This is not part of the Church's program for children or youth.

Where to Begin

The first thing to consider when preparing to register a potential Scout with disabilities is what kind of unit to join. At this writing, there are 100,000 Scouts with disabilities registered across the United States. BSA prefers that boys be mainstreamed as much as possible, which means attending the pack or troop in your ward or branch. There may be special packs or troops in your area. You can locate these by contacting your local council. When deciding placement, take into consideration the following:

- What type of placement does the boy have at school? This is the setting in which he will feel the most comfortable during Scouts.
- Ask the boy what he prefers. He may request to be with his friends from church.
- Speak to the parents and find their preferences. They will be most in tune with the needs of their son and their family.
- Consider any limitations caused by the boy's disability, especially if he is medically fragile.
- The boy's age must be considered. For example, BSA does register Scouts over the age of eighteen if they are cognitively disabled, but they should be in a special troop. BSA policy is to modify membership requirements to fit the needs of the Scout.

In extenuating circumstances, a boy may be registered as a Lone Scout. This is a boy who typically does not live near a pack. He needs an adult counselor, and both will register with the council. The boy wears the regular uniform except for a special neckerchief and a Lone Scout patch worn where pack numbers would usually be. Lone Scouts will generally be invited to local activities with other packs and may even lead to the formation of a new pack. Only choose this option after visiting with your bishop or branch president. An adult must be approved by the council and registered to serve as the Lone Scout's counselor. The boy and counselor work together to advance in rank and earn merit badges. See www.scouting.org for more information on this program.

I have seen boys with disabilities be successful in both types of

packs. I would encourage you to participate within your ward or stake whenever possible, but these kinds of decisions need to be made prayerfully within the family.

Do Your Best, Modify the Rest

One of the most important positions in the pack is the den leader, who will do the best he or she can to plan and carry out the program. A great leader will love the boys!

One mother sent us this story about her Cub Scout:

> When Colt was a Bear in Cub Scouts, he had an awesome den leader. She had den meeting every week on the same day, at the same time, and at the same place whenever possible, which was awesome for Colt as he needed consistency and sameness with his autism. She always had everything well planned and organized with a monthly calendar of what they were doing each week. This was a blessing, as I could tell Colt what to plan on each week and could read a social story with him, if necessary, so he would not get stressed. She always made him feel welcome at den meetings and did whatever she could to accommodate him. She never forced him to do something he did not feel comfortable doing. She would not allow the other boys to tease but instead encouraged them to be his friend. When she saw him at church, she would go out of her way to say hi and take a few minutes to chat with him. My son absolutely adores her.

How do you become this kind of leader? Organization is key. As you plan your den and pack meetings, BSA suggests that you follow an agenda. For den meeting, I used the following:

- Gathering activity (flexible enough for boys to join at any point, such as a word search, a puzzle, questions that send them around the room, or other activity)
- Prayer
- Flag ceremony
- Snacks (provided by parents—for food allergies, I taped a warning and a list of do's and don'ts to the lid of the snack can)
- Announcements (it's easier to hear when the boys' mouths are full!)
- An "active" game to burn off extra energy
- Something to pass off toward an award
- Closing prayer

The whole thing took about an hour and a half. Having a routine makes the boys feel comfortable and helps them know what to expect. You may want to post an outline so that Scouts with special needs can see what comes next. This also helps you stick to the routine.

The Cub Scout motto is "Do your best." Each Cub is encouraged to complete activities as well as he can. Den leaders should determine what modifications may be necessary for each Cub before the meetings and make those accommodations. Handicap awareness activities may be used in den or pack meetings to help Cubs develop empathy. One den became more understanding of friends with writing problems after they placed a paper on their heads and tried to write their names. Most were too embarrassed by the mess they made to show anyone and very sympathetic to those who write like that all the time.

Another Cub Scout with emotional problems had frequent meltdowns during games in pack meeting. His friends knew the Cubmaster would have to take him aside and give him a little time to regain his composure. They learned patience as he found ways to cope and learn good sportsmanship with his fellow Scouts.

Some Scouts with disabilities have a hard time understanding change. One Cub Scout with autism helped his Cubmaster prepare the bridge for a crossing-over ceremony. Through misinterpretation, this Cub Scout believed he would be the one moving onward. He sat, in tears, during pack meeting as he watched his friend participate in the ceremony he had anticipated. His parents had mixed emotions as their hearts ached for his disappointment, yet they experienced pride as he handled his feelings appropriately, without throwing a tantrum. As this story shows, Scouts with disabilities need careful preparation for changes, especially if those changes involve friends moving out of the program.

Other Cubs may be overwhelmed by den and pack meetings. Giving parents instructions for any games or activities and supplies for crafts can allow all boys to participate and advance through ranks. See if your special Scout can attend for at least part of the meeting and then build from there. Don't be discouraged if this doesn't happen as easily or as quickly as you anticipate. Remember that any progress is still progress. Ask the leader if you can take projects home so your Scout can make the same progress through ranks as his friends.

LDS Cubs may also work toward the Faith in God award. This

award is based on the principle that children learn by doing. This program encourages children to live gospel standards, participate in meaningful activities, and earn recognition. By learning to live gospel standards and keeping the covenants they made at baptism, children set important patterns for the rest of their lives. Meaningful activities help children learn and live the gospel, serve others, develop talents, and prepare for the future. By earning recognition, special spirits feel valued by their peers, leaders, family, and Heavenly Father. This process encourages them to keep working on goals and provides positive feedback about their efforts. This program reinforces righteous gospel teachings learned at home and therefore strengthens the family.

Requirements for the Faith in God Award and Cub Scout achievements have been aligned and are available at http://pack152.net. You can also adapt these requirements to meet the needs of the boy. For example, if he can't read a general conference talk, he could listen to one from the www.lds.org site and repeat one thing he learned. If this Cub struggles to memorize an article of faith, he could sing it, or read it to the leader.

Meeting the Family

A great way to get to know your Scout is to meet with him and his parents before he joins your pack or den. This is a good time to introduce yourself to the Scout and have a conversation about what types of things he likes. You may be surprised by his interests and find he can help teach the den something to pass off a requirement. For example, one Cub Scout with special needs loved everything to do with dinosaurs. He knew their common names and scientific names, where they lived, what they ate, and more. The leader and Scout put together a fun den meeting where the Scout taught them about four of his favorite dinosaurs. Then the den participated in an "archaeological dig" in the leader's backyard.

Working together with parents will help the Scout with special needs achieve his full potential. I've seen many boys earn their Eagle when supported by family and troop, despite struggling with disabilities. During the parent interview, make a list of what works for the Scout at home, school, and church. This will help you to have a better picture of how to help him fit into your troop. A suggested outline for this interview is on pages 146–47 of the *Scouting for Youth with*

Disabilities Manual, as well as the chapter titled "Getting to Know You" in this book. If you have more questions about the Scout's disability after meeting with the parents, you can find more answers in "Demystifying the Diagnosis," also found in this book.

Outdoor Activities and Day Camp

Please take extra care when planning outdoor activities. BSA recommends that you have at least one adult for every three disabled Scouts.[4] Some activities may need modification. One young man with cerebral palsy kept up with his pack while hiking but couldn't do a crab walk. His Cubmaster had him do it with his stomach toward the ground rather than his back and shortened the distance by half. This young man was able to participate to the best of his ability.

Activities that involve swimming require extra precautions. See the Scouting website for more information on lifeguards, buddy boards, and other safety recommendations. One Cub with a fear of water initially refused to let go of the side of the pool during pack meeting. Gentle encouragement from his Cubmaster and friends helped him gain the confidence and skills to jump off the diving board by the end of the evening. Please remember that if you plan to take Cubs swimming, you need to complete the safe swim defense course. See www.scouting.org for details.

Day camp directors go through extensive training and detailed planning to make sure the Scouts have fun and learn in a safe environment. Consider having medically fragile Cubs attend part of the day or attend a "twilight" camp held in the evening if they struggle with heat. Give all the boys plenty of water breaks so they don't become dehydrated. Be sure parents provide any medications their Scouts may need and that they are given to the camp nurse for administration. You may want to keep a list of the Scout's food allergies for camp cooking classes.

During day camp, be aware of how the Cub Scouts are interacting with each other. One pack discovered that while their Cub Scouts interacted well with one of the Scout members with special needs during den and pack meetings, they teased and purposely made this particular Scout frustrated during day camp. The day camp leaders didn't fully realize what was happening until the Scout with special needs became so frustrated, he cried and ran away. The boy's mother arrived to volunteer about the time her son ran away. She also became frustrated while

she chased her son through other campsites and struggled to help him calm down—without any help from the other day camp leaders. After a twenty-minute struggle, both mother and son left in tears and have not returned to a day camp since because they are afraid of a repeat experience.

It is the responsibility of pack, den, and other volunteer leaders to make sure that all Cub Scouts are being treated in a kind and loving way. If a boy is struggling, there should be an immediate response to help. The goal of day camp is for the boys to enjoy the outdoors, learn new skills, and work together. If you have a boy with special needs, be sure to consider what he may need in order to have a successful camp experience. This may include having a camp leader who works directly with the one Scout, assisting him throughout the day and monitoring the interactions between him and the other Scouts to be sure they are appropriate and friendly. You may consider having a leader shadow some special Scouts, especially for activities such as shooting BB guns or arrows. This does not mean they are alone with the boy but simply that they are available to assist during the activity. Some boys with cognitive disabilities may wander, so you will need to assign a den chief or adult to keep an eye on them.

Being aware of your environment and surroundings is important when outside. One day camp director made announcements and then blew the air horn that signaled the beginning of classes. She routinely aimed it behind her and up so it wouldn't blast the ears of nearby campers. Unfortunately, that's where her husband, the program director, was standing, and it blew his hat right off. She hadn't taken the time to look around before she acted.

Another important tip is to have a valid phone number for all parents. One Cub Scout skinned his knee and then was left behind by his assigned ride home. Contacting the parents immediately was very important in this case.

Scout-to-Scout Relationships

Encourage other boys to include your special Scout in discussions and games. Point out things they have in common and help the Scouts discover each others' strengths. One pack had a scavenger hunt. At first, they were very competitive, but with encouragement from the leaders, the Cubs worked with the boys with special needs so everyone was included.

After they all finished, they celebrated as a pack and played together.

When you think an activity might be too difficult or frustrating for your Scout with special needs, work with the parents and other pack committee members to find an appropriate modification or another activity he can do that is similar. If the other Scouts ask about the different activities, explain that fair does not always mean equal. Each boy is expected to work as hard as he can, and sometimes another Cub may do something differently as he works toward the same goal. Remind them of the Scout motto to "Do your best."

Words of Caution

Always remember that the Church owns your pack. As the chartering organization, your bishop or branch president has the ultimate say about what happens in your unit.

As you work with your Scout with special needs, don't try to do everything for him. When you allow him to do as much as he can on his own, this teaches him that he is valued, competent, and worthwhile. In short, you are demonstrating your respect for that boy.

Another way of demonstrating your high opinion for your Scout is to be consistent and firm. Don't use force, but share your high expectations for all the boys and encourage them to behave in a Christlike manner.

Be careful about making promises you can't keep. It's an easy way to solve problems at the time, but if the boys learn they can't rely on you, it eats holes in your relationship.

Don't allow challenging behaviors to provoke you. Remain flexible and avoid patronizing, sarcastic, or insulting behavior. I try to remind myself that everyone is a child of God and that He loves them. Then I look for reasons why. This allows me to see the unique individual within.

Positive discipline prevents problems. Have the boys work toward a reward for good behavior. Praise good habits and accomplishments and learn to ignore undesirable actions that aren't very important. Remember to hold behavior discussions in private—never in front of the other Scouts or during the problem.

Focus

As a Cub Scout leader, you are an example to the boys and have an

opportunity to enhance their self-esteem. When my Cubs made bird-houses, they were each unique. I'm not very good with wood myself, and so we all just did our best. When one parent was worried that they didn't look very professional, I explained that I was more concerned with building boys than building birdhouses. The boys' Scouting experiences will remain part of their characters long after the craft projects have turned to dust.

Resources

- www.lds.org has training videos about working with Scouts.
- www.NetCommish.com is an excellent resource with lots of great suggestions for working with Scouts with disabilities.
- Your council advisory committee on youth with disabilities. See page 9 in *Scouting for Youth with Disabilities Manual.*
- For a dictionary of disability terms, see *Scouting for Youth with Disabilities Manual*, pages 45–46.
- Considerations for specific disabilities are found on pages 45–106 of *Scouting for Youth with Disabilities Manual.*
- Leader presentation on dealing with disabilities is found on pages 144–46 of *Scouting for Youth with Disabilities Manual.*
- Forms are also available in the manual. Dealing with persistent problems is found on page 148 of *Scouting for Youth with Disabilities Manual.*

Notes

1. Charles W. Dahlquist II, "Message from the Young Men General Presidency," *LDS Relationships Newsletter* 3, no. 2 (May 2008): 1. http://www.ldsbsa.org/pdf/newsletters/May%202008%20Newsletter.pdf.
2. "History of Scouting in the Church," *The Church of Jesus Christ of Latter-day Saints*, http://www.lds.org/pa/display/0,17884,5169-1,00.html/.
3. "National BSA Policy on Advancement for Youth Members with Special Needs," *MeritBadge.com*, http://www.meritbadge.com/info/policy5.htm.
4. *Scouting for Youth with Disabilities Manual* (2007), Dallas: Boy Scouts of America, 84.

Young Men &
Young Women

Teaching Youth with a Broader Gap in Needs

by Lynn Parsons

I love teaching youth. I spent six years teaching high school and even more teaching seminary. Dealing with the effects of teen drama, hormones, and their struggles to find their way in the world wore me out some days. On the other hand, their enthusiasm, sense of fun, and sense of anticipation frequently energized me.

Being able to watch as youth learn and grow is a blessing like no other. In order to work with teens with special needs, you need to prepare, understand their behaviors, and adapt your lessons for them.

Preparation

You need a variety of resources to get information on your special youth. Their parents, the presidency of your organization, www.lds.org, and Heavenly Father are all great sources.

Check the "Lead Me, Guide Me, Walk beside Me" chapter of this book for the kinds of questions you should ask the parents. Make note of their answers for later reference—it can seem like a lot of information at first. Keep these details confidential and share them only with those working with this young man or young woman.

Be careful as you interview the parents. Remember, you are trying to serve that youth—not offend the family! Pray before you go and try to work with the parents. Ask questions in a nonjudgmental way and be sensitive to their feelings. Try not to ask about topics that may be too personal. For example, questions about how the family pays for treatment or equipment are not related to your teaching situation. Stick to

behaviors, medical information, and other things you need to know to help that special spirit.

Your organization's presidency or bishopric may already have many helpful ideas about this teen. Ask them what worked well in past classes, what was unsuccessful, and for any other counsel they may feel impressed to share.

The Church has a very useful website with information on specific disabilities, helps for teachers and leaders, family resources, scriptures, quotes, and materials. This site is being expanded all the time, so return there often. The home page is found at disabilities.lds.org.

The last source of information, the Holy Ghost, is the most important.

"Seek not to declare my word, but first seek to obtain my word, and then shall your tongue be loosed; then, if you desire, you shall have my Spirit and my word, yea, the power of God unto the convincing of men" (D&C 11:21).

As you study your lesson materials, keep your students in mind. Through prayer, fasting, and inspiration from the Holy Ghost, you will learn what your students need.

Understanding Behavior

Youth with special needs may blurt out random answers impulsively, leave class (and sometimes the building) to wander, pick fights with other class members, and have other challenging behaviors. This conduct can frustrate not only the teacher but also other members of the class. Everyone needs a chance to feel the Spirit and learn the gospel, but one class member may be so disruptive that this seems almost impossible. What can be done?

Determine the source of the behavior problems, set some goals, and enlist help when necessary. These steps should make this a win-win situation. One young man I had in seminary would leave class and go downstairs to the restroom. He would get involved looking at the pictures in the hall and forget to return. I spoke to him after class and taught him to repeat "bathroom, back up to class," as he left the classroom. This helped him to remember not only to return but also not to dawdle in front of the paintings.

All behaviors have a purpose. Is your student being rewarded, fulfilling a need, or trying to avoid something? I've had students who were

uncomfortable feeling the Spirit, so they would leave when it became too intense for them. Others would search the kitchen for leftover treats. Some had to use the restroom frequently and would simply forget to return to class. Visiting with the parents, talking with the student, and seeking inspiration through prayer will give you some answers. Then you can work with the student to find other ways to meet their needs.

How do you determine motivations? Look at the situation and try to track what happens before (antecedent), during (behavior), or after the behavior (consequence). If the student is avoiding something, the same types of things will happen just before they leave (announcing a class activity, reading, and so on). Rewards come either during or after the behavior. If they are leaving to raid the kitchen or other classes with treats, food will be their prize.

Fulfilling a need is a more difficult motivation to determine. If the teen is walking around, they may be using this behavior to calm down. If you speak to the parents about behaviors, they can help you discover which are meeting a need.

Your special spirits may need to set a goal to improve their classroom behavior or learn gospel lessons. Visit with the parents and child to set these goals. Charts can help you track progress, and rewards may motivate the students.

Some youth may require more help to participate in class. An aide may be called to support this young man or young woman. For more information on this topic, see the chapter titled "Lead Me, Guide Me, Walk beside Me."

Adapting Lessons

Everyone learns differently. Some need to see information in order to absorb it, so they are visual learners. Auditory learners do best when they can hear the lesson. Kinesthetic learners need to physically move during the lesson. When you plan a variety of activities during your class, all will learn more.

To determine each class member's learning style, print out the chart found at www.chaminade.org/inspire/learnstl.htm and either help them circle their responses or ask parents to fill them out.

When teens are taught exclusively one way (for example, through teacher presentation or lecture), youth with nonauditory learning styles may miss out. For example, for many years my seminary class

memorized Scripture Mastery verses by writing them on the board, repeating phrases, and then erasing it piece by piece. This doesn't work for all students. These verses have been set to music online (available at http://lds.about.com/od/seminary/a/scripture_songs.htm), and teens who have given up on memorization may more easily learn this way. One group even sang to their Young Women leaders and shared the songs with nonmember friends at school.

How do you use activities that will help all learning styles in one lesson? If you were teaching lesson 32 from *Aaronic Priesthood Manual 1*, "Tithing," having a visual learner write down the group's list of blessings would help them understand the concept. Auditory learners benefit from the discussion, and kinesthetic learners can move to the front of the room and present the reports to the class. Each type of learner has a good chance of learning this way. Similar techniques could be used in "Maintaining Chastity through Righteous Living," lesson 37 in *Young Women Manual 2*.

If special spirits in your classes are still struggling, you may want to make additional changes. Adapted materials, simplified assignments, object lessons, and concrete analogies will all help. Christ taught with everyday objects familiar to His disciples. You can compare feeling the Spirit with listening to soft music and have a tape of common noises playing in the background. They have to make an effort to listen to the music through all the distractions. This exercise makes the abstract concept of inspiration more clear.

When teaching how to keep your thoughts pure, you can use a visual aid. For example, hold up a CD to teach that what you see, hear, and experience are "burned" into your brain and are very difficult to erase. Analogies with familiar objects—especially when they relate to special interests—can make even the most abstract ideas easy to understand. Search "LDS object lessons" for many analogy suggestions on the Internet. The Church has adapted many materials that help make the gospel accessible to all. Scripture readers are written on a simplified level and are available on DVD. Resources for the blind, deaf, and those with other disabilities are available at disabilities.lds.org.

When giving an assignment—like reading a scripture block—consider giving your special spirit a shortened version, such as part of the scripture reader or a chapter heading. For example, if class members are

making a list of how many times the word "prayer" appears in a set of verses, ask your student to look through one verse. This way, everyone can participate in the lesson.

Preteaching is another great way to include special spirits. Also, some who struggle to read need additional time to practice. A week ahead of time, give these students a very short verse to practice, and allow them to read it during the lesson. Be sure not to skip that scripture as you move through the material! Look at the questions you will ask that week and teach one answer to the teen. You can do this just prior to the lesson or at their home. Only those with good long-term memories should be told their answer a week before.

I taught one young man in Primary whose answer to every question was "Joseph Smith!" He understood what was going on—he was being the class clown! But you can be sure when the answer really was Joseph Smith, I called on him. The whole class cheered! A little planning can have huge rewards.

Helping these students fit in with the rest of the class can be one of the most rewarding parts of teaching teens. Let them help in any way they can—pass out materials, hold pictures, keep score during games, and so on. Encourage class presidencies to make extra efforts to greet each class member and even work as peer tutors during activities. As you prepare your lessons, pray to find different ways to allow everyone to participate.

As you seek the Lord's will in serving your special spirits, you will be blessed with great insight and wisdom. You will "strengthen your brethren in all your conversation, in all your prayers, in all your exhortations, and in all your doings" (D&C 108:7).

THE YOUNG WOMEN CONNECTION

by Lynn Parsons

> "Our youth activities should reflect our belief that 'men are, that they might have joy,' and we should be willing to share that joy with others."
>
> *Spencer J. Condie*

Each week, LDS young women gather all over the world to participate in activities that share the joy while learning the gospel and preparing for their future lives.

Mutual

"And all this for the benefit of the church of the living God, that every man may improve upon his talent, that every man may gain other talents, yea, even an hundred fold" (D&C 82:18).

Everyone has a unique set of talents. I've met young women with special needs who are musically gifted, amazing readers, or very empathetic. Mutual nights allow teens to share their talents. It draws young women closer together as they learn to appreciate each other. Each young woman should participate in some way. There are many kinds of activities at Mutual, including relationship builders, service projects, sports, talent development, camps, and youth conferences. Young ladies may use some of these activities to pass off requirements for their Personal Progress awards. Everyone can benefit from these programs with a few modifications. You may find it helpful to meet with the parents of your teens with special needs to see how they can best take part.

One young woman with a disability was especially excited to attend

Mutual because she had seen the fun activities her mother had planned as Young Women president. She sometimes struggled to control her excitement during the meetings. She really wanted to participate, and as the leaders learned how to redirect her energy, she made friends and had a great time. This young woman also enjoyed being in class presidencies and did very well in her callings. She was especially good at activating her friends.

One way to promote positive relationships among the youth is to have an "Empathy Dinner" similar to the one hosted yearly at Texas Christian University. Guests are given "disabilities" such as blindfolded blindness and artificial arthritis (where Popsicle sticks are taped to their fingers). They must cope with these challenges as they eat their meal. Those who participate come away with experiences they never forget and are better able to relate to their friends with disabilities.

President Spencer W. Kimball said, "When we are engaged in the service of our fellowmen, not only do our deeds assist them, but we put our own problems in a fresher perspective. When we concern ourselves more with others, there is less time to be concerned with ourselves. In the midst of the miracle of serving, there is the promise of Jesus, that by losing ourselves, we find ourselves. (See Matt. 10:39.)"[1]

I believe every adolescent should give service. It teaches that his or her problems aren't the worst ones on the planet, it is excellent job training, and it builds self-esteem. I believe teens with disabilities have even more need for these experiences because they face so many challenges. Opportunities to serve allow them to feel competent as they help others and moves the focus from "can't" to "can." The projects don't have to be elaborate. One young woman can make a phone call to a sick friend. Another can greet class members as they enter or help set up for an activity. No effort is too small.

Some wards have more involved service projects where many youth are simultaneously doing different things. For example, one youth group set out to help fix up the home of a new member. Some teens took out bags of trash, others moved furniture, a few cleaned, and one group worked to do repairs. When working on a large project, a young woman with special needs may need to work with a buddy. She could do a simple task, such as washing windows, and then report to a supervisor for her next assignment. Sometimes working alongside a leader is more appropriate. You can also create a checklist she can mark as others

report what they have completed. Remember that having a cheerleader who encourages others can be very important to the success of your project. Look for the strengths of your special spirits, and you will find the perfect place for them.

When teens with special needs serve, they learn many different skills. They may learn to make change during a fund raiser, do manual labor during a car wash, provide child care during a mother's day out, or serve food at a shelter. Each of these experiences gives real-life training and valuable job skills. The teens also learn to show responsibility by being on time, getting along with peers, and treating those they serve with respect. Those who give service inevitably feel good about their efforts. One young lady with a cognitive disability was able to babysit for a family as they made funeral arrangements. She was very touched as they expressed their appreciation for her service. It made her feel valued and respected.

Sports activities are fun, build teamwork, and provide exercise. Some teens with special needs may find sporting events a challenge. You need to "bend" the rules to allow them to participate, such as allowing assistance from a teammate or letting them be the scorekeeper. For example, if you're playing basketball, a young woman with special needs might have difficulty dribbling and walking at the same time. She may dribble, then walk a few steps, and dribble again. Rather than calling her for "traveling," recognize that she is doing her best and encourage her to continue. Visit families to see what adjustments can allow these youth to participate and have fun. Most young women with disabilities want to play.

Young Women Camp and Youth Conference

Young Women Camp is a time of fun and very little sleep! Even so, young women are blessed to attend. When youth are separated from their normal environments, cut loose from technology, and living in a natural setting, they are better able to feel the Spirit.

Teens with special needs may have problems adapting to camp. I worked with one ward whose young woman with special needs refused to get out of bed on the first morning of camp. This young lady hadn't been prepared for any changes and felt overwhelmed. She was given a daily schedule, which allowed her to know what to expect and when things would end. Her comfort level increased, and she was then able

to participate. Others may need modified facilities, a shorter program, time inside, sensory breaks, or other adaptations. For more information, see the chapter titled "The Scouting Adventure."

If young men and women are over the age of fourteen, they also have the chance to attend youth conference. This is more than a coed version of Young Women Camp. Each stake will run its course a little differently, but programs can range from classes at the stake center followed by a dance, service at the Special Olympics, trips, pioneer-type handcart treks, and other activities. There is generally a dance, so teens with special needs may need preparation to learn how to do some basic steps. One great bishop's counselor was very talented at introducing youth to those from other wards. He would look around for someone looking lonely, introduce himself, and walk them over to a group of youth. He would bring the young man over to a young woman and say, "Hey, this is my new friend. He wants to ask you to dance." Many potential wallflowers were saved by his efforts.

Personal Progress

The Personal Progress program encourages young women to live the standards set in "For the Strength of Youth" as they set goals to complete six value experiences and one project in each of the eight value areas. This program is flexible as far as young women with disabilities are concerned. Leaders should counsel with the young woman's parents and priesthood leaders to determine what modifications would be appropriate. Some young women may not have the reading or comprehension skills to read the volume of Church talks required. In this case, each young woman may read fewer articles, have them read to her, or listen to the audio versions available at www.lds.org.

One young lady with a disability couldn't use the journal provided by the Church because the spaces between the lines were too small for her handwriting. Her mother simply provided her with another journal that had larger spaces. Other young women have "written" their journals by using audio recordings and pictures or by dictating to someone else. Young women who struggle with abstract concepts, such as divine nature, could describe good things a friend or family member does or how they act rather than describing the divine qualities of a daughter of God. A young lady who has difficulties with memorization might be able to read the thirteenth article of faith from a card or state the

meaning from a series of pictures. If you prayerfully seek alternative ways to meet the requirements, you will find them.

One mother shared,

> There were a few things in the Personal Progress program we had to modify. My daughter has dysgraphia. She has to have an outline or she can't write, and she can't write long passages. I had her write one sentence with bullet points underneath. She also used a spiral notebook so she didn't have to worry about making it fit the small book.
>
> One of her projects was to modify a dress to be more modest. I allowed her to read the instructions and do it herself. She is good at putting things together by sight. Technically it was a mess, but it looked pretty good. For other projects, I drew out instructions.

This mom helped her daughter participate by making just a few changes.

The blessings from the Personal Progress program are almost too many to count. One young lady with special needs grew tomatoes, which the whole family worked together to can. This increased her knowledge, raised her feelings of self-worth, and pulled her family closer together while teaching them to keep the commandment to store food.

The inspired programs the Church has implemented for our youth are the best available on the earth today to prepare young men and women for their future. When all are included, their feet will be set upon the path back to their Father in Heaven.

Notes

Quotation on p. 112 from Spencer J. Condie, "Becoming a Great Benefit to Our Fellow Beings," *Ensign*, May 2002, 44–46.

1. Spencer W. Kimball, "Small Acts of Service," *Ensign*, Dec. 1974, 2.

The Scouting Adventure

Helping Boy Scouts with Special Needs

by Lynn Parsons

Scouting has been called a game with a purpose. Lord Baden-Powell, one of the founders of Scouting, really had three purposes in mind—to help the boys grow in moral strength and character; promote citizenship; and develop physically, mentally, and emotionally. Leaders should use the eight methods of Scouting as they plan for fun and learning. These methods are:

- advancement
- ideals
- patrols
- outdoors
- adult association
- personal growth
- leadership
- uniform[1]

Advancement

The first decision is which troop to join. Whenever possible, have your Scout join the troop in your ward. In some areas, there may be troops for boys with special needs. You can call your local council office to locate one of these groups. You may wish to visit before joining to learn about fees and what time will be required of the parents. Please consult with your local leaders and pray before making your decision.

Leaders, work together with the parents to open the lines of

communication. Partner with the parents to help the boy achieve his full potential. I've seen many boys earn their Eagle when supported by family and troop, despite struggling with disabilities. During the parent interview, make a list of what works for the Scout, both at home and at school. For more information on this process, see the "Getting to Know You" chapter. This will help you have a better picture of how to help him fit into your troop. A suggested outline for this interview is on pages 146–47 of the *Scouting for Youth with Disabilities Manual*. Some disabilities may intimidate newer leaders. My son was allergic to pecans. He avoided all nuts and carried an EpiPen. This easy solution reduced the stress for us as his parents and also for his leaders.

Some Scouts will need modifications as they pass off requirements for merit badges or rank advancements. One change from Cub Scouts is that the BSA requires a doctor's medical statement to verify and clarify the condition or diagnosis if you need to make changes to requirements. This document needs to specify that the disability is a permanent condition. Parents are responsible for obtaining this documentation. You will need a parent's written permission to contact their medical professional for additional information. BSA does not have a form for this, but a letter stating that the leader can contact the doctor and obtain records should suffice. The doctor's note is required when you prepare the written request to the council for program modifications. Please remember that if your special Scout has a physical problem, outdoor or strenuous activities need to be approved by the doctor.

After you've learned all you can from the doctor and parents, do some research on your own about the specific disability. As you understand more about your special Scout, you will be able to make better plans for him. Schoolteachers are a great source of information. Some other good places to start gathering information include

- www.disabilityinfo.gov
- www.nichcy.org
- www.cdc.gov

For tips on how to include a Scout with disabilities, see www.Net-Commish.com.

Ideals

The ideals of Scouting include the Scout Oath, the Scout Law, the

Scout Motto, and the Scout Slogan. It's important for parents to sit down with their boys, explain the meanings of the Oath, Law, Motto, and Slogan, and encourage the boys to live the ideals.

A unique opportunity to strengthen the morals of our young men is the Duty to God program offered to LDS Scouts. It strengthens the youth spiritually and prepares them for future priesthood duties. Young men must live priesthood standards, participate in quorum and family activities, give service, and keep a journal. They must also complete goals in four areas, including spiritual growth; physical development; educational, personal, and career development; and citizenship and social development. As they work with family members and priesthood leaders to complete their goals, these young men may earn a certificate as a deacon, another as a teacher, and one as a priest. After being awarded all three, they are eligible for the Duty to God Award.

Requirements may be modified with prior permission from parents and priesthood leaders. A deacon-aged boy with a cognitive disability may not be able to reach the goal of washing and ironing his clothing for a month. Perhaps he could assist the person who does his laundry to sort clothes, load the machine, or fold. A teacher-aged young man with an educational challenge may not be able to read from Alma through Moroni in the Book of Mormon in the traditional manner. Perhaps he could listen to it on tape or have the chapters read to him. Please remember that all modifications must be approved by the bishop.

Because this award is presented in sacrament meeting, this is a great opportunity to let special spirits shine. One young man with a cognitive impairment and physical disability worked hard to earn the Duty to God award, but his older brothers did not. He was very proud that, despite the fact that his brothers could do many things he could not, such as drive a car, this was one area in which he excelled. What a wonderful experience and self-esteem builder for this young man.

Patrols

The patrol is the peer group the boys work with to solve problems. In the Church, the patrols are formed in the priesthood quorums. This means there is both a spiritual and a Scouting relationship between the boys. The quorum gives the boys the opportunity to provide service and leadership to each other, to the ward, and to the community. The Scout with special needs should do the same program as his patrol

whenever possible. Tasks or activities that are more difficult may require extra time or need to be broken down into individual steps. Aids, such as tools with special grips, picture instructions, or preassembled parts, may be needed. Pair the boys up with a buddy. Some boys with special needs may find meetings too stressful, so arrange for them to attend for a few minutes, and see if that can be gradually expanded to the entire meeting. Leaders can make project kits to take home if the Scout cannot attend and can offer alternate ways to fulfill requirements.

Creating a routine for meetings is essential. It ensures you will do all your activities and allows special Scouts to be calmer. Many agendas are available in leader handbooks. Posting your routine will allow boys to see what to expect next and keep leaders on track.

One patrol has three members with special needs, including a boy in a wheelchair. All the Scouts help him and prefer not to participate in activities that don't include him. When an overnight cave activity was planned, his father chose to go along and carry this eighty-pound Scout in a backpack. The whole patrol worked together to help both of them. Another Scout with Tourette's syndrome hesitated to join group activities, so the others made an extra effort to include him. The third struggled with the dark, so the Scouts in his patrol worked together to guide and help him. These boys learned to live Christlike lives while advancing through Scouting together.

Outdoors

The idea is to get the boys outside and away from the electronics that complicate their lives and block the Spirit. On one campout, the Scoutmaster walked with a young Scout and his dad through the woods on a clear and moonless night. They were discussing how to find their way if they got lost. The scout confidently replied, "I would pick a star and follow it," just as they cleared the trees. His Scoutmaster pointed to the sky and asked, "Is there one in particular that you had in mind?" The look on the boy's face was priceless as he looked up and saw the beauty of the Milky Way.

Some activities, such as hiking, may need to be shortened. You may also want to give the boys a longer time to climb ropes or complete other challenging tasks. Make sure you have emergency transportation nearby at all times. One family was concerned about their Scout with cognitive impairment. His father chose to attend every outdoor activity

to ensure the safety of his son. Another young man struggled to attend campouts because they disrupted his bedtime routine. When his father attended, this Scout saw the campout as an adventure instead of a series of broken rules.

Adult Association

Scout leaders have an opportunity to impact the boys in their troop by being role models. Some of the boys may not have a worthy priesthood holder at home. Even if they do, teenage boys often do not listen to their parents. One young man with a disability had a father who frequently traveled for work and was therefore unable to attend troop activities. He often left troop meetings nearly in tears because he didn't feel like a member of the group. The situation changed with his new Scoutmaster, who treated this Scout with respect and gave him a job within the troop. Furthermore, this leader looked for reasons to give praise and encouragement as the Scout fulfilled his responsibility. As he prepared for his future, this Scout was more willing to listen to counsel from his Scoutmaster because of their ongoing positive relationship.

Personal Growth

Personal growth comes from learning and giving service. Some Scouts may serve as they allow others to serve them. With written council permission, changes to requirements for Tenderfoot, Second Class, and First Class can be made. Also, alternate merit badges that require similar effort and learning experiences may be substituted for Eagle Scout rank, with permission. Check with your Council Advisory Committee on Youth with Disabilities for more information. If the local council does not have such a committee (most do, but not all), you can find more information at www.scouting.org about forming one.

One young man with significant cognitive disabilities was able to complete the requirements for Eagle Scout with only a slight modification. When a merit badge required something to be written, he dictated to his father. This young man also did a wonderful Eagle project. A home for children with disabilities in his area had been burglarized. He led a drive to replace what had been stolen. He made telephone calls, took containers to church buildings for donations, gathered materials, and delivered them. When he received his Eagle Scout Award, many people attended his Court of Honor. Administrators and teachers from

his school were there, as well as family, ward members, and friends. Many tears of joy were shed as we watched the recognition ceremony to celebrate the accomplishments of this special spirit.

Another young man struggled to follow through with merit badge requirements on his own. He could set the goal but had a difficult time understanding the steps involved or moving independently between different stages. He needed frequent prompts to advance and was very proud when presented with an award.

Leadership

A major difference between the Cub Scout and Boy Scout programs is the focus on leadership. Adults plan and carry out the activities for the younger Scouts, but Boy Scouts are expected to provide leadership for their peers.

When Scouts are asked to accept responsibilities within their patrol or troop, they feel valued and, as with the Scout mentioned above, respected. This training prepares each young man to lead in his quorum. He plans activities, reviews advancement, and looks for ways to activate those who don't come. Scouts who take ownership of the program are also more likely to participate.

Uniform

Wearing the uniform shows commitment to the program and gives the boys a group identity. Check thrift shops for "experienced" shirts when Scouts may not be able to afford a new uniform. Having the troop dress alike is one of the best ways to help all the boys feel included. A buddy can be assigned to a Scout with a disability to help him wear the uniform correctly. It's important that the leaders set an example by also being properly uniformed.

The Scouting program is currently one of the best ways to prepare boys for their future. I have seen young men change from acting like juveniles to shouldering adult responsibilities. As we include those with special needs, we are allowing them to grow into their full potential.

Note

1. National Eagle Scout Association, http://www.nesa.org/methods.html.

Deacons, Teachers, and More—Oh My!

by Lynn Parsons

Each Sunday, little boys watch the young men pass the sacrament. They wonder what it would be like to have the priesthood and carry the trays of bread and water. In order to pass the sacrament, each young man must be ordained to the office of a deacon in the Aaronic Priesthood.

Youth who have not been baptized because of severe cognitive disabilities cannot be ordained to the priesthood. While unable to pass the sacrament or perform other priesthood ordinances, these special spirits are considered worthy young men, unaccountable here on earth. Bruce R. McConkie stated, "Becoming accountable is a process, not a goal to be attained when a specified number of years, days, and hours have elapsed. In our revelation the Lord says, 'They cannot sin, for power is not given unto Satan to tempt little children, until they begin to become accountable before me.' (D&C 29:47.)"[1]

LDS parents look forward to the time when their sons turn twelve and can be ordained to the office of a deacon. Preparation for this ordinance is important for any young man, but it's vital for those with disabilities. You can begin their preparation by reviewing the restoration of the gospel and the priesthood. Remind your young man of how he prepared to be baptized and the covenants he made at that time. Explain that the priesthood covenant is an extension of his baptismal covenant.

Teach this youth that the priesthood is the authority to act in the name of God on the earth and that it is given so he may serve others. The twentieth section of the Doctrine and Covenants describes the duties of

various priesthood offices. Another resource that may help is found in *Primary Manual 5: Doctrine and Covenants and Church History*; *Primary Manual 6: Old Testament*; and *Primary Manual 7: New Testament*. In each of these manuals, you will find lesson 47, "The Priesthood Can Bless Our Lives." This is a lot of information to cover, so do it over several sessions. This would be a great topic for family home evening. Finish each lesson by bearing your testimony and sharing personal stories of priesthood blessings. If there is no priesthood holder in the home, consider involving the home teacher or other priesthood holder in your discussions.

Young men with special needs may need extra information on how to dress and act as they fulfill their priesthood responsibilities. They should understand that they represent Heavenly Father and should be following the dress code in "For the Strength of Youth." These boys may not be able to learn how to act by observing others. For example, one deacon with a disability would pass the sacrament by holding it in front of the member's face. He had to be directly taught to hold it down lower. During Mutual, they practiced having him hand it to someone sitting in the pew until it was a habit. Role plays and practice sessions are especially helpful to find the gaps in learning and fill them.

Young men have an interview with the bishop in which they discuss questions similar to those used in temple recommend interviews. Special spirits need to understand these questions and feel comfortable speaking to the bishop during their visit. Help them remember their baptismal interview. As part of this meeting, the bishop will make sure the young man understands the covenants he will make as he is ordained to different priesthood offices and that he will be able to complete at least a portion of his duties.

One young man with a disability was very excited to be ordained to the Aaronic Priesthood. He understood the importance of the covenants he was about to make. His concern was that his leaders would think he was too immature to advance to the office of a teacher. Visit with your youth to learn his worries so you can work together toward this important goal. These concerns may change as he is ordained to other priesthood offices and has new duties.

Deacons

Deacons are to assist teachers. "They are, however, to warn, expound, exhort, and teach, and invite all to come unto Christ" (D&C 20:59). These young men assist the bishop with temporal matters, such as collecting fast

offerings and cleaning and maintaining buildings. They are also responsible to pass the sacrament. Consider having your deacon come to the chapel during the week to learn how to pass the sacrament. Think about having him just do one row at first, carrying a card with written or picture instructions or arranging hand signals with the other boys. I know one young man with a disability who does the same route each week. These small steps should allow most deacons with special needs to participate in this important priesthood duty. I know one boy who passed the sacrament as a team with another boy. They walked side by side, and the one boy gave the deacon with special needs reverent prompts on where to stand, how to pass the trays down the rows, and where to go next.

Teachers

"The teacher's duty is to watch over the church always, and be with and strengthen them; And see that there is no iniquity in the church, neither hardness with each other, neither lying, backbiting, nor evil speaking; And see that the church meet together often, and also see that all the members do their duty" (D&C 20:53–55). Teachers may do all the same duties as deacons. In addition, they prepare the sacrament and serve as home teachers. A teacher with special needs may still provide the sacramental bread or make a home teaching visit with a companion who holds the Melchizedek Priesthood. For more information on working with a companion with a disability, see the chapter titled "Love One Another: Home and Visiting Teaching."

Priests

Priests, in addition to the duties performed by deacons and teachers, bless the sacrament, baptize, and ordain others to the offices of priest, teacher, or deacon.

> The priest's duty is to preach, teach, expound, exhort, and baptize, and administer the sacrament,
> And visit the house of each member, and exhort them to pray vocally and in secret and attend to all family duties.
> And he may also ordain other priests, teachers, and deacons."
> (D&C 20:46–48)

A priest with special needs may need extra time to learn the sacrament prayer or a cue card with pictures to help him memorize. Parents and leaders should take care that he understands the words of the prayer

as he learns it. Home teaching is also an appropriate way for these young men to fulfill their priesthood responsibilities.

Melchizedek Priesthood

The Aaronic Priesthood, which is composed of the offices of deacon, teacher, and priest, is a preparatory priesthood. "The power and authority of the lesser, or Aaronic Priesthood, is to hold the keys of the ministering of angels, and to administer in outward ordinances, the letter of the gospel, the baptism of repentance for the remission of sins, agreeable to the covenants and commandments" (D&C 107:20). Young men who hold the Aaronic Priesthood are preparing to hold the Melchizedek Priesthood.

> The power and authority of the higher, or Melchizedek Priesthood, is to hold the keys of all the spiritual blessings of the church—
>
> To have the privilege of receiving the mysteries of the kingdom of heaven, to have the heavens opened unto them, to commune with the general assembly and church of the Firstborn, and to enjoy the communion and presence of God the Father, and Jesus the mediator of the new covenant. (D&C 107:18–19)

Young men with special needs must also have careful preparation to receive the Melchizedek Priesthood and be ordained to the office of elder. Start with the steps outlined above for Aaronic Priesthood preparation. Also explain that while Aaronic Priesthood duties are temporal, those of the Melchizedek Priesthood are spiritual. "The elders are to conduct the meetings as they are led by the Holy Ghost, according to the commandments and revelations of God" (D&C 20:45).

Exercising the power of the Melchizedek Priesthood through the Holy Ghost impacts every duty of an elder. Each young man preparing to become an elder needs to learn how to live so the Holy Ghost will be his constant companion. This means you will have to give specific instructions on personal prayers, worthiness, tithing, and Sabbath day observance. "For the Strength of Youth" is an excellent resource for lessons on these topics. Please remember to bear your testimony as you teach these truths. Bearing your testimony of the priesthood will help boys with special needs also feel the Spirit and the importance of honoring the priesthood.

Note

1. Bruce R. McConkie, "The Salvation of Little Children," *Ensign*, Apr. 1977, 3.

EARLY TO BED, EARLY TO RISE

The Seminary Alarm Clock

by Lynn Parsons

A former seminary teacher shared the following story with me:

"What would my daughter get from attending seminary?"

I was the principal at a seminary for students with disabilities, and the question caught me off guard. Generally, when I told parents about our small class sizes and personalized teaching methods, the response was excitement and anticipation. This time, a mother wanted to know how gospel instruction would help her daughter as much as the important life skills she was learning at school.

I knew the answer to the question, but I wasn't sure how to put it into words.

I had seen the answer on a daily basis as I observed a teacher, well-prepared, provide lessons for a classroom of four students who were able to respond to the lesson only in spirit. Even though her students sat silently, unresponsive in their wheelchairs, she knew that each was a child of God and deserved the opportunity to hear the word of God.

I had seen the answer from the light in the eyes of a young man named Robert, who, over the course of many months, had learned to say and feel the meaning of the words, "Jesus loves Robert."

I had seen the answer each day as countless expressions of service and love were exchanged between teachers, students, and classroom missionaries.

Instead of attempting to answer the mother's question, I simply invited her to come and sit in one of our classrooms so she could feel the Spirit that is there.

I taught early morning seminary for six years. Like this seminary teacher, I have seen miracles happen in the lives of my students. This program is a blessing in the lives of our youth. Those with disabilities can also benefit, although they may face special challenges with attendance, class participation, scripture reading, and scripture mastery.

Attendance

As a youth, I was unable to attend early morning seminary because my parents didn't want me to attend. I wish I could tell each of you individually my testimony of the benefits of the seminary program. I've seen near-miraculous changes in youth who attend. One young man who was expelled from seminary for behavior problems not only returned but also served a successful mission when the time came. Others recalled scripture mastery verses at times when they most needed them. I have missionaries speak to my class each year just after they return home from their missions, and most say they wished they had paid more attention in seminary.

Seminary attendance is a challenge for many families when release-time (available during the school day) is not available. Transportation is often difficult and now costs more than ever before. I rely on the faith of the parents who struggle to find a way to allow their children to come. Some teens with special needs are physically unable to attend early morning seminary. One young man had seizures when he was too exhausted. He completed makeup work, and the class members tried to recognize his efforts whenever they saw him. They even made a video showing an empty chair they said the class had reserved for him. He was given a copy of the video to watch on his computer. This way, he was able to participate in at least some of the fellowship and relationships that develop between class members. He now attends a seminary class that meets later in the day.

Class Participation

I've had teens who wandered around the building during class. I explained to their parents that, for security reasons, being out of class during early morning seminary is a big problem. Reminders, either in the form of phrases to repeat or notes written on cards, helped these special spirits remember to stay in the room.

Some seminary students struggle to get along with classmates. I

try to keep them separated for a while and then get them involved in a project together (building the Tower of Babel from graham crackers is a good one) so they will learn that cooperation works better than opposition.

Involving these students is another challenge. Peer support, active learning experiences, preteaching, and lesson modifications allow them to participate, learn, and feel successful.

Peers can be a wonderful support during seminary activities. During a scripture mastery Easter egg hunt, one young woman with a disability was paired with a nondisabled peer, who helped her play the game. They had fun, collaborated, and won! Youth with low self-esteem had a boost if asked to help another student.

Active learning is good for all youth. Role playing, acting out scripture stories, drawing pictures, and creating ads for gospel principles are all examples of ways to get everyone involved in the lesson. Those with learning disabilities learn more through participation, especially if they struggle to focus. One young woman with autism felt like the most popular student in the class when she played Queen Esther.

Preteach by looking ahead a day or sometimes a week for your lessons. You can do this at the end of a class, send something home, or contact the parents. Then just call on the student to make their contribution during class. Others won't know they were set up and will be impressed by their answers. I've had some students who were so excited to be able to give the correct answer that they were more willing to participate in class discussions later.

I've found a few modifications to be most useful. They include scheduling and creating guided work. Other ideas can be found in the chapter titled "Teaching the Spirits."

Setting up a schedule is very important for special spirits. They know what to expect next, and the consistency is comforting. When he or she learns the routine and can anticipate change, many meltdowns can be prevented.

If the class will be taking notes or a test, creating a guided assignment will help those who struggle with writing. You can give them a scripture verse missing key words that can be found in a word bank at the bottom of the page. Or create a fill-in-the-blank test rather than asking essay questions. Multiple choice tests can be modified by reducing the number of answer choices to two. For additional ideas, visit

with the parents and see what modifications are done at school.

Scripture Reading

Some teens with special needs struggle with reading. The scriptures are available on CD, and there are software programs readily available that read text aloud. Scripture readers are another good alternative, as are the scriptures (audio and text versions) available for download at no cost from www.lds.org. The most important part of reading the scriptures is not to complete a set amount each day but to spend time with inspired words and feel the Spirit. Parental support is key. One family wouldn't allow their daughter with autism to go on her first date unless she finished reading the New Testament. She made it by the deadline with no problem. Motivation!

Scripture Mastery

This is a program that truly works miracles in the lives of our youth. One young woman with autism memorized Deuteronomy 7:3–4:

> Neither shalt thou make marriages with them; thy daughter thou shalt not give unto his son, nor his daughter shalt thou take unto thy son.
>
> For they will turn away thy son from following me, that they may serve other gods: so will the anger of the Lord be kindled against you, and destroy thee suddenly.

She not only took it to heart but would also use it to remind the other young women not to seriously date nonmembers.

Memorizing the scripture mastery verses is a challenge for everyone. I've been blessed many times as these verses have popped into my head just as I needed some inspiration. Some people find it easier to memorize one phrase at a time. Others begin memorizing with the last phrase. They add sections from the bottom up until they have completed the verse or verses. That way, when they start from the beginning, they are reciting the end—the part they know best—when they are tired.

A few of my seminary youth felt overwhelmed by the thought of memorizing twenty-five verses each year. I found the verses put to music online (available at http://lds.about.com/od/seminary/a/scripture _songs.htm), and they were able to learn the songs and pass them off that way. This group was so excited about the song for Deuteronomy 7:3–4 that they sang it for their Young Women leaders. Another idea

is to reduce the number of verses done at one time or to have your students try memorizing just the first line. Some youth may be able to identify a picture that goes with the verse, put pictures in order, or find and read the scripture after being given the reference. Reading the verse from a 3x5 card or retelling it are other good options, Don't be too concerned that they have it letter-perfect. If your teens put forth their best effort, Heavenly Father will give them the words when they are in need.

We are truly blessed to live in a time when so many programs and resources are available to our youth. As you earnestly seek Heavenly Father's will for these special spirits, you will be inspired to make the changes necessary to help them prepare to live with their Father again.

Blessings

The blessings of seminary participation can be either immediate or long-term. One young man had been given a glow-in-the-dark CTR bracelet as a prize in a game. At the end of the class period, every student was given one, so he ended up with two, which he wore constantly on both wrists. One night while standing in line for an R-rated movie, he looked down and saw the glow. He chose to leave his friends and return home. This was shortly before he turned in his mission papers, and it helped him be a little more worthy of the call.

After learning about millstones, the youth in another class were asked to wear a large metal washer on a string around their necks as a reminder of something they either needed to do or shouldn't do. The next day, a young man with ADHD remarked that he talked so much to his friends about the Church while explaining the washer, he knew he could be a missionary. He later completed a successful mission.

In the words of President Gordon B. Hinckley, "I hope all of you who are eligible are attending seminary. This organization provides wonderful opportunities to learn the doctrines that will make you happy."[1]

I know as you seek to find ways to help your special spirit thrive in seminary, you and those you serve will be blessed in unimaginable ways. I pray that as you create a safe zone for learning that you will find ways to build their testimonies for a lifetime.

Note

1. Gordon B. Hinckley, "Stand True and Faithful," *Ensign*, May 1996, 91.

I Love to See the Temple

by Lynn Parsons

Unbaptized Youth

Some youth have delayed their baptisms or haven't been baptized because they are afraid of the water. They can participate in temple trips by preparing names for the group to baptize. They may also go along on the trip and tour the temple grounds and learn about the history of that particular temple. Your local temple presidency can tell you about those who sacrificed time or talents as the temple was built, special significance of how the grounds are laid out, or other information that will impress your youth with the importance and sacredness of the temple.

For example, the ceiling of the baptistry in the Dallas Temple looks like marble. It was actually painted with feathers. After the artists completed their work, they decided it wasn't good enough for the House of the Lord, so they started over, demonstrating their love and respect for Heavenly Father. There may also be a visitors' center that the unbaptized youth can tour or a room where church videos are shown. Another option is to call the temple ahead of time to ask if there is some sort of service the youth can provide while the others are in the baptistry.

Perhaps a unique opportunity with a youth leader or member of the bishopric can be arranged. They could tour the grounds and discuss the importance of temple work. This way, your youth with special needs have an experience to relate on Sunday when others are reporting their temple stories, and they will feel included in this activity.

Preparing the Way

I've participated in many youth temple trips and found they can be a turning point in the lives of youth. As young men and young women walk through the temple doors, they can feel the world fall away. The Spirit is felt very strongly. Each young man and young woman feels a stronger desire to return to the presence of their Heavenly Father and resolves to work toward a temple marriage. Before attending the temple, there are a few key things you can do to prepare your youth with special needs for what will happen and what will be expected of them.

First, you should explain the sacred nature of the ordinances performed in the temple. Your youth may remember his or her baptism, but make sure they understand that they are being baptized for someone who didn't have the chance to learn the gospel while they were alive. Answer any questions your teen asks as honestly as you can. I was baptized at age sixteen and heard a few weeks later that the youth were doing baptisms for the dead. Not understanding what that involved, I believed coffins would be brought to the chapel, and we would have to help wheel them around. Needless to say, I didn't show up that night. Don't assume that everyone knows what you're talking about.

Next, every youth will need a temple recommend interview with the bishop. You can go over the questions ahead of time to be sure the youth understand what is being asked. You may need to clarify what some questions mean so they will feel more comfortable with the process.

Explain that they will wear Sunday dress to the temple and change into white jumpsuits with white underwear after they arrive. Reassure them that they will have a private changing area to protect their modesty and that when they are wet, you will not be able to see through the clothes. Some people are nervous about that. Girls with long hair will need to tie it back with a white band provided by the temple.

If needed, your teens can practice before the trip. They can rehearse holding onto a priesthood holder, plugging their nose, and leaning back. Some may prefer to sit down. If the priesthood holder puts his foot over the toes of the youth, it's generally easier to bring him or her down and back up again. Practice this process as often as your teen needs to for reassurance.

Please remember to review each step in the process a few days before the trip. Remind them how the youth are expected to act in the temple.

You may want to consider using power cards, narrative stories, or PECS to make this an even better experience.

Temple Power Cards, Narrative Stories, and PECS

Power cards can be used to help youth know how to behave and what to expect, especially on the first visit. Carefully select which graphics to use on the cards so they will be appropriate for the temple. A good reminder would be a picture of the Savior with text such as, "Jesus knows Rachel can remember to be quiet in the temple," or "The Savior is proud of Mary for wearing white while doing baptisms for the dead."

Some youth may need a narrative story to have a positive experience. For example:

"Billy is going with his ward to the temple. They are going to do baptisms for the dead. He knows he will see the bishop for a recommend interview before he goes. Billy will dress in church clothes. He will wait quietly in the lobby with the rest of the group. After listening to a talk, the group will get special white clothing. Billy will follow the young men into the men's locker room, wait his turn, and then change in a stall. Brother Pilgrim will help Billy put his things in a locker and keep the key.

"Billy and the other youth will sit quietly in the baptistry area, and he will wait for his turn. Then, Billy will go down the stairs into the font and hold hands with the leader just like he did when he was baptized. The leader will read the prayer from the computer monitor and baptize Billy. Billy will nod at the leader if he wants to do more names or shake his head if he thinks he has done enough.

"After being baptized, Billy will walk up the same set of stairs, get a towel, and go back into the men's locker room. He will squeeze water out of his clothes in the first area and use the shower to rinse them out, and Brother Pilgrim will help him with his locker. Billy can go into the stall and dress himself. Brother Pilgrim will help Billy put his clothes into the laundry chute.

"When Billy is dried off and dressed, he will go back into the waiting area. He will wait for a leader to call his name to go be confirmed. Afterward, he will sit quietly until everyone is finished. He will be proud to help people receive their temple blessings!"

PECS can be used in much the same way. A picture schedule

following the same order of the narrative story can be set up. You can use pictures of the group gathering, a car for travel, and people in white clothing, listening to a speaker, waiting for a turn, getting baptized, changing into church clothes, and participating in confirmations. For more information about a PECS schedule, please see the chapter titled "A Picture Is Worth a Thousand Words."

Attending with Support

One young woman with special needs was very excited to participate in baptisms for the dead for the first time. She prepared her great-grandmother's name with help from her mother. This created a more personal connection with this sacred experience. Her mother also chose to go on the trip with her daughter. The number of girls going in and out of the dressing room was a little disturbing, but the opportunity to perform ordinances for her great-grandmother made a lasting impression. This young woman now has a testimony not only of temple work but of genealogy as well.

A young man who struggled to sit still during meetings went on this same trip. When things were difficult for him, he frequently made noises. On this particular temple trip, he brought a family name. This young man had been named for this ancestor, and he had looked forward to this trip for a long time. Because his father knew it might be hard for his son to sit quietly as others were baptized, he chose to attend the temple trip with his son. It was hard for this young man to be quiet, but with gentle reminders from his father, it was a positive experience.

After your trip to the temple, encourage the youth to record their feelings. Youth with special needs can participate by drawing pictures, dictating or writing in a journal, or making an audio or video recording. This will become a treasured memory they will use to refresh their testimony during challenging times. This experience can be a stepping stone to remind them to return to the temple for more baptisms, to receive their own endowments, and achieve a temple marriage.

I Hope They Call Me on a Mission

Missions and Youth with Special Needs

by Danyelle Ferguson

Our prophets and apostles have taught us that every able and worthy young man should serve a mission. Many young women also choose to serve missions. In recent years, requirements regarding missionary health have changed. Speaking on this topic, Elder M. Russell Ballard said,

> We recognize that it may not be wise for some of our young men and young women to face the rigors and challenges of a full-time mission. If priesthood leaders excuse any of you from full-time missionary service, we ask you and your families to accept the decision and move forward. You can prepare to participate in the saving ordinances of the temple and find other ways to be of service. And we ask all of our members to be supportive and to show great love and understanding in assisting all of our faithful youth in their various Church callings.[1]

Called to Serve

In your calling as a Church leader or teacher, you may work with young men and women who will not have the opportunity to serve a full-time mission, but that doesn't mean they can't serve. In the chapter titled "Mission Possible," you'll find many stories of young men and women who have completed wonderful part-time service missions and have made an incredible impact on those they served. While that chapter is written for the prospective missionary, Church leaders, teachers, and family will find the information and resources helpful as they

support the young man or woman in a search for service opportunities.

The Church has many full-time missionaries with disabilities, such as missionaries who are deaf. It's not necessarily the fact that the young man or woman has a disability that may preclude them from missionary work but rather if he or she will be able to physically, socially, and emotionally handle sixty to sixty-five hours per week of demanding work surrounded by unfamiliar people and locations. In general, Church leaders, teachers, and family will not know which type of mission the youth will serve until they reach the required missionary age.

Teach Everyone to Serve

Missions are a popular topic of conversation during the teen years. During this time, continue to encourage and support your youth with special needs to read the scriptures, pray, attend seminary, and prepare to serve a mission, just as you would the other youth. When you teach or talk about missions, it would be helpful if you shared a variety of stories and experiences about both full-time missionaries and missionaries who served part-time service missions.

It's especially important for youth with special needs to be aware of the different mission opportunities available to them. In recent years, some were caught off-guard when their mission applications were returned, saying they were not required to serve a full-time mission. They were hurt, confused, and not sure what the response meant. Some didn't realize there were other options for serving. All youth should be taught that they each have a special mission to serve here on earth. Each mission and act of service given is important to Heavenly Father, and it's important that we fulfill those missions. Elder Richard G. Scott said,

> If you are a young man wondering whether you ought to fulfill a full-time mission, don't approach that vital decision with your own wisdom alone. Seek the counsel of your parents, your bishop, or stake president. In your prayers ask to have the will of the Lord made known to you. I know that a mission will provide extraordinary blessings for you now and throughout your life. I urge you not to pray to know whether you should go; rather, ask the Lord to guide you in whatever may be necessary to become a worthy, empowered full-time missionary. You will never regret serving a mission.[2]

Support Your Missionaries

Receiving a mission call is such an exciting moment for a young man or woman. Celebrate these calls with your ward. When a young man or woman with special needs is called to a part-time service mission, make the announcement just as you would for other mission calls. If the missionary will be serving away from home—for example, as a host at a Church historical location—coordinate a "Going Away" open house if you do this for other missionaries.

If the missionary will live at home while serving locally, encourage him to wear his badge to church. When you address your missionary, always refer to him or her as "Elder" or "Sister." If your ward writes letters or puts together missionary boxes to send out for the holidays, don't forget to include your missionary with special needs, even if he or she is serving from home. You may ask your missionary if there's something specific he'd like donated to the program in which he's serving. For example, if your missionary is serving at the bishop's storehouse, he may prefer the ward to donate canned goods to families for their holiday meals. All missionaries love it when you show genuine interest in their work.

Most importantly, show love and appreciation to your missionary no matter where he or she serves. There are very few things as exciting as serving a mission for The Church of Jesus Christ of Latter-day Saints. The missionary work those missionaries do will create a rolling effect of blessings that will carry on into eternity.

Notes

1. M. Russell Ballard, "One More," *Ensign*, May 2005, 69–71.
2. Richard G. Scott, "Now Is the Time to Serve a Mission!," *Ensign*, May 2006, 87–90.

Let's Get Together

A Guide to Teen Socializing

by Lynn Parsons

It can be difficult to be a teen under the best of circumstances. It may be exponentially harder to be an adolescent with a disability. Some of these challenges include getting along with others, making friends, and forming dating relationships.

Classmate Relationships

Some teens with special needs struggle to develop positive relationships during Church classes. It's hard to get to know others during class, but friendships can begin during this association. Teens with special needs may need specific coping strategies, a chance to participate, or help from a peer to build connections to those in their Church classes.

Many special spirits get upset because of lighting, classmates' behavior, or other things beyond their control. There are many ways to deal with anxiety. These may include using a "fidget." This can be a soft ball to squeeze, a stone to feel in their pocket, or something scratchy to rub with their thumb. Others can repeat a calming phrase to themselves, and some may need to walk down the hall for a drink to take a break. As long as these supports are approved by the parents and teachers, any strategy that works for your adolescent to help him or her remain calm and not lash out at others is good to implement. One young man with ADHD repeatedly fell asleep during seminary. He was choosing to do this rather than yell at classmates when angry. He was given a small ball to keep in his pocket that he could squeeze to keep his emotions under control. This was the best alternative in his situation.

Giving your teen a job to do during class helps him work with others and feel like he's an important part of the group. As you prepare lessons each week, look for ways to involve him. One young woman with autism was great at drawing. Her teacher asked her to draw pictures on the board that went along with the lesson. This involved her, made her feel valued, helped the others learn, and gave her classmates a way to value her input.

Involve your class president to help any teens with special needs get involved in the class. They can model good behavior, help explain difficult ideas, cheer during games, and act as a calming friend. Remember that they will be blessed for their service as well. I've had success encouraging conversations among teens by pointing out similarities. For example: "Sarah saw a movie last weekend. Did you see that one?" Once these bonds are forged, you will be impressed with how well youth with special needs are accepted by their peers. A young lady with autism was frequently shunned by her classmates because she would initiate conversations on random topics. After learning about her talents and making the effort to get to know her better, these loving youth were willing to interact with her more, even on her preferred topics.

Special Friendships

I've watched my four children go through the teen years. I've spent six years teaching high school special education and six years as a seminary teacher. During this time, I've realized that making and keeping friends is a huge struggle at this age. Youth with special needs have many of the same desires as their peers, suffer from the same social anxieties, and wonder about their futures.

Teens make friends with people they see often, who share their interests, and who act like them. You can help your special spirit make friends by inviting him or her to attend different activities. Church gatherings, sports teams, school clubs, and community groups are a great place to start. Some teens feel uncomfortable in a new place and might need support from a parent, sibling, or friend to get started. Remember, friendships can't be forced, but you can put your young adult into a position to meet and make new friends.

After he or she gets to know some people, encourage your adolescent to invite a new friend to your home and get to know them better. Have talks with your teen about how to keep friends, use good manners, and

other social skills. Let them benefit from your experiences. This will help them know how to build a positive relationship with their new buddy. Encourage them to make friends with people both with and without disabilities. With a little facilitation, your special teen can build relationships that may last for decades. Don't be upset if some friendships fade. This happens to everyone. Use the previous relationship to encourage the youth to form new ones.

As a teen, I constantly felt that all eyes were on me. I was sure I was the ugliest, stupidest, and clumsiest person on the planet. Every adolescent thinks they're being watched and that they may be ridiculed for any mistake. Try to reassure your special spirit that it's normal to feel this way and that most people are too concerned about themselves to worry about others.

If problems or arguments happen, try to stay out of it. My mother-in-law gave me some great advice when my children were small. She said that when adults get mixed up in children's problems, everyone loses. I only stepped in when there was physical danger or when my child might feel forced to act against our standards. Small squabbles are a great chance for teens to practice the social skills they will need later with family and coworkers.

Dating

Dating is a difficult time for teens, parents, and Church leaders. Following the standards set by the Church can bring you comfort and safety. For more information, see "For the Strength of Youth." Have family discussions on this topic often. If they talk to other teens, watch television, read magazines, or surf the Internet, they are already learning about boy/girl relationships. If you start conversations on this topic, they will feel better about asking questions, and you will have the chance to teach gospel-centered values.

My own children were not allowed to date until they were at least sixteen years old, and then they had to group date until age eighteen. Some were not ready until they were older. I've seen many special adolescents who were not ready for a boyfriend/girlfriend relationship during high school. Some were pushed by their parents into situations for which they were not ready. Just relax! I've seen eighteen-year-olds who just wanted to watch Disney videos and play with dolls. They were not developmentally prepared to date. There is

no hurry. Encourage friendships by inviting peers over, but don't try to force a more mature relationship. They will let you know when they are ready.

Letting my girls go on dates was much more difficult than seeing the boys drive off. I knew how well my sons could drive and where they were going, and I felt more in control of the situation. I was pretty freaked out with the girls. I had a huge advantage in that I worked at their high school and could check out their dates pretty thoroughly. And I did! Meet the teens prior to the date, if possible, and this will lessen your anxiety.

Siblings worry about their brothers and sisters with special needs on dates. One was afraid that her sister with autism appeared to be too affectionate, which could be misread by a teenage boy. Another worried about her brother acting so interested, a young lady might mistake him for a stalker.

Daddy-daughter or mother-son evenings are a great chance to practice for "real" dates. Teens can learn how to behave, make conversation, and eat politely. Parents also have an opportunity to teach dating behavior directly while having fun and spending time together.

Some teens may be unable to date at all unless their parents intervene. I've had students whose parents drove them to the prom, stayed in the shadows, and then took them home early when they'd had enough fun. One family with two children on the autism spectrum has already told them they will have a parent or sibling chaperone when they date. You have to decide as a family what is appropriate for your situation. Try to remember that just as you can't force friendships, you can't force romantic relationships.

Dating Typical Peers

This is a very challenging area. I was unable to find any studies or research on this topic. I know many families worry that typical peers may try to take advantage of their teen with special needs. I have known those who have dated teens with disabilities. The outcome seems to depend on the character of the peer and the expectations of the adolescent with special needs. If this date is just a one-time outing for a special event, this needs to be explained clearly. Some teens with special needs get very attached to new people quickly. Joan, a teen with two siblings with special needs, has often struggled to explain to her family how

and why many teen relationships are so short-lived. On the other hand, peers can serve as a model for good dating behavior and may teach some good social skills.

Social relationships in the classroom, friendships, and dating are all challenging for teens with special needs. Pray often and follow Church guidelines, and you will have the inspiration you need to help your teen grow in this area.

Adults

Church Callings

by Danyelle Ferguson

When I receive a new Church calling, I'm always filled with excitement mixed with a little bit of fear. I can't wait to serve, but at the same time I'm intimidated by the unknown. No matter what my calling is, I know it was given to me from Heavenly Father as an opportunity to grow into the person He wants me to be. I've had callings that, to others, may have seemed simple and easy to accomplish. In actuality, those callings were sometimes a challenge but always a huge blessing. Each Church calling gave me a sense of accomplishment as I did the best I could to serve the Lord.

Likewise, Church callings are very important for individuals with special needs. Callings give them a sense of accomplishment, of being needed and included. Callings and responsibilities also give these individuals the opportunity to grow personally. Some assignments may enhance favored talents, while others may help develop talents or skills the individual hasn't mastered yet.

It's important for Church leaders to take the time to consider prayerfully how Heavenly Father would like these individuals to serve. Consider their talents, hobbies, and the activities they enjoy. Through sincere prayer, Heavenly Father will give you promptings and direction in areas where the individual can be blessed as he serves. In 2 Nephi 26:28 we read, "All men are privileged the one like unto the other, and none are forbidden." Each individual has talents and gifts, and each thrives when presented with opportunities to contribute.

In an article titled, "Encircled in the Savior's Love," Elder W. Craig Zwick spoke of his son's disability and the blessings each member of his family has received as a result. He also goes on to say,

> The Lord spoke in plainness, "Be faithful and diligent in keeping the commandments of God, and I will encircle thee in the arms of my love" (D&C 6:20). We all want to feel the comfort of the Savior's embrace.
>
> During His ministry, the Savior, with great compassion, saw beyond the imperfections of body and mind and looked upon the heart. Our discipleship includes the sacred responsibility to follow His example of reaching out and loving those with disabilities. Valiant disciples seek meaningful ways to stretch their souls in service and love to others.[1]

Elder Zwick then goes on to give examples of members with special needs and how they have served in the Church.

> Jamie Wheeler is an exceptional sixteen-year-old. He was born with Down syndrome. Jamie has a calling in the ward and helps the bishop in other meaningful ways. He participates actively in the Boy Scout program. Truly he contributes and also receives genuine love and appreciation.
>
> Four young men with severe disabilities work in the São Paulo Temple. Each has a different challenge, but each is blessing the lives of thousands as they contribute to the sweet spirit within this beautiful temple. *"Remember the worth of souls is great in the sight of God"* (D&C 18:10).[2]

I've met many individuals with special needs who serve diligently in their wards and stakes. One young lady with Down syndrome serves in the temple folding laundry each week. Another young man served in the office of the local institute building. I've met members who have served in the Missionary Training Center, and others who sent out birthday cards to the Primary children. The size of the calling is never what's important—it's the love and fulfillment that comes from serving that impacts and enhances lives.

Working Together

Once a calling is extended and accepted, the leader and the individual accepting the calling will need to talk and figure out a system of communication and follow-up.

An important note to leaders: Remember, you are working directly with the individual with special needs, not his parents or siblings. Develop a relationship with him. Be sure to address him when you have questions, comments, or assignments. Also, let him know when he does a good job and express your appreciation often.

Leaders will need to know how the individual prefers to have tasks recorded. Tasks could be given verbally, written on paper, emailed, or even recorded on a mini-cassette player. Also, you'll need to decide how many tasks to assign at a time. This will most likely need to be adjusted often in the beginning. As you serve together, you'll get to know each other's strengths and abilities. When you work together and divide up the tasks, choose a date for both of you to report on what you've accomplished. As the leader, you may find that one or two reminders partway through could be helpful.

As an example, let's say a young woman is very good at organizing and has been called to serve on the committee for additional Relief Society meetings. She has been given the assignment to organize donations for table decorations. The committee leader may then email the task list to the young woman with a note that the leader will email again in a week to follow up.

You may also find that reminders aren't needed at all.

An excellent resource for leaders is an article by Carmen B. Pingree titled, "Six Myths about the Handicapped."[3] It can be found on the Church website. The article discusses common misconceptions members tend to have about the handicapped. You'll find good tips and information that will help as you serve with an individual with special needs.

Notes

1. W. Craig Zwick, "Encircled in the Savior's Love," *Ensign*, Nov. 1995, 13.
2. Ibid., italics added.
3. Carmen B. Pingree, "Six Myths about the Handicapped," *Ensign*, Jun. 1988, 19.

LOVE ONE ANOTHER

Home and Visiting Teaching

by Lynn Parsons

Home and visiting teachers can be a great blessing to families with special needs. One great home teacher brought object lessons for my young children. They anticipated his visits, enjoyed the lessons, and remembered them long afterward. He really tried to meet our needs as a family by considering our interests, ages, and abilities. As parents, we felt very blessed—our offspring wanted to participate, so we didn't have to struggle to control their behavior during this time. See the chapter titled "Teaching the Spirits" to learn how to adapt your messages for different needs.

Home teaching and visiting teaching are unique opportunities to serve the Lord and each other. Some may serve with a companion who has a cognitive disability—another unique opportunity. Those eighteen years of age or older who live with their parents may enjoy their family's home or visiting teachers, while others may want separate sets of teachers, especially if they attend different wards. Check with the families to see which they prefer.

Serving the Family—Home Teaching

President Harold B. Lee said, "Home teaching, in essence, means that we consider separately each individual member of the family who constitutes the entire home personnel."[1] As a home teacher to an individual with special needs, you will need an attitude of love and patience. You may need to adapt your message in a way the individual will understand more clearly, perhaps with more visual and concrete examples.

Before you visit, pray with your home teaching companion for the

guidance of the Holy Ghost. This will allow you to be more empathetic and sympathetic to the needs of the family. For example, when you make an appointment, ask about bedtimes. Many families find that disrupting bedtime schedules can create chaos in the household. Please remember that their household may not run like yours. Children with special needs come with special challenges, which each family faces differently. A loving attitude creates a trusting relationship. This, in turn, encourages your assigned families to request help when needed.

The monthly message should be tailored to the needs of each family. As home teachers, you are the eyes and ears for the bishop, looking for needs and ways to serve this family. Being the family member of a person with special needs can be very stressful. Parents may need babysitting, help with chores, or just a listening ear. Offer assistance in chores when you can help—such as mowing the lawn if the husband travels for work or raking up autumn leaves. The family may enjoy an afternoon excursion to your house if you have a fenced-in backyard their children would like. Ask how you can serve them, but don't make assumptions. For example, one family may love to have you mow their lawn, while others may not. My coauthor, Danyelle, looks forward to mowing her lawn each week. Her children all think the lawn mower is too noisy, so it's her opportunity to be outside in the fresh air with no children chasing after her!

The children of some families you may visit could be grown and gone. One or both people in the couple may have special needs. You will need to be sensitive to the individual with a disability as well as the caregiver. This family may need help with household repairs, transportation, or respite care.

Other members may be in a group home or care facility. They may need fellowship and love more than any actual assistance. A telephone call, visit, or card in the mail can mean the world. Rather than dealing with physical needs, you may just want to stroll with them down memory lane as they turn the pages of a scrapbook. You can consult the staff to see what they suggest to meet the needs of the member or family you teach.

Serving the One—Home Teaching

As a home teacher, you may be assigned to visit the home of a single person with special needs. He or she may be living in a home, an

apartment, or an assisted living center or care home. Begin by building a relationship with him or her. Then seek to be uplifting. Finally, try to be a facilitator who meets his or her needs.

Building a relationship with a person with special needs can be a challenge. Communication is vital to this effort. You may have to learn an alternative form of communication, such as sign language. If picture communication is used in the home, see the chapter titled "A Picture Is Worth a Thousand Words" for more information about the PECS program. Be sure to speak in a respectful manner and treat the other person as an equal.

If the person you are home teaching has a specific interest they continually mention, you may need to do some research and learn how to use that interest to teach them gospel principles. For example, let's say you are teaching an adult with special needs who is a huge Lego fan. He often tells you about the newest Lego themes and his favorite Lego characters. When you become familiar with them, you can print pictures of the Lego men and use them to tell scripture stories to teach a gospel principle. If he has a large supply of Legos, you may even be able to create Lego men and buildings together to create the scene for the scripture story.

Yes, this will take more time and effort on your part, but can you even imagine what joy you would instill in this person's life by sharing something he loves and teaching the gospel in a way he understands? Not only will you gain his trust and open lines of communication, but you will become his new lifelong friend. Just imagine the greeting you will receive from him when you are together after this life, when all his capacities are fully functioning. That is reward enough for any effort.

For those living in some type of assisted living facility, be sure to make contact with the staff. You may ask them to call you about needs, ask them about special interests or favorite things, and ask when is the best time to visit. They can be a gold mine of information.

Challenged Companions—Home Teaching

Young men are called to be home teachers when they become teacher age in the Aaronic Priesthood. Their companions have a sacred responsibility to lead by example as they serve their families. Some companions with special needs may feel inadequate, while others may struggle to figure out how to help their families.

Your companion with special needs may relate to William Cahoon, who was a convert of six months when called to teach Joseph Smith. He was seventeen years old at the time. He describes his first visit:

> Finally I went to his door and knocked, and in a minute the Prophet came to the door. I stood there trembling, and said to him:
>
> "Brother Joseph, I have come to visit you in the capacity of a teacher, if it is convenient for you."
>
> He said, "Brother William, come right in, I am glad to see you; sit down in that chair there and I will go and call my family in."
>
> "They soon came in and took seats. He then said, "Brother William, I submit myself and family into your hands," and then took his seat. "Now Brother William," said he, "ask all the questions you feel like."
>
> By this time all my fears and trembling had ceased, and I said, "Brother Joseph, are you trying to live your religion?"
>
> He answered, "Yes."
>
> Then I said, "Do you pray in your family?"
>
> He said, "Yes."
>
> "Do you teach your family the principles of the gospel?"
>
> He replied, "Yes, I am trying to do it."
>
> "Do you ask a blessing on your food?"
>
> He answered, "Yes."
>
> "Are you trying to live in peace and harmony with all your family?"
>
> He said that he was.
>
> I turned to Sister Emma, his wife, and said, "Sister Emma, are you trying to live your religion? Do you teach your children to obey their parents? Do you try to teach them to pray?"
>
> To all these questions, she answered, "Yes, I am trying to do so."
>
> I then turned to Joseph and said, "I am now through with my questions as a teacher; and now if you have any instructions to give, I shall be happy to receive them."
>
> He said, "God bless you, Brother William; and if you are humble and faithful, you shall have power to settle all difficulties that may come before you in the capacity of a teacher."
>
> I then left my parting blessing upon him and his family, as a teacher, and took my departure.[2]

You can share this story with your companion and explain that, even today, someone home teaches the prophet and General Authorities.

If you and your companion earnestly try to fulfill your duties, your efforts will be enough.

Some companions with special needs may not be able to drive, or they may have limited resources to help. As you come to know them better, you will discover talents that can bless the lives of your families. Young men have come to my home and remained silent. Others have borne strong testimony of gospel truths that touched our hearts. Your companion with special needs could call to make appointments, phone for reminders, or pray during appointments.

Others may feel comfortable enough to give all or part of the lesson. This requires advance planning so they may coordinate their message.

Serving the Family—Visiting Teaching

Sister Julie B. Beck, Relief Society general president, said, "Visiting teachers minister in behalf of the Savior. Our hands are His hands, our love is His love, and our service is His service. They focus on fortifying homes and lives."[3] As we visit sisters "in behalf of the Savior," we are really serving the entire family. We can fortify homes by supporting the sisters in word and deed.

Using words to support a sister with special needs is more than just delivering the monthly message. Use your voice to uplift, comfort, and cheer. Using your gospel lesson as a beginning, you can convey the reality of the Savior's love and His promises of future blessings and kindle faith in our eternal life to come. Continue by relating positive, hopeful stories that will encourage and enlighten.

Words are often not enough. Sister Elaine L. Jack said, "In visiting teaching we reach out to each other. Hands often speak as voices can't. A warm embrace conveys volumes. A laugh together unites us. A moment of sharing refreshes our souls. We cannot always lift the burden of one who is troubled, but we can lift her so she can bear it well."[4]

Create a relationship with the sisters you visit in which the sister is comfortable sharing her needs with you. Ask what is needed and offer not just advice but also practical help. Most people can buy their own prepared food, but having a meal arrive at the door brings feelings of comfort and support. The food doesn't have to be homemade to be a blessing. Elaborate or expensive efforts are not required. You may be asked to visit an adult daughter and her mother together. Make sure you present the message in a way that is beneficial to both. Refer to

the chapter titled "Teaching the Spirits" to see how to modify the lessons. The sister with special needs may require extra attention while the caregiver takes a much-needed break. Offering a respite is a great way to get to know one while assisting the other. There may be other times when it would be appropriate to visit each sister separately in order to serve them better.

Serving the One—Visiting Teaching

"Good visiting teachers know the sisters they visit. They love them, serve them, and help them learn the gospel by the Spirit."[5] Love is of supreme importance. As you learn to love the special spirit you visit teach, you will discover how to deliver the message. Those you teach will be more receptive to you as they feel your care and concern. You will be able to discern any needs and find ways to meet them. Communicating as equals will help you develop the respect Heavenly Father feels for each one of us.

As you serve this special sister, not only will your love increase, but you will also feel appreciation for the blessings in your own life. Meeting her needs will help you develop Christlike qualities. One young companionship felt they had little to offer the elderly lady they visited. She was an accomplished homemaker and mother and was very well educated. The years had taken a toll on her health, however. She often expressed appreciation for the opportunity to offer advice. While unable to help physically, she felt useful as she counseled with these young mothers.

Gospel teaching is an important part of visiting teaching. There may be times when you feel chatting is enough, but don't skip the chance to expound on eternal truths. As you lift your sisters, the messages you leave will also have a profound effect on your life. There have been many months when I felt impressed to make changes in my own life as I offered the lesson to others. I have also learned much as I listened to the experiences and testimonies of those I had been sent to instruct.

Challenged Companions—Visiting Teaching

"No matter what our individual circumstances are, we all have the opportunity to edify and nurture others."[6] This will also come true for your companion with special needs. Given the opportunity, she can

testify of God's love through her example of good works and service.

It may be tempting to shoulder all the responsibility yourself. This might seem easier, or you may feel you are lifting a burden. Can your companion set up appointments? Prepare a thought? Make an encouraging phone call during the week? Sit with someone who is alone at church? Provide a warm smile and a friendly greeting? Her example can provide a much-needed lift to a struggling sister.

How can you provide opportunities for your companion to magnify her calling? First, prayerfully consider her gifts. One young adult sister with autism bakes wonderful cupcakes. She will stay up late into the night if she thinks someone needs a fresh batch. Visit with relatives and the Relief Society presidency to see what untapped talents your companion may have. Then prayerfully consider each sister you visit and ask how you both may best serve her. I promise you will be inspired to find a perfect solution.

Don't forget to praise the unique talents of your companion. She will feel valued and accepted and will be encouraged to perform further service. As you seek out her unique abilities, your love for her will become truly charitable.

Conclusion

Home and visiting teaching are inspired programs with the potential to bless the lives of each member of the Church. As you and your companion seek for ways to include those with disabilities, the Lord will bless your efforts with promptings from the Spirit and strong relationships with those you serve.

Notes

1. Harold B. Lee, *Stand Ye in Holy Places* (Salt Lake City: Deseret Book, 1974), 298. Used by permission.
2. *Juvenile Instructor,* vol. 27: 491–92.
3. Julie B. Beck. "Focusing on the Lord's Work of Salvation." *Ensign,* Mar. 2009, 18–22.
4. Elaine L. Jack, quoted in Jaclyn W. Sorensen, "Visiting teaching—giving selfless service in a loving sisterhood," *Church News,* Mar. 7, 1992, 5.
5. Beck, "Focusing," 18–22.
6. Silvia H. Allred. "Feed My Sheep," *Ensign,* Nov. 2007, 113–15.

MISSION POSSIBLE

by Danyelle Ferguson

When I think about missionaries, I remember the knock on my door that introduced my family to two elders who taught us about the Church. While this is the traditional way to think of missionaries, I now know there are many ways to be a missionary. In this chapter, we are going to delve into the different types of missions to which men and women with special needs can look forward and how their service blesses the lives of others and the Church.

There is one very important concept I want each prospective missionary to remember as he or she ponders and considers mission opportunities: *Each and every mission is important.* One mission opportunity is not more important than another. Each missionary, no matter how or where they serve, is a beloved child of God, an example of our Savior, and an inspiration to bring others closer to Christ.

I know that as prospective missionaries keep this thought in mind while they search and pray about a mission, they will be led to serve Heavenly Father in exactly the right way.

Full-Time Missions

The Church Handbook explains that those who have disabilities—whether physical, mental, or emotional—are not called to full-time missions if their disabilities prevent them from being able to serve effectively.

The focus of this statement is not "are not called to full-time missions" but rather "if their disabilities prevent them from being able to serve effectively."

Full-time missions are rigorous and demanding. On average, these missionaries are out walking, riding bikes, knocking on doors, and interacting with strangers sixty to sixty-five hours per week. That's more time than most adults put in during a regular work week. Social, emotional, and physical abilities need to be realistically considered before choosing which type of mission is the best way for you to serve Heavenly Father.

Depending on the disability, a person with special needs may be able to apply for a full-time mission. The individual's stake president can call the Church Missionary Department to ask more specific questions and talk with someone about his or her situation. Before a call is extended, the individual with special needs may be asked to meet with different doctors for evaluations. In an interview with the *Salt Lake Tribune*, Quinton Harris, former director of the LDS Missionary Medical Committee, said,

"We (the Church) would like anyone with emotional problems to be evaluated, then get stabilized on medication before he goes, then stay on it in the field. Any condition you have before you go gets worse when you get out in the field. If they're stable on medication, chances are they are going to succeed."[1]

During these evaluations, be honest and open with the doctors. If given the go-ahead, the individual may be asked to serve a trial mission for one to three months. This is a wonderful opportunity for a person to step into the hectic life of a missionary and be confident he or she has made the correct choice before being called to a full-time mission.

As I spoke with missionaries with special needs who served trial missions, many expressed gratitude for the experience. Some found it helped them be better prepared for when they moved to their full-time mission, and others found that the stress of missionary life hindered their social and coping skills. In the latter scenario, these missionaries were given time and help from their mission presidents and companions. Some were able to overcome their obstacles while others, through prayer and fasting, chose to return home honorably and serve in another capacity.

During a trial mission, one missionary with autism found that there were so many things he wanted to express while teaching investigators, he couldn't move the words from his thoughts to his mouth. After weeks of prayer and trying to overcome this new trial, he came

to the peaceful knowledge that he should return home and seek out another mission opportunity. His mission president was very impressed with this young man and sent him home with a wonderful referral letter for the elder's next mission opportunity.

Other missionaries found they encountered struggles with routine and flexibility, or social interaction in large groups of missionaries and new Church congregations. When these missionaries were paired with patient and kind companions, they became less stressed and were able to relax enough to become comfortable with the adaptations and changes necessary to be successful.

Part-Time Service Missions

Many individuals with special needs will participate in service missions, either through the Church Service Missionary Department, local seminary or institute directors, their stakes, or their wards/branches. These part-time missions are served while living at home, giving the missionaries a familiar place and support system at the end of each day. The work service missionaries do is very important. Without them, the Church would not be able to complete necessary work assignments unless they hired more employees, which would take funds away from other important Church programs.

The Church Service Missionary Department has a website devoted to listing part-time service missions. It can be found at http://servicemission .ldschurch.org. Missions listed on this site require between eight and thirty-two hours per week, and normally last anywhere from six to twenty-four months. Service missionaries must also provide their own transportation and financial support. When you visit the website, be sure to read the "FAQ" and "How Do I Get Started" sections first. This will help you understand how to find and apply for programs in your area.

Examples of these missions include assisting in your local mission office, working with seminary or institute directors, or being a host at a local Church historical site. The Church Educational System has many part-time missionary opportunities. Teachers often need assistants or aides to read with students in class, help with lessons, and assist students to and from school. If you don't see a listing for your local seminary or institute program, call the CES leader directly to ask what opportunities they have available.

One young man with Down syndrome called his local institute director and talked with him about serving there for his mission. The director was excited and even wrote an official letter detailing the mission expectations, such as no dating, finding bus transportation to and from the institute location, grooming, and so forth. This young man served a two-year mission working with and assisting the institute director, singing with the institute choir, and participating in one class each day.

This same young man later served a part-time service mission at one of the Church historical locations. While there, he was a host and tour guide. After only a short time, he was called to be an ordinance worker at the local temple, where he served two days a week throughout his mission.

If you have difficulties with transportation, there are also opportunities on the website that allow you to serve from home. For example, you could receive phone calls and referrals for different programs, such as answering questions about family history programs. Simply follow the "At Home Service Opportunities" link.

Some mission opportunities through your ward or stake leader might include MTC, temple, and genealogy missions.

To qualify for a temple mission, you must have a temple recommend. Some areas of the temple only admit endowed Church members, while others do not—such as serving in the baptistry or as a garden aide. One woman with Down syndrome serves a temple mission and helps patrons rent their temple clothing. Another young woman assists in the prayer roll department answering phones and recording names on the prayer roll list. One young man who loves the outdoors assists with the gardening and keeping the temple beautiful.

If you live near a Missionary Training Center (MTC), they usually need service missionaries to work in the Training Resource Center (TRC). When I was in college, I was a service missionary at the TRC. Usually this involved role playing as a nonmember investigator. Each week, I met with a group of volunteers for that day—some of whom actually were nonmembers. We would sing and have prayer together, then one of the TRC coordinators told us what the missionaries were working on that day. There were many different scenarios, such as teaching a certain discussion, following up with a new member, or visiting with a Church member and asking for referrals.

The service missionary's job is to act out the scenario without giving away if they are a member of the Church or not, as well as to make the missionaries work a little bit to get the information they need. This is a wonderful program to help missionaries prepare before leaving the MTC.

If you do not live near an MTC or temple, talk to both your bishop and stake president to find out what other opportunities are available in your region. One option could be a genealogy service mission through the Family and Church History Department. They often need individuals to work in local genealogy centers to help patrons who are unfamiliar with computers and new genealogy programs, and also with extracting names from microfilm. Another option is helping your local missionaries if they host a weekly literacy night or assist in another ward or stake class assignment.

Two young men—Elder Jared Cassity and Elder Paul Hansen—were called to serve stake missions and help teach their stake's missionary preparation class. Both elders have mental and physical disabilities. Together, they helped the class teacher with various responsibilities and were asked to extend their missions beyond the typical two years. One of the returned missionaries who took the stake class said,

"Paul and Jared might not be full-time elders, but they are serving real missions. I think it's all just serving the Lord. They do a tremendous job. They really do bring the Spirit into the classroom."

You can read more about Elder Cassity and Elder Hansen in the March 2001 *New Era*.[2]

Called to Serve

As you can see, there are numerous ways to serve. In D&C 4:3, we are promised, "Therefore, if ye have desires to serve God ye are called to the work." Depending on your abilities or the area where you live, you may need to be creative. But, if you have a desire to serve the Lord, work with your Church leaders, and pray for guidance, you will be led to wonderful missionary opportunities. May you desire to serve and be blessed with the Spirit through your service.

Notes

1. Peggy Fletcher Stack, "Unintended consequence of church's 'raising the bar,'" *Salt Lake Tribune*, July 26, 2005.
2. Shanna Ghaznavi, "They Also Serve," *New Era*, Mar. 2001, 12.

Will You Remember Me?

Older Adults and Mental Illness

by Danyelle Ferguson

I once had an institute teacher who said that we are born into this world with no teeth, wearing diapers, and remembering very little about our premortal existence, and that if we live long enough, we leave with no teeth, wearing diapers, and remembering very little about our life here on earth. As a college student, I thought his comment was rather funny. As an adult, watching my parents and grandparents age, I find myself pondering the prophetic value of his statement from time to time.

Mental illness comes in many forms, some of which don't occur until much later in life. Even then, it's a gradual process, and you may lose some memory before you realize there's anything wrong. Alzheimer's disease and dementia are two examples of illnesses that affect your memory and the ability to function and care for yourself.

In one congregation I attended, we had a Relief Society sister who developed dementia. She didn't remember much of her daily life, and most of her memories were of events from earlier in her life. Each week during the lesson, she would answer one of the questions with the very same story from when she was a little girl, waiting for her slowpoke brother to join their parents and siblings for family prayer. After a while, I began to doodle on my program or do some other activity while this sister shared her story.

But one day after the weekly story was finished, the Relief Society teacher paused in her lesson to thank this sister for always sharing her testimony of family prayer. She commented on how it had increased her

own desire to have consistent family prayer with her children so that they too would develop a strong testimony of this principle. Tears came to my eyes as I learned a great lesson that day. This sweet sister wasn't just telling a story—she was bearing her testimony. It made me wonder what events must have occurred in her life that created this powerful memory to which she clung. I realized that her testimony of family prayer showed how much she deeply loved and valued her family and their relationship with Heavenly Father. From that moment on, whenever this sister stood to tell her story, I listened intently, hoping to gain more insight from her wonderful testimony and faith.

Other illnesses, such as depression, can affect the way you view yourself, your relationships with others, and your surroundings.

One sister shared with me her struggle with depression when she was in her midforties. She became depressed to the point she attempted to end her life. She just wanted everything to be done and to rest. Fortunately, she had a loving husband who followed a prompting to return home, and he helped save her.

During this sister's recovery, many sisters from her ward showed an outpouring of love. They sent cards and emails to ask how she was and update her on their families, which added a bit of cheerfulness to her day. Other sisters dropped off flowers, meals, and sweets, or just stopped by for a quick hug and chat. A few even shared their own experiences of dealing with depression, their testimonies of being a daughter of God, and how Heavenly Father helped them find the love and joy of living again.

Through her experience, this sister's testimony was renewed. She found strength in Heavenly Father and went on to share her story and experiences with others who have similar struggles.

Sometimes it's confusing or frightening to know how to interact with other adults who have mental illnesses, especially if they reach a stage that is so very different from the friend with whom you shared both inspiring and funny stories. In one stake, an older sister with special needs always sat with the same family because she remembered the husband as her former bishop. This family's daughter was sometimes frightened when the sister wanted to sit next to her. The little girl would scoot toward her mother and then the sister would scoot closer. The process was repeated until the little girl was squished between her mother and the sister with special needs. Over time, the little girl came

to know the sister with special needs, felt more comfortable, and more important, stopped scooting! Now when they meet at stake meetings, the little girl—who is now a young lady—saves a seat for this special sister.

Here are a few ideas of how to support adults with mental illnesses:

- Remember them as the person they were before their illness began. Love and serve them.
- They may ask questions or tell the same stories repeatedly when you are together. Be patient, loving, and genuine when you respond.
- Take a moment of extra time out of your week to call or send a note to say you are thinking of them.
- Invite their families to join you for family home evening or an occasional friendly BBQ.
- Invite them to sit next to you during church meetings.
- Find out what hobbies they still enjoy and then form a small group to meet once a week and enjoy that hobby together.
- If they have a difficult time reading, they might enjoy listening to you read the scriptures or Church magazine articles to them.

For more information about some common adult mental illnesses, you can visit the following websites:

- National Institute of Neurological Disorders and Stroke
  http://www.ninds.nih.gov
- Alzheimer's Association
  http://www.alz.org
- National Institute on Mental Health
  http://www.nimh.nih.gov
- National Alliance on Mental Illness
  http://www.nami.org

The most important thing you can do is remember that an adult with mental illness is a child of God. Underneath his mortal body is the soul of someone wonderful and perfect—your friend. Continue to love him and be his friend because your relationship will continue on after this life. And just think of all the memories you will share with each other then!

Families

SACRAMENT MEETING SURVIVAL

by Lynn Parsons

Before I had children, I was sure my little darlings would never act up in sacrament meeting. They would hang on my every word of advice and be the most talented on the planet! Heavenly Father chose to send me real children, not imaginary ones, so we had many behavior problems. During one particularly bad week, my husband came down off the stand and took one child out. As they made the long walk down the aisle, this child—with arms stretched out toward me—said, "Daddy, don't spank me! I'll . . . be . . . good!"

This is hilarious now but was somewhat painful then. Two of my four children had special needs. During most of the time they were growing up, their father was in the bishopric, was the stake clerk, or held some other leadership calling. I found that planning, humility, and flexibility were the keys to a successful Sunday.

Planning

Sunday preparation is important for any parent but essential when you have children with special needs. I tried to begin on Saturday to create schedules, gather important materials, lay out clothing, and pre-teach important skills. Sunday, for most families, is a drastic change from the rest of the week, and many children with disabilities struggle to adapt. I found that this planning prevented many potential problems and lessened others.

Laying out clothing (after checking for stains, missing buttons, and so on) and getting scriptures and other needed supplies ready minimized

frustration for my children and myself. Not having to search for a lost shoe made it easier for the whole family to feel the Spirit on Sundays and gave me time to deal with any last-minute problems that could (and did) happen. I, like most parents, have been covered in bodily fluids when walking out the front door. In fact, my mother-in-law said diaper bags should hold a change of clothing for Mom. I've also listened in horror as a child remembered a talk assignment at the last minute, and I've sighed in frustration when a teen decided that what they were wearing wasn't good enough. Preparation can help you, in the words of Rudyard Kipling, "Keep your head when all about you are losing theirs and blaming it on you."[1]

Much of the Saturday work needs to involve your child. Include him in the preparations discussed thus far and help him practice what will happen at church. If you are unable to sit in the same location each week, rehearse looking for a pew. Then practice sitting down quietly without arguing about who sits next to Mom and Dad. I tried to encourage my children to sit without toys until the sacrament had been passed, but you can adjust your strategies to meet the needs of your children. You may try role playing, Applied Behavior Analysis, Discrete Trials, or social tales to help children learn proper church behaviors.

Applied Behavior Analysis is a method of behavior modification that has proven very successful for children with many disabilities, including autism. Children are rewarded for either engaging in or avoiding certain behaviors. This process is all about the "paycheck," so the reward must be worth whatever the outcome needs to be.[2]

Schedules

Creating and reviewing a schedule with your child prepares her for what will be happening, especially if there will be an unusual event such as a confirmation or baby blessing. Contact your child's schoolteacher to see what kind of classroom schedule is used and create a similar one for church. This may take the form of a written, picture, or more concrete schedule that uses objects rather than pictures.

Older children who can read may use the sacrament program as a schedule. If the copy machine is not working, you may have to get the information from the bishopric and write your own to avoid a meltdown. The pattern of sacrament meeting (opening hymn, opening prayer, announcements, the sacrament hymn, the sacrament, speakers,

intermediate hymn, speakers, closing hymn, and closing prayer) could be taught to some older children. Be sure to include changes for fast Sunday, ordinations, ward and stake conferences, and so forth.

Picture schedules may be created in a permanent form and laminated for sacrament meeting. These should follow the pattern given above, with possibly a different version for fast and testimony meeting. The pictures may come from a variety of places. You can take pictures of your child or family or use generic pictures available at any of the free LDS clip art sites on the Internet. Boardmaker software is perfect for creating picture schedules but is not necessary. You may use pictures that have been copied and pasted into word processing software or even cut out pictures drawn by your child.[3]

Concrete schedules work well for children who struggle with abstract concepts. The items on these schedules must be three-dimensional. For example, a dollhouse-sized pew or chair may be used for the first symbol, followed by a doll with folded arms, and then a doll with an open mouth (singing).

As you prepare on Saturday, go over the schedule with your children. Then you should review it Sunday morning and possibly again during the car ride, if necessary. This will help all the children make the mental shift to a Sunday routine and feel more confident about the upcoming gathering, and it will make sacrament meeting a better experience for everyone.

Busy Bag

Every family with small children needs a sacrament meeting busy bag. It should be filled with things your children enjoy but only see on Sundays. As you make your selections, consider carefully whether each item will enhance or detract from the meeting. For example, small coloring books and crayons are appropriate, while permanent markers are obviously not! Always test each toy at home to see how loud it will sound in the meeting. There are many patterns for Church busy books and completed editions available commercially. My children loved busy books. Small, quiet toys such as cars and dolls will also keep little hands busy. You can buy scripture story action figures and let your children act out the tales they have learned. Keep snacks to a minimum and always make sure they're not messy. But if sacrament meeting falls during mealtime, some dry cereal or fruit snacks may save your life.

Humility

As I mentioned before, there were many weeks when I struggled alone. On particularly bad days, I would leave the chapel with one child, take her to her father in the clerk's office, and return to sacrament meeting. I often wondered if the ward members thought I had given her away! During one point, there was a family who would help me, but most of the time I had no offers. That's why I now send my teen girls to help young mothers who are alone. I always tell them I've been there, and it's no reflection on these young parents—we're just trying to help in a tough situation.

Please don't let your pride interfere. I should have asked for more help! Often, others *want* to help but don't know what to do. Ask for specifics—entertain a toddler, hold a baby, or just sit with your kids.

In one ward, there were several older members who routinely came to church and occupied the seats in the hall rather than entering the meeting. As I held my fussy baby and watched several sisters balancing in their high heels while trying to take care of small children, I realized those chairs were occupied by the wrong people. I told them, "You're out here by choice. We (indicating myself and the other sisters) are not. Get up!" They did and went into the meeting. We had no further problems with this after my speech. You and your helpers will be blessed for their service, just as I'm sure those hall-sitters were blessed by attending sacrament meeting.

Your pride may also be offended by those who offer unwanted advice. This will happen to you no matter what your situation. I have a chronic condition and have been offered free medical advice from many who meant well but who came across as judgmental and offensive. You may be offered parenting tips from those who have stood in your shoes and others who may never comprehend even one percent of your situation. If you see these intrusions as offers of caring, despite the rudeness of the speaker, you will keep the Spirit with you and avoid many hard feelings. This is difficult to learn but vital in your relationships with ward members.

Flexibility

We all have to give up our imaginary flawless children at some point. Instead of expecting everything to go perfectly during sacrament meeting, we need to deal with what's really happening. I learned

to accommodate the needs of my children and to put them ahead of my pride, expectations, or concerns about others' thoughts. Some of the areas in which we may need more flexibility include sensory issues, minimizing change, and expecting the unexpected.

Sensory Issues

Children with sensory issues frequently struggle to get through large assemblies like sacrament meeting. Loud sounds, unsettling fluorescent lighting, and crowds may be upsetting. Muffle loud noises with earplugs sold in drugstores for airline passengers. Be sure to practice with these at home to see if they can be tolerated. Lighting can be altered by where you sit, a hat with a brim, or sunglasses, if necessary. Arriving early and spreading out in the pew so that you won't be crowded may help decrease the sense that there are too many people in the room. Sensory issues are serious enough that they should be explained to your priesthood leaders so they can provide whatever help you need.

Minimizing Change

There are other ways to minimize the potential negative effects of change on Sunday. Plan to sit in the same pew each week. Many families do this anyway. Ask your priesthood leaders to support you—most will be accommodating. Some wards even place a "reserved" sign so visitors or new members will sit elsewhere. This routine will provide some additional continuity for your child and will help him be calmer. You may also extend the sense of routine by having the same parent take them to the restroom while the other (or a sibling or friend) takes them to class.

Expecting the Unexpected

Some off-days can be predicted, while others will catch you by surprise. If there has been a disruption to the household routine (for example, sickness or a traveling parent), the resultant stress may cause your child to act out at church. This may be the time to use your backup plan, including an emergency bag, special reinforcers, tag team parenting, and hanging on to your sense of humor for dear life.

Your emergency bag should be in your trunk every Sunday, even if you don't plan on using it that week. You can include special Church-oriented file folder games (search Google for "LDS file folder games" for more information), special treats, small books of family photos, special

interest toys or books, and sensory items. Things in this bag should not be readily available during the week so they will be more attractive to the child.

File folder games are fairly easy to make and can be created from coloring book pages, Internet pictures, or special reproducible books. They may be laminated with clear shelf liner, and the smaller pieces may be plastic-coated with wide packaging tape. If you use Velcro, be sure it's not the heavy-duty type, as this will make a great deal of noise as the pieces are removed. Pieces may be stored in a half-sized manila envelope glued to the back of the folder.

Special treats may be small, easy-to-handle items such as fruit snacks, a favorite toy, or stickers. This should be something the child does not usually have during the week so it will be truly special. These things may lose their appeal over time, so check frequently with your child through questioning or observation to be sure you have chosen the correct food or object.

Small books of family photos are wonderful distractions. Most children are thrilled to see pictures of themselves and loved ones. A homemade laminated copy or small photo album will work fine.

Many children with disabilities have a special interest. These topics range from cartoon characters, types of transportation such as trains, or animal species, to movies and movie stars. A small book or toy on that special interest is a surefire hit.

A child who is agitated in new situations may benefit from calming sensory stimulation. Wrap the child firmly in a blanket to help her reorganize her central nervous system. Use a soft paintbrush to stroke her arms. There are two different results depending on how you stroke. Remember that stroking away from the heart—down the arm—calms a child, whereas stroking toward the heart—up the arm—will excite a child. Squeezing a soft ball reduces angry feelings. Stim toys—designed to help someone with autism stimulate her senses—can help a child who is raging. This can help her calm down, concentrate, or block out something upsetting, such as a loud noise.[4]

Above all, try to remember that the problems experienced by most children during sacrament meeting are short-term. I often wondered why I went to church if I spent most of the meeting out in the hall. It turns out that almost every parent feels this way at some point! Hang in there, try to enjoy spending time with your child, and remember that

most phases end in a relatively short time. If you are doing all you can and still feel you are getting nowhere, pray earnestly for the Lord's support, and you will feel His peace as you work together with others to give your child a positive church experience.

Notes

1. Rudyard Kipling, "If," *Rewards and Fairies*, http://www.poetryfoundation.org/archive/poem.html?id=175772.
2. For more information on Applied Behavior Analysis or Discrete Trials, go to http://www.autismspeaks.org/whattodo/index.php#aba.
3. For more information on picture schedules, see http://www.do2learn.com/picturecards/howtouse/schedule.htm.
4. For more information on sensory stimulation, see http://www.livestrong.com/article/76136-sensory-stimulation-activities-autism/.

A House of Prayer

by Danyelle Ferguson

"Let our house be a *house of prayer*."

President Thomas S. Monson

Take a moment to create a picture in your mind of what the perfect family prayer would look like:

All the children are kneeling reverently in a circle. Perhaps their heads are bowed and their eyes are closed. Their little arms are folded. The expressions on their faces are simply angelic. A soft voice gives a beautiful, heartfelt prayer. The Holy Spirit touches each family member's heart.

It's a wonderful picture, isn't it? And then there's reality. Or at least, this is my family's reality.

Picture this:

We're all sitting on the floor, however is most comfortable. Our eighteen-month-old bounces on my lap while trying to unfold my arms. Our three-year-old watches to be sure everyone's eyes stay closed during the prayer and immediately tells us if anyone peeks. My husband shushes our seven-year-old, who starts to hum. And our eight-year-old gives a quick, rather loud, prayer.

Short, sweet, and rambunctious—that's our family! And that's okay. When raising a family, the important part isn't necessarily having the "perfect picture" but simply taking the time to actually have prayer and develop our communication skills with Heavenly Father.

It's easy to get distracted during the day and forget to have prayer. I've found it easier to schedule prayer when I know my family will be in the same place at the same consistent time throughout the week. For us, it's during supper. When we sit down to the table, we first talk about

anyone we should pray for (a sick relative or a friend who had a rough day) and then if there's anything we need to prepare for in the next few days. Each member of our family has an assigned day to say the prayer at the dinner table. Once we are finished talking about things or people to remember, the assigned person says the prayer.

Immediately after dinner, before we even clean up the dishes, we sit on the floor between the dining room and kitchen for family scripture study and prayer (which is the scenario I described a few paragraphs ago).

Every family's schedule is different. Perhaps morning or later in the evening works better for you. I knew one family who had prayer huddles. As each person got ready to leave for the day, he'd reach the front door and call out, "Prayer huddle!" Anyone nearby and available would come to the door, and together they would have a quick prayer. Several prayer huddles would occur each morning as younger children, teens, and parents got ready and left for the day. Find a solution that works for your family. And don't be afraid to be creative!

Teaching Prayer

In the May 1984 *Ensign*, President Thomas S. Monson told the following wonderful story about his young son and prayer:

> When our oldest son was about three, he would kneel with his mother and me in our evening prayer. I was serving as the bishop of the ward at the time, and a lovely lady in the ward, Margaret Lister, lay perilously ill with cancer. Each night we would pray for Sister Lister. One evening our tiny son offered the prayer and confused the words of the prayer with a story from a nursery book. He began: "Heavenly Father, please bless Sister Lister, Henny Penny, Chicken Licken, Turkey Lurkey, and all the little folks." We held back the smiles that evening. Later we were humbled as Margaret Lister sustained a complete recovery. *We do not demean the prayer of a child. After all, our children have more recently been with our Heavenly Father than have we.*[1]

How many of us have heard similar prayers from our children? Prayers thanking Heavenly Father for beloved toys and snacks instantly come to my mind. One of my favorites was from our son with autism, given just recently after scripture study. He said, "Dear Heavenly Father, we're done reading the book. Now it's time for bed. Amen." As I said before, short and sweet—that's our family.

I love to hear my children pray. I'm humbled by their faith and trust that Heavenly Father hears them and cares about all the things they care about. I grew up in a home without prayer. As a convert to The Church of Jesus Christ of Latter-day Saints, I learned to pray when I was sixteen years old. Teaching my children how to pray has been a daunting and intimidating task. But I've learned several things along the way.

- Teach children that prayer is just like talking to Mom or Dad, except in this conversation, they are talking to their Heavenly Father.
- Children learn to pray by praying. Be sure to give everyone an opportunity to pray. Our kids fought over whose turn it was to pray until we set up a schedule for our dinnertime prayers.
- Share stories of times when you needed help and Heavenly Father answered your prayers.
- Get caught praying. There's no better way to teach kids than to let them find you praying on your own. This shows them just how important prayer is to you, and then they'll want to make it an important part of their lives as well.
- Remember that prayers aren't just the formal ones we hear from other adults. Heavenly Father can read our hearts and understands our desires and needs through even the simplest words. Encourage your children to express their wants and desires in words and phrases that are natural to them.
- Remind children that prayer is not a test. There isn't anything they can't say to Heavenly Father. He understands their feelings, no matter if they are happy, sad, or all the emotions in between.

Stages of Prayer

I found a wonderful article on www.TeachKidsHow.com titled, "Teach Your Child to Pray." In this article, the author discusses how children learn to pray at different age levels. While this article is generalized to any religious denomination, I am going to share a few of her ideas and add examples for my church and also for children with special needs. Each stage will be grouped by ages. Rather than looking at the age group, look to see which stage your child fits in. Prayer has a natural learning progression, and each child is at a different stage.

Stage One (Preschool)

Learning to pray begins with routine. In this stage, children learn about prayer through consistent schedules (prayer at the dinner table, bedtime, and so on) and also through simple repetition. Help your child learn a few very simple phrases, such as:

- Dear Heavenly Father
- Thank you . . .
  - for my family
  - for the Church
  - for our food
- Please bless
  - me to sleep well
  - the food
  - our family
- In the name of Jesus Christ, Amen.

Start with just a few short phrases and help your child repeat them each time he says a prayer. When he gets the hang of it, start to prompt him to use new phrases or to make a phrase a bit longer, such as, "Please bless the food to make us healthy and strong."

The most important part of this stage isn't how the prayer is said but having a consistent prayer schedule so the child learns the importance of prayer in his life each day.

Stage Two (Grades K–3rd)

In this stage, children start to understand why we pray and the correct pattern of prayer. They also gain a testimony of how prayer helps them and that Heavenly Father will answer them when they pray. During this time, children will begin to change the simple phrases they've been taught to more complex or heartfelt expressions.

A few points to remember:

- Allow your child to pray in his own words. Don't stop him during the prayer to correct his sentence structure. For example, if Emily said, "Thank you for the sleep of my nap," don't stop her and prompt her to say, "Thank you for my nap." Allow your child to learn that Heavenly Father understands her, no matter how she expresses her thoughts.
- Help your child remember to pray daily. Heavenly Father is

always there. He wants to hear from your child every day, not just when there's a problem.

- Remind your child about sick relatives or others in your family who may need help. If Aunt Sally broke her arm, you could ask your child to pray for her to be able to do her chores with just one arm and to feel better soon.
- Let your child develop his own prayer voice. That doesn't mean using all the correct thee's and thou's, but rather, figuring out how to pray to Heavenly Father from his heart.

Stage Three (Grades 4th–6th)

Children who feel close to Heavenly Father have a better chance of resisting peer pressure and other preteen or teen risks. Their testimony of prayer and receiving guidance from Heavenly Father will benefit them by relieving the heavy load on their shoulders.

A few points to help your child develop prayer skills at this stage:

- Talk with them about reasons for prayer.
  - Giving thanks—not just for the cool stuff they got, but for opportunities to serve, difficult lessons they learned, and so on.
  - Asking for forgiveness. Talk about how to ask for forgiveness, what to do while repenting, and how to know when Heavenly Father has forgiven them.
  - Asking for personal wants and desires.
  - Remembering others who need support or guidance.
- Help them feel comfortable praying.
  - Encourage your child to talk with Heavenly Father like a friend and mentor, someone they greatly respect and love.
  - Tell your child stories of times Heavenly Father has answered your prayers, as well as stories from friends, family members, or other church members.
  - Encourage your child to turn to prayer more often for guidance as he is faced with peer pressure, Church callings, and other things he has questions about.
  - Teach your child how to address Heavenly Father more reverently (thee, thou, and so on), and practice using those terms.

Silent Prayers

In a home with deaf family members, you won't find the parents and siblings with their heads bowed and eyes closed. Instead, they slightly incline their heads, and their eyes remain open to "listen to" (watch) the prayer.

Using this example, any child can pray by using a Picture Exchange Communication System (PECS). The child would pull out his PECS cards and place them to create sentences. The cards can have pictures with words along the bottom to represent each phrase or concept. An interpreter (for example, a family member or teacher) can be the voice of the prayer.

PECS cards should include:

- Basics
  - Dear Heavenly Father
  - In the Name of Jesus Christ, amen
  - We Thank Thee
  - I Thank Thee
  - We Ask Thee
  - I Ask Thee
  - Bless

- Examples of Simple Phrases
  - Food
  - Travel Safe
  - Sleep Well
  - Family
  - To Feel Better
  - Our Teachers
  - Bishopric
  - Primary Leaders
  - Friends
  - Missionaries
  - Prophet
  - Church

Using these cards, the child may arrange them like this:

- Dear Heavenly Father
- We Thank Thee
  - Our Teachers

- We Thank Thee
  - Prophet
- We Ask Thee
  - Bless
    - ○ Primary Leaders
- We Ask Thee
  - Bless
    - ○ Travel Safe
- In the Name of Jesus Christ, amen.

The interpreter would read this prayer as:

"Dear Heavenly Father. We thank Thee for our teachers. We thank Thee for the prophet. We ask Thee to bless the Primary leaders. We ask Thee that we can travel safely. In the name of Jesus Christ, amen."

Activities to Encourage and Develop Prayer

The following activities are ideas to help encourage your child to pray and to develop a better understanding of prayer.

- Create a Picture Book—Sometimes children aren't sure who to remember in their prayers. Putting together a small book filled with pictures of family members, friends, and Church leaders will help the child remember and decide whom he would like to include in his prayer.
- Sentence or Circle Prayers—This is a fun group activity, especially for families who have several children who love to pray. The family sits close together on the floor and then holds hands. One person starts the prayer, chooses one thing he is thankful for, and then squeezes the hand of the person on his left (going clockwise). After completing the circle once, start one more round, this time to ask for Heavenly Father's help with something or for blessings.
- A Prayer Notebook—Take a five-subject notebook and label each section with one of the following:
  - Thankfulness Section
  - Remembrance Section—For people who need help (sick, sad, and so on)
  - Problems or Protection Section—For you or others
  - Wants/Needs Section

- Answered Prayers Section—Record how your prayers were answered

Young children can draw pictures or have their parents help write in each section. You can make the notebook more fun by decorating it too.

As with anything you are teaching your child, remember to enjoy the journey. Parents, keep your own notebook and fill it with funny or touching prayers to look back on in the future. One mother sent me the following recollections of her son's prayers:

"For the longest time, all our son would say was, 'Heavenly Father, Thank you for the list.' The only thing I can think of is that it was too hard to think of creative things to say, so he just put it into a huge category called 'the list.'

"As his ability to communicate increased, he became more specific—sometimes extremely specific.

"Late at night when he was about seven, he had a terrible earache. I suggested we pray, and I said a prayer that he would be able to feel better and get back to sleep. He was very angry and told me I 'said it wrong.' He then said, 'Heavenly Father, please bless the white blood cells to win the war in my ear. In the name of Jesus Christ, Amen.' He then rolled over and went right to sleep. Now that is direct!

"Finally, this story is much more personal, but once when our son was praying, he stopped and gasped out loud. We asked what was wrong, and he said, 'I heard Jesus talking in my heart.' Dumbfounded, my husband and I asked him, 'Well, what did he say?' He acted surprised and responded, 'Jesus said, "I love you, JT."'"

Another parent shared the following story:

"I love family prayer, especially when it is the children's turn to pray. When children pray, it's an example to me of how we should pray. When Madeline says the family prayer, she is having a conversation with her Father in Heaven. Early on, I would try to get her to end the prayer but then got an impression, 'I'm listening. I want to hear about her day too.' So now I listen too as she tells her Father in Heaven about her day and about the people she loves.

"One neat experience we had was the day before a surgery. I cradled her in my arms to tell her about what was going to happen, and we talked about prayer. I asked her if she was a child of God. She replied, 'yes.' I asked, 'Does Heavenly Father love you?' Again, she replied, 'yes.' I then asked her if Heavenly Father would help her to be brave, and she said, 'yes.'

"That evening when she said her personal prayers, she asked Heavenly Father 'to help me be brave.' After her surgery, while still in pain, she looked at me and said, 'Heavenly Father helped me be brave.'

"Many times since, she has prayed asking Heavenly Father to help her be brave, and the smile that comes on her face when she sees how Heavenly Father helped her is priceless and an expression that is etched in my memory forever."

I'd like to end with this quote from President Thomas S. Monson's talk, "Precious Children—A Gift from God."

"A happy home is but an earlier heaven. President George Albert Smith asked, 'Do we want our homes to be happy? If we do, let them be the abiding place of prayer, thanksgiving and gratitude.'"[2]

May all your homes be filled with happiness, thankfulness, and prayer.

Notes

Quote at chapter start from Thomas S. Monson, "Building Your Eternal Home," *Ensign*, May 1984, 16.

1. Ibid., italics added.
2. Thomas S. Monson, "Precious Children—A Gift from God," *Ensign*, Nov. 1991, 67.

Scripture Power

by Danyelle Ferguson

I have spent the majority of the past ten years serving in Primary in one capacity or another. One of my favorite Primary songs is "Scripture Power." I love how it reminds us that scripture study helps keep us safe and that we need to study the scriptures daily so we can receive "power" from Heavenly Father to guide us.

During the early preschool years, our family life was in constant upheaval as my husband and I learned about autism and worked with our oldest son. Some days, it was hard to think about even picking up the scriptures. Just looking at them made me feel tired and overwhelmed—another task on my to-do list. There were mornings when my husband would shake me awake so we could read together, and all I wanted to do was roll over and go back to dreamland where life wasn't so hard.

Then there were days when all I wanted was to sit on the couch and soak up scripture after scripture. One of the reasons scripture study was so difficult for me was the fear that my son would never understand the scriptures or the stories and lessons within. I finally came to the conclusion that even if our son wasn't able to read the scriptures or understand the stories, I still needed to try. I needed to provide as many opportunities for him as I could to learn scripture stories and lessons.

An amazing thing happened. As my son and I read together— which meant I was reading my scriptures out loud while he ran around the room—I felt peace. One day, I realized that even if his physical body didn't understand, *his spirit did*. So when he was running around

or playing in a corner while we had scripture study, his spirit was still receiving nourishment from the spirit in our home.

Introducing Scripture Study

Like prayer, there are stages of scripture study.

First, we start with routine. Choose a consistent time for family scripture study. Your child may play while the rest of your family reads—that's okay. The important thing is that he's there. He knows the scriptures are valued just from the fact that each day, the whole family gathers to read. That in itself is an important part of the process.

Second, you may want to choose a goal and reward for your child to work toward. Perhaps you want him to sit for the first five minutes. Choose an appropriate reward. Maybe he'd like to serve the family treats or choose the person to say closing prayer. Be sure your child knows what he's working for and what he needs to do to earn it. Then set a timer—the wind-up timers that ding are great for this activity. When the five minutes are up, be sure to praise him for doing a great job. The first time most likely won't be perfect. But praise him for what he did well. Then follow through with the reward. As your child masters the goal, make it a little harder. Maybe you'd like him to sit with the family for ten minutes.

If your child needs time to move around, you may want to include breaks. Perhaps he does well in five-minute intervals. Set a timer for five minutes. When it dings, no matter where you are, everyone could stop, stretch, sing a Primary song or Church hymn, and then resume reading until the chapter is finished. Some people find being read to very soothing and enjoy being together listening to the scriptures.

Third, when your child starts to read, start teaching him words from the scriptures he won't learn at school. Through scripture study, family home evening, and Church classes, he'll already be familiar with words like "Jesus," "Nephi," and "prophet." He knows what they *sound* like, but now you'll need to teach him what they *look* like. You'll love it when he suddenly points to a word on a page and exclaims, "That says 'Jesus'!"

Fourth is understanding the scriptures. This will vary, depending on your child's developmental growth.

We found that the Church's scripture readers were fantastic for teaching our son to read the scriptures. First, he liked to look at the

pictures while we read. Then he started pointing out words he learned at school or that we'd taught him. Next, we chose one or two verses from the real scriptures and then read the story in the scripture reader to illustrate. Then gradually, we read more and more from the scriptures until he understood most of what he read.

Reading is often a challenge for children or adults with special needs. No matter what reading level your child (young or old) is on, he can always enjoy the scriptures, even if it's simply by turning the pages of the scripture reader and looking at the pictures. His mind will be filled with the wonderful, inspiring art—and maybe that's all he needs at that time.

Bringing the Scriptures to Life

It can be difficult to capture a child's attention during scripture study. But did you know that family scripture study doesn't have to mean sitting in a circle and reading? It can be something more interactive and fun where you're all together learning scripture stories and principles. Mixing things up and bringing some fun into scripture study will benefit not only your child with special needs, but also all his siblings. Try some of these fun ideas:

Puppet Theater

Turn a coffee table on its side or drape a table with a cloth to create a theater. *Easy puppets*: Use paper plates as the puppet. You can cut, color, and even glue on fabric or other fun stuff to create people, animals, buildings, and so on. You can also print pictures on card stock or construction paper to make collages and cut them out. Then glue craft sticks to the back. Lynn's kids (currently in their late twenties) still talk about the time they used puppets for Noah's Ark.

Scripture Notebook

Give each child a notebook to write or draw his or her own version of what they learned during scripture study each night. If your child doesn't draw, he or she may like using stickers to create pictures.

Scripture Chart

Make a scripture study goal each week. Perhaps your goal is to read ten verses each night. Make a chart to track your progress and show it to your children. Be sure to have a reward at the end! Homemade treats,

art projects, and board games all work well at my house. The goal you set could also be time related, such as to read each day—no matter how many verses—for a month.

Scripture Hide and Seek

This is a fun twist on an old favorite game, played either individually or as teams. Write scriptures on small pieces of paper. Everyone leaves the room except for whoever is "it." This person draws one scripture and then hides it. The rest of the family comes in and searches for the scripture. Whoever finds it reads it aloud. Also, that person or his team gets a point. When all the scriptures have been hidden and then found, whoever has the most points wins!

Story Time

Get ready for some story time fun! Turn the scripture account you want to teach into a fun, simple children's story. Be as animated as possible while you retell it—whisper, use hand motions, change your voice for different characters. Think about what your child likes when you read to him, and do that with your scripture story time. To involve your kids more, make puppets during the week. For example, if you're telling about Noah's Ark, let them make puppets or pictures of the animals. Then when it's time to gather the animals and put them on the ark, be sure to let each of the kids show off the creations and make fun animal noises.

Costume Trunk

Collect clothing articles the kids can use to dress up and act out scripture stories. Secondhand stores and yard sales are great for finding low-priced items. Look for things like bathrobes, towels (to wrap around a head like the shepherds), sandals, ropes (to use for belts), plastic "armor," and so on. Even teens will join in the dress-up fun, especially if you give them some "bling!"

Homemade Picture Books

Children love to show off and look at things they've created. Try creating your own scripture picture books. All you need is some construction paper, white card stock, crayons, glue, and a stapler. First, break the story into small sections, like a children's picture book. Then cut your card stock into two pieces. On one, have your child draw the

picture. On the other, write a sentence or two about the story. If your child doesn't like to color, he may like cutting out pictures and gluing them onto the card stock. Then put together the pictures and words on pages of construction paper. After putting all the pages together, staple down the left side several times so it opens like a book.

Prop It Up

Surprise your kids with some fun props the next time you tell them a scripture story. For example, if you were telling about Lehi and his family at sea, you could have a CD of ocean waves and seagulls playing softly while you read. You could make sure they stay awake by occasionally misting them with a spray bottle filled with water.

Timelines or Maps

Create your own timeline or map of where you are reading in the scriptures. This could be the chronological year the story happened or the location where events are taking place. You would need butcher paper, tape, and crayons. Tape the paper to a wall or door. Then use the crayons to work on your timeline or map. For example, let's say you were reading about Lehi's journey to the promised land. One group could make a boat and figures of Lehi and his family out of construction paper. Another group could draw land for Lehi's starting location near the bottom of the paper and then draw the ocean and finally the destination of the promised land. As you read the story, you can act out the events on the map. This may take several days, depending on how many verses you read each day, but the kids will have fun watching the boat get closer and closer to land. It's a great way to visualize scripture stories.

Thoughts about Scripture Study from Other Parents

"My family as a whole has benefited greatly from reading the scriptures daily. For one thing, all children like to feel conformity, so when their Primary teacher asks them if they read the scriptures daily, they can confidently answer, 'Yes!'

"Hopefully they will also feel the Spirit as we read. That, in itself, is quite secondary at the moment, because they are still very young. The most important reason we read the scriptures is because the prophet has told us to do so. And in doing it, we are establishing good habits that they will continue when they leave home.

"Our son often leaves the room when we are reading the scriptures. I am not too fussy about that. I don't want to force him. I just ask him gently if he can stay with us, but most of the time, he goes. Still, he is being exposed to the habit of family scripture study."

⁂

"We tried reading the scripture readers before bedtime each night. My daughter began associating scriptures with bedtime, which she hated, so she would have nothing to do with scriptures for a long time. Now we have someone read a scripture story every family home evening, but we are still working on daily family scripture study.

"I will say that I found the scripture readers to be wonderful and inspired, right down to every little emotion on the characters' faces. We also like the videos made from them."

⁂

"My daughter has begun to read the scripture readers on her own now and then. Currently, our morning devotionals include repeating an article of faith, singing a Primary song, saying a prayer, and having me report about what I read that morning in my scriptures."

⁂

"My husband is not an active member of the Church, so we don't do scripture study together. My personal scripture study has helped me to understand my son Colt's needs by knowing that he is a child of God and that Heavenly Father and Jesus love him just as They love everyone else.

"I especially love the New Testament and Third Nephi in the Book of Mormon because these stories focus on Jesus Christ. My favorite parts are when Jesus gathers the little children around Him and blesses them. I think of Colt being in that circle of children and being blessed. Also, I think of Jesus healing the sick, and it reminds me that when my son passes away later in life, he will be healed and perfect. I can't wait to see him in the next life, without autism!

"I don't read the actual scriptures to Colt, but we use the scripture readers so he can learn the scripture stories more on his level. The most memorable scripture study experience was when we were reading the

New Testament reader. Colt saw the picture of Jesus on the cross when He was crucified. Colt looked at me with a really sad look on his face and said, "Jesus has an owie." Then he leaned over and kissed the picture. I always kiss Colt's owies when he gets hurt, so he wanted to kiss Jesus's owie all better."

No matter how your family holds scripture study, you will be blessed for your efforts, and your children will feel the Spirit and love from Heavenly Father. President Gordon B. Hinckley taught,

> Read to your children. Read the story of the Son of God. Read to them from the New Testament. Read to them from the Book of Mormon. It will take time, and you are very busy, but it will prove to be a great blessing in your lives as well as in their lives. And there will grow in their hearts a great love for the Savior of the world, the only perfect man who walked the earth. He will become to them a very real living being, and His great atoning sacrifice, as they grow to manhood and womanhood, will take on a new and more glorious meaning in their lives.[1]

Note
1. Gordon B. Hinckley, "Messages of Inspiration from President Hinckley," *Church News*, Dec. 6, 1997, 2.

FAMILY HOME EVENINGS

A Night of Blessings and Fun

by Danyelle Ferguson

In 1915, the First Presidency of the Church issued the following statement:

"We advise and urge the inauguration of a 'home evening' throughout the Church, at which time fathers and mothers may gather their boys and girls about them in the home and teach them the word of the Lord."[1]

Save the Date

Family home evening (FHE) is a challenge for any family but can be especially difficult for a family with a special needs child. The first thing you need to do is establish a routine. FHE is traditionally held on Monday nights, but this isn't set in stone. If Mondays don't work well for your family, choose another night. I know families with busy teens who meet together each Sunday. I know another family who changes the time each week depending on the father's day off work. The thing each of these families has in common is that they all devote one night a week to FHE.

If FHE doesn't already happen consistently in your home, it may be difficult in the beginning. As time goes by, you will get into a comfortable routine.

Something that helped us was to purchase a calendar like preschool and elementary teachers have in their classrooms. It's white and completely blank except for the days of the week above rows of squares where the dates belong. There's also room at the top for the months of the year. We purchased numbers, months, and holiday cards to go with it. At home, I made additional cards for FHE, church, family birthdays,

and so on. For FHE and church, I made four or five of each. Then I put the cards on the calendar.

At the beginning of each month, the calendar is blank except for the special cards showing holidays, FHE, church, or birthdays. Then each day, our family would put on the date. If there was a special card, we would talk about what was going to happen that day.

For example, if we placed an FHE card, we would say, "Look! Tonight we have family home evening. We're going to talk about temples and make temple collages." Our kids then had an idea of what to look forward to that night. After school, I'd remind them about the activity later that evening. Then after dinner, we'd say, "Okay, let's clean up and have FHE." We found this helped our son with autism to be ready when it came time to gather for family night.

On Your Mark, Get Set . . . Go!

It can be frustrating to prepare a lesson and then watch your child with special needs run around the room distracting the other kids. I have great news for you, though! When President Joseph F. Smith and his counselors introduced family home evening, they also said:

"Formality and stiffness should be studiously avoided, and all the family should participate in the exercises."[2]

There you go—the perfect reason not to stress!

Yes, it may still be frustrating at times, but keep in mind that's just the way your family home evening is. There is no right or wrong way to act during FHE. Of course, we'd all love to have our kids be perfectly reverent and completely absorbed in our lessons. But realistically, that just doesn't happen very often for any family.

To help your child with special needs sit with the family, try creating an FHE bag filled with gospel-centered activities, such as file folder games or a picture from the *Friend* magazine cut up to make a puzzle. This may keep your child's attention while you teach the lesson.

You may find there's something specific your child really enjoys doing. For our son, it's passing out the treats. Our family rotates responsibilities for song, prayer, scripture, lesson, and treats. We've found that when it's our son's turn to pass out the treats, he stays with us for the entire lesson, anxiously waiting so he doesn't miss out.

If your child continues running around the room or prefers to play in a corner alone, that's okay. He's still with your family, and his spirit

is benefiting. I've often been surprised by the things my kids later say to me when I thought they weren't paying attention at all. Just relax and enjoy having your family together.

Preparing Lessons for Everyone

Understanding each of your children's learning styles and capabilities is an important part of preparing a lesson. Take the time to prayerfully ask the Lord for insights into your children's lives and how to prepare an FHE lesson that will connect with them. In the case of your child with special needs, think of what helps him learn at school. Incorporating these techniques into teaching at home will help him focus on the lesson.

Tips for preparing lessons:

- Keep lessons short (about five to fifteen minutes).
- Break up the lesson with activities such as a song, a story with puppets, or a game.
- Use visual aids. You can even let your kids draw pictures to illustrate a scripture story during the week.
- Include all your children by having an activity for younger ones such as a flannel board story. Then ask your older kids more meaningful, in-depth questions about the lesson.

Plan Ahead

My husband and I came up with a system that makes our family nights much easier.

Each December, we choose four general topics we want to teach for the next year. Some general topics include the articles of faith, Young Women values, stories of Jesus's life, the prophet, preparedness, or baptism.

After choosing our four topics, we assign each to a certain week of the month. For example, the first week might be the article of faith we want to memorize that month, the second week a lesson about baptism, and so on. On months with a fifth week, we schedule a fun family outing.

Each month, we look at who is giving the lesson and help that person choose a specific lesson to go along with the topic for that week. Once we have the schedule figured out, there's no more guesswork or last minute, "What are we going to talk about for FHE tonight?" worries.

Creating Family Unity

Elder Marvin J. Ashton once said:

"One of the greatest purposes of family evenings . . . is to have family members realize that a brother can be a friend, and that a sister can be a friend, and that a father and a mother can be more than parents, they can be friends."[3]

In the generations of our grandparents and great-grandparents, families ate the majority of their meals together and spent time talking or reading out loud at the end of every day. In today's busy world, families are running from work to doctor appointments to extracurricular activities, and so on. FHE is meant to be a casual time for the family to learn and have fun together. Making time for each other each week is what helps create those strong bonds of friendship.

I read a really fun idea on Families.com[4] to help promote family unity—birthday family home evenings. For FHE before a family member's birthday, you plan an activity centered on that individual. Someone would give a short talk about why that person is special to your family. You may also want to include his talents, hobbies, and any accomplishments from the past year. Then each person shares something they like about that family member.

Blessings for All

We are promised that if we do our best to hold weekly family home evenings, "great blessings will result."[5] These blessings include more love at home, eternal friendships, and the power to overcome evil influences and temptations. Through focus and good planning, we can each do our best to receive these wonderful and great blessings.

Notes

1. The First Presidency of the Church, 1915, "Family Home Evening: Counsel and a Promise," *Ensign*, Jun. 2003, 12.
2. Ibid.
3. Marvin J. Ashton, Conference Report, Oct. 1969, 28–29.
4. Miriam Caldwell, "Five Resources for Ideas for Family Home Evening," http://lds.families.com/blog/five-resources-for-ideas-for-family-home-evenings.
5. First Presidency, "Family Home Evening," 12.

Can I Make It Through Another Day?

by Danyelle Ferguson

R aising a child with special needs can be difficult. We have good days, bad days . . . and sometimes what feels like bad week upon bad week. Here are a few tips to make it through those rough moments.

You Too?

The most important thing is to know you're not alone, whether it's dealing with Individualized Education Program meetings (IEP's), sibling rivalries, or shampooing the carpet for the third time that day because "someone" decided to use poop for paint. Yes, this really happens. Some of you are thinking, "Yuck! Thank goodness I don't have to deal with that!" and others are thinking, "Wow! You mean it's really not just my child?" In each situation, you can almost always find another parent somewhere who is going through—or has already gone through—a similar phase. These parents can be found in your child's class or school, support groups, disability societies, online groups, disability conferences, and workshops—even stories in books or magazines. You may find sympathetic ears in your child's teacher, therapists, Special Olympics coaches, or Church leaders. My experience was that once I found one or two people who understood what I was going through and I began to talk about it more openly, more and more people sought me out to share their experiences too.

Laughing It Out

Finding humor in the middle of all the stress is sometimes difficult.

Often it takes a few weeks, months, or even years before you can see the humorous side of a particularly difficult trial. When our son Isaac went through his poop-painting stage, I seriously thought I was going to pull all my hair out. But my husband was able to turn it into something funny. While venting to some friends at a support group meeting about cleaning the carpets several times a week, my husband chimed in, saying, "Well, it certainly gives new meaning to having a crappy day." Everyone laughed, including me. Suddenly, the situation wasn't quite as heavy and burdensome as it had been five minutes before.

Time-Out for Grown-Ups

When everyone's running around like crazy, screaming at levels only dogs should be able to hear, and you feel as though your head is going to erupt, it's definitely time for a break. Start enforcing quiet time in your home. This doesn't need to be a specific time every day—or it can be, if that's what you need. Generally, the kids are sent to their separate rooms to play and calm down. For the kids who share a room, I tell them they need to play nicely for the next twenty minutes. Then I put myself in a time-out.

Try going to your room or somewhere you would only hear the kids if they were fighting or really needed your help. If you choose your bedroom, lie down on your bed and relax. Take deep breaths and clear your head. You may like to play soft music or pick up a book. No matter what you do, just take some time to relax and calm down before leaving your sanctuary to face normal life again.

My coauthor, Lynn, asked me if I planned my time-outs or kept them in the back of my head, or if, like her, it was something I dreamed about as I cleaned the toilets. My answer was yes, yes, and yes.

There were some planned time-outs. I found that some planned quiet time each day helped everyone in our family have a better day—or to at least tolerate each other better on off days. I also kept my time-out plan in the back of my head. It's a good idea to mentally rehearse how you would handle different situations, what you would say, and how you would act. This helped me not to overreact to difficult or stressful situations. As for the last, there were lots and lots of times I dreamed about the sanctuary of my bedroom while I diligently scrubbed our toilets for what seemed like the umpteenth time that week.

Write It Out

Keep a notebook for your own personal venting. When it's full, throw it away or send it to the recycling bin. You may want to keep your notebook in a safe place where it can't be found by others.

No one else should ever read it, and you shouldn't go back to read what you've previously written. It's just for your own use to get out any negative, stressful feelings. Write it all down, then close the book and move on. You'll be surprised at how much lighter your shoulders feel.

Call 9-1-1

I don't mean this literally. Call a family member, friend, or your visiting teacher—someone who will listen to you vent and not be judgmental. It feels good to hear another adult's voice as you unload some of your stress.

Chocolate!

Chocolate bars, hot chocolate, chocolate cake, chocolate cookies, chocolate kisses—the list goes on and on. Find your favorite and occasionally indulge.

Sweat It Out

Exercise is not only a great stress reliever for Mom and Dad, it also helps the kids to go to bed at night. Here are some exercise ideas to try with or without the kids.

- Tie up your sneakers—Walk at the park while the kids play.
- Join a gym—Go while the kids are in school. Many gyms now have child care at a low cost or even for free.
- Learn yoga—We had a mini-yoga class at a Relief Society meeting, and I found it to be very relaxing. A great book for beginners is *Yoga for Wimps* by Miriam Austin. I can pull it out and do a quick fifteen-minute session when I need a fast and easy relaxer. My kids even like to copy some of the stretches with me.
- Exercise on TV—No, I don't mean start your own exercise show. But you could start your own class with your kids or perhaps another friend and her kids. Find an exercise tape with upbeat music. My kids love *Sweatin' to the Oldies*. By the end of the tape, we're all ready for a nap, but we had a great time

singing and dancing together. What better exercise could there be? Jazzercise has fun music. Also, ask your librarian. Many libraries have either free or low-cost rentals. This way you can try lots of different exercise programs.

- Dance in the kitchen—I love to turn on my favorite radio station during lunch. My neighbors often see me dancing around the kitchen. My daughter usually joins me, and we have a great time singing, dancing, and making PB&J sandwiches together. Another great benefit: upbeat or soothing music promotes endorphins in your brain. So not only is it fun, but carefully selected music is also a pick-me-up that leaves you feeling better than you did before.

- Smell the roses—Try gardening with your spouse while the kids play. You may even consider creating a special flower bed that's just for the kids. They could each choose some flowers or plants and then tend them while you work on your own flower beds. This also works well for vegetable gardens.

- Goal!—A quick game of soccer, baseball, or tag in the backyard with your kids can help relieve some of your stress and some of their energy.

This Too Shall Pass

It may seem like the phase you're experiencing is never going to end, but generally it does. Most children with special needs continue to grow as they experience new things, develop better social awareness, or add another year to their age. Like all children, they learn and grow at various rates. What may take one child a week to learn, may take another a year, or another a lifetime. But have faith and patience. Even if it's taking a long time to accomplish one goal, your child is usually making great strides in another. Sometimes we focus too much on the end results and forget to enjoy the journey. Celebrate all the wonderful things your child enjoys doing, the areas in which he's making progress, and the uniqueness that is your child. There's lots of work on this road we travel, but there's also plenty of joy when we look for it.

Remember Who You Are

The most important thing to remember during these stressful moments is that you are the adult and need to act responsibly. If you

ever find that life truly is overwhelming and you need a break, call someone you trust who is willing to let you drop your child off for an hour or two while you decompress. *Never feel guilty* when you need help. Every single one of us has moments or days like this. You're not the only one who sometimes can't take another moment. Part of being a great parent is knowing what your limits are and taking time to nurture yourself. When you nurture your body, mind, and spirit, you create a reserve of extra strength and love so you can nurture your family. When parents are happy, the whole family is happy—possibly off-the-walls hyper, but happy.

RELATIONSHIPS MATTER

Strengthening Your Marriage

by Danyelle Ferguson

Our marriage relationships ought to be a top priority. Our marriages ought to come before everything but our relationships with God."1

This quote can be found on page sixteen of the July 7th, 1990 issue of the *Church News*. If this issue was in your home today, it would look old, with yellow-tinted paper and faded photographs. But this quote is as true today as it was at the time of publication.

Each couple needs to make their marriage a priority. With all the time and energy that goes into raising children, you need to recommit to each other.

Recommit to making your marriage happy, not just functional.

Recommit to becoming closer in friendship.

Recommit to making each other laugh more and scowl less.

Recommit to loving each other more each day.

There is an often-quoted statistic that couples raising children with special needs have a divorce rate of 80 percent—80 percent! Does that scare you? It did me, the first time I heard it. While researching this chapter, I scoured the Internet and emailed special needs foundations and reporters—and couldn't find a reliable source or study to back up the 80 percent quoted above.

I did discover that the National Autism Association has pioneered a program called Family First. This program provides family support and marital counseling to families raising children with special needs. I had an opportunity to talk more on this subject with Lori McIlwain,

cofounder and Vice Chairman of the National Autism Association. She said:

> There appears to be no source for the high divorce rate often quoted. Our Family First Program was created based on the need we saw within the community—so, although there is no specific number, the percentage does seem to be high within the autism community.
>
> The 80% rate is mainly used for the special needs community as a whole. Even so, there is no source for that number either. Because of the rise in autism, it would be a great challenge to maintain accurate data on the divorce rate. I think it's generally recognized as a problem, so whatever awareness that can be raised about the high risk of divorce certainly couldn't hurt. We just like to point out that we do not blame divorce on the child, rather the financial and extra stresses that seem to affect communication between couples.[2]

In April 2008, Elder M. Russell Ballard gave an excellent talk titled "Daughters of God." While his talk was directed to the women of the Church and their husbands and children, he gave some wonderful advice that would strengthen any relationship. When you read this, please fill in "spouse" wherever you see "husband" or "wife."

> The second question: What more can a husband do to support his wife, the mother of their children?
>
> First, show extra appreciation and give more validation for what your wife does every day. Notice things and say thank you—often. Schedule some evenings together, just the two of you.
>
> Second, have a regular time to talk with your wife about each child's needs and what you can do to help.
>
> Third, give your wife a "day away" now and then. Just take over the household and give your wife a break from her daily responsibilities. Taking over for a while will greatly enhance your appreciation of what your wife does. You may do a lot of lifting, twisting, and bending!
>
> Fourth, come home from work and take an active role with your family. Don't put work, friends, or sports ahead of listening to, playing with, and teaching your children.[3]

Often, couples find it difficult to carve out time from their already busy schedule to spend time alone, without their children. They decide that being together as a family is just as good—but it's not. There are

conversations and experiences you and your spouse can only share when alone together. It's important that you continue dating each other—especially now that you are married!

If you feel guilty for leaving your child with special needs or your other children, remember this: They will see that you value your relationship, are dedicated to each other, and love each other enough to organize your busy schedules to include time together, which gives them a sense of comfort knowing their parents have a strong relationship.

There are many ways to strengthen your marriage.

- Weekly date nights
- Going to the temple
- Couple scripture study and prayer
- Daily "listen up" sessions
- Mommy and Daddy's special time
- Pillow talk
- Getting away together
- Girls' or guys' night out

Date Night

Date nights are a ritualistic must. Church leaders have continually counseled couples to have weekly date nights. My coauthor, Lynn, told me that during temple recommend interviews, her previous stake president used to ask the brethren if they were taking their wives out. This same stake president was also known for giving "date night" talks during stake conference, when he'd remind the couples that going to Home Depot or shopping for new golf clubs didn't count.

Elder Joe J. Christensen said:

"Keep your courtship alive. Make time to do things together—just the two of you. As important as it is to be with the children as a family, you need regular weekly time alone together. That takes commitment, planning, and scheduling."[4]

So, here are your date night rules:

- No talking about work.
- No talking about kids.
- Enjoy being together.
- Have fun!

Making date nights successful can be as easy as saying your ABC's. Together with your spouse, decide how often to have date nights. Will it be every week or perhaps twice a month? Then see if there's a particular evening that would work best. My husband and I like Thursday nights. This way we avoid the weekend traffic, and it doesn't conflict with our ward Young Women weekly meeting, so our babysitter will be available.

Choose a babysitter you feel comfortable caring for your child with special needs. There are several ways to go about this search. Some options include

- Look for a responsible young woman in your ward. If you don't know the Young Women well, ask other mothers in your ward who they like to have babysit and why. Find out if any of the girls have taken first aid, CPR, or a community babysitting class.
- Ask your friends who have special needs children for a referral.
- Check into local respite care nights. For example, an early intervention center in Orem, Utah, sponsors Friday's Kids Respite. Parents can sign up for one Friday night each month. On that night, you drop your child off at the care center. Generally, there will be arts and crafts, a sensory area, and so forth for the children to enjoy. You may need to get a separate babysitter for your other children, but you would know your child with special needs is in good hands.

I often get asked how much I pay our weekly babysitter. Instead of naming a price, I suggest figuring out how much you can budget. Tell your babysitter that each date night should be about three hours long (or however long you and your spouse agree on). Then talk to her about payment. I once left my kids with a babysitter so I could attend a meeting and then run errands. When I returned and got out the checkbook, the babysitter told me she charged $2 per hour per child. After this experience, I made it a point to talk first and agree on an amount we both felt was fair. My friends—some have two kids and others have up to five kids—on average spend anywhere between five and fifteen dollars per date night on a babysitter.

What if weekly dates don't work for you and your spouse or you can't afford to pay a babysitter *and* go out on a date? Then here's another great solution:

Call up your friends and ask who would be interested in trading babysitting services. Then neither of you are paying for a babysitter, and you both get to enjoy going out with your spouses every other week. Follow the advice from above about choosing date nights so there isn't any confusion about when either of you will be going out.

Still at a loss of what to do? Try stay-at-home dates interspersed with occasionally getting a babysitter to go out. Dates at home can be a lot of fun. They give both of you the chance to be creative and find new things to do together—all within the comfort of your own home.

Sister Emily C. Orgill tried this with her husband while they were in college. Later, she wrote an article for the *Ensign*. She said:

> My husband and I, with our two toddlers and small baby, lived in a university ward. Often, our leaders stressed the importance of weekly dates for Mom and Dad alone. As students on a limited budget, however, we couldn't afford a date, not to mention a babysitter. We decided we would have to wait to apply the counsel when we could afford to do so.
>
> One wise leader changed our minds. He convinced us that weekly dates are vital to a young couple's marriage. Time spent together sharing interests helps a couple grow closer and gives them a chance to relax and take a break from daily stresses. Perhaps most important, dates help a couple build a reserve of love. Filled with memories of good times and strong positive feelings, this reserve can help them through difficult times of stress, disagreement, and trial.
>
> My husband and I finally determined to follow this leader's counsel, even though most of our dates would need to be the stay-at-home type. Alternating the responsibility of planning the dates, we scheduled these evenings on the calendar just as we would any important meeting. We tucked the kids into bed a little early on the night of our date, then began to build our reserve of love.[5]

Even though Sister Orgill's experience was as a young married couple going through college, her stay-at-home date idea is great for those who can't afford to go out every week or who don't quite feel comfortable leaving their child with special needs yet.

Now, what to do on your date nights? How about making a date night can? This is a great place to keep ideas of things you and your spouse want to do. Find a container that has a removable lid. I used an empty formula can. Then cover it with construction paper and decorate

it. *Voila!* Jot ideas down on strips of paper and drop them in the container. Clip coupons from the paper for places to eat, discounts for activities, and so forth. This is also a good place to keep your date night money. Be sure to keep your cash in an envelope so you aren't digging for coins or misplacing dollar bills.

Speaking of date night money, keep in mind that your dates don't need to be expensive. Depending on what type of activities you and your spouse enjoy, you may occasionally want to save up and go on a big date. Often, you can find activities that cost little or no money. To save money, you may want to eat dinner at home and then go out for an activity. Also, bargain hunt. Check your local newspaper for free community activities. Local colleges and universities often have great programs you can attend for free or at a low cost.

To keep from getting into a rut, take turns planning dates. This is a great way to learn more about each other's interests. But the very best part is spending time together—without kids!

Date Night Ideas:

- Mission Impossible Night: Do something you've never done before (rock climbing, skiing, scrapbooking).
- Watch a sunset from the park.
- Go on a hike.
- Go to a community concert or play.
- Attend a sporting event together.
- Plan a treasure hunt.
- Kidnap your spouse for a night out.
- Plan a scavenger hunt.
- Go to the Family History Library.
- Do a service project.
- Take a weekly class.
- Sketch out your dream house.
- Share your favorite conference talks.
- Play board games.
- Plan a surprise date with notes or poems during the day to heighten the anticipation.
- Paint T-shirts.
- Attend the temple.
- Go stargazing.

- Double date with friends you don't see often.
- Put together a puzzle.
- Take a personality test and then talk about what strengths you bring to your relationship.
- Send the kids to the babysitter's house and have a romantic dinner for two at home.
- Blindfold your spouse and take them on a tour of places you went when you were dating.
- Time Capsule Goals: Make a list of goals you'd like to accomplish in one year, five years, ten years, and so on. Label each envelope with the date it is to be opened, then seal the goals up in their respective envelopes and place them in a box.
- Make holiday decorations together for yourself, family, or friends.
- Have a "This Is Your Life" night. Get friends and family to write down memories of your spouse's life. Then take turns reading letters about each other.
- Take dancing lessons together.

Going to the Temple

In May 1992, Elder David B. Haight counseled couples to attend the temple in the following quote:

> May I invite those of you who are sealed to a spouse, whether living or departed, to recall for a moment your memories of that day of days when you knelt together at the altar and were sealed as husband and wife for time and all eternity. Do you remember any of the words of the ceremony? Do you recall sacred feelings, a glimpse of eternal promises? Can you feel again the power that created a relationship which will transcend death? Can you recall the feeling of love of our Heavenly Father for you and your companion, which was manifest on that occasion?
>
> If time and the realities of everyday life have eroded your recollections of what you felt and received when you were sealed, you should return to the temple and participate again as proxies for the departed in that same sealing ordinance. Take advantage of that opportunity. Do it together as husband and wife. In this manner you may deepen your understanding of the covenants you made and renew the promises you received on that day when you were sealed as eternal companions.[6]

Together with your spouse, make a goal of how often you will attend. If you live near a temple, then your goal may be one, two, or three times a month. Many Latter-day Saints still need to travel several hours or even days to get to a temple. In these instances, make a realistic goal that works for you and your family. Perhaps it will be once a month or twice a year.

Whatever you decide, look at your calendar and choose the dates. Then set whatever goals necessary to get there—babysitters, saving money, transportation, lodging, and so forth.

For example, if you live in central Pennsylvania and your closest temple is in Washington DC, start by choosing two Saturdays that would work for you. Then find a babysitter who can help on one of those Saturdays. Sometimes, Young Women will babysit for service while you attend the temple. You could even make arrangements for a neighbor, family member, or friend to babysit for half the day and for the Young Woman to take the other half. Be sure to leave a list of contacts for the babysitter in case of an emergency or if she has questions.

Once child care is arranged, plan what you can do to keep costs down. Pack a cooler with sandwiches and bottled water so you won't need to eat out. The rest is money for gas. Leave early in the morning to get to the temple at a reasonable time to do a session or two.

Then there's the drive back home. You'll arrive home late in the evening. To make driving easier and cut down the cost of gas, you may want to invite another couple to come with you. Many couples find that when they plan ahead to attend the temple, Satan puts as many road blocks in their way as he possibly can. Keep focused on your goal. Whatever it takes for you to get to the temple, it's worth it.

Scripture Study and Prayer

Ah, yes—the standard Sunday School answers. I once felt as though they were all I heard: family scripture study, personal scripture study, couple scripture study . . . then repeat that list for prayer and say it ten times as fast as you can!

When I paused in the midst of life and analyzed my daily and weekly schedules, I realized the amount of time I spend reading scriptures and having prayer every day is minuscule in comparison to doing chores and running kids to activities and therapy appointments or working on Church callings.

Then I thought about all the blessings my family receives from that small portion of time—more patience and love toward each other and, most important, feeling the Holy Spirit in our home. Amazing, don't you agree?

Elder L. Tom Perry said:

"I promise you that daily family prayer and scripture study will build within the walls of your home a security and bonding that will enrich your lives and prepare your families to meet the challenges of today and the eternities to come."[7]

What a wonderful promise for your family and home. But let's think about how prayer and scripture study can make your relationship as a couple better. President Ezra Taft Benson said:

"Prayer in the home and prayer with each other will strengthen your union. Gradually thoughts, aspirations, and ideas will merge into a oneness until you are seeking the same purposes and goals. Rely on the Lord, the teachings of the prophets, and the scriptures for guidance and help, particularly when there may be disagreements and problems."[8]

When you study the scriptures as a couple, you are taking the time to learn the gospel together and to discuss the principles and concepts you read. You will have opportunities to share your thoughts and feelings about what you are reading. You will both have moments to share your testimony with each other.

One of the greatest adhesives of your marriage will be kneeling in prayer and expressing the love you feel for your eternal companion to Heavenly Father. Praying for each other will pull you even closer together as you express your desires and thanks. On sunshiny days, it's your expression of gratitude to Heavenly Father for His blessings in your lives. On rainy days, it's a balm and a healer.

No matter what kind of day you've had, when you pray together for each other's individual needs and the needs of your family, the Spirit will create the adhesive that strengthens the bond of your hearts.

Here's one last quote to end this section:

> Many Church leaders as well as professional counselors have indicated that they have never seen a marriage in serious difficulty in which the couple was still praying together daily. When you invite the Lord to be a partner in your union, there is a softening of feelings, a moderation of tension that occurs through the power of the Spirit. See what happens when, as you kneel together, you hear your

companion express gratitude and love for you. Pray that you, working together, may overcome whatever difficulties you may have so that your love can increase.[9]

Listen Up

James 1:19 says:

"Let every man be swift to hear, slow to speak, slow to wrath." Let's break that scripture down.

- We should be swift to hear.
- We should be slow to speak.
- We should be slow to wrath.

Really listening to each other doesn't mean you always have to agree. But you should listen to each other's point of view and respect the other's opinion. If you're trying to make a decision but have differing viewpoints, then hit your knees. Pray together. Spend some time apart rethinking everything and then come together and discuss it again. Sometimes you may be able to compromise. Other times you may need to agree to disagree. Perhaps then you should try one person's solution and see how it works. If it doesn't bring about the desired results, then try the other person's solution.

Remember, you are each other's natural sounding boards. Talk to each other about your day—the stresses, the funny stuff, and so on. Go over your schedules for the next day. Often the husband is working and doesn't attend therapy appointments, IEP's, and so forth. Wives, be sure to fill your husband in on challenges and successes of your child with special needs—and your other children, of course! Husbands, remember to tell your wife how much you love her and share your appreciation for all she does in the home and with the family.

Mommy and Daddy's Special Time

This is my favorite time of the day. After you get your kids into bed (or at least in their rooms), you and your spouse should take about forty-five minutes together to decompress from the day. Relax on the couch, play a board game, talk about the day's highlights, and go over the next day's schedule.

Our son often comes out of his room and wants to share this time with us. But we tell him it's Mommy and Daddy's special time and send

him back to his room, where he plays until he eventually decides it's time to sleep. If you have wandering kids, don't let it stress you out. Just herd them back to their respective bedrooms and go on.

A fun activity for this time is to listen to LDS audio talks. A variety of subjects are available, and they generally last about one hour. You may be able to check one out from your library, borrow one from a ward member, or purchase them at an LDS bookstore. Another idea is to work through a seminary or institute workbook or read talks or Church books together.

Pillow Talk

In the April 1982 General Conference, Elder Robert L. Simpson said:

"Every couple, whether in the first or twenty-first year of marriage, should discover the value of pillow-talk time at the end of the day—the perfect time to take inventory, to talk about tomorrow. And best of all, it's a time when love and appreciation for one another can be reconfirmed. The end of another day is also the perfect setting to say, 'Sweetheart, I am sorry about what happened today. Please forgive me.' "[10]

Getting Away

We love our families, but let's face it. With all the stress in our lives, we occasionally need a break that lasts longer than a trip to the grocery store. Besides that, when is the last time you and your spouse went away without kids tagging along? Your honeymoon? Try planning an annual overnight trip for you and your husband.

Now, lots of us would like to go, but money can be hard to come by. Try putting aside fifteen to twenty dollars a month. By the end of the year, you should have 180 to 240 dollars saved for your overnighter. Or you could plan to use part of your tax return for this purpose. A hotel room or a room at a bed and breakfast will cost 110 dollars on average, depending on where you live. If you plan your trip for the middle of the week, rooms are usually priced lower. You may also be able to find a midweek special package that includes dinner or a movie. You shouldn't have to worry about breakfast, as most hotels have a free continental breakfast in the lobby. Grandparents are great for overnight babysitters, but if they aren't available, plan to use the rest of your allotted money for childcare.

Your destination doesn't need to be far away. You can stay in town or another town close by. The purpose of the trip isn't sightseeing as much as it's about being away from home, with your spouse, for a whole twenty-four hours!

Some couples may try going away together for a longer period of time. I say, go for it! My husband and I have gone away a few times for two or three nights. The first time we planned an extended trip, we ventured about two hours from home, far enough away that we could visit places we generally don't go, but close enough that if we were needed back home, we could cut our trip short. While we enjoy the time together, we miss the kids, and they miss us. It's always fun to return to shouts of "Mommy! Daddy!" and plenty of hugs and kisses.

No matter where you go or how long you stay, enjoy being together as husband and wife—best friends who are free to roam and relax at their own pace.

Girls' Night Out or Getting Together with the Guys

Developing friendships outside of your marriage is important. Your friends are people you feel comfortable calling and telling funny stuff your kids just did, telling about an exciting upcoming event, or venting when your day is not going the way you want it to. If you're lucky, you will have another couple who are friends with both you and your spouse. Then you can have fun going out on double dates and getting your families together for barbecues.

More often, though, you each will have nonrelated friends. The wife may meet other mothers at play groups, and the husband will have friends from work. In these instances, you may enjoy getting together with the guys or the girls. Be respectful of each other's desire to spend time hanging out with friends, but at the same time, don't try to escape by spending as much time as possible away from your home. Your family relationships should be your first priority.

My husband and I differ in the amount of time we spend getting together with friends outside of our home, without the other spouse tagging along. My husband spends five days a week at work, where he has a lot of friends. His company does fun things like foosball tournaments and other contests between the employees. I, on the other hand, stay at home with my kids, work from home, and see less of my friends.

My husband and I talk often about our schedule and things we'd like to do. Occasionally, my husband goes out for a movie night with the guys. But most often, he likes to hang out with the kids and give me an opportunity to go out.

Once a month, I attend a scrapbooking night and a monthly writer's group meeting. I also get together with my old college roommates about every three or four months. I have other friends who like to get together a couple of times a year to go out for ice cream or the movies.

The important part about spending time with friends is this: balance. You and your spouse should be honest about how you're doing. There are times when I'll go for two or three months without getting together with friends or going to any of my meetings if my family has a lot of activities planned, the kids are sick, or my husband has a deadline at work and is working a lot of overtime. Be flexible. Remember that first comes Heavenly Father, then comes your spouse, and then comes your family. All other activities fall in the "other priorities" or "fun stuff" categories.

Notes

1. "Strengthening a marriage," *Church News*, July 7, 1990.
2. Email correspondence with Lori McIlwain, National Autism Association (www.NationalAutismAssociation.org), 13 June 2008. Used with permission.
3. M. Russell Ballard, "Daughters of God," *Ensign*, May 2008, 108–10.
4. Joe J. Christensen, "Marriage and the Great Plan of Happiness," *Ensign*, May 1995, 64.
5. Emily C. Orgill, "Date Night—at Home," *Ensign*, Apr. 1991, 57.
6. David B. Haight, "Come to the House of the Lord," *Ensign*, May 1992, 15.
7. L. Tom Perry, "Back to Gospel Basics," *Ensign*, May 1993, 90.
8. Ezra Taft Benson, "Salvation—A Family Affair," *Ensign*, Jul. 1992, 2.
9. Joe J. Christensen, *One Step at a Time: Building a Better Marriage, Family, and You.* (Salt Lake City: Deseret Book, 1996), 15–16. Used with permission.
10. Robert L. Simpson, "A Lasting Marriage," *Ensign*, May 1982, 21.

BUILDING PARENT-CHILD RELATIONSHIPS

by Lynn Parsons

The parent-child relationship is one of the most important, and most intense, relationships we will have in our lifetimes. It begins before the child is born, as the parents dream of the possibilities for this little spirit. The relationship changes with a disability diagnosis and continues to evolve throughout the child's life.

When a child is diagnosed with a disability, the parents' expectations may undergo many drastic changes. I experienced this with my own children. You are suddenly thrust into an unexpected and strange world. The consequences of this mind-shift vary from family to family and from parent to parent. Losing the "dream child" is so traumatic that, for many years, it has been compared to the grief cycle experienced at the loss of a child. There have been many theories formulated to explain this process with similar types of stages.

Stages of Coping

Each stage has its own unique feelings and must be experienced in order before the person can move on. The levels include:

- Denial Behavior
- Repair Mom
- Adapting
- Coping

Like many parents, I began with denial behavior. I made my decisions based on a lack of information. My children with special needs didn't talk as much or as clearly as their siblings. I "blamed" this on

their early ear problems. This was a cause but not a reason to ignore the problem. I took comfort in popular tales such as "Albert Einstein didn't talk until he was three years old." When my children were teased at school (a fact I found out from a neighbor child), I had a transformational experience. This moved me on to the next stage.

Then I became "Repair Mom." I was determined to "fix" my child. A first-grade teacher told me she didn't expect that one of my children would learn to read. My child would be tested but not for several months. I was concerned how much ground she would lose in the meantime and about her quality of life if she never learned to read. I was most concerned that I felt I had lost control of my daughter's life.

I had returned to school to finish my bachelor's degree, but I put it on hold to teach my child to read. Her wonderful speech language pathologist told me what she thought was wrong. I went to the teacher supply store, purchased books, and began to teach my child phonics. By the time she was tested, she was reading at a level too high for special services, and by the end of the school year, she was reading at grade level. I was so convinced I had "fixed" her that I became a special education teacher.

During my experience in the adaptation stage, I had my children included in as many things as possible. They have unique talents, and I still feel that others benefit from knowing them. This was an especially easy phase for my family because they fit in with their peers. Other families will find this more of a struggle as they try to get their children included in activities at church. It may help to remind teachers and leaders that it's okay for your child to have different goals from the rest of the children.

I have only recently experienced the coping level. I sincerely believed I had "fixed" both my children with special needs and that they were well on their way to living the best life possible. It wasn't until I took classes to become certified as a diagnostician that I learned that my child still had difficulties identifying letters with sounds—the same disability diagnosed when she was three! She had learned ways to compensate for her struggles. I had provided tools, and she had made great strides, but she wasn't "fixed"! I have now learned that "different" is not better or worse than "typical" and that my children can advocate for themselves to meet their needs. I am currently able to work from a standpoint of reality rather than dreams and illusions.

These levels are just a model. They are useful for understanding many struggles and are especially helpful if one parent is on a different level than the other.

The Blame and Shame Games

One nonproductive activity is the blame game. With each of my kids, I blamed myself for their disabilities. I thought I had eaten the wrong things while pregnant or hadn't talked to them enough. I even wondered if my child was being punished for something I had done, forgetting that "We believe that men will be punished for their own sins, and not for Adam's transgression" (Articles of Faith 1:2).

I found that their struggles had nothing to do with my parenting. One child, who didn't speak, had enormous adenoids that would swell, blocking her Eustachian tubes and making her temporarily deaf. After years of mentally beating myself, I learned it was not my fault! I wasted precious time and energy torturing myself rather than commending myself for the things I *had* done right.

Cousin to the blame game is the shame game. Never be embarrassed to admit that your child has a disability. You will prove to your child you are proud to be their parent and can serve as an educator to others.

Faith

As a teacher, I've seen many dysfunctional parent/child relationships. I've spent hours wondering why some parents and children get along very well (for the most part—hormones excepted!) while others falter. The one thing I've identified that is common in all good relationships is trust. In fact, trust is the most important thing in this relationship.

I tried to establish trust early in my relationships with my children. They know I will be there to help them because of past experiences. If you make every effort to be consistent and reliable, you will create an atmosphere of trust. I worked to earn and keep their trust as we expressed our love, spent time together as a family, and worked through positive discipline.

All children need to be told they are loved on a regular basis. They need to hear the words and see the deeds. Physical expressions (hugs, and so on) are important, as are consistent words and actions. Take time to enjoy your child. All children love to have a one-on-one "date" with Mom or Dad, and this is a perfect time to show your feelings and

learn to appreciate your child as an individual.

Every family needs to develop a unique culture. We have jokes no one else gets, reminisce about different events, and spend time together. Quality time is a misleading concept, for there is no quality without quantity. This culture will bind you together and really make each person a *member* of your family.

Every child needs discipline. He needs to learn responsibility to the best of his abilities and that actions are followed by consequences. James E. Faust said,

> A principal purpose for discipline is to teach obedience. President David O. McKay stated: "Parents who fail to teach obedience to their children, if [their] homes do not develop obedience society will demand it and get it. It is therefore better for the home, with its kindliness, sympathy and understanding to train the child in obedience rather than callously to leave him to the brutal and unsympathetic discipline that society will impose if the home has not already fulfilled its obligation."[1]

Part of discipline is teaching responsibility. Each child needs to participate in the work of the family. Having chores will help him feel like an important member of the family while learning valuable life skills.

Hope

There is always hope. My own children exceeded predictions made by others. Keep despair away with a focus on your child's potential. Search out experiences that will allow him or her to grow, and it will be easier to maintain hope during difficult times. Participating in temple ordinances and family history work can also help you develop an eternal perspective. Temple experiences expand your view beyond today's challenges to the blessings of the future. This allows you to see family members as Heavenly Father's children with unique talents and abilities so you can better appreciate them.

Time off is necessary. You need to take time alone and with your spouse to recharge your batteries. I find I'm a better parent when I've had a break and can return refreshed.

Charity

This topic is the most important. The pure love of Christ is important in any relationship. You are not just the instructor or therapist,

you are the parent. While mothers and fathers are the first and most important teachers, your role covers so much more than that. It's often hard to be understanding when your child is struggling with new skills or old behaviors. As you extend charity toward your special spirit, your patience and teaching ability will increase. You will see this child as a son or daughter of God and will appreciate her true worth.

Let your charity also extend to those who work with your child. Don't bad-mouth teachers, leaders, or care providers in front of your child. This creates a conflict between their natural feelings of love for their teachers and a desire to align with your opinion. Let adult problems be discussed among adults, and leave the child free to develop his own relationships.

Building Blocks

How do you find things to do with your children? First, use their interests. Maybe there is a railroad museum or local station you could visit with your child who enjoys trains. Check with your local chamber of commerce or visitor's bureau for attractions you may not have seen yet. Many families are opting for budget-friendly "staycations" instead of expensive vacations. Do an Internet search for local zoos, libraries, hands-on science museums, and community events. Familyfun.com also has a list of low-cost ideas for families, with lists arranged by age.

Babies and toddlers can participate in music and finger plays. Mold creations from peanut butter clay or make art projects from handprints, footprints, or thumbprints. Play at identifying things, for example, body parts, facial expressions, and family members. Take them on adventures with the rest of the family and build verbal skills as you tell them about your trips. My grandson loves this!

Preschoolers can create craft projects from food, do puppet shows, sort household items, and go on adventure hikes to find insects or animals. My kids loved to paint the house. I saved plastic food containers and bought cheap paint brushes. They painted the outside of the house with water, "wrote" on the driveway, and had a ball. I usually had half the neighborhood over, and the cleanest aluminum siding in the neighborhood (from three feet down).

Elementary-age children can create cars from boxes and watch a "drive-in" movie or play water games in the backyard even if you don't

have a pool. Try doing a regular activity in the "wrong" place such as dinner in the bedroom, tents in the living room, or reading stories in the car.

There are also Internet activities for elementary-age children at AbilityOnline.org and Bandaides and Blackboards (www.lehman.cuny .edu/faculty/jfleitas/bandaides). AbilityOnline.org is a free online community for kids aged four to twelve created by a doctor. Online tutors are provided in a safe and secure environment. Bandaides and Blackboards was designed by a registered nurse. It's filled with fun information about living with disabilities. See the notes below about Internet safety.

There are many activities even teens will do with their families. They love to blow things up. Plans for water bottle launchers, foaming soda sprays, and other safe activities can be found on Cub Scout websites. My children enjoyed geocaching, which uses a GPS unit and information from www.geocaching.com to find hidden "treasures." LDOnline has stories, art, and more by teens with disabilities. Activities that take them back to a simpler time (tricycle races, acting out scripture stories) are a big hit, especially if food is involved.

Internet safety is an enormous concern right now. Teach your children never to give out personal information. Use one of the many filters commercially available. Allowing the Internet into your home without a filter is the same as leaving the front door wide open. *Never* allow a computer in your home that is not in a public area. If you are concerned about what your children do on the Internet when you are not at home, take the mouse and keyboard with you. NetSmartz.org and SafeKids.com are two great places to start if you aren't Internet savvy. I promise that your kids know way more than you do about the Internet and how to get to their favorite sites.

Kids of all ages love to read together. I read the Harry Potter books to my children. I started out with the girls (aged ten and thirteen at the time), and then my fifteen-year-old son joined in. Pretty soon, we had to wait until the eighteen-year-old son came home, and finally Dad got with the program. I would read until I thought the lower half of my face would fall off, and they would beg for more. See your local librarian or bookstore or the American Library Association for ideas. Also, many local libraries now have websites with suggested books for each age group. Here are some book suggestions:

Babies and Toddlers:

- *Brown Bear, Brown Bear, What Do You See?* by Bill Martin Jr.
- *Good Night, Spot* by Eric Hill
- *Where Is Baby's Belly Button?* by Karen Katz
- *Whose Baby Am I?* by John Butler
- *Can You Moo?* by David Wojtowycz

Elementary Age:

- *Click, Clack, Moo: Cows that Type* by Doreen Cronin
- *A Series of Unfortunate Events* by Lemony Snicket and Brett Helquist
- *If You Give a Mouse a Cookie* by Laura Joffe Numeroff
- *Clifford the Big Red Dog* by Norman Bridwell
- *The Treasure Tree: Helping Kids Understand Their Personality* by Dr. John Trent

Teens:

- *The Giver* by Lois Lowry
- Mary Higgins Clark mysteries
- *Holes* by Louis Sachar
- *Speak* by Laurie Halse Anderson
- *Nothing But the Truth* by Avi

Many novels have been written featuring a main character with a disability. These include:

- *Joey Pigza Swallowed the Key* by Jack Gantos
- *Blue Bottle Mystery: An Asperger Adventure* by Kathy Hoopmann
- *The Curious Incident of the Dog in the Night-Time: A Novel* by Mark Haddon
- *Haze* by Kathy Hoopmann

Special Occasions

Special occasions are an important time for family bonding. Create a family tradition for your kids' birthdays, such as taking that child out to breakfast or lunch, serving food on a special plate, decorating, or having a holiday food. Be sure to attend important events such as plays, recitals, games, and award ceremonies. These are important to

your child, and your presence says that you value your child as a person. Think back to your childhood programs and how you scanned the audience for the faces of your loved ones.

Weekly family councils are also special occasions. As my children got older, it was very easy to get lost in the activities and forget to take time to talk as a group. Consistency will teach your children that the household members are important to you, and having everyone participate to the best of their ability will make them feel a vital part of your clan.

Connecting with your teen can be a struggle. First, you need a basis for conversation. Listen to their music, watch their movies, and listen as they tell you about their friends and activities. Psychologists know about the late night/early morning effect. For some reason, adolescents are more open and honest during the late night and early morning hours. Waiting up for teens is very difficult. More than one night, I was so tired I thought my head was going to fall off and roll around the floor. But I also knew if I went to bed, I would get responses such as "fine" and "nothing" the next day. Once the opportunity has passed, you may not get it back.

What if you are the one who needs to talk? I talked to my girls about boys at the local drive-in restaurant. It's private because you're in the car, it's too hot in Texas for them to get out and walk home, and everything you say goes down better with a liberal dose of sugar, fat, and salt. Of course, they're now suspicious if I offer to take them out to dinner!

Driving your teen to activities is a great time to talk. I don't allow headphones or cell phone conversations in the car, and they don't like my radio stations, so they have no option but to talk or listen. This is when not buying your adolescent a car can be an advantage. If they do have a vehicle, consider a road trip without electronics—that's one of the reasons why iPods aren't permitted at Church camps!

Some of those talks should be about disabilities. I firmly believe that children should be told (to the best of their understanding) about their disabilities. In a high school social skills class, we interviewed twenty students with autism. Many of them had never heard the word autism, a few described it as a "brain problem," and others said they thought a classmate had it. How can you begin to deal with a problem you don't know you have? LDOnline has great information about how to explain disabilities to your children.

Siblings also need information about disabilities. Autism.org tells how to explain it to your children at various ages and has an exercise (Aunt Blabby) where siblings write advice to other siblings.[2] The National Sibling Research Consortium has good information as well.[3] Children's Disability Information is another good resource.[4]

There is more information on this topic in the "Sibling Relationships" chapter of this book.

Being a parent is one of the most rewarding things in life. It can also make us feel the most lost, confused, and overwhelmed. Every parent feels this way, but it can seem more intense when you have a child with a disability. Remember that you have a partnership with the Lord in this, and He can make up for whatever you think you may lack. As I sent my oldest son off on his mission to Mexico, it felt the same as when I had sent him to kindergarten, only I was more scared and unprepared. I wondered if I had taught him enough and prepared him for this huge step. The fact that he would be in Mexico, only a few hundred miles away from our home in Texas, was some comfort, but at the airport, I wanted desperately to wrap my arms around his legs and keep him home. The only thing that stopped me was that it wasn't what was best for him. By placing my focus on what he *needed* rather than what I *wanted*, I was able to do the right thing.

The scriptures teach us, "Train up a child in the way he should go: and when he is old, he will not depart from it" (Proverbs 22:6). If you rely on the influence of the Holy Ghost and the inspiration God *will* give you in your parenting responsibilities, you will develop an eternal relationship with these special spirits and help them return to our Father again.

Notes

1. James E. Faust, "A Thousand Threads of Love," *Ensign*, Oct. 2005, 2–7.
2. http://www.autism.com/fam_page.asp?PID=349.
3. http://kc.vanderbilt.edu/kennedy/research/siblingconsortium.html.
4. http://www.childrensdisabilities.info/parenting/siblings-disabilities.html.

SIBLING RELATIONSHIPS

by Lynn Parsons

A s with any unique situation, being the sibling of someone with a disability has blessings and challenges. Along with great maturity, these children experience many of the same concerns as their parents and need additional support. Reading more about sibling experiences will help you understand what they need.

A good place to start is the sibling section under disabilities at www.lds.org and www.siblingsupport.org.

Blessings

I've seen many siblings who are loyal, mature beyond their years, and who really appreciate their blessings. Living with someone with a disability has helped them see past differences to the spirit underneath. They are very proud of their brother or sister's accomplishments and bravery when facing challenges. They are strongly bonded to their families and remain devoted to each member. They are also thankful for their own health and for those who help their brother or sister. This may cause them to choose a helping profession (such as a teacher, doctor, nurse, or social worker) for their career.

I interviewed "Joan," a young lady with two siblings on the autism spectrum. (Her name has been changed to protect her privacy.) I was impressed with her level of maturity and was interested to learn the advantages she has discovered because of her experiences with her brother and sister.

Joan is very matter-of-fact about the challenges her siblings face and her role in the family as a secondary caregiver. Instead of feeling sorry

for herself or other family members, she looks to discover ways to help.

Joan says she gets a lot of babysitting jobs for children with special needs because she has so much experience dealing with disabilities. It has also helped her at work in a local water park, where she's better able to help children with disabilities. She's also able to deal with the embarrassment that having siblings with disabilities can bring and has great coping skills. How wonderful to meet a teen who is not only a tremendous help to her family but also sees opportunities in her challenges.

Teaching about Disabilities

Each parent will have his or her own method of teaching non-disabled siblings about the special children in their family. Here's an experience from Sandra Cooper, talking about her son Anthony, and how she has taught him and his little brother about his sister, Madeline:

> Anthony knows Madeline is a child of God, just like he is. She might be different on the outside, but it doesn't take away from the fact that she is a child of God. We also never describe her heart as being bad or sick. We always talk about it as being "special." Madeline's abnormalities are *not* different; they are special. After all, we are all children of our Heavenly Father, no matter our shape, size, or color.
>
> We also don't draw attention to Madeline's challenges. In our house you are not allowed to say *can't*, but you can ask for help. With Madeline, we tell her she can do anything she wants, and then we stand back and give her the room she needs. Seeing that Madeline wants to do what she sees her brother do, we have adapted our house to allow her to reach all her desires. Our playground at home has been adjusted so that Madeline and other kids can run around together. In her room, everything has been brought down to her level so she can feel independent. We have stepstools in our house so she can access what she needs.
>
> Last, we don't treat her any differently than we do her brothers. She has chores that are age-appropriate, and we are there to help her as she needs. If she needs help, we use the opportunity to show and talk to her older brother about service and helping each other because we are a family. We love, support, and respect one another. Madeline is also disciplined age-appropriately. It is important for her brothers to see that she doesn't get away with things.
>
> Because of all this, I believe Anthony doesn't see his sister as

different. When asking him if his sister is different, he said, "Yes, because she is a girl and wears different clothes." As parents, we try hard to have the world around Madeline fit her needs so she doesn't feel that she lives in a world not made for her.

Some teen siblings worry about the potential for embarrassment when their disabled brothers or sisters are around. Joan's siblings remember the death of family pets with a flood of strong emotions. Whenever anyone mentions the subject of death, they become tremendously upset. To others who don't understand the situation, this appears to be an overreaction. Her siblings also act overly excited when they see Joan at school and generally run over and jump on her. This can be physically dangerous, as they are both taller than Joan even though they are a few years younger. When she sees them coming, she holds up her hands and reminds them not to jump on her. This reminder generally does the trick. If not, she tries to have a quick sidestep ready.

Adult Worries

Siblings without special needs often share worries with their parents. They don't want strangers to stare at their brothers and sisters or they worry about bullying. They feel alone and wish for a friend who understands their struggles. Children with disabled siblings may be forced to grow up too fast. This can cause resentment, grief, and guilt.

The family may be so overburdened with child care that older siblings take on the roles of mini-parents. Parents may be worn out from taking care of a child with special needs, and the nondisabled children may be left mostly to fend for themselves. Many marriages dissolve due to the stress of challenging parenting, and single parents may use older children as confidants. Too much information about adult problems (money struggles, challenges with medical professionals, school struggles) can stress these children beyond their ability to cope. They might resent the adult roles thrust on them, for which they are not prepared.

Joan told me she gets upset when others come to her to vent about something one of her siblings may have done. She doesn't appreciate her peers at school saying upsetting things about her family members.

Teachers may see nondisabled siblings as a resource for information about a special spirit. These leaders may inappropriately vent about behaviors they find upsetting or ask for advice. Rather than including

a minor in your comments, seek out the parents. Joan agrees with this, preferring to be treated as just another teen rather than a mini special education teacher.

Siblings worry about all the challenges faced by their loved ones with disabilities. My twin brother was born with one kidney. My mother constantly worried that he would be hit in the back during sports, damage his only kidney, and die. I worried that he would be injured in a fight and took it upon myself to do everything in my power to make sure that he was never involved in one. My parents didn't ask me to do this—I just assumed that responsibility. I wasn't always successful, and I felt very guilty whenever he fought.

Siblings worry about who will take care of their brother or sister after their parents die. Parents need to make plans for the brother or sister with a disability. Providing for future care is an important consideration, whether guardianship is given to a relative or family friend. Consider having finances controlled by a person separate from the physical caregiver. Share this information with all the other children in the family. Answer any questions, and don't just say, "You can take care of him after we're gone." Providing a satisfactory explanation for living arrangements will alleviate anxiety and provide reassurance about the future.

These children mourn the loss of a more normal family life, activities their friends have, and a more typical sibling relationship. They are aware of what's happening in the lives of their friends. They know how others interact with their brothers and sisters. Provide opportunities for conversation, and try to do this without making them feel guilty for having natural feelings.

In these situations, there is plenty of guilt to go around. Children may resent the time and effort parents put into one child and then feel guilty about that resentment. They may feel guilty about being nondisabled. Some may need counseling or at least a chance to vent during especially tough times.

Hope for the Future

The best way to help these children is to simply be aware of their challenging situation. Don't waste time worrying about their struggles—take action. Give them information, support, and resources for their own needs.

Age-appropriate information is the single most important thing they need. Some parents may deny the problems of the disabled sibling, but this makes brothers and sisters confused and agitated. When children reach adolescence, they will wonder about their role in their sibling's future, if they will become disabled, and if the condition can be inherited by their children. Let them ask questions, and answer them honestly as best you can. If you don't know an answer, tell them so, along with any reassurances you can. Your plans for the child with disabilities definitely need to be discussed. These conversations need to be closed with expressions of love for all family members.

Important support includes good communication, help with relationships, and assistance in meeting their own needs. Encourage your child to talk with you, typical peers, and those with disabilities. This will encourage them to find help before little problems become big ones.

The website www.siblingsupport.org holds workshops for siblings, and there are many online communities where teens can chat with others who understand them. Sib shops are held to educate and support children who have brothers and sisters with disabilities. Kids aged eight to thirteen can have fun while getting peer support, discussing concerns, learning coping skills, and finding out about their siblings' challenges. Parents can also learn during these events. Check with your local support group to see if they have classes available.

Siblings sometimes need encouragement to forge a better relationship with their brother or sister. Teach them appropriate ways to interact, and they will be able to develop a lasting and worthwhile relationship. Some children may be uncomfortable bringing friends home. Help them work out a script or explanation they can share with their friends before coming to the house, and this will help them become more comfortable sharing with everyone.

Children are not mini-adults. They need help coping with school, dealing with friends, and other problems that arise. Ask about their schooling, listen to them talk about friendships, and teach them coping strategies for stressful situations. Sometimes just being heard can be enough.

Joan says she's had to become independent because her siblings require so much attention. All children need special time with their parents. Even if it's just a few minutes, it makes them feel valued and keeps them from becoming "shadow siblings," or invisible members of

their own families. This gives them time to discuss how to deal with reactions from strangers, the pressure they may feel to be "perfect," and freedom to follow their own dreams. Especially during adolescence, when they are trying to establish their own identities, they need to be grounded in their own family as they develop outside relationships. This time and attention can prevent children from acting out in an attempt to recapture parental attention.

Most of these siblings will be better people because of their relationships with a brother or sister with special needs. Joan has developed many coping mechanisms. She doesn't let things bother her, when possible, and she leaves the situation when she can't handle it. She does struggle to explain social skills to her brother and sister, which she admits is pretty difficult. But, despite all the hardships, Joan wouldn't trade her siblings for any others. She appreciates the lessons she has learned. Among these are increased patience, a better ability to explain processes in detail (such as math solutions), a perspective that allows her to let go of little problems, greater independence, an appreciation for the talents of all people, and a profound ability to deal with responsibility.

With the right support from family, friends, and leaders, these siblings can be blessed in ways beyond our imagination.

Extended Family and Friend Relationships

by Lynn Parsons

Discovering a child has a disability affects more than the parents and siblings in that family. It can have a major effect on your relationships with extended family and friends. The challenges you may face include communication breakdowns, differences in expectations, and future family gatherings.

Communication Breakdown

Telling your family and friends about the challenges your child may face could possibly be one of the most difficult things you have done in your life. It's fine to take time at the beginning to process everything and experience the many emotions that come with changing life circumstances. When you are ready, ask for help from your family and friends, educate them, help them feel comfortable, and teach them how to feel the joy your child will bring into all your lives.

Getting help will probably be your most immediate concern. It's natural to turn to your own parents when something happens—you've been doing this your whole life. Ask them to help you communicate with others. This will give you time to focus on your immediate family needs while they find some help for you. These assistants may make offers of help, while others wait in the background for you to contact them.

I still struggle to accept help. I'd rather serve than be served. If I needed an appendectomy, I would prefer to drive myself to the hospital, take it out myself, and then drive myself home. When I was sent to bed

for a month toward the end of my pregnancy, several friends came to my house and cleaned it. I was terribly hurt until one friend explained that they had done it out of love, not a criticism of my housekeeping. It also helped me to understand that when I didn't allow others to help, I denied them blessings.

Be specific in your requests. Most people will want to do something but will not know how to help. If you are feeling overwhelmed, have a family member or close friend act as a coordinator for rides, meals, or whatever else you need.

Everyone will have a natural curiosity about what is happening to your family and your child. At first, you may have little information to share. As you learn more, consider having family meetings. This spares you from repeated conversations and allows all members to be on the same page. These meetings may be held electronically through email updates describing how the child is doing, progress, and challenges. Some families have blogs that require passwords. My daughter-in-law has set up a blog that allows me to see pictures of my grandson, videos, and stories of his life many times each week even though we live in separate states.

What happens in these family meetings? First, explain all the information you have about the disability. Be sensitive to those who will feel uncomfortable in this situation. They may need more time to adjust their thinking. If you give too much information at once, they may feel overwhelmed and distance themselves from you as a defense. You may want to give them a list of resources they can read as they're ready, such as disabilities.lds.org plus other websites specific to your child's disability. For example, if your special spirit has Down syndrome, you might refer them to the National Down Syndrome Society.

Give practical strategies and information such as how to feed your special spirit, manipulating medical devices, or dealing with behaviors. After learning how to help your little one, those you love will feel more comfortable interacting with your family. The more involved they are with the care of your child, the more they will become a support team. Don't forget to offer frequent, heartfelt thanks for all they do. Nothing keeps volunteers coming like appreciation!

With friends who might be uncomfortable, take time to help them build a relationship with your special spirit. Show them how they can communicate and interact just as with any other child. This helps them

see the sweetness underneath and will encourage them to get to know your little one.

Differing Expectations

Some family and friends may want to jump in right away and do everything they can for you. This may seem overwhelming at first. Give them something specific to do. This will allow them to show their love without adding to your burden. Others may feel you need your privacy and could seem to be pulling away. The solution for both extremes is to talk. Have a conversation about needs on both sides, and you will be able to find a solution.

You may be hesitant about sharing setbacks and other bad news. It's natural to want to protect loved ones from more pain. One of my sons was in a car accident while on his mission in South Africa. At first we knew only that he had been hurt but not how badly. I chose not to notify my family until we had more details, sparing them unnecessary worry. The mechanic who repaired the car said John's pelvis should have been crushed, but he was fine. I felt much more comfortable sharing the good news than sharing concerns based on inadequate information. Differing expectations may come out in reactions. Aunt Mary may get upset when your daughter can't go to sleep without a special doll. Uncle Fred might think your son is spoiled if you don't force him to eat certain foods. These opinions and emotions will be felt on both sides. Be aware that your feelings may change based on the level of awareness you are experiencing at the time. See the chapter "Building Parent-Child Relationships" for more information on the stages of coping. A remark that would have had you crying for days may make you laugh later. One of my daughters didn't talk much until she was over three years old. I was told repeatedly by well-meaning family members that I should "make" her talk. Two years later, we learned that she had periodic hearing problems that had to be cured by surgery. She became a chatterbox by sixth grade, and my other children kept saying, "You were the one who taught her to talk!" This was a tears-to-laughter experience.

What if you get caught up in a round of the "blame game"? "This wouldn't have happened if . . ." "You should have . . ." "You need to . . ." Try to remember that this is an effort to make sense of the situation and you may have experienced some of the same feelings. It will be difficult to deal with these reactions. When this happened to me, I moved the

focus from me to what the child needed. Talking about what might have been, or even what "should" have been, only creates bad feelings. It really does nothing to help your special spirit.

What if you've talked and they still don't understand? Your conversations may include unwanted advice, questioning of your parental authority, or social isolation. You can still deal with these problems in a positive manner.

I've dealt with a chronic medical condition for years. I've found that people offer advice because they want to help, need to feel smart, or want to take control of a situation. Every remedy from the ridiculous (copper bracelets) to the impractical (build a swimming pool) to the potentially harmful (leeches) has been offered. I find I deal with this best if I assume these "advisors" care about me and are genuinely trying to help. Sometimes I thank them and just walk away. If they press, I tell them I'll discuss it with my doctor (She always enjoys a good laugh!).

Having your authority as a parent questioned is more difficult to understand. You are entitled to inspiration as you take care of your children, and others may have a hard time accepting this. Parenting special spirits requires you to be both a dreamer and a realist. This split requires careful balance, but try to keep a hopeful outlook while not raising your expectations too high. One of my daughter's friends from school was three when I met him. He was given little hope of walking, but his mother kept working with him as best she could. The kids went to different schools, and we lost touch. I saw him again when he was thirteen, and he was walking, talking, and attending mostly regular classes. He may never make the track team, but he is living his best life.

If you feel no one understands your situation, seek out community parent support groups, other families with special-needs children, and those who work with your child. In addition, there are many chat rooms and message boards on disability websites filled with those in similar circumstances. Hearing echoes of your words and feelings from someone else can ease isolation, validate your emotions, and help you through tough times.

Be very careful during your adventures in cyberspace. Many misrepresent themselves in order to prey upon the vulnerable. As a teacher, I've seen countless terrible situations that started with an innocent chat. If you keep your computer in a public area and remember to pray and read

your scriptures daily, you will be inspired to cut off communications that may become inappropriate.

It may seem easier to avoid those who don't easily understand your situation. This is a short-term solution, however. Being isolated from your family and friends will take a toll on your relationships and your health. Even if it's sometimes painful to deal with them, try to keep in touch. Some people may not ask about your child. Don't view this as a rejection. They may want to respect your privacy and not appear nosy. Some will feel uncomfortable bringing it up or have grief about your situation. Others may wonder if you exaggerate your problem, or they don't want to seem to brag about their own children.

Family Gatherings

Getting together for holidays and special occasions can be joyful or stressful in any family. Prepare carefully, be patient, and try to keep an eternal perspective. Also remember that every family has problems, but they are usually not long-term.

Just like any other activity with a special spirit, family parties need special preparation. The Boy Scouts plan for the worst and expect the best. This is a great way to deal with gatherings. If you've met with a few family members and taught them how best to interact with your child, the way will be smoothed. While there is no way to anticipate every possible situation, you can make reasonable plans, bring the supplies you think your child will need, and therefore reduce everyone's stress.

Don't forget to prepare yourself. Pray that you may be patient and forgiving with family members who don't understand the situation. Set the tone by being upbeat and using humor. Try to put yourself in their shoes. Be ready to tell them what you need. You may grieve as others experience milestones that your child will meet differently. You may feel left out of some activities. Your child's unusual behavior may be embarrassing at times. Focus on your goal of building family relationships, and this may help you as you struggle.

Children in the extended family may have questions about your child's special needs. Be as up-front and honest as possible, but remember to keep the information age-appropriate. You may even want to practice answering difficult questions. Role-play this with your other children so they will also be prepared.

Remember that there are strained relationships at times in every

family, but they are usually not permanent. The family is the basic unit of all creation, and it can be an eternal one. Give your extended family and friends the blessing of getting to know your special spirit. As you seek the inspiration of the Holy Ghost in your efforts, you will be blessed, and your relatives will be able to understand your sweet youngster.

The Holiday Survival Guide

by Danyelle Ferguson

The holidays are coming! The holidays are coming!"
Depending on what your past experiences have been, this statement can either be exclaimed in excitement or uttered in dread. Our family has been very lucky during what is normally a busy, stressful holiday season. When our son was diagnosed with autism, we made a few family rules that have worked really well for us. Perhaps a few of them will help you too. If not, later in this chapter you'll also find a whole list of tips and advice from other parents to help you survive. These tips are great, not only for the holidays, but also for any large family get-together, such as birthdays, anniversaries, picnics, and so on.

Ferguson Family Rules:

- *No traveling from November to January.*
- *Let family come to us.* We travel back east several times each year from April through August to visit our families, so we don't feel too guilty asking family to visit us during Thanksgiving and Christmas. This is also nice because we can control the number and frequency of visitors coming through our home.
- *Holidays are for fun, not stress!* I love to cook a great big holiday meal, but sometimes that just doesn't work. For example, three years ago at Thanksgiving, I discovered that the smell of cooking turkey didn't agree with my morning sickness. I ended up stuck in our bedroom, away from my family, for the whole day! When Christmas Day rolled around, we all went

to Denny's for our holiday meal. Another option is to order your ham or turkey already baked from a restaurant. One year, just after we moved, our oven died halfway through cooking the Thanksgiving turkey. Luckily, we were able to get into the church to let it finish cooking. But once again, we headed off to Denny's for dinner and postponed our official Thanksgiving celebration to Friday. Be flexible, and don't forget your best sense of humor!

A Few Tips to Surviving the Holiday Season

Meals with the Extended Family

If your child is on a special diet, then getting together for meals with extended family can be stressful. Find out in advance what the menu will be and then volunteer to bring some of your child's favorite items. Our son loves mashed potatoes, which are generally made with milk, to which he is allergic. In this situation, I volunteer to make a huge bowl of mashed potatoes made with chicken broth rather than milk.

Also, don't be afraid to ask others to adapt their recipes. I often take packages of Nucoa margarine and other milk-free substitutes when friends invite us to dinner. Be sure to check that the spices being used for the turkey or other dishes fit your diet.

Some of you may run into family members who don't want to make changes "just for your child." This can be very frustrating for you and others who don't want to get caught in the middle of a family feud. One parent told me that her family doesn't attend the big meal on holidays. Some members of her extended family resent making changes, so she has her own Thanksgiving and Christmas dinners with her husband and children. Later that day, they drive to Grandma's house to visit the rest of the extended family during dessert hours. This is much easier for them to handle, since they can easily bring an appropriate dessert for their son.

Visiting Family

Thanksgiving and Christmas are the busiest "running around to visit others" days of the year. Try to calm down your day by spreading visits through the whole two-week Christmas break. You won't get to see everyone at one time, but your visit will be more rewarding as you'll

actually be able to have a meaningful conversation without forty or fifty other people vying for attention as well.

If you do attend a large get-together, be sure to bring plenty of activities or toys your child enjoys. When we attend family parties at Grammy's house, we know we'll be in a smaller home filled with lots of people. Generally, this atmosphere provides too much stimulation for our son. Grammy always sets aside her spare bedroom just for our son's use. When things get too loud and crazy, he takes his toys into the spare room for some peace and quiet until he's ready to return.

Family Visiting You

Follow your child's lead. Ask family members and friends to call before coming over. If your son or daughter is having a bad day or has already had too much stimulation, then ask visitors to come another day. Don't push your child more than you know he can handle. Too much overstimulation in one day will upset him for days afterward and make the holiday even more stressful.

A good rule of thumb for scheduling visits: Pick two of the best times of the day for your child. If he does great in the morning and afternoon but by evening is generally cranky and overstimulated, then schedule one visit for morning and one for the afternoon. Also, don't be shy about asking visitors to put a time limit on their visit. This way, you'll be able to schedule naps, snack times, or anything else that would help your child throughout the day.

Traveling

Airports are packed during these holiday months. If you are traveling during this time, plan for bad weather delays that could last up to five hours. If possible, try to schedule layovers in airports that have play areas. You can find this information by looking up the airport on the Internet. You can also check out what restaurants fit your family's needs. This way, if you have a long layover or delay, there will be some entertainment for your children.

The #1 Tip for Surviving the Holidays . . .

Don't be afraid to say no! Don't stress about baking treats for all the neighbors *and* your extended family *and* your kids' friends *and* your coworkers. Don't feel as though you have to make it to every Santa appearance in town. Just say no . . . and enjoy being together with your

family. Each day, have a calm family activity such as reading holiday books, coloring holiday pictures, writing letters to Santa, or making snowmen and snow angels in the front yard.

By staying relaxed and flexible, your holidays will be filled with memories you'll treasure for a lifetime!

I Am a Child of God

Expressions of Faith and Love

Compiled by Danyelle Ferguson & Lynn Parsons

By Small Means

---

by Thomas Knowlton

My wife and I have a three-year-old named Isabelle with some developmental delays. She does not walk or talk—yet.

She's learned how to blow raspberries. She is fixated on anything that stimulates her mouth, whatever it may be, and does it all day long. I didn't know you could keep up something like that for so long, day after day, week after week. You'd think your mouth would become tired, but it does not seem to be that way for her. She never seems to tire of it. It's interesting when she decides to blow a big raspberry in the middle of a bite of squash. I've given up on clean shirts.

I don't know if my daughter will ever talk, but her progression has gone from complete silence to raspberries to "uuuuunh," and I suspect she is not done yet. The other day while in the middle of an "uuuuuuunh," she interjected an "mmm," and it seemed to sound like "Maaa" as in, short for Mother. My wife and I just looked at each other, and we were so excited, for the Lord had mercifully allowed us to hear what her voice and her words will sound like one day when, or if, she ever starts speaking. I love my daughter's little voice. Any of you who have been blessed with similar challenges while raising "special" children will understand just how much the little things mean.

I love the lessons the Lord is willing to teach us if we are willing to receive them according to His goodwill and pleasure.

My daughter continues to teach me and my wife important lessons about how to come unto Father via the Son—how it will happen and how He views us as He looks upon us, as children, as we struggle to come home and become like Him and His Son, Jesus Christ.

Each of us is just like my "special needs" daughter right now in the eyes of our Heavenly Father. Our progress is sometimes slow and painful. We don't seem to contribute much to the process. It is three steps forward and two back. But the Father and the Son rejoice at each small bit of progress we make toward home. They take it, and bless it, and return it to us an hundredfold.

I also want to say that in order to contribute meaningfully to someone's life, all you need to do is be yourself. Our daughter does no chores. She can't talk. She can't walk. In the eyes of some, she would not seem to be of much use. But we still feel so much love for her and *from* her every day. She has always been this way, so for her, her existence is normal. She does not complain or murmur. She is just happy to be here—happy to exist and be a part of our family.

She laughs when played with. She loves to snuggle. She loves to explore. She has the whole house to crawl around, but we will often find her peacefully sleeping in a solitary patch of sunlight that comes through the back door in the mornings. She gives us so much; it is natural and effortless.

Some people are just here to love and quietly teach us lessons from heaven.

A Special Spirit

by Kimberly Job

As I sat in the foyer, holding Alyssa crying on my lap, I wondered why I had been chosen to be her teacher. Alyssa was born with Sotos syndrome. She was a beautiful little girl with many challenges.

The Primary presidency decided she needed some one-on-one attention, so in addition to her regular Primary teacher, they called me to be her teacher. My assignment was simply to be with Alyssa while the other teacher presented the lesson, which Alyssa and I rarely heard.

I was instructed not to get her mother unless it was absolutely necessary. The first few weeks, we alternated between sitting in the foyer, Alyssa screaming on my lap, and going to the bathroom to wipe her nose, which was constantly running from crying.

I received many looks of sympathy from other adults who walked by. They all appeared to be glad it was me and not them who had to deal with Alyssa's behavior. It was difficult, and I felt helpless. The first few weeks, Alyssa's mom finally came out to rescue me. I think the whole ward could hear Alyssa crying.

If Alyssa's mom brought her to Primary, we never even made it into sharing time because she cried and refused to leave her mom. When her mom finally tore herself away, Alyssa was left screaming and crying at the top of her lungs. I finally figured out that if I took her outside, she seemed to calm down, so we spent a lot of time walking around the church outside, talking about Heavenly Father and all the beautiful things He created for us. Slowly, Alyssa seemed to be warming up to me.

Eventually, Alyssa and I were the best of friends. She always came to find me after sacrament so we could go to class together. She even stayed in class and participated, as much as she was able to, in the lesson.

Her mother and I were Cub Scout leaders for the Wolf den, and Alyssa started coming to Scouts every week. She proudly wore her mom's Scout shirt and joined in all the activities. Alyssa's mom said she talked about me all week, wanting to know when I was coming over to her house.

I came to realize that, although I had been called to help Alyssa, the calling was more for what she could do for me than what I could

do for her. I was at a tough juncture in my life. I was in the process of repenting for some serious mistakes, and I wasn't feeling very worthy or very loved. Alyssa's smile filled my heart each week. She needed me and relied on me to feel safe in Primary. And I needed her. I finally figured out that if someone as sweet, loving, and innocent as Alyssa loved me, then I must be worth loving. She helped me heal from years of heartache.

It was a privilege to be her anchor, to keep her safe from the perceived threats in Primary, and to feel her healing love in return. She will always hold a special place in my heart. I now know why Heavenly Father sends his most special spirits to the earth clothed in bodies and possibly minds that are not quite whole. It is for the benefit of those of us who are privileged to be part of their world.

I Often Sit and Wonder

by Julie Presley

I often sit and wonder what you would say.
I have a feeling that you would talk for days.
Would you tell me that it hurts so bad,
Or would you say, I love you Mom and Dad?
Don't worry, my son, I know what you want to say.
You tell me in your own special way.
The way you wrap your arms around me tight.
The way you smile as we cuddle every night.

I often sit and wonder what you would want to be.
I have a feeling you would say I just want you to be proud of me.
A teacher, a great leader, a salesman or a fireman?
But there was Someone who had a much bigger plan.
Don't worry, my son, I know what you were sent here to be.
A special gift to love and cherish just for me?
No, you had a special mission from the day of your birth.
A special angel sent to teach of peace and love to all of us on earth.

I often sit and wonder how I can be so blessed
And if I am passing this very important test.
To love and protect someone so special and dear
To trust in God's will and trust that He is near.
Don't worry, my son, I will walk beside you every step
And when you are weak in my arms you will be kept.
You are my special angel and were sent to me on loan
But for all eternity a family we will be known.

My Brother, My Friend

---

by Kimberly Daley

As any family's oldest child can explain, there is a lot of pressure when you're the first. The oldest child needs to be a good example. The oldest child needs to be the peacemaker. The oldest child needs to be responsible. This is a tall order for any kid, but what about children who have a sibling with special needs?

When I was eleven years old, my parents explained to me that my younger brother, Jonathon, had been diagnosed with autism. The words didn't mean much to me at the time—I just knew that my brother needed a lot of extra help. Since I had no idea how to directly help Jonathon, I tried to contribute to my family by taking care of my baby sister and doing other chores to free up my mom's time.

I watched in wonder as therapists came into our home to teach my brother. I heard his screaming protests as they tried to get him to sit in a chair and attend to tasks, even very simple ones. As frustrated as they might have been, they came back day after day, and slowly Jonathon began to change. I couldn't help but wonder how these women helped him when I couldn't. As his older sister, I wanted so badly to understand him and be able to teach him. But how could I reach this little boy?

One afternoon, several years later, I was babysitting my siblings when Jonathon had a meltdown. As the responsible older sister, I tried to calm him down using words, but everything I said escalated his tantrum. In frustration, I finally grabbed his shoulders, looked him in the eye and yelled over his screams, "I don't understand you!"

And suddenly, I did. For a split second, I understood my brother. I looked into his eyes, and I saw an upset little boy who was tired of not being able to communicate his wants and needs, tired of not understanding what was happening, and just plain tired.

Without another word, I dropped next to him, put my arms around him, and cried with him. I realized that he didn't need more words, and he certainly didn't need my frustration. He needed my love. And as a big sister, love was something I could give him. That could be my contribution.

In that unforgettable moment, I knew that my Heavenly Father

had given me an opportunity to look past my brother's behavior and see into his heart, allowing me to understand what I could do for him.

I have gone on to work with many other children with special needs, first as a tutor and then as a teacher. There are moments of frustration and times when I want to give up. But sometimes, when I feel that there is nothing more I can do, I will look into the eyes of a child and remember that, although I don't know their heart, there is Someone who does; and although He won't always give me all the answers I may want, He knows the hearts of these children and will teach me what I need to know. And for now, that is enough.

Sterling—Our Personal Blessing

by Lanni Graf

Sterling came into our family when he was two and a half years old. He was born with a chromosome translocation, which causes mental retardation. In spite of the challenges that come with handicaps, we cannot imagine our family without him. Sterling has taught our family so many qualities that are needed to get back to our Heavenly Father.

We took Sterling to the temple to be sealed to us when he was three and a half. My grandfather performed the sealing. When they brought our little boy into the room all dressed in white, the Spirit was so strong, almost everyone in the room began to cry. I knew he would be a great blessing to our family.

He has taught me about kindness. It is a very rare thing to see Sterling get angry, and if he does, he has a good reason. He never says any mean or ugly thing. When he gets mad at a sibling, he will simply say, "Stop!" or "That's not nice!" Sterling is our gentle giant.

Scouting was great for our son. He had the opportunity to associate with the "normal" kids, but I think the biggest blessing was that they had the opportunity to associate with him. Most of the boys were very kind, but in all honesty, I don't think they recognized all the good in his gentle spirit. As a parent, I've often prayed that people could see all the good and realize that many of the struggles are things that we need to overcome.

As Sterling worked toward his Eagle, we supported and helped him complete all the requirements. Some of the requirements had to be modified, but we knew that if Sterling did his best, which is the Scout Motto, it was enough. We can personally say that Sterling did do his best. For Sterling's Eagle project, he was able to collect items for the Autism Center, which had been burglarized. It was a great service project that he was capable of doing with only a little help and direction from his parents. Sterling is definitely an Eagle Scout. He lives the law, and as he matures, is really trying to do his best.

Sterling has advanced to the office of a priest. We feel he needs to mature more before he becomes an elder. He has blessed the sacrament and has always done a good job. He just requires a bit of direction. I feel

that at times he seeks direction because he lacks confidence in himself. He is a home teacher with his father. Sterling graduated from seminary and will graduated from high school in 2010. He will go on to a transition school and desires to serve a home-based mission in the future.

Sterling is truly one of our family's greatest blessings. He has things to overcome, as do all of us. As I said before, many of the serious things that will keep us from our Heavenly Father, Sterling has already mastered. He is a great example of kindness, charity, patience, and being able to forgive. He has changed my life and the life of our family. We are so grateful for him. Our family has been blessed with a celestial spirit.

Special Children of God

by Lynn Parsons

I never intended to work with children with special needs or even to become a teacher. Heavenly Father has placed me in positions so that I may come into contact with special needs children and their parents. From my BYU thesis to my current job, He has led me down an unusual path.

Two of my own children have special needs. Although they have only minor disabilities, being their mother helped me learn to look past differences to the spirit within each child. This continued as I worked in school and at church to help my students develop their full potential.

Working with those with disabilities is challenging and frustrating, and at times, the problems seem insurmountable. I have been fortunate enough to see some of my students grow and learn from age three to high school, or even beyond. I have seen how they influence others for good—bringing joy to family, friends, or even strangers, and encourage others to be their best. Heavenly Father and Jesus Christ truly love these special spirits. They are watched over, cared for, and blessed in ways we can only imagine.

Above all, I have learned that nothing is impossible if it is in line with God's will. I've seen children learn to walk, speak, and interact with others against seemingly impossible odds.

As you seek to serve those with special needs, remember that Heavenly Father knows your situation. He will bless you as you serve in love.

An Unexpected Gift

by Danyelle Ferguson

The business of parenting is not what I had expected it to be.

Yes, I had expected the stinky diapers, the crying, and sleepless nights blended in with snuggles, singing, and expressions of love. But I had not expected the complete change of thinking, change of everyday life, change of world. I had not expected autism.

Together, my husband and I faced the struggles and trials that came with trying to pull our son out of his own little world. Some days I felt as though my knees knew no other purpose than to kneel as I prayed and prayed for guidance. And yes, some days were very dark and difficult. On those days, I just wanted to soak in my big bathtub until our hot water heater and my tears both ran dry.

But these difficult days and emotions were overridden by the joy our son brought into our lives. Just to hear him laugh and smile made my heart swell until it felt as though it would burst. Watching the progress he's made over the past seven years has been amazing. To see him participate in Special Olympics, play with his friends, succeed in school, develop lasting family relationships, and to hear him pray to his Heavenly Father—I couldn't ask for more. He has such enthusiasm for life. Every year, his teachers comment on it and tell me how much they love his expressions of friendship.

I love the scripture "Adam fell that men might be; and men are, that they might have joy" (2 Nephi 2:25). I know that all the trials our family experiences are the refining fire, which intensifies the feeling of joy and happiness in our home. Through these experiences came a rock-solid testimony that Heavenly Father knows exactly who my son is and what he needs. That He loves him, forever, and will always be there for our son. What an unexpected gift and blessing. It gives me peace each and every day as I pray for guidance to raise my family.

And so, yes, the business of parenting is not what I had expected it to be.

It's even better.

BIBLIOGRAPHY

Allred, Silvia H. "Feed My Sheep," *Ensign*, Nov. 2007, 113–15.

Answers to Gospel Questions, comp. Joseph Fielding Smith, 5 vols., Salt Lake City: Deseret Book Co., 1979, 3:19. Used by Permission.

Ashton, Marvin J. Conference Report, Oct. 1969, 28–29.

Ballard, M. Russell. "Daughters of God," *Ensign*. May 2008, 108–10.

———. "One More," *Ensign*, May 2005, 69.

Beck, Julie B. "Focusing on the Lord's Work of Salvation." *Ensign*. Mar. 2009, 18–22.

Benson, Ezra Taft. "Salvation—A Family Affair," *Ensign*, Jul. 1992, 2.

Christensen, Joe J. "Marriage and the Great Plan of Happiness," *Ensign*, May 1995, 64.

———. *One Step at a Time: Building a Better Marriage, Family, and You.* (Salt Lake City: Deseret Book, 1996), 15–16. Used with permission.

Condie, Spencer J. "Becoming a Great Benefit to Our Fellow Beings," *Ensign*, May 2002, 44–46.

Dahlquist, Charles W., II. "Message from the Young Men General Presidency" *LDS Relationships Newsletter* 3, no. 2 (May 2008): 1.

"Family Home Evening: Counsel and a Promise," *Ensign*, Jun. 2003, 12.

Faust, James E. "A Thousand Threads of Love," *Ensign*, Oct. 2005, 2–7.

Ghaznavi, Shanna. "They Also Serve," *New Era*, Mar. 2001, 12.

Haight, David B. "Come to the House of the Lord," *Ensign*, May 1992, 15.

Hinckley, Gordon B. "Messages of Inspiration from President Hinckley," *Church News*, Dec. 6, 1997, 2.

———. "Stand True and Faithful," *Ensign*, May 1996, 91.

Juvenile Instructor, vol. 27: 491–92.

Kimball, Spencer W. "Small Acts of Service," *Ensign*, Dec. 1974, 2.

Lee, Harold B. *Stand Ye in Holy Places* (Salt Lake City: Deseret Book, 1974), 298. Used by permission.

McConkie, Bruce R. "Salvation of Little Children." *Ensign*, Apr. 1977, 3.

Monson, Thomas S. "Building Your Eternal Home," *Ensign*, May 1984, 16.

———. "Miracles of Faith," *Ensign*, Jul. 2004, 2–7.

———. "Precious Children—A Gift from God," *Ensign*, Nov. 1991, 67.

Orgill, Emily C. "Date Night—at Home," *Ensign*, Apr. 1991, 57.

Perry, L. Tom. "Back to Gospel Basics," *Ensign*, May 1993, 90.

Scott, Richard G. "Now Is the Time to Serve a Mission!," *Ensign*, May 2006, 87–90.

Simpson, Robert L. "A Lasting Marriage," *Ensign*, May 1982, 21.

Stack, Peggy Fletcher. "Unintended consequence of church's 'raising the bar,'" *Salt Lake Tribune*, July 26, 2005.

"Strengthening a marriage." *Church News*, July 7, 1990.

Zwick, W. Craig. "Encircled in the Savior's Love," *Ensign*, Nov. 1995, 13.

About the Authors

Danyelle Ferguson is the mother of a son with autism and the cofounder of *Friends of GIANT Steps,* a nonprofit organization that benefits the GIANT Steps Autism Preschool. Over the years, she's learned that prayer and a sense of humor are the keys to not only enduring but also enjoying the special needs journey.

Danyelle is a wife, mom, book editor, reviewer, and writer. She and her hubby, John, are raising four angels-in-training. She grew up surrounded by Pennsylvania's beautiful Allegheny Mountains but is currently experiencing mountain-withdrawal in Kansas. She enjoys reading, writing, dancing and singing in the kitchen, and the occasional long bubble bath to relax from the everyday stress of being "Mommy."

Danyelle is available as a keynote speaker or to teach training classes for churches, parent support groups, book clubs, writers groups, and other organizations. For more information, she can be contacted at Danyelle@Danyelle Ferguson.com.

Website: www.DanyelleFerguson.com
Blog: www.QueenOfTheClan.com

Lynn Parsons, M.S., is a wife, mother, grandmother, educational diagnostician, and writer. She entered the field of special education because two of her four children have special needs.

Lynn received her Bachelor of Independent Studies from BYU, where her thesis was titled "Non-Drug Treatments for Attention Deficit Disorder." She then became certified as a special education teacher, primarily working with students with autism. Her classes and teaching methods were featured in "District Administration Magazine," "Edutopia," and several websites on disabilities. After six years of classroom experience, Lynn currently works as an Educational Diagnostician.

Lynn earned a master's degree in Education and Technology from Walden University. Her collaborative research project, "Using Video to Teach Social Skills to Secondary Students with Autism" was also published by the Council for Exceptional Children. She is currently a doctoral candidate at Northcentral University.

Lynn's experience as a speaker and presenter includes teacher in-services, presentations on using technology for students with special needs, and community presentations on disability awareness. She was also a community columnist for the "Fort Worth Star-Telegram."

Lynn grew up in the San Francisco Bay Area but now calls Texas home. She enjoys spending time with her family, reading, and needlework. Lynn continues to seek out and develop innovative methods for teaching children with special needs. You can contact her at www.lynndparsons.com or ldparsons60@gmail.com.

Made in the USA
Monee, IL
09 February 2021

59997226R00152